PRAISE FOR GLOR

"Duane Schultz has recreate̶̶̶̶̶̶̶̶̶̶̶̶̶ ̶̶̶̶ ̶̶̶̶̶̶̶̶̶̶̶̶̶̶̶̶̶̶̶̶̶̶̶̶̶ in superb, totally engrossing detail. A memorable book."
—Lamar Herrin, author of
The Unwritten Chronicles of Robert E. Lee

"The denouement is not only effective, but powerful. If in this notable contribution to military fiction, there is glory enough for all, then there is also stupidity, drunkenness and cowardice."
—*New York Times Book Review*

"Authentically detailed and tightly paced, this is an absorbing novel."
—*Publishers Weekly*

"A highly readable and informative bit of history. Mr. Schultz's work is highly recommended."
—*Civil War Roundtable*

"Riveting...A horrific episode."
—*Austin Chronicle*

"Schultz describes vividly and with deep feeling the emotional and physical challenges and frustrations the Union men faced."
—*Richmond Times-Dispatch*

more...

"Schultz's histories read like fiction. Here, he takes the next step, metamorphosing history into exceedingly realistic and suspenseful fiction. Readers who prize good war stories won't be disappointed."

—*Kirkus Reviews*

"Successfully weaves facts with real and fictional characters to present both the bravery and brutality of war."

—*Ocala Star-Banner*

"Schultz has full command of the history of this bizarre and devastating battle. He has created vivid and often sympathetic characters. *Glory Enough For All* is a powerful and compelling novel."

—Peter Burchard, author of *One Gallant Rush*

"A riveting account...A tale of jealousy and insecurity and indecisiveness among the Union's leading generals...A story of grandiose plans gone awry because commanders couldn't—or refused to—command. And it is a tale of blood, gore, and guts that is war...A fine novel."

—Gannett News Service

"All the elements of an engrossing novel: a daring plan successfully completed, intrigue, characters that could only be found in the Civil War...In Schultz's hands, it makes for a quickly paced and enjoyable story."

—*Orlando Sentinel*

GLORY ENOUGH FOR ALL

A NOVEL OF
THE CIVIL WAR

• DUANE SCHULTZ •

ST. MARTIN'S PAPERBACKS

To My Father

GLORY ENOUGH FOR ALL: THE BATTLE OF THE CRATER

Copyright © 1993 by Duane Schultz.

Library of Congress Catalog Card Number: 93-21811

ISBN: 0-312-95579-0

Printed in the United States of America

St. Martin's Press hardcover edition/September 1993
St. Martin's Paperbacks edition/August 1995

10 9 8 7 6 5 4 3 2 1

Take the white men, kill the niggers!
CONFEDERATE BATTLE CRY

It is the saddest affair I have witnessed
in this war.

U. S. GRANT

History will record what we do here.
There will be glory enough for all.

JAMES H. LEDLIE
BRIGADIER GENERAL
ARMY OF THE POTOMAC
PETERSBURG, VIRGINIA
JULY 30, 1864

1

THE empty coffin sat next to the empty grave. Around it, massed to form a large rectangle, the 4,300 men of the Fourth Division, United States Colored Troops, stood at attention. The soldiers waited, grim and quietly at attention, blue uniforms and black faces all except for the officers, occasional specks of white in the sea of blue and black. No one moved. No one spoke. They seemed frozen in time, as if Mathew Brady, that fashionable and nearly blind portrait photographer from Washington, had captured them on a photographic plate, imprisoning them stolidly forever.

The war in the background turned silent. The rebels knew that a nigger was about to be executed, and their sharpshooters and the men at the mortars and cannon were glad to take a holiday from their work. For now, only one man would die, and the rebs as well as the white soldiers on the Northern side were in a mood to celebrate. They climbed to the tops of the parapets and stared across the desolate battleground at one another. They waved and laughed and exchanged jokes, knowing they would live at least another fifteen minutes, until the fighting resumed and someone else died from a bullet or a mortar round.

Halfway up an incline leading to the Union trenches, two officers watched the proceedings.

"Poor dumb bastard," said Henry Pleasants, clenching and unclenching his fists. "Bad enough to die this way, but to wait around all morning just because some damn reporters have to be escorted to the front. . . ."

Lieutenant Colonel Pleasants, thirty-one years old, was a slim, dapper man of average height. Born in Argentina, he had sharp features carved in a dark complexion, outlined by luxuriant wavy black hair, a thick mustache, and a thin line of beard from ears to chin that widened to form a neat goatee. Some might have called him a dandy, but not to his face. His mother was the daughter of a Spanish aristocrat, and his father an adventurer from Pennsylvania who made his fortune running guns to the revolutionaries.

As Pleasants's dark brown eyes glared at the scene below, his companion, Lt. Jack O'Brien, knew it was not the time to speak.

"Barbaric," Pleasants said, "trussing a man up and shooting him down on his own coffin. Poor devil doesn't deserve to die at all, much less that way."

"But he killed two white men," O'Brien said, regretting the remark before it was out.

"He killed two soldiers who were wearing the same uniform he's wearing, serving the same country he's serving, and he killed them in self-defense. If he were white, he'd be in the stockade instead of preparing to die. You know I'm no abolitionist, Jack. I don't care one way or another about the colored race. But this is wrong. Hell, I'd feel the same way if he was Irish."

O'Brien chuckled.

"You heard how it happened?" Pleasants asked, then answered the question before O'Brien could speak.

"The black division was kept in the rear guarding the wagon trains until Burnside brought them up two days ago. Two drunken cavalrymen came upon this fellow and decided to have some fun, only he didn't think it was fun being run down by horses and beaten with the broadsides of sabers. Cavalrymen always overdo things. The colored fellow stood it as long as he could, until one of them turned the saber and sliced open his shoulder. He pulled the cavalryman off his horse, grabbed his pistol, and shot them both, killing one and wounding the other.

"He carried the wounded man to the field hospital. That was his big mistake, aside from being black, of course. He should have run away and kept quiet. The trooper died, but not before saying that he and his friend had been attacked by the colored. The court-martial lasted fifteen minutes. Everybody was eager to believe that this scrawny, unarmed former slave, described by his commanding officer as a model soldier, went out of his way to gun down two brawny cavalrymen."

Pleasants was clearly disturbed by the unfairness of the episode, but few of the Northern troops cared about the man who was about to be executed. They didn't know him. He wasn't one of theirs. He was just one more, or soon one less, of Burnside's Niggers, the name the Southerners had been shouting across the killing ground since the Fourth Division joined Gen. Ambrose Burnside's Ninth Corps. Until they came along, life in the trenches had been marginally tolerable.

The men on the opposing sides had worked out an informal arrangement. You fire some and we'll fire some, but we'll all aim high. After dark, we'll venture out and carry on some barter. Coffee and sugar for tobacco and newspapers, and I'll show you some pictures of my kids.

When the colored troops arrived and set up camp behind the Union lines, life in the Ninth Corps became deadly serious. The rebs were furious to be facing black troops and they took revenge on every white face they saw in a frenzy of shot and shell aimed to kill. The only barter now was dying for dying and death for death. Until 12:45 on the afternoon of June 23.

"Rest easy a spell, Yanks," a Southerner yelled. "Now you got the right idea. The only thing to do with niggers is kill 'em, not set 'em free. Hell, you boys give 'em guns, there's no telling what they might go and do."

In other parts of the line, shots rang out and shells shrieked and exploded. Men screamed in pain and slumped in the dirt.

But along the Ninth Corps trenches, soldiers laughed and talked and stayed alive a little longer.

The men of the Fourth Division, United States Colored Troops, stiff and sweaty in the sweltering sun, waiting to watch one of their own die, heard the Southern voices. Although the words did not carry the half-mile distance, the meaning was easily understood. They heard the jibes from the Northern voices, too, and they knew their meaning as well. They had heard the talk every day since they had put on their uniforms and had known it all their lives, slaves or freedmen, and that was the reason one of them was about to be shot. Mr. Lincoln may have set them free, but he had not changed anyone's mind, not even those wearing Union blue.

From the woods beyond the coffin, Gen. Patrick Franklin, provost marshal of Burnside's Ninth Corps, urged his horse forward at a stately pace. Behind him appeared the band, playing the chilling, hypnotic notes of the "Dead March." Twelve armed guards marched in formal procession in a column of twos, followed by the chaplain and the condemned man, flanked by additional guards. The firing squad, twelve soldiers from the provost guard, brought up the rear, each man convinced that his was the musket that carried the blank charge.

As the parade passed the grave, several guards detached themselves to form a line, in case the prisoner attempted to escape. Pleasants remarked to O'Brien on the orderliness, the rhythm, the established set of military procedures. Each man, including the condemned, knew his role and performed flawlessly. Most had done it before; executions were now commonplace. What was different about this one was the color of the condemned man's skin, and there were few true and righteous abolitionists in the army by 1864 to be upset by that. They had joined up early and been used up fast.

The players took their places. The prisoner's escort bound his hands and feet with rope and tied a white linen blindfold over his eyes. The men of the firing squad marched twenty paces beyond the coffin, did a smart about-face, and stood at attention. General Franklin dismounted, pulled the official warrant of execution from his pocket, and waited while the guards led the prisoner to the coffin, gesturing for him to sit on the edge. The chaplain hovered nearby, prayers at the ready, as the black soldier threw his head back as though he could see the intense blue sky. The band finished one more monotonous round of the "Dead March" and double-timed away, relieved that their part was finished.

Pleasants turned away, disgusted by the proceedings. A sudden wail, deep and clear, stopped him. The prisoner was singing. The provost marshal looked up from the warrant of execution he was reading, and a murmur of recognition ran through the ranks of the black troops.

"I walk in the moonlight," the prisoner sang.

"I walk in the starlight."

A few voices joined in the response.

"Lay this body down."

"Jesus," Pleasants whispered.

General Franklin faltered, fumbling to find his place. He continued to read, but his words were overwhelmed as the prisoner's voice rose.

"I know moon rise. I know star rise."

The chaplain placed a hand on the condemned man's shoulder and whispered to him. The soldier shook him off. The chaplain looked around wildly as more of the black troops joined in the old spiritual, the sound massing like thunder.

"Lay this body down."

A few of the Fourth Division's white officers shouted orders, but they could not be heard. The provost guard and the firing squad tightened their grips on their weapons. General Franklin's hand moved to his holster as he finished reading the warrant aloud.

The chaplain patted the prisoner's shoulder lamely, trying to offer whatever comfort can be given to those who are about to be shot, but the man seemed oblivious. His body rocked in rhythm with the music. His soul was offering its own prayers in its own spirited way. The man did not need, or heed, the voice of the white preacher. General Franklin brusquely motioned him out of the way.

"I walk in the graveyard," sang more than four thousand voices in joyous harmony.

"I walk through the graveyard."

The provost marshal shouted an order to the firing squad. They could not hear him, but they knew what he was saying. They raised their muskets and took aim.

"To lay this body down."

General Franklin mouthed the word *Fire* and dropped his right arm to his side. Nothing happened. The men did not fire. Rooted in place like toy soldiers, their fingers froze on the triggers.

"I'll lie in the grave and stretch out my arms. Lay this body down."

Franklin's mouth contorted and his face turned red. He took one step, then another toward the firing squad, screeching the order to fire.

"I go to the judgment in the evening of the day. When I lay this body down."

Still the men held their fire.

"And my soul and your soul will meet in the day. When I lay this body down."

As the last word of the Negro spiritual spun away into silence, the prisoner cried, "Hallelujah!" General Franklin raised his arm. The soldiers fired and the prisoner crumpled to the ground. "Fire," yelled the general into the sudden stillness.

Pleasants looked at O'Brien and shook his head. In the aftermath of the volley of shots, they could hear the rebels cheering.

"I've got to find a way to end this goddamn war," Pleasants said. He turned away and headed for the trenches. He knew what would happen next. He did not have to stay to see the Fourth Division march single file past the blood-soaked body stretched out in the coffin. It was the final object lesson for the troops, as if the sight of a man being torn apart by bullets was not graphic enough. After the last of the 4,300 soldiers passed, the body would be buried facedown in an unmarked grave, the final and eternal punishment.

Pleasants stalked toward the front line with O'Brien hurrying to keep pace with him. When they emerged from a thicket of trees within sight of the long zigzag lines of Union and Confederate trenches, Pleasants stopped. The gunfire had resumed on both sides. Mortar rounds exploded in the trenches and threw up clods of dirt, bark, and bits of uniformed bodies. Stray bullets, fired high above the trenches, thudded into limbs of the thin trees behind them. O'Brien spied several places that would provide good cover, but he did not dare move while his commanding officer remained in the open, glaring at the rise beyond the rebel line.

"Look at that goddamn hill, Jack," Pleasants said. "I've never hated anyplace so much in my life."

On Union maps, the slope was called Cemetery Hill, the burial ground for Blandford Church. It was the highest point of land as far as anyone could see. The key point in the five-mile line of Confederate defenses, it stood directly opposite the position of Colonel Pleasants's regiment, the Forty-Eighth Pennsylvania Volunteers. Halfway up the hill between the rebel trenches and the peak perched an ugly, imposing, solid earthen fort, the strongest defensive work anywhere on the line. General Grant had tried to take it when he reached Petersburg two weeks ago. He had failed.

No troops could charge the hill in the face of the Confederate guns, and the weary, trigger-shy remnants of Grant's army, now huddled in their trenches deep in the earth, no longer had the will to try. The hill taunted Pleasants. It mocked him; it challenged him; it set his teeth on edge. At times, it damn near drove him crazy because he knew that the hill was all that stood between him and the end of the war, between him and the new life he wanted to make with Anne Shaw. If the Union forces could take Cemetery Hill, no more than a half mile away, the war would be over.

Once Union troops occupied Cemetery Hill, they would

have the high ground. They would be behind the rebel line and could walk on to Petersburg unchallenged. And once they held the town, Pleasants knew, they would have the railroad lines that supplied Richmond. The Confederate capital would fall. Lee's army, split in two, would have to abandon its fortifications and surrender or try to run south and west, where Grant's army would outflank them. It could all be done in a week.

"I hate that damn hill," Pleasants said again, oblivious to the rebel bullets.

O'Brien sighed, squinted as though to see better which bullet was heading toward him, and hurried after the man he had vowed to follow anywhere. He wondered whether Pleasants, in his fury at the obstacle of Cemetery Hill, would even notice if he got shot.

Henry Pleasants hated death, not on abstract intellectual or moral grounds but for personal reasons. Twice death had shattered his life, the first time forcing him to leave his home and make his way in an alien world, and the second time driving him to court his own destruction. Death was the reason he was wearing the blue uniform and striding across the open plain, railing at the forces that might now take his life.

As a boy, he had idolized his flamboyant father, cherishing the stories of his Pennsylvania boyhood. The old pirate died when Henry was thirteen, leaving his son bereft of hope, stipulating in his will that Henry be entrusted to an uncle, a wealthy Main Line Philadelphia physician. With a stern warning from his mother to behave and not embarrass her, Henry stepped aboard a ship bound from Argentina for the United States and never saw her again.

Uncle Henry and Aunt Emily were warm, loving people with a large family of their own, and they happily embraced the wild, fearful boy who spoke little English. Although he learned the language quickly, he was sensitive about making mistakes and quick to respond with his fists to taunts from his classmates. Out of respect for his father's wishes, he applied himself to his studies and graduated from high school in 1851, second in his class. Uncle Henry urged him to go to college, but the boy was restless and tired of school. He wanted to build things, to make things work, and he decided to become an engineer, not by studying in a college classroom but by learning on the job.

Railroads were booming. The companies needed bright, ambitious young men. Pleasants was hired by the Pennsylvania Railroad as a surveyor's assistant. He camped out in the wilderness with the work crews and took pleasure in executing precise, orderly calculations and drawings, seeing how the results of his efforts tamed the forests and rivers and led to mile after mile of shiny new track. He was good. He had a knack for the detailed work and for getting along with the men. Within two years, he was senior assistant engineer.

A year later, at the age of twenty-one, he was sent to work on the Allegheny Mountains project, constructing one of the longest railway tunnels in the world, 4,200 feet cut through rock. Promoted over several older and more senior engineers, Pleasants was given the task of maintaining adequate ventilation for the men and equipment as the long, dark shaft was blasted out of the mountain. He had no guidelines to follow, no precedents, no generally accepted way of providing fresh air. He solved the problem by digging vertical shafts to the tunnel. Heated air from a fire lighted at the bottom of each shaft drew the stagnant, noxious fumes out of the tunnel.

When the job was completed three years later, Henry Pleasants, rising young star of the railroads, quit. The chief engineer, who had befriended and encouraged him, was fired. Rumor had it that Pleasants would replace him, a phenomenal opportunity for a twenty-four-year-old. But Pleasants refused to stay with a company that had treated his friend unjustly.

He went to Pottsville, an area said to be bursting with coal. He'd heard that a good mining engineer could make a fortune. Within months, he was recognized in that grimy, dreary coal town as one of the best in the business. He specialized in deep-shaft mining and had more work than he could handle. His economic future was set, and when he married Sallie Bannan, daughter of the local newspaper publisher, life seemed complete. Until the October night when Sallie died in childbirth.

He returned to his aunt and uncle in Philadelphia to try to heal. He spent most of the winter wrapped in silence, staring into the fireplace, mesmerized by the flames. Far away, South Carolina seceded and the union of states began to unravel, but Pleasants took no notice until the day Aunt Emily stood by his armchair and suggested that he join the army. It was a way to save himself, she said. He watched the fire a few minutes longer, rose, and kissed her on the forehead. She didn't realize that she was offering him a way out. A rebel bullet would end his suffering.

The men of the Forty-Eighth Pennsylvania Volunteers worshiped Pleasants. They were a tough lot, most of them unschooled, quite a few illiterate. All were from Schuylkill County, Pennsylvania, mining country. An independent bunch, they were not about to take orders just because some officer had rank on his shoulder straps. He would have to earn their respect, affection, and loyalty to prove that he had the right to boss them. Pleasants, appointed a captain in the regiment in the first year of the war, earned that right quickly. Any officer who did not measure up was hounded out of the regiment. Or if he didn't leave of his own accord, he might take a bullet in the back. That knowledge, the men said, focused the mind wonderfully.

The Forty-Eighth had had a strange war, different from the usual pattern of battle after battle, march after march, one dreary encampment following another. They started out at Hatteras Inlet, North Carolina, building a causeway connecting two forts. They never fired a shot in anger or saw a man in gray. Captain Pleasants was furious. He had joined up to fight and die, not to build bridges.

The regiment finally came under enemy fire in August 1862, at the second battle of Bull Run. Pleasants fought recklessly, repeatedly taking foolish chances. The men of his company were worried. Sure he had a lousy temper and drilled them until they dropped, but he was fair, and they didn't want to lose him. He would not eat until he saw that his men were fed, he lived with them in the mud, and he never put on airs. It was understood that he was seeking danger as some sort of expiation for his grief, but if he was fixing to get himself killed, they were not going to stand for it. They began to cover for him when he tried to lead a charge, to find shelter during a rebel counterattack. Once when Pleasants stalked back and forth behind a stone wall, exposed to enemy fire, a lanky Irish sergeant, who had been reading law before the war, took charge. The young man carefully laid down his rifle so no dirt would get in the barrel, stood up, and lunged at Pleasants, bringing him crashing to the ground.

"Stay down, you damn fool," he shouted.

Pleasants, enraged, untangled himself and brushed off his trousers. He glared at the soldier, his voice low and menacing.

"What did you say to me, Sergeant?"

The man swallowed hard and forced himself to look the captain in the eye.

"I said, 'Stay down, you damn fool,' sir!"

Pleasants said nothing for a moment, then grinned and laughed aloud. And that was how Sergeant Jack O'Brien became a second lieutenant.

The Forty-Eighth Pennsylvania fought at Chantilly and South Mountain, and Pleasants continued to court rebel bullets, as much as his troops would let him. Many of those who wanted desperately to live did not, but Pleasants escaped unscathed, with nothing to show for his determination to die but a bullet in his hat and another through his sleeve. Promoted to lieutenant colonel for bravery under fire, he would not face enemy soldiers again for nearly two years.

The regiment camped and marched and drilled and waited while huge armies clashed throughout the East and West. The Union forces kept losing. In March of 1863, the Forty-Eighth was posted to Lexington, Kentucky, as provost guards—policemen—to keep the peace between Northern and Southern sympathizers. They built their own barracks, improved the town's defenses, and drilled until they were such a smart outfit that they impressed friend and foe alike. But first, they got stinking drunk on corn whiskey. Pleasants summoned uncharacteristic diplomatic skills to soothe the city fathers. By the time the regiment was ordered out, the good citizens of Lexington petitioned the commanding general to let these fine, well-behaved young men remain. The general consented, and the Forty-Eighth settled down to the best wartime duty a soldier could hope to have.

This did not suit their self-destructive commanding officer. He grew even more ill-tempered and withdrawn. One night, he was invited to the home of wealthy merchant Hiram Shaw for a glittering social evening, the kind he had known in his uncle's house in Philadelphia—sophisticated company, cultured conversation, the finest of foods and wines, and an enchanting girl of eighteen. She was Anne Shaw, the niece of his host.

Anne wore her blond hair parted in the center, with a cascade of spiraling curls over her ears. To Pleasants, her hair reminded him of showers of golden sunlight. Her fair complexion glowed in the candlelight and her soft blue eyes sparkled when she was introduced to him. She was not a perfect beauty. Some said her eyes were a bit too close together and her cheekbones a touch too imposing. But Pleasants noticed that men of all ages stared at her, admiringly and longingly.

So did he, and it was disconcerting when she returned his look, though not in the coquettish way Southern women are born knowing. She stared frankly, openly, as if she was appraising him. And when she smiled, her eyes lighted up with such radiance, such dazzle, that Pleasants felt a joy that shook him so firmly, he felt dizzy.

"This is my little niece," Hiram Shaw said. "She's growing up much too fast. It's this war. It's changing everything."

"I was grown up long before the war, Uncle Hiram, and you know it," Anne said.

"I guess you were, honey," her uncle said. "You always were older than you was supposed to be. Your daddy would be real proud of you. Your mama, too."

"Now, Uncle Hiram, you know Mama expects me to stay a child forever."

She linked her arm in Pleasants's and led him away.

"My daddy," she told him, "taught me to grow up fast, to read books, and to have my own opinions and not be afraid to express them. Poor man—he's dead now—he wanted a son so badly but had to make do with me. He said he didn't raise his daughter to go to quilting bees or make frivolous conversation or stay home and have babies. Mama says I'm much too forward to get a husband anyway, but if I have to act like a ninny to capture one, I'd rather be an old maid. I think most men are afraid of a woman who speaks her mind. What do you think, Colonel Pleasants?"

"I think you're right," he found himself saying, swept along by her words and her charm, and the blue eyes that saw into his soul.

"I thought you would," she said.

She patted his arm and inched closer to him than was proper for a first meeting. She guided him around the ballroom, talking about the war and President Lincoln and the Union and Confederate commanders in their various campaigns, all with a passion and confidence that unnerved him. And she told him of her conviction that women should be able to do anything they chose. She was determined to be a modern woman, whatever that was, and that unnerved him, too.

He had never met anyone like Anne Shaw. He was torn by an urge to flee and a desire to be alone with her and take her in his arms. It made him feel disloyal to the memory of his wife, but Sallie's image was growing dim and Anne was here and so alive and vivacious.

They were separated at dinner, Pleasants held captive by a judge's boring wife, who lamented the state of the town's magnolia trees. He stole glances at Anne at the far end of the table in conversation with Colonel Simmons, Lexington's military governor. After port and cigars, Simmons sidled up to him.

"Best be wary, Henry. That little lady has designs on you."

Panic-stricken, he decided it was time to leave. Anne found

him, tucked her arm in his, and guided him toward the open French doors leading to the garden.

"Walk with me a ways, Colonel Pleasants," she said.

She led him to a painted wooden bench in the far corner of the piazza and studied him seriously for a moment. Pleasants felt uncomfortable. The April night was warm, the scent of the dogwoods heavy.

"Tell me about your wife," Anne said.

He was stunned by her directness and momentarily resented the intrusion into his private life. He had never talked about Sallie before, but suddenly he found he could not hold back his thoughts. They burst forth like a summer storm, uncontrollable, unstoppable. Anne reached over and placed her hand on his. When he noticed it, when he became aware of the warmth of her skin against his, it made him want to cry. When he was finished and had said everything that had been locked inside him for so long, a feeling of peace came over him.

"You have lovely memories," Anne said. "That's more than many people have. You should cherish them and keep them alive."

"I do," he said.

"Then why does Colonel Simmons tell me that you keep trying to get yourself killed? I don't think that's what your wife would want. She would want you to get on with living."

Anne stood up and plucked at the puffed sleeves of her off-the-shoulder gown, as if surprised that it stayed up.

"Do you plan to come calling on me?" she said.

Before Henry could answer, she linked her arm in his again and walked him toward the house.

"If you do, I hope you will not be slow about it, Colonel Pleasants. We do not have time to waste on formalities. With this awful war, we don't know when you'll get orders to leave, so if you plan to come courting, I do hope you'll get on with it."

He did not know what to say, but Anne did not wait for an answer.

"Tomorrow is Sunday," she said. "We'll be back from

church at half past eleven. Dinner is at noon. That is as good a time as any to meet Mama and get that over with. Now, she'll carry on some, you being a Yankee from Pennsylvania and almost twice my age, but if you just keep looking at me the way you are now, I think you'll do fine."

Anne kissed him lightly on the cheek, and within a month their engagement was the talk of Lexington. Pleasants had found a reason to live.

Pleasants cast another angry glance at Cemetery Hill, looming above him like some haunted mountain. He turned away and gestured for Jack O'Brien to follow him into the deep-pit passageway that stretched diagonally from the rear to the trenches. It was one of several passages used by the troops to reach the front in relative safety, a lot safer than crossing the open ground in full view of the rebel line.

A stench hit them as soon as they neared the front. The trenches were foul, open, stagnant sewers simmering in the heat. They stank of sweat, unwashed bodies, urine and excrement, rotting food, and decaying, purulent corpses, bloated and unburied, lying just beyond the deep scars scratched out of the red Virginia soil. The dead and the wastes drew flies, huge, angry, buzzing blue-black monsters that clung to every surface, adding to the soldiers' misery. At night, the flies were replaced by mosquitoes, and the lice kept the men itching around the clock.

Bugs, rats, and other vermin got in the food. The hardtack, sometimes all the soldiers had to eat on the line, was usually infested with maggots and weevils. The joke was that the crackers did not have to be transported in wagons—the stuff could walk on its own. Many men toasted the crackers over a fire to drive the pests out, but some never bothered, claiming that the bugs had no flavor and at night you couldn't see them, anyway. Army food was a constant source for complaints, and, eventually, for disease, which proved as deadly as enemy bullets. The men of the Forty-Eighth Pennsylvania were more fortunate than most, thanks to Pleasants's efforts.

With the odors from the front line came choking dust as powdery and fine as cake flour. It piled up inches thick in and around the trenches where the trees had been felled, and where shells and marching feet had chewed up the thin layer of topsoil. Like the smells, the dust hung over everything and stuck to sweat-soaked uniforms, making its way inside shirt collars and trousers, irritating the skin. The men could taste it with their mouths closed. It grated against the teeth like grains of sand. The grit stained faces and uniforms a dull yellowish gray and, worse, it jammed rifles at critical moments and added to the minute-by-minute wretchedness of life in the trenches.

Pleasants and O'Brien plodded down the subterranean path, raising dust clouds, wiping sweat from their faces. They kept their eyes half-closed against the dirt and the glare of the sun. Rifles cracked and cannon roared. An occasional bullet whined overhead and shells burst off to one side. Once in a while, a stray shot hit squarely in the deep walkway, killing whoever happened to be there at the time. There was no defense against that, only blind belief that such misfortune happened only to someone else. That idea was strong in Pleasants's mind. If no rebel bullets or shells had found him when he longed for them to release him from his grief, surely none would find him now that he wanted to live.

Still, he increased his speed as they neared the line of trenches. He might feel invincible, but a little common sense never hurt. O'Brien went off to check on his men while Pleasants sought the quiet of his dark bombproof shelter. Whoever had misnamed these caves bombproofs had never seen one after a direct hit. They kept out the sun, and might keep out rain if it ever rained, and bullets and shrapnel could not penetrate them, but a direct hit from a mortar round pulverized a bombproof and everyone in it as completely as if they had been standing on the parapet in full view of the enemy.

The bombproof shelter was a hole in the ground ten feet long, six feet across, and five feet deep, roofed with logs and a layer of dirt. A number of bombproofs had been built at regular intervals along the line as officers' quarters and as refuges for the men during heavy shelling. Some officers rarely emerged from their shelters, but not in the Forty-Eighth. Pleasants insisted that his officers show themselves to their men at every opportunity. He said he would bust any officer who spent too much time underground.

He threw himself into a legless camp chair propped against the dirt wall. He nodded at the shelter's other occupant, Lt. Robert Lee, a large, bulky man who took a lot of kidding about his name. Bobby Lee's head was bald, the result of daily efforts with his razor. "It was only a home for lice," he announced when he first shaved off his dark hair.

Lee's skin was pitted the color of coal, the result of spending fourteen of his twenty-eight years in the Pennsylvania mines. With his shaved head, dark skin, broken nose, and a jagged scar the length of one cheek, Bobby Lee had a sinister appearance, frightening to children, old ladies, and drunks in bars. His injuries had come from a mining accident, not from fights. Bobby Lee was the gentlest of souls, particularly with children, old ladies, and drunks in bars, two of which he had once been. He reserved his animosity for rebels, Union generals, and mine owners.

Lee was stretched out on the floor, hands clasped behind his head, staring at the log ceiling. He didn't attempt to rise when his commanding officer entered. He was too tall—over six feet—to come to attention in a five-foot hole, and Pleasants did not insist on military formalities on the line. Like Pleasants, Lee was a natural leader, and there was little about coal mining he did not know.

The colonel had no objection to finding Bobby Lee resting in the shelter in the middle of the day. Lee had spent the last twenty-four hours on picket duty with his men, stuck out in front of the trenches in shallow holes. Their job was to give advance warning if rebels tried to sneak across from the other side. It was grueling duty, and Pleasants believed that a man was entitled to try to get some rest if he made it back.

Lee held up two fingers, indicating the number of casualties since Pleasants had left for division headquarters early that morning.

"O'Connor's dead," Lee said, "and Johnson's got some shrapnel in his shoulder. He'll be back in a couple of days. Any day we lose only two by one o'clock can't be all bad."

Pleasants nodded again and closed his eyes, hoping for a quick nap. A shell exploded close by, loosing several pounds of dirt from the roof. A moment later, as if the explosion were announcing his arrival, a portly man in his mid-forties, with white muttonchop whiskers and an upturned mustache, materialized in the shelter, nonchalantly brushing dust from his jacket. If anyone deserved to make general on appearance alone, it was William Lawrence Cabot III. "Of the Pottsville Cabots," he was fond of saying, "the poor but proud branch of that noble family."

Before the war, Bill Cabot clerked in his father-in-law's dry-goods store while pursuing his education privately in his library of more than two thousand volumes, his sanctuary in a noisy household overrun by a wife and eight children. They were the reason he had enlisted.

Cabot slipped off his jacket and shook it out before he noticed Pleasants. The jacket sported a lieutenant colonel's insignia.

"Oh," he said. "I didn't expect you back so soon, Colonel."

"Obviously," Pleasants said. "You know, you're going to go to jail for that one of these days."

"For what, Colonel?"

"Impersonating an officer. Who were you this time?"

"Edwin M. Stanton, Jr., sir. Eldest son of our illustrious secretary of war."

"I don't want to know about it," Pleasants said. "The less I know, the less I'll have to lie at your court-martial."

Cabot returned the jacket to Pleasants, revealing his true rank of corporal, to which he had been demoted several times. Cabot was Pleasants's unofficial adjutant and chief of staff, his clerk and scrounger. Pleasants knew he could not run the regiment without him.

This morning, he had given Cabot sixty dollars for a trip to City Point, the army's supply depot, to buy lemons and oranges and whatever other fruits and vegetables he could find to supplement the regiment's diet. Tobacco would be welcome, too. The sutlers' stores at City Point, run by civilians who followed the army for considerable profit, sold everything from foodstuffs and frying pans to boots and medicines, supplies that usually did not get as far as the front line but that were always available in the rear, for a price.

"Did you get the stuff?" Pleasants asked.

Cabot raised himself to his full height, bumping his head against the log ceiling, and looked offended.

"Of course, sir," he said. "Everything you asked for and some extras I thought the men might appreciate—eggs, tinned salmon, sardines, and oysters."

"All that for sixty dollars?"

"Not exactly, sir."

"What does that mean?"

"I didn't exactly purchase them, sir."

"Are you telling me you stole them?" Pleasants asked, apparently not surprised.

"Oh no, sir. Think of my reputation. Let us say that I appropriated them, right off the boat."

"I don't think I want to know about this."

"Young lieutenants will do anything to please the son of the secretary of war, sir, particularly when he makes a show of taking their names and promising—"

"I have never seen this man before in my life," Pleasants said. "That's what I'll say at your court-martial."

"Here's your sixty dollars back, sir."

"How long have you been a corporal this time, Corporal Cabot?"

"Approximately three weeks, sir."

"I hereby promote you back to sergeant. I'll sign the orders whenever you have them ready."

Cabot opened his file box, pulled out the appropriate form, already completed, and handed it to the colonel.

Pleasants chuckled, scribbled his signature, and hoisted himself out of the camp chair.

"It's time for our rounds, Sergeant Cabot. And tell me, just out of curiosity, does the secretary of war have a son?"

"Do you think I would make up something like that, sir?"

"Absolutely."

Several times each day, and at least once every night, Pleasants visited the line held by his men of the Forty-Eighth Pennsylvania Volunteers. Cabot trailed behind, taking notes. There was always something to repair or rebuild as a result of shell damage. They walked the length of the trenches the men had fashioned out of raw earth and reinforced with logs after hours of backbreaking labor. The pits were three feet deep and eight feet wide. The dirt dug out was piled several feet high atop the lip that faced the enemy. That wall of the trench was lined with thick tree trunks. Slits or loopholes for firing and observation had been hacked through the top portions of the logs, and a fire step had been built so they could raise themselves to see through the openings. At regular intervals, stout timbers were wedged horizontally against the logs and braced against the trench's rear wall to prevent cave-ins.

In front of these timber-backed walls, facing the enemy line, the men had dug a dry moat six feet deep and ten feet across. The dirt from that ditch was added to the embankment until it was a good eight feet high and at least a dozen feet thick. Farther forward—in some places halfway to the rebel lines—the Union troops had built complex and deadly abatis and chevaux-de-frise. Most of the men couldn't pronounce the words, but they had no trouble constructing them.

Abatis were thin tree trunks honed to needlepoint sharpness embedded in shallow trenches, with the tips facing the enemy. The men planted rows of them, leaving narrow, winding passageways so that their one- or two-man picket details could reach the forward positions. Short of blowing them up, it was almost impossible for an attacking army to penetrate the maze fast enough to avoid being picked off by rifle fire and falling on the deadly stakes.

Equally effective were the chevaux-de-frise, made up of interlocking timbers tied with chains and studded with sharpened six-foot-long stakes. The stakes projected at right angles. No matter how a soldier tried to scale them, they would tear his skin to shreds. His body would quickly become pinioned, an easy, stationary target.

No army could hope to take such a fortified line. Of course, the rebel line was equally strong, and, as a result, neither side could advance. The troops and their officers knew it would be suicide to charge either line, and Grant's men in blue were too tired and discouraged even to try.

The thought of stalemate, of weariness and fatigue, plagued Colonel Pleasants as he and Cabot worked their way from one end of the line to the other. He stopped to ask a soldier how he was doing, another whether he'd written home or what he'd heard about his new baby. He didn't hesitate to criticize when necessary, and he laughed and joked with them, grinning when they asked after Miss Anne. He showed her photograph to two men just returned from the hospital. One boy blushed and doffed his cap.

"You better get this damn war over with quick, Colonel," said Sergeant Watkins, the oldest man in the outfit. "That little lady's not gonna wait for you forever."

"I know, Sergeant," Pleasants said. "General Burnside asked me just the other day how to end this war. I told him I'd ask you."

The men around them snickered until the old sergeant raised a hand and hushed them.

"It's about time somebody in charge asked me. It don't take no genius to figure it out. You blow up that hill and we'll have a wide open road right into Petersburg. That would wrap up this war in a couple of shakes."

"It would indeed, Sergeant. Are you volunteering to carry five tons of dynamite up there and set it off?"

Watkins cocked his head and frowned at Pleasants as if the colonel were a dim-witted child.

"No need for anybody to get himself killed," he said quietly. He waved his arm around at the troops. "Most of these boys ain't worth much as soldiers, Colonel, but they've been bragging since the war started about being crackerjack miners. If they're half as good as they say, put 'em to work digging a mine shaft from here to there, pack enough dynamite in the far end, light the fuse, and run like hell. You'll blow that hill and all the rebs on it to smithereens."

Pleasants was stunned. Watkins's idea was so simple, so obvious, so inevitable—as if fate had arranged it. Of all the regiments to be stationed opposite Cemetery Hill, a bunch of men who made their living digging mines. He had been playing soldier for so long that he had forgotten who and what he really was, a mining engineer, and one of the best.

"Why didn't you tell me this before, Sergeant?"

"You never asked me before, Colonel. Are you gonna do it?"

"Hell yes. I'll do it if I have to go all the way to General Grant himself to get permission."

He looked around at his men, grinning like a kid out of school when the fish were biting.

"The Forty-Eighth is going to win this war, boys, and we're going to do it the way we know best, with shovels and pickaxes, and sweat."

"About time," the old sergeant grumbled.

2

"YOU mean that's General Grant?"

"That's him, all right," another reporter said. "I saw him outside Vicksburg in '63, during the siege. He looks just as seedy now as he did then. And he was whittling a stick then, too. Seems like nothing's changed."

A few of the men started to laugh.

"One thing has changed," said Grant's aide, Lt. Col. Horace Porter, five years out of West Point. "General Grant now wears the three stars of a lieutenant general, the highest rank in the army, all of which he now commands—east, west, north, and south."

Porter spoke quickly and forcefully, with no small amount of pride in the man he had served for two months. Still, he wished the general would dress more fittingly for the second-most-powerful person in the United States. Grant appeared pretty unimpressive, shabby, really, and old beyond his forty-two years, sitting up the hill in his shirtsleeves. He had carelessly left one front button undone. A black felt slouch hat was pulled low over his eyes and a cigar stuck out of his mouth as he worked with his penknife at the pile of sticks near his dusty boots. Except for the three stars on his shoulder straps, Grant could have been mistaken for an old farmer, down on his luck, reduced to wearing secondhand army clothes, and the outfit of a private at that.

Porter pulled out his handkerchief and wiped the sweat from

the inner band of his hat. Only one o'clock in the afternoon and already the temperature was well over ninety degrees. The sun beat mercilessly on him and the dozen journalists sprawled on the ground, glassy-eyed and hung over from General Hancock's party. There was not a tree or a cloud to give the promise of shade, not so much as the breath of a breeze. The upstate New York reporters, here to interview men from their local regiments, were not used to the damp, clinging heat that had held the Army of the Potomac in its grip for more days than its men could remember.

Porter had taken the men on a tour of those portions of the five miles of trenches manned by New Yorkers. They had stumbled across the broken fields and into the long, jagged trenches, like graves waiting to be filled, flinching and ducking whenever a rebel shell fell within a half mile or a minié ball spun overhead. The stench hanging over the trenches left most of the reporters, already sick from late-night drinking bouts, retching and gagging. Gratefully, they had cut short their visit to the troops and staggered back to City Point's supply depot, gasping for air and checking their pocket watches to see how soon they could board the gleaming white paddle wheeler that would bear them out of this purgatory and north toward civilization. Now they sagged on the ground, no longer bothering with the charade of taking notes as Porter, just as anxious for their departure as they were, explained the organization and logistics of the Army of the Potomac.

One of the reporters noticed the bent figure on the hill and asked whether that was General Grant. They had been disappointed on their arrival yesterday when the general had been too busy to talk to them. Now that he was in sight, a few straightened up, but no one seemed to have the energy to ask for an interview. And that was how Colonel Porter found himself defending the man the Union expected to work a miracle by ending the three-year war, defending the man who was being denounced for failing to end it in three months.

"Since General Grant took command three months ago, on

March eleventh," Porter said, "he personally has led the Army of the Potomac—"

"To its destruction," a reporter finished.

Porter blinked and his cheeks flamed as he scanned the writers' faces, searching for the one who had spoken. They gazed at him innocently and he took a deep breath. It would not do to get angry at reporters. They always had the last word, their own, in print.

"As I was saying, General Grant has led the Army of the Potomac from the banks of the Rapidan almost ninety miles to the very gates of Richmond. Through four major battles—the Wilderness, Spotsylvania, Cold Harbor, and here, against the fortifications at Petersburg. We have pushed back what remains of Lee's men time after time, and now we have them pinned down. You saw this morning in the trenches that at some points we are as close as one hundred fifty yards from them, and daily we are wearing them down."

"But at what cost, Colonel Porter? My God, at what cost?"

The man who spoke this time made no effort to conceal his identity. Tall and thin, with a cadaverous face and a pronounced limp, he was the only one who had not joined the party last night.

"It's Mr. Gilbert?" Porter asked.

The man nodded.

"John Gilbert, from Utica," he said.

"Well, Mr. Gilbert, it is an unfortunate but ineluctable fact of war that we cannot have victories without casualties. We cannot expect to win battles without losses."

"We can no longer sustain casualties on such a scale," Gilbert said. "The American people won't tolerate it."

Grunts of assent broke out. Porter started to reply, but in response to the look on Gilbert's face and his upraised hand, the colonel remained silent.

"I have the figures here," Gilbert said, waving a wrinkled sheet of paper. "From May fourth, when General Grant began this campaign and headed toward the Wilderness, until a week ago, when his troops tried to assault these trenches, he has lost more than sixty thousand men in seven weeks. If we add the casualties from the West, from Sherman and the other forces, the Union has lost ninety thousand men since Grant took command of all the armies. At Cold Harbor, seven thousand fell in the first half hour alone, trying to assault entrenched rebel positions. And here at Petersburg, in the attack on these trenches, another ten thousand have been lost."

"That's true, Mr. Gilbert, but we now have the rebels with their backs against Richmond! Don't forget they've suffered grievous losses, too. It is a war of attrition, sir, and the South cannot win. They can no longer replace their losses, while we can."

Gilbert seemed not to have heard him.

"Every day, every newspaper in the North printed the names of the dead," he went on. "Can you picture how many pages we needed to list ninety thousand names?"

"Don't forget how far our troops have marched in that time," Porter countered, "and how much rebel territory they have captured."

"How far our troops have marched," Gilbert mocked. "You know what they call it in the North, Colonel? Grant's Funeral March. It is being said that he has provided either a cripple or a corpse for half the homes in the Union."

Porter glanced up the hill, fearing that the stooped figure might overhear the reporter's remarks, but if Grant did, he gave no sign of it.

"You tell us to look at how far our men have advanced since they left the Rapidan," Gilbert said. "This is the twenty-third of June in the Year of Our Lord 1864, and right now, this very ground on which we stand is where Union soldiers stood two years ago during McClellan's campaign. How many have died so that the army could be right back where it was?

"The people are tired, Colonel Porter. They are disillusioned. They are sick unto death of this war. Patriotism is played out. Mr. Lincoln himself said, 'The heavens are hung in black.' The war is bankrupting the nation. Four million dollars a day. That is what it costs us to kill our sons and fathers and brothers."

Porter let the words wash over him. He knew he should be protesting, refuting the man's arguments, but he could not. Deep within himself, he sensed that Gilbert was right. And he believed that the weary, taciturn little man up the hill felt the same way. He had seen Grant sobbing after learning of the losses at the Wilderness. But Porter also believed that Grant's way of waging war, his relentless pursuit of Lee's army, was the only way to end the killing. Hammer, pound, assault, never let up. No other Union general had shown the courage to persist. Pope, McClellan, Burnside, Hooker, Meade—all of them too timid to press the attack until the other side had nothing left.

"Colonel?"

"I'm sorry, Mr. Gilbert. I didn't hear what you said."

"I asked if you had participated in any of the assaults. Have you charged across an open field to face a solid sheet of flame from an army hidden behind barricades? Have you seen your friends mowed down like a field of wheat at harvest time?"

"I have indeed been under enemy fire, sir, and so has General Grant. He has cheated death on many fields of battle and—"

"Not in a suicide charge," Gilbert snapped. "Not in an attack you knew in your gut was hopeless. I tell you, Colonel, there is no feeling of doom, of inevitability and tragedy and futility, quite like it."

"How would you know, Mr. Gilbert? You only write about war. How can you talk with such certainty?"

Porter realized as soon as the words were out, as soon as he saw the faint smile of triumph on the reporter's gaunt face, that he had made a mistake. He had, in his anger, rushed into a trap that was about to be sprung.

Gilbert slowly reached down and tapped his right leg below the knee. The series of hollow wooden cracks hit Porter like pistol shots.

"Fredericksburg, 1862. I left this leg and my brother there, following that damn fool Burnside's orders to keep attacking across an open field. A field that by day's end was covered with bodies and blood. All night, the wounded lay in the cold, crying for their mothers, cursing God, and begging for someone to shoot them to end their misery. I was one of them, Colonel.

"That was a year and a half ago, and the soldiers were more idealistic then. We didn't fully appreciate how inept our leaders were, and we still thought it was a grand and noble thing to die for the Union. We believed in glory. Most of those men are dead or crippled, or rotting away in some Southern prison."

He gestured toward the trenches and shook his head.

"The men on the line today aren't like we used to be. They aren't even like *they* used to be, not after taking forty percent casualties, not after Cold Harbor and the Wilderness and Spotsylvania. They've changed. They're dug in deep in those trenches and I don't think you'll get them out in the open again."

"You don't know these soldiers, Mr. Gilbert. They're the finest—"

"No, Colonel, *you* don't know them. I talked to them this morning, and from what they told me, I wouldn't be planning an assault anytime soon."

Gilbert raised his hand again to forestall Colonel Porter's interruption.

"They told me about last week's attack against the rebel line. It wasn't too spirited, was it? Even corps commanders weren't aggressive because they didn't want to see their men used up for no purpose. Oh, some of the new men charged, the replacements, poor devils—they didn't know any better. But the Cold Harbor veterans didn't go. They hugged the ground or advanced at a crawl and warned the new ones to take cover. The attack fizzled out and fell to pieces."

Porter knew Gilbert was speaking the truth. The colonel had watched the failed attack. The men no longer had the stomach for it. They had changed since Fredericksburg. Even since Cold Harbor, only a few weeks ago. He had read General Meade's report: "Our men are tired and the attacks have not been made with the vigor and force which characterized our fighting in the

Wilderness." Just yesterday, General Franklin, the provost marshal, had told Porter that the troops were demoralized. "We'll have to prod 'em with bayonets to get them out of the trenches."

It was no secret. Meade knew it. Grant knew it. The truth scared Porter almost witless. Had they all fought for three years and come so far only to fail within cannon range of the Confederates' capital at Richmond?

The presidential election was coming in November, and Lincoln stood to lose to General McClellan, the Democratic candidate, who promised to negotiate a settlement with the rebels. All those deaths, all that suffering, for nothing? Porter glanced toward the lines of trenches and the white spires of Petersburg's churches just beyond and realized that if the Army of the Potomac did not get from here to there by autumn, the Union could lose the war by having failed to win it.

The reporter followed the colonel's gaze and seemed to read his thoughts.

"Yes, we are so close. It would be a greater tragedy than we've already suffered to lose now, for want of sufficient spirit to see it through. But an old sergeant told me this morning that he would not charge the rebel line again unless he saw a chance of winning. I asked what he would do if ordered to attack the trenches. He declared that he'd refuse, even if it meant the firing squad. The worst thing, Colonel Porter, is that this fellow was speaking openly, in front of his whole platoon. I tell you, sir, if General Grant orders another frontal assault on entrenched positions, an awful lot of his men won't go."

Porter watched the steamer back away from the dock and head out into the James River, near the spot where Pocahontas saved John Smith in an earlier troubled time. The reporters disappeared into the main cabin to find the bar. Gilbert leaned on the railing, nodding at Porter on the riverbank.

"I hope to God this is the last field of battle I ever see, Colonel."

"So do I, Mr. Gilbert," Porter answered, but he did not

believe it would be. General Lee had escaped from too many traps. All he had to do was wait, secure behind his fortifications, until the federal election in November. After that, the Confederates might not have to worry about any more battles.

Porter watched the steamer surge forward, threading its way through the mass of shipping, at least 150 vessels of all descriptions, from sailing ships to riverboats, tugs, and barges. They jostled for position at City Point's seven wharves, almost 3,600 feet of dock, to discharge their supplies and return for more.

City Point was a bustling, noisy, primitive place chockablock with tents, huts, sheds, and warehouses, hundreds of them. Over it all hung a dank pall of dust raised from the dry ground by the hooves of horses drawing wagon trains of provisions for the men in the trenches. The newly completed City Point & Army Line Railroad added to the din and haze as its locomotives chugged uncertainly over uneven tracks, hauling boxcars and flatcars that groaned under the weight of the army's goods, artillery pieces to beans to boots.

Horsemen and troops of cavalry, riders and animals alike wilting in the sun, raced in all directions, each loosing another stream of dust and a chorus of curses from the men on foot left choking in its wake. Porter walked carefully. It was dangerous to wander absentmindedly here; the seven-thousand-bed hospital was filling up with soldiers who'd been ridden down while daydreaming. Not a few accident victims had taken up residence in the army cemetery, just as dead and grieved over back home as if rebel bullets had found them.

He walked past the Bullpen, glancing at the thick iron bars across the open windows and the hopeless faces of the men confined in that already-notorious stockade. Many had died in that strongbox of a building, beaten by guards or fellow prisoners, yet no one acknowledged it officially or appeared to care. There had been more prisoners since Cold Harbor, soldiers charged with desertion, cowardice in the face of the enemy, disobeying orders, insubordination, mutiny, all signs of declining morale.

There had been more executions, too, since Cold Harbor,

but the one scheduled for this morning had been postponed until one o'clock. It wasn't the sort of thing the army wanted visiting reporters to witness and write about back home, particularly when the condemned was a black soldier.

Porter strode past the stables and the smithies, pausing on a knoll to look out over the hastily built structures that had transformed this once-quiet village. Warehouses, bakeries, slaughterhouses, photography parlors—pictures snapped for two dollars—sutlers' stores, carpenter shops, repair shops. Stacks of lumber, logs, shells, and crates of all sizes. And way over there, almost out of sight, the shed in which men labored all day, every day, making coffins.

He started uphill toward a bluff on which perched a large, comfortable old house, as out of place as a dowager in a dance hall, gazing with disapproval on the crude, upstart town. The chief quartermaster lived and worked in the house, while the commander of all the Union armies chose to work from a hospital tent erected on the front lawn. He slept in a smaller tent behind it. Porter and the staff lived in a cluster of tents nearby, and most of their meetings with General Grant took place where he sat whittling a stick beneath the raised tent fly of his office. There, on folding camp chairs, under a perpetual cloud of cigar smoke, the business of war was transacted.

Porter reached the top of the bluff and slowed his pace when he saw fiery John Rawlins, Grant's chief of staff, hand the Old Man a piece of paper. Major General Rawlins, like most of Grant's aides—Porter was an exception—had no military background or training. A poor boy who became a successful attorney, Rawlins first met Grant in Galena, Illinois, where the future commander of all the Union armies was clerking in his brothers' store.

Rawlins was indispensable to Grant, not only as an organizer and expediter but also as his moral keeper, his conscience, because Rawlins had a fanatical hatred of whiskey. His father was an alcoholic, and he was determined not to let Sam Grant be brought down by drink. He cursed at the general and watched him like a zealous nursemaid, descending in fury on anyone, regardless of rank, who offered Grant a drink. He had made it clear that he would resign if Grant took to the bottle again. Grant believed him.

Porter watched as Grant read the message Rawlins handed him. Grant shook his head sadly and slipped the paper into his shirt pocket, the usual place for filing dispatches. He had no patience with paper and stuffed orders and memoranda in his pockets until they fell out and Rawlins rescued them. The two men exchanged a few words, Rawlins haranguing, Grant taking no notice. When Rawlins left, Grant slouched in his chair, picked up a fresh twig from the pile at his feet, and began slicing it carefully to a point.

Porter crossed the bluff to report to the general on his morning mission, chaperoning the New York reporters.

"Good afternoon, General," Porter said, snapping to attention and saluting smartly. West Point training survived, even in such a casual camp as Grant maintained.

The general raised his penknife in the direction of his hat and motioned for Porter to pull up a camp chair.

"Didn't lose any of those reporters, did you?"

"No, sir. They're safely away."

They sat in silence for a moment, then Grant sighed. He took off his slouch hat, mopped his brow, and looked at Porter.

"Sounded like you had a spirited discussion."

Porter peered into the dark gray eyes, the left one slightly lower than the right, both expressing frankness, almost wonder, as if Grant found it hard to believe he was the army's commander after so many years of failure. Grant stroked his brown chin whiskers with his left hand, running his fingers up and down both sides of his full, neatly trimmed beard. The weight of the Union's fate was imprinted in the wrinkles that crossed his forehead like plowed furrows in a field.

"I hope we didn't disturb you, General," Porter said, alarmed that the reporter's angry words had carried up the hill.

"Well," Grant drawled, "you've been here long enough to know that not much disturbs me, but, confound it, it gets my dander up when people expect me to beat General Lee without taking casualties."

He turned away from Porter and burrowed deeper into his canvas chair.

"Don't they think I'd like that more than they would? More than even Mr. Lincoln would?"

Grant glanced toward the rebel trenches, seven miles away.

"Grant's Funeral March," he muttered. "Don't they realize that if I knew how to win this war in a week without losing so many lives, I would do it? Or if I thought somebody else could do the job better, that I wouldn't step down? Do they think I like seeing fresh graves and hearing wounded men scream and riding past miles of ambulances carrying my boys to the hospital so the doctors can butcher them?

"Butcher!" he repeated. "That's what the newspapers call me. My popularity in the North is on a par with John Mosby or Bedford Forrest, or maybe even Robert Lee. It's a good thing I'm not running for President."

Grant toyed with his beard.

"They call me a butcher for staying on top of the rebels, for keeping at their throats. And now that we're stalemated here at Petersburg, they complain that I'm not aggressive enough. Doggone it, sometimes I think that election in November depends more on me than on Mr. Lincoln. If I don't give the Union a victory and some reason to believe we can win this war, the people will vote Lincoln out and we can all go home. Us and the rebs, back to our separate countries."

Grant fished in his pocket and pulled out the dispatch Rawlins had brought him.

"We didn't win any victories today."

"General Wright, sir?" Porter asked.

"And General Birney," Grant said.

He had sent them off two days ago with orders to sever Confederate supply lines to the south and to extend the Union lines around Petersburg. It was the kind of flanking movement Grant had used successfully on the drive down from the Rapidan.

"They were both driven back. Birney lost near to three thousand men. We'll try again tomorrow or the next day to outflank them. It's either that or assault the trenches, and I don't want to do that any more than that newspaper fellow. I know the men have got trench fever and I'm not sure we could pry them out. I have to keep stabbing at General Lee's flanks, but for now I think most of the men had better stick to their shovels for protection, until a new vein can be struck."

"Anything I can do, General?" Porter asked.

"Nope. Why don't you go have lunch."

"Aren't you coming, sir?"

"Not hungry. Go on and amuse yourself as best you can. One of these days, we'll get busy again."

"I wish there was something I could do, General. I feel so useless."

"Feel the same way myself, Colonel," Grant said.

Grant threw down his finished stick, picked up a fresh one from the diminishing stack, and attacked it with his knife. With each frenzied stroke of steel through wood, he heard the same word in his mind: *Useless! Useless!*

The shouts of the other children haunted him. What else would they call an outcast, a misfit named Ulysses?

The word rang within him like the clang of a hammer on the bottom of a metal washtub, jarring, discordant, insistent. The word had pursued him for years, and he knew it would be with him until he died, as much a part of him as the color of his hair and eyes, with him always like the stench of the slaughtered animals, hides, rendering vats, and acids of his father's tannery.

He thought about the backward and unsociable boy with no ambition or talent beyond being able to handle a horse. Young Ulysses had been certain of only one thing, that he would get away from the tannery with its bloody sights and sounds of death. To this day, he could eat meat only if it was cooked so thoroughly that not a trace of pink remained. And he still averted his face from the sight of bloodied, wounded men.

He had never wanted to be a soldier. His father had obtained the appointment to West Point and commanded him to go. If the boy could not work in the tannery, then he had to get an education. The Military Academy was free. Grant hated it, and he eagerly followed the congressional debate about whether to close the place down. It was his only hope for an honorable way out of a life in which he would not fit. He persisted, however, determined not to be useless, not to return home a failure. He graduated twenty-first in his class of thirty-nine. When he went home on leave, resplendent in his dress uniform, he was teased by the children and the town drunk. Humiliated, Grant donned the plainest uniform he could find and vowed to leave the army as soon as his obligation was finished. He planned to become a schoolteacher.

But he didn't leave the army. He fell in love with Julia Dent, his roommate's sister, who made him feel useful, and he never stopped loving her. Forced to leave her in 1844, when the army was sent to the Mexican border, he saw her only once in four years. He passed the time drilling his troops and playing cards with his buddy Pete Longstreet. The army crossed the border into Mexico, and Sam Grant was made quartermaster, buying mules and loading them with supplies, more clerk than soldier.

He went forward against orders during an attack, came under fire, and volunteered to ride through enemy lines for reinforcements. Although his mission was successful, he returned to his quartermaster duties through battles in which others achieved glory. The only time anyone noticed Grant was to criticize him for his shabby uniform. The man who admonished him was a colonel, an impeccably dressed staff officer with patrician manners and a noble bearing, a man already known to be brilliant. His name was Lee. Grant never forgot the incident.

When the army left Mexico after four years, Grant, now a captain, rushed to St. Louis to marry his beloved Julia. Longstreet was best man. For a while, life was good and the work undemanding for a quartermaster stationed in Detroit. But when the regiment was shipped to the West Coast in 1852, Julia, with one child and another on the way, went to live with her parents.

Fort Vancouver, Washington, for one year, and Fort Humboldt, California. Grant's existence was dreary, and it was too expensive to bring Julia and the children to live with him. He tried to supplement his army pay with various business ventures and failed every time, losing his small savings. He treasured a letter from Julia bearing the outline of his baby son's palm and he showed it to everyone, with tears and trembling hands. He sat alone for hours, rereading her letters, and in his loneliness and despair, he drank.

Nothing unusual about that in the army. Almost everyone drank. Old-timers warned that you couldn't trust a man who didn't drink, but Grant could not hold it. On a spree, he irritated a visiting officer, George McClellan, a man obviously destined for success. The evening he got drunk at the home of his commanding officer, the man prepared a letter of resignation. In the morning, Grant's army days were over.

He was thirty-three years old, with no savings, no business savvy, and no prospects. He caught a boat from San Francisco to New York and looked up Simon Bolivar Buckner, a friend from West Point, who passed the hat among classmates and fellow officers and collected enough money to send Grant home to St. Louis.

Grant's father wrote to the secretary of war asking that his son be reinstated, but Jefferson Davis turned him down. Julia's father gave them sixty acres on the outskirts of St. Louis and Grant's father bought them seed and horses. They lived in a primitive cabin Grant built himself while he tried to make a living as a farmer. The crops were poor. He cut cordwood and hauled it into town to sell on street corners, dressed like a derelict in his old blue army overcoat, caked with mud and dirt. His beard grew scraggly, he pawned his watch, and he saw embarrassment on the faces of his army friends when he ran into them around Jefferson Barracks. By 1858, he was forced to auction his remaining goods and send Julia and the children to her parents.

Grant tried selling real estate but was as useless at that as farming. He took lodgings in a room with no stove and walked twelve miles every Saturday to be with his family, and twelve miles back the next day. After he lost the real estate job, he wandered the streets looking for work, stopping acquaintances to ask for a loan. He came across an army buddy who had also left the service—Sherman was doing no better than Grant.

Grant returned to Galena, destitute, and begged for a job clerking in the leather-goods shop run by his brothers. The war saved him from failing at that job, too. Despite the army's need for officers, however, too many people had heard the stories about Grant's drinking. Finally, he was accepted in a volunteer regiment, first as a colonel, then with the single star of a brigadier. He paid off his debts, visiting every person and every shop that had advanced him money. His father warned him to be more careful this time.

"You're a general now," the elder Grant said. "It's a good job. Don't lose it."

"Useless," Grant said aloud.

A chill went through him. The war seemed like a dream. Used up at thirty-nine, he had been given the opportunity to redeem himself in the army, only to see it fade in the dreary months outside Vicksburg. A newspaper described him as the "foolish, drunken, stupid Grant."

When Vicksburg fell, Grant was a hero again. Four months ago, Lincoln had made him general in chief of all the armies. Mobbed wherever he went in the capital city, he could not walk through the lobby of Washington's Willard's Hotel without causing pandemonium. People flocked to touch him as though he was their savior, staring at him in open-eyed wonder, plucking his sleeves, pumping his hand. Politicians asked him to run for President—a man who had delivered cordwood door-to-door! It was fantasy. It was madness. And it had all come tumbling down in the trenches at Petersburg, and the realization that he was useless, failing once more, and this time on a gigantic scale. His men stared in silence when he rode by. They no longer cheered him. The newspapers were calling him a butcher again.

He stared off in the distance, in the direction of the front. "I've got to find a way to break through that line."

3

THE rebel sharpshooter burrowed in the earth like a mole. He lay motionless, part of the dead landscape, as inconspicuous to any eye that sought him out as a blasted tree stump or the bloated carcass of a horse. That was why he had been so successful these past six weeks in the lines around Petersburg. He could blend into the scenery, disappear in the dirt, and wait, frozen like a statue for all the hours of daylight if need be, until a Yankee face appeared in the gun slit he had selected as his target for the day. So far, twenty-seven Yankee faces had appeared. Caleb Caffee had hit them all.

Caffee was used to waiting for game. He had been doing it since he was six or so. He was not sure exactly how old he was, but he thought he was maybe twenty by now, or so he told the army. He remembered when he was a skinny slip of a kid back in Jasper County, South Carolina, when his daddy handed him an old flintlock musket that was taller and heavier than he was. His daddy told him not to come home until he bagged something to eat. It took four days before Caleb killed a fat possum, and he ran home proud as could be to show it to his daddy, who beat him for taking so long.

It didn't take long the next time, and by the time the boy was ten, there was no better shot in the county. Caleb had learned to think like his prey. No rabbit or squirrel, coon, deer, or possum was safe if he came within a half mile of its scent. His daddy still beat him. The meat was too stringy, the rabbit too small, the bullet had lodged in the animal's liver—his daddy loved nothing better than liver. Sometimes he beat Caleb for no reason at all, just because he was in one of his dark moods.

The army offered Caleb a way out. His daddy beat him one last time when he said he was going. His mama cried and his daddy beat her for crying and Caleb wished he had a gun in his hands. He vowed never to go back, to kill as many Yankees as he could. Not that he knew for certain what a Yankee was, but the fellows in the regiment said they were coming down south and setting the niggers free, and Caleb knew that wasn't right. The Yankees had to be stopped.

He had chosen his new spot the day before, after he had to abandon his last hiding place when Yankee sharpshooters fired at the puff of smoke he made when he killed an eighteen-year-old lieutenant from Massachusetts, a youngster new to the line who wanted to see what rebel territory looked like. Caffee selected his site with the natural cunning and instinct of an animal choosing its lair. It was above and to the right of the earthen fort on Cemetery Hill, on a patch of ground chewed to bits by a flurry of Union shells that pulverized it after two rebel twelve-pound howitzers, smoothbores more than twenty years old, fired a couple of rounds.

In the final half hour before dawn, which Caffee knew without the aid of a pocket watch, he hauled himself over the rubble until he reached the edge of a small shell hole. Brushing aside the dirt with his hands, he fashioned a trench wide enough to hold his lanky frame.

Caffee unrolled the India rubber poncho he had taken from a dead Yankee soldier, so long ago he had forgotten where, and took out his .45-caliber English Whitworth rifle with its telescopic sight. The Whitworth was the most beautiful gun Caffee had ever seen, and he lavished more love and care on it than he ever had on any human being. Every night he cleaned it and polished the mahogany stock and the long blue-black barrel, ignoring the jibes of the others. He never paid them any mind. He didn't care to be friends with them. He was a sharpshooter, a hunter, which was why his commanding officer had given him the outfit's best rifle and let him go his own way.

He blew imaginary dust from the telescope's eyepiece and placed the gun delicately, as if it were an egg, on the hub of a half-buried cannon wheel, in the V formed by two spokes. With the poncho beneath the stock to protect it, he built up a pile of dirt to rest it on. He reached into his shirt pocket and pulled out enough food to sustain him through the day. It was corn bread and beef. Hell, it was always corn bread and beef, the bread coarse from unsifted meal and the beef sticky and blue. The men called it mule meat. Caffee folded one corner of the poncho over it to protect it from the sun and placed his canteen of ersatz coffee, made of parched peanuts, next to it.

He rolled over on his back and brushed loose dirt over his body for camouflage, covering himself from feet to chest. Carefully, he turned over and wriggled his way deeper into the soil. There was sufficient daylight to make out the Yankee fortifications, and he squinted through the telescope until he found the Yankee gun slit he wanted. He lined up the rifle and focused the sight until he could make out the bark on the logs in the Union trench and the splinters left when an ax and chisel had cut the hole through which a Yankee might look this day. He hoped it would be an officer. He hated officers and if he thought he could get away with it, he would just as soon kill his own as any Yankee. But as long as he had his Whitworth rifle and prey to stalk and bread and beef to chew on, Caffee gave no more thought to his task. He would wait and stalk and kill. He was a happy man.

As early in the morning as he dared, Henry Pleasants went to see Brig. Gen. Robert B. Potter, commanding officer of the Second Division, to which the Forty-Eighth Pennsylvania Volunteers was attached. Pleasants had spent most of the night awake on his bedroll, his mind alive with facts and figures, thinking about digging the tunnel under Cemetery Hill. He had consulted the chief engineer in the Eighteenth Corps, which held the line next to Burnside's Ninth, feeling the need to talk the idea over with a colleague, to make sure he had not overlooked anything, before taking his plan to his division commander. They reviewed Pleasants's sketches, chewed over the obstacles, and listed the tools and equipment the regiment would need. The chief engineer shook his hand and wished him well.

Bobby Lee was enthusiastic, too. He had spent half his life digging mines.

"Do you think it can be done?" Pleasants had asked him.

"Nothing to it," Lee said. "All we need is the right tools and enough timber to shore it up. We could have it dug in two weeks."

"And if I ask you to take charge?"

"Beats the hell out of lying around here getting shot at."

"We'd have to work around the clock, just like the coal mines," Pleasants said. "Three shifts, with a foreman for each one."

"Already picked them out," Lee said, "only they don't know it yet."

He rubbed a hand over his bare scalp as though brushing hair out of his eyes.

"When do we start?"

"As soon as I get permission," Pleasants said.

"Life never changes," Lee groused. "We're always at the mercy of the mine owners."

Brigadier General Potter, thirty-five years old, had been a New York lawyer before the war. He was a sincere and affable man with the saddest eyes Pleasants had ever seen. He resembled his chief, General Burnside, with those same peculiar muttonchop whiskers, thick and full, descending from his ears and ending before his clean-shaven chin. Pleasants had noticed that several of Burnside's senior officers had adopted that style, which they'd taken to calling sideburns.

Potter waved Pleasants to a camp chair inside his tent. The heat was stifling. Pleasants tugged on his goatee and stroked the thin line of beard, a look none of his own officers had imitated. He idly wondered whether he should feel hurt.

As he explained his plan to blow up the Confederate fortifications on Cemetery Hill, he was careful to give credit for the idea to its source. Potter was amused.

"This Sergeant Watkins," Potter said. "Is he a miner?"

"No, sir. He's the only career army man in the regiment. Enlisted in '35. I doubt he's ever seen a coal mine."

Potter chuckled.

"Sometimes it takes a man with a different point of view, a fresh perspective, to point out the obvious. Show me on the map where this tunnel of yours would go."

Pleasants leaned over the wobbly table and traced a line with his finger from a point behind the trenches occupied by his regiment, straight as an arrow to the rebels' earthen fort.

"I estimate the distance to be approximately five hundred feet to the fort, sir. Once we reach it, we'll dig two lateral tunnels, one right and one left, each about seventy-five feet long. Most of the explosives would be packed in the laterals, with some at the end of the main tunnel."

"Where would you start digging? It has to be out of sight of the rebs perched on that blasted hill."

Pleasants moved his finger to a place some forty yards behind the Union trenches.

"There's a deep tree-lined gully that drops to an abandoned railway cut. We could start digging straight in through the west bank and no one on the Confederate line would be able to see us. Also, that way we won't have to dig down twenty feet or so before beginning the horizontal shaft. Since the terrain rises from there to Cemetery Hill, we can dig at a slight upward angle. If we get water in the mine, it would drain out naturally."

"Sounds good," Potter said. "Do you have enough men to do the job?"

"Yes, sir, more than enough. Over a hundred of my men worked in coal mines before the war, and the others can haul out the dirt and cut timber. Of course, we'll have to move out of the trenches. We can't work a twenty-four-hour day and defend the line as well."

Potter nodded.

"That's no problem. What about supplies?"

Pleasants handed the general a neatly hand-printed list of equipment.

"Pickaxes and shovels, lots of timber, saws, drills, some simple surveying instruments, fuses, and a galvanic battery. About twelve thousand pounds of powder for the explosion should do the job nicely."

"And how long do you think it will take to dig this tunnel of yours?"

"Not long, sir. The subsoil is mostly red clay, and that's not too hard to hack through. Working three shifts, we should be able to excavate twenty-five to fifty feet a day."

Potter whistled.

"That means you could have the job done in two weeks?"

"Yes, sir. Providing we get the tools we need and don't strike a vein of solid rock."

"When could you start?"

"Within the hour, General. My men are ready to go. I haven't seen them so excited since we got our reenlistment leave last year. They know we could win the war by blowing up Cemetery Hill. That's a powerful incentive."

"That and getting out of the trenches for a while," Potter said, smiling. "Well, we all want to get out of those trenches, Colonel. I have to tell you that your idea is the first I've heard that makes sense. I'll send a dispatch up the line to General Burnside recommending that he approve it."

"Do you think he will, General?"

Potter threw up his hands.

"I gave up trying to predict General Burnside's reactions a long time ago. But I do know that he's as frustrated and impatient about this stalemate as I am. He and General Meade and General Grant are all under a great deal of pressure to figure out a way to break through the Confederate line. I can promise nothing, Colonel, but off the record, I think Burnside will approve your plan. Also off the record, I think he'd be a damn fool to turn it down. General Burnside may be many things, but a damn fool is not one of them."

"Does that mean we can start today, sir?"

"You don't have any shovels yet."

"The men are so eager that they'll weigh in with bayonets and bare hands. It would be great for morale just to burrow in a few feet."

"I hate to dampen your enthusiasm, Pleasants, but I cannot authorize you to start this project."

"That's too bad, sir," Pleasants said as he stood and prepared to take his leave.

"Of course," Potter added, tapping the map at the abandoned railway cut, "I won't have time to be in this area in the next day or so, and what I don't see, I don't know about."

Pleasants gave a smart salute.

"Yes, sir," he said.

"You know, Colonel, a couple of days ago General Grant was talking about being shut up here at Petersburg and the men being too played out to attack the reb defenses. He said, as best as I can remember it, that the men had better stick to their shovels for protection until a new vein could be struck. By God, it sounds to me like you're going to strike that new vein for him."

Pleasants walked up the hill and glanced back at the mound of earth heaped over the grave site. The soldiers of the Fourth Division, United States Colored Troops, were drilling in formation around it. He wondered what they thought of the execution and whether they could ever bring themselves to sing that hymn again? "Lay this body down." He watched their precise, orderly movements, the best drilled soldiers he had ever seen. How many of them would lay their bodies down before this war was over? And how many of his own men would die with them? He knew that if he could dig his tunnel, many fewer men on both sides would die and he could start life anew with Anne Shaw.

He tapped his shirt pocket where he kept Anne's picture in a silver frame. He smiled at some private memory of his last leave with her in Lexington and continued on to the crest of the hill. It was eleven o'clock in the morning, and the sun, as it had for a blur of days and weeks, shined mercilessly from a cloudless sky, outlining the desolated landscape in harsh, glaring relief. He scanned the irregular outlines of the Union and Confederate trenches and the earthen fort on Cemetery Hill, a spiteful, malevolent animal hovering over its prey. He shaded his eyes with his hand and squinted at the rubble surrounding the fort, pausing for an instant when he thought he glimpsed a flash of something in a half-buried cannon wheel, its spokes radiating from the hub like the ribs of the delicate silk fan Anne had carried the night they met.

Fury erupted within him as he looked at the church spires of Petersburg, so near in the brilliant shimmering light of the sun. If he set off on foot, and if there were no rebel troops, he could be in town in a half hour. And if his mine worked, if he blew the top off that damn hill, Union troops could capture Petersburg in less time than that. Or so he had written to Anne, feeling like a boastful schoolboy.

He mentally corrected himself. Not *if* his mine worked. *When* it worked. He had been certain from the moment the old sergeant spoke up. Now the decision was out of his hands. All he could do was wait, and that was something he did not do well.

Nor did his men. Word of the plan for a tunnel spread from one end of the Forty-Eighth Pennsylvania's line to the other. It raced along the trenches like the sputtering flame on a fuse, and wherever Pleasants and Cabot stopped on their inspection tour, the news preceded them. Every man wanted to be part of it, even those who were not miners and who had no idea what it was like to hack at hard earth with ax and shovel twenty feet underground, in a world so tight and small that a man could not stand upright. Anything sounded better than staying in the trenches. There would be no shortage of willing hands, experienced or novice.

* * *

Caleb Caffee glanced up from his gunsight and looked along the low crest beyond the trenches on the Yankee side of his world. It appeared as bleak and ugly as the Confederate side of the landscape, but he did not seem to notice. Caffee saw targets and little else. He watched a lone figure climb to the top of the rise. Caffee took a quick glimpse through the telescopic sight and shifted his gun toward the man.

He focused the figure in the lens and saw that he was an officer, a lieutenant colonel. He centered the cross hairs on Pleasants's head and smiled. There was no better feeling for a hunter than having a target square in your sights. He pretended to squeeze the trigger. His target was too far away even for Caffee's Whitworth.

"You're a lucky man, Colonel," he said aloud. "But I've got all day. Maybe you'll decide to take another peek once you're back in the trenches."

Caffee lowered the rifle barrel and realigned it on the gun slit as Pleasants dropped from view. He lifted a corner of his poncho, tore off a piece of mule meat, and set to chewing. His jaws worked the tough beef slowly and mechanically. There was no sense in doing anything in a hurry.

Laughter reached him from the rebel trench below his position, and he wondered whether the troops were laughing at him. He was tempted to turn his gun on them and pick off three or four before they knew what was happening. Even though they were all on the same side, Caffee's fellow soldiers had been making his life miserable since he'd joined up. They called him ignorant and said he smelled. They accused him of being a shirker when the outfit went into combat because he hung back from the others. An officer threatened to shoot him for skulking in the rear while his unit held on against a Yankee charge.

He would have been shot for cowardice long ago if he was not the best shot in the regiment. He would never forget the look of contempt on his platoon leader's face the day he turned over the Whitworth and told him he was on his own as a sharpshooter.

"Captain's orders," the lieutenant sneered. "If it were up to me, you'd be drummed out of here. Sharpshooters are no better than murderers. Take this and get on with your killing."

Union and Confederate soldiers despised sharpshooters. It was a cowardly way to fight, like sneaking up on a man in the dead of night and shooting him in the back. The fair way to fight a war was to slug it out in the open, both sides exchanging shots and may the better man win. It was true that the war had changed. Troops no longer marched across open fields in massed formation, shoulder to shoulder, like Burnside's men at Fredericksburg and Pickett's at Gettysburg. Nowadays, they charged, running and taking cover where they could find it to shoot. But war remained a contest, an honest fight. It was not lurking and hiding and picking a man off when he was not shooting at you. War was decent and honorable, noble and chivalrous.

Sharpshooters had been known to hit a man while he was answering a call of nature. That was unfair; it was contemptible. No wonder men like Caffee were shunned. Nobody mourned when a bullet or a shell took them in their lairs. Served them right.

Every man Pleasants met in the deep-pit passageway leading back to the trenches asked him about the tunnel.

"We gonna be miners again, sir?"

"We gonna blow up that damn hill, Colonel?"

"Where are the shovels, sir?"

"When can we start digging?"

He answered "yes" and "soon" so many times that when he finally reached his trench, he had begun to believe it himself.

A burst of bugles, trumpets, trombones, tubas, fifes, and drums, a caterwaul of noise, broke his good mood. Moans, groans, and catcalls erupted from thousands of men in the trenches, North and South, but their cries were inaudible over the din of what the troops called "Ledlie's Serenade."

Brig. Gen. James Hewett Ledlie, a civil engineer from New York, became, and remained, a general solely because of his political connections. He commanded the First Division of Burnside's Ninth Corps, and Pleasants thanked his lucky stars more than once that he was not in Ledlie's command. He would have been tempted to shoot the general long ago. He was surprised no one else had.

Renowned as the Army of the Potomac was for its inept generals, Ledlie was outstanding. He was a poltroon, a base coward, who sat out every battle behind the line, getting drunk while his men fought and died. His troops had no confidence in him, and their morale was the lowest of any outfit in the trenches. It was said that rot in an army begins at the top. Men who have no faith in their commanding officer have little faith in themselves.

Pleasants did not understand why Burnside kept the vain, pompous, arrogant sot in place, but Ledlie stayed, putting his men through dress parades and white-glove inspections, subjecting them, and everyone else within hearing distance, to his raucous concerts. Ledlie, drunk or sober, loved his band music. Every day, he ordered his musicians out to entertain the troops.

"Good for morale," he liked to say.

Ledlie's First Division band was the largest in the army and, like him, the least competent. Believing that bigger was better, Ledlie kept more than sixty musicians, twice the regulation number. The general accepted anyone who claimed to play a musical instrument, relieving him of all other military duties. That decree prompted a flood of ill-trained volunteers, and their discordant shrieks and ragged tempos set tempers on both sides on edge.

The repertoire included no more than a dozen tunes, at Ledlie's request, mostly patriotic and martial airs like "Yankee Doodle," "The Battle Cry of Freedom," "Holy Land of Canaan," and the lively "Pop Goes the Weasel." Ledlie loved toe-tapping music. The only time the band attempted a sentimental favorite, "Home Sweet Home," the result was so disastrous that Ledlie, in a drunken rage, threatened to court-martial them all.

Pleasants remembered the day of "Home Sweet Home." As soon as the haunting melody became clear, the soldiers on both sides fell silent. Then the rebs started to sing. A few men at first, and others picked it up. Before the first verse was finished, the entire Confederate line was singing. The men of the North joined in, and soon more than thirty thousand voices rang out in a chorus of longing and lamentation.

A single unarmed Confederate soldier climbed atop the parapet, and in twos and threes, and finally by hundreds, the men of North and South left their trenches and sang in unison. Pleasants stood solemnly among them.

Ledlie went wild, ordering his men to shoot the rebels down. When no one obeyed him, he yanked his pistol from its holster and charged out of the trench. Someone stopped him. Some said it was a couple of privates in the band; others swore it was two of Burnside's aides who happened to be visiting. Ledlie was so drunk that he never recalled who it was. They took his gun away and shoved him back in his bombproof.

The soldiers repeated the song twice. There was hardly a man who was not in tears. After the last note and the last voice faded, the lines of enemy troops stood still a moment longer, staring at one another. Some waved before scrambling down into their trenches, and it was almost an hour before a zealous Union lieutenant fired his cannon and war settled over the scarred earth once more.

Pleasants shook his head as Ledlie's band continued its din, and across no-man's-land the rebel sharpshooter Caleb Caffee cursed when a Confederate band in the earthen fort below him blared forth its own tune, "Bonnie Blue Flag." Other outfits picked up the same tune. Ledlie's bandmaster, angered at the competition, stopped in the middle of "The Girl I Left Behind Me." He gave the downbeat for "The Star-Spangled Banner." Cheers erupted from the Union trenches when the band took up the national anthem. The rebels quickly countered with "Dixie."

"Sons a bitches!" Ledlie yelled from the doorway of his shelter, but no one knew which side he meant.

Caffee saw movement out of the corner of his eye and risked a quick glimpse away from his gunsight. From the safety of his trench, a lone rebel soldier was waving the Confederate colors back and forth over his head in a long arc. Other flags fluttered up and down the line as the men shouted the words to their most beloved song. Shots came from the Union side, and Caffee looked back through his rifle's telescopic sight, tightening his finger on the trigger. This was his chance. All along the Union line, rifle barrels poked through gun slits and pale faces behind them took potshots at the waving flags. It all appeared to be good fun, as if the boys were shooting for prizes at the county fair.

"Get down from there, you damn fools!" Pleasants yelled when some of his men jumped up on the firing ledges. "That's just what the reb sharpshooters want you to do."

The troops climbed down sheepishly, embarrassed at being caught out and disappointed to be missing the fun.

"I hit one," a corporal down the line shouted.

Pleasants ran toward him, detailing a sergeant to go in the opposite direction, ordering everyone in the trench to keep away from the gun slits. Rifles popped off up and down the line. The bands continued their racket, blaring in patriotic fervor, until only snatches of the two songs could be distinguished.

Pleasants raced around the corner of each trench in the zigzag line, shouting as he ran. More and more men were standing on the firing ledges, laughing and yelling taunts as they aimed and fired at the Confederate Stars and Bars. They backed down from the gun slits in response to Pleasants's orders like sullen boys called in from play.

Caleb Caffee, covered to his neck in dirt, winced when stray bullets whined over him. One thudded into a spoke of the wheel on which his rifle was propped, showering him with tiny splinters. He had not bargained for this. Sharpshooters rarely came under fire until after they had fired and the puff of smoke gave away their location. He cursed and refocused on the Union gun slit.

Pleasants rounded another corner, panting and shouting to

be heard above the racket of gunfire and band music. He waved his arms wildly, gesturing for his soldiers to get down, not to linger on the firing ledges. One man at the far end was just stepping up. The man turned toward him and Pleasants recognized the thick fringe of bright red hair beneath his cap. It was Jack O'Brien.

"Get down, Jack," he called between cupped hands. "Get down, you damn fool!"

O'Brien grinned and jumped up on the ledge.

"Just a quick look, Colonel."

"No!" Pleasants screamed.

O'Brien peered through the slit and turned back to Pleasants. A lock of red hair appeared to have fallen over one side of his face. Pleasants realized it was blood.

By the time Pleasants reached him, O'Brien lay writhing on his back, making unintelligible noises.

"Stretcher bearers!"

The colonel shouldered his way through the crowd gathered around O'Brien. The bullet had entered his head below the right eye and traveled down, tearing at the lower part of his face. One eye was swollen shut and the other gazed upward, wide, terrified, unseeing. Pleasants knelt and felt at the neck for a pulse. It was weak but still pumping. O'Brien was trying to speak, but great bubbles of blood erupted from what had been his mouth.

"You'll be all right, Jack, I promise. We'll get you to the hospital."

O'Brien uttered a strangled, gurgling sound, shook his head once, and sighed.

Two soldiers lifted the body onto a stretcher. Pleasants reached for one end, but a tall, stocky lad of eighteen gently pushed his hand away.

"That's my job, Colonel. You wouldn't want me trying to do yours, would you, sir?"

Pleasants felt someone help him to his feet. It was Bill Cabot. Pleasants shook him off.

"Go find Bobby Lee," Pleasants said. "Tell him to get his

men ready. We're going to start that tunnel when I get back."

He hurried to catch up with the stretcher bearers, reaching down to take O'Brien's hand.

"Bastards!" Caffee shouted as a stream of bullets plowed into the dirt in front of him. These were not stray shots. They were a steady, well-placed stream of fire from Yankee sharpshooters, hidden killers like himself, who enjoyed nothing better than smoking out one of their own. He wriggled backward, dragging his Whitworth and poncho, until he reached the edge of the shell hole and slid down into it, as safe from any Yankee bullet as if he was home in bed.

He leaned against the crater wall and wolfed down two pieces of corn bread, drowning the taste with swallows of the peanut coffee. Killing, and almost getting killed, made Caffee ravenous. If he did not have to ration his food until nightfall, when it would be safe to leave his hole, he would gulp down everything he had. He took out his penknife, cut off a chunk of mule meat, and popped it in his mouth. By the time he managed to finish chewing it, his hunger had dissipated.

Caffee the hunter had taken his prey. There was one less Yankee to face tomorrow. The thought did not linger or make him feel good. He felt the same when he killed a deer or a rabbit, or hit a tin can tossed in the air on a bet. It was the shooting, the killing, the winning that made him feel gloriously alive. Everything else was just waiting, passing time, until the next Yankee face appeared in his gun sight.

Corp. Stan Michnik of Pleasants's Forty-Eighth Pennsylvania Volunteers slumped against the logs that formed the wall of his trench. He tugged his cap down over his eyes and drew his knees against his chest, hugging them with his muscular arms. He wanted to hide, to make himself invisible, but there was no place to go. Bobby Lee would find him soon. Stan glanced up briefly when the band music ended abruptly, as if the musicians on both sides were being conducted by the same demented leader. The music died and the shots trailed off and stopped.

Stan lowered his head and tensed his body, waiting for Lee to call his name, to tell him to get up and follow him and take up a pick and a shovel and burrow into the bowels of the earth. And Stan would have to tell Bobby Lee that he could not do it anymore, that he couldn't go in a mine again, because the last time he had he'd left his best friend there to die.

The men had nicknamed Stan Michnik "the Barrel." They said it good-naturedly because everyone liked him, even if he was a Polack and a Papist, one of the first of that foreign breed to grow up in Pennsylvania coal-mining country. They learned to forgive him for that, and Stan eventually learned to tolerate being hassled.

But when he was growing up in Pottsville, the kids ragged him about his name, Stanislaus, and his bulky stature and made fun of his father's thick accent. The boy learned to fight before he learned to read.

"You will dig in the earth like your father and my father, and his father before him, and every man in our family as far back as there has been coal to mine," Stan's father had told him. His father gave him shovels and picks, the implements bigger than he was, and set him to digging in the backyard of their company-owned frame house close by the mines. The boy grew up on dinner-table talk of seams and veins and coal faces, stories of men underground. To his father, miners were valiant soldiers in a war, in a holy mission to wrest the black coal from the earth. He made it seem like a crusade, a mission to which only the most faithful and able are called.

"You will dig, boy," Stan's father said in his heavily accented English.

Stan's mother, a sweet, gentle soul who never accepted her new country as her home, who yearned for her family left so far behind, acceded to her husband's wishes. Such was the way of the world. The priest had made it clear on her wedding day that her vows called for obedience.

She wanted a better life for her child. She lived in fear of the day he would enter the pits the way her father and uncles and brothers had done in the old country, men with blackened skin that never came clean and hacking coughs that carried them away long before the biblical three score and ten. She urged Stanislaus to study so that someday he might clerk in a store and wear a white shirt. Or even become a priest. Her husband would not tolerate such crazy ideas, and she knew her dream for her son was lost.

"You will dig, boy."

And the boy dug coal like his father, starting at age thirteen, eager to live up to the old man's dreams.

"The mine is fierce," his father said, "like a wild animal. You cannot show fear or it will devour you. The animal never gives up. He is like Satan, waiting to take your soul. You must be strong, boy; you must never give in. If you stop believing in yourself, the devil will take you."

The devil took his father one day, and thirty-seven others, in a massive cave-in. His mother was left with nothing but work clothes that never came clean. Not even her house was hers. It belonged to the company. She died of grief within the month, after telling Stanislaus that she was finally going to be with her God. He had never seen her look so happy.

By then, Stan had his own family, a wife four years his senior. Her Protestant family disowned her for marrying a Papist, although they relented when the first of four sons was born. Life was good to Stan. Life was full. Until the day in March of 1861 when the animal that was the Number Four mine caved in and took his soul. The horror and shame had never left him.

He had stepped back from the coal face, with its beautiful jet black formations, to take a drink of water. Three other men, including Casimirz, his best friend, continued to swing away with their picks. Bobby Lee had stood beside Stan, waiting for his turn at the bucket of cool water.

Stan sensed rather than heard the sudden change. It made the hairs on the back of his neck stand up. The most minuscule vibration, a change in the tension of the air, a feeble shower of dust, a subtle moderation in the pressure, only a man who had been in the mines for years could feel it coming. Bobby Lee felt it, too. Stan dropped the dipper in the bucket. The two men instinctively glanced at the beams overhead. They saw the fissure and heard it snap simultaneously.

"Get out," Stan yelled.

The miners at the face started to run, but the roof beams groaned and split and shattered, burying them under tons of coal and dirt.

"Come on, Stan," Bobby Lee called. "Leave it."

As Lee's footsteps receded, Stan glanced toward the cave-in, a solid wall of dirt and coal only six feet away. From the center, beckoning him, a hand thrust out of the debris. It was Cas. Stan recognized the cheap silver wedding band, black like the hand, caked with coal dust. The hand moved, the fingers groping for him, clawing at the air, twitching and trembling. Stan froze. The timbers groaned like a human voice in pain, threatening to close off his escape route. He stared at the hand and reached toward it, then turned and ran, scrabbling down the tunnel as the roof timbers gave way behind him.

"Come on, Stan," Bobby Lee said.

He grabbed Stan's arm roughly and the two men ran through the choking dust. In Stan's mind, Cas's hand still stretched toward him.

"Come on, Stan," Bobby Lee said, reaching down and shaking the husky man's shoulder.

Stan opened his eyes and looked around at the blue sky and the timber-lined walls of the trench and the large figure of Bobby Lee blocking out the sun. Stan was panting, as though he had been running down a long tunnel, and his back was sore from leaning against the logs.

"Good-for-nothing Polack," Lee said. "Sit around and sleep all day."

Lee sat down next to him and stretched out his long legs.

"Colonel wants us to dig a mine," Lee said. "Just like old times. I want you to be foreman of the day shift."

Stan said nothing. After a moment, Lee nudged him in the side.

"You awake?"

"I haven't been in a mine since the accident."

"Well, neither have I," Lee said. "We both decided to join up instead, remember? But this army works in strange ways. Now we've got the chance to be miners again."

"I cannot go down in a mine," Stan said. "Never again."

"Come on, Stan, we've been through cave-ins before. It's a fact of life. Remember your old man. 'You can't show fear or the devil will take your soul.' Something like that."

Lee laughed and shook his head.

"Quite a guy, your old man."

"He was right," Stan said. "I showed fear and it took my soul."

"Hell, I was afraid, too," Lee said. "I got out quicker than you did."

"I left Cas to die," Stan said in a whisper. "I could have saved him."

"Was that whose hand it was?" Lee asked.

Stan gaped at Bobby Lee. He had never told anyone about the hand.

"I saw it, too," Lee said, "just before I ran. If you're passing around awards for cowardice, don't leave me out."

"I was so close," Stan said. "I could have pulled him out."

Lee shook his head.

"No, Stan. Cas was beyond help. If you'd stopped to pull his body out, you would have been crushed yourself. What the hell good would that have done for your wife and kids?"

"I've been no good to them anyway since the cave-in," Stan said. "Or to anybody else."

"You're a hell of a soldier, Stan. Best in the regiment. The guys all look up to you, especially since Chantilly when you rescued those poor wounded bastards out in front of our line. They were screaming their guts out in pain, and you were the one who brought them in. I was too scared, just like all the rest."

"I don't believe that," Stan said. "Nothing frightens you."

"I've got an advantage," Lee said. "I just look like nothing scares me. An accident of birth gave me this size and made me look mean as hell. But you conquered your fear and dragged those guys in. You gave them back their lives, Stan. You didn't lose your soul to the mine."

"That was different. That was out in the open, not down in a pit. I can't do it, Bobby. I can't go down again. You'll have to find somebody else."

"I don't want anybody else. Goddamn it, I need you. I've picked three guys I can trust to be foremen and you're one of them."

Lee got slowly to his feet and looked down at Stan. He knew that if Stan did not face his devil, he'd be lost forever.

"I'm not asking you, Corporal Michnik; I'm issuing a direct order. You will take the day shift and dig the mine. If you don't, I'll bring you up on charges. You want to wallow in shame and pity? Think about a court-martial for refusing to obey orders. You want disgrace? You'll get it, along with a dozen years in the stockade and knowing your family's starving because their allotment's gone. The choice is yours, Corporal. We start in about three hours. You better be there."

Later that afternoon, Bobby Lee led two dozen handpicked miners of the Forty-Eighth Pennsylvania down the deep-pit passageway from the trenches and along the railway cut to the site chosen for the mine entrance. Stan Michnik was not among them. Lee considered going after him but thought better of it. If Stan would not come on his own, then he would be of no use as a foreman.

Lee had sent a work detail to scour the trenches for tools. They found a few shovels, two axes and a saw, and more than thirty good-sized logs. The men hauled their prizes with them to the mine site.

Lee gathered the group around him and shook his head.

"Hell of a way to dig a mine," he joked.

"What are we waiting for?" one asked.

"For the colonel to get back from the hospital," Lee said.

Bill Cabot had brought the news that the rebel sharpshooter's bullet had shattered when it hit O'Brien's skull, shearing off his jaw, teeth, and part of his tongue. A fragment of the bullet had ricocheted into the base of the brain. The doctor said it would be a blessing if O'Brien died soon.

Cabot had left Pleasants sitting alone on a camp stool, his uniform spotted with O'Brien's blood. Only when the surgeon went to work did Pleasants let go of O'Brien's hand.

The miners sat around the railway cut smoking their pipes and speculating about the mine, how long it would take to dig and what would happen if General Burnside nixed the idea. A few absentmindedly patted the grassy, weed-choked bank where they would work their special skills, feeling the mixture of excitement and apprehension that greeted the burrowing of a new hole in the earth. It was not unlike combat. Some would survive and some would not, and the decision was more often than not a matter of chance and caprice. But it was what they did, what defined them as men. Miners were a special breed, a proud clan of artisans. There was no better thing for any man to be.

When Pleasants arrived an hour later, Lee called the men to attention, rendering what was, for him, a smart salute. Pleasants returned it, looked at the men and their motley collection of tools, and told them to stand at ease.

"Lieutenant O'Brien died a half hour ago," he announced. "The funeral will be at the new City Point Cemetery at nine o'clock tomorrow morning. The men of his company will be released from duty to attend. Everyone who can be spared is welcome."

"We're ready to start digging, Colonel," Lee said, anxious to divert Pleasants's attention from his loss. "Where do you want it?"

Pleasants climbed atop the bank, shaded his eyes, and stared at Cemetery Hill. He walked ten paces to the right.

"Here," he said, pointing to the ground.

He clambered down to the railway cut and borrowed a bayonet from one of his men.

"We want it five feet wide along the bottom, three feet across the top, and five feet high."

He jabbed the bayonet into the hillside and carved a line five paces long. He gestured at the small pile of logs.

"One thing about this mine is that we can't nail the supports together. The rebs would hear the hammering. The logs will have to be notched and fitted together. These logs will take us a couple of feet into the hillside. And that's about as far as we can go, anyway, without the proper tools."

Bobby Lee offered Pleasants an ax.

"Why don't you do the honors, Colonel, and break ground?"

Pleasants took the ax and whacked a hole in the earth. The men cheered as dirt flew in the air. He heaved the ax several times, digging about a foot into the ground.

"Who's next?" Pleasants asked.

Lee stepped forward and took the ax. He noticed Stan Michnik at the edge of the crowd.

"I think the day-shift foreman should get her going," Lee said. "Come up here, Corporal Michnik, and get to work."

A roar of approval greeted Stan's name. A couple of the miners grabbed his arms and shoved him forward. He shook his head and started to back away. Lee placed the ax in his hand.

"Do your duty, Corporal," he said.

Stan stared at the hillside as if he could see through it, into the long, dark shaft that waited for him inside, waited for his soul. He glanced at Lee, his eyes appealing for help. Finding no answer there, Stan shrugged and plunged the ax into the hole Pleasants had begun.

The miners wielded their few shovels and bayonets, and in no more than a half hour, they were ready to set the first supports, anchoring each log to its neighbors to form a cham-
ber of wood.

"ready starting to look like a mine," Pleasants said.

pt for one thing, sir."

Bill Cabot stepped forward, holding out a foot-long board wrapped in muslin.

"I'm not a miner, Colonel, but I've been around mining country long enough to know that mines have names."

"Coal mines are named after their owners," Bobby Lee said. "We don't have any goddamn mine owners here and we don't want any."

Cabot turned to Pleasants.

"With your permission, sir?"

Pleasants had no idea what Cabot was up to, but he knew that if the men did not like the name, it would spook them. The operation could become jinxed before it was even five feet deep. He looked at Cabot for a long moment and nodded.

"You may christen the mine, Sergeant."

Cabot centered the board on the log across the top of the entryway and nailed it in place. With a dramatic flourish, he tore off the muslin. The men were silent. Pleasants blinked and grunted his approval as he mouthed the name etched into the board: The John Francis O'Brien Mine.

4

June 25, 1864

My dearest Anne,

We buried Jack O'Brien this morning. It was the saddest thing I have had to do in this war. My heart aches with grief at the loss of this bright shining star, for that is what he was. Not only to me but to his men, as well. All the men in his company were in tears at the grave site, and I do not mind admitting that I cried along with them.

I remember how famously the two of you got on at the regimental dance, so well that I confess to having felt more than a twinge of jealousy, even though I knew there was no need of it. You made such a beautiful couple dancing together. I can still hear his laughter ringing out over the music in response to something you said. And how he blushed beet red, matching his flaming hair, when I introduced you. Do you remember? You kissed him on the cheek and thanked him for saving my life.

How many like Jack spun happily around that dance floor and now live only in our memories? But this loss is worse for me, not only because his spirit dispelled many a dark mood of mine, leaving laughter in its place, but because of the terrible, wasteful way he died.

I know that every death is a tragedy and a waste, but at least lives given in battle can be said to be for a purpose, to end this war and preserve the Union. But Jack was killed for no purpose. His death brought us not one step closer to victory. He was larking. In a moment of frivolity, he jumped up on a firing ledge to see the sights and a sharpshooter's bullet brought him down. I watched it happen. I yelled the same words he shouted at me two years ago when he saved my life, but I was not close enough to drag him out of harm's way. Another ten seconds and I would have been, and that is a sorrow I shall carry with me forever.

How do I tell his wife that his death was in vain? I've written more letters to wives and mothers than I can remember, than I want to remember, and I have always said their loved ones died heroically, gallantly, or with some other such palliative. I could almost believe the words myself, for most of them died in action, in battle. If there is such a thing as a purposeful death, I suppose death in combat comes closer than anything else.

But to die on a whim, because the rebs are playing "Dixie" and waving their flags to taunt us, and everybody's laughing and taking potshots at the rebel flags and Jack just wanted to see the fun? It seems so senseless.

He is buried near a grove of trees, mostly hickory and locust, at the edge of the City Point Cemetery, a spot facing the juncture of the Appomattox and James rivers. The green countryside beyond is a vista unspoiled by war. The trees hide City Point itself and the trenches in the distance. It is a place of peace.

Some families ship their loved ones home for burial, but that is expensive and Jack's wife has little money. Even if she did, I would have resisted sending him back for fear she would open the coffin. He is better off where he is, in a soldiers' cemetery, hallowed ground. And so is she.

I said some words over the grave and the men joined me in reciting the Lord's Prayer. One played on his harmonica the most mournful "Taps" I've ever heard. When it was over, we filed past to drop a handful of earth on the coffin. What a bleak, lonely sound is dirt falling on wood. The harmonicist played "Danny Boy," a tune Jack was always whistling.

A trail winds through the trees by the grave site, and during the services General Grant and his retinue thundered through on horseback, drowning out my eulogy. When the general saw us, he reined in his horse and shushed an aide who loudly reminded him they were late. Grant took off his hat, bowed his head, and waited in silence until the service was over. It was a gracious thing for him to do and speaks volumes about the man.

So, Jack is gone, but even our commanding general paid his respects. I'm sure the men were wondering who would be next. Perhaps they even wondered if they would all end up like Jack before this war comes to an end. It is egotistical of me, I know, but I believe I can keep them alive because of the mine I wrote you about. I have become obsessed by it. Morning, noon, and night, I think of how to improve it. I will go to any lengths to complete it so we can end this war and come home, and I don't care who I offend in the process.

We are off to a good start, at any rate. General Potter endorsed the idea and we broke ground not long after. General Burnside sent word that he wants to see Potter and me this afternoon. I suppose that means he has not rejected the idea out of hand.

I must be my most persuasive when I see him. If Burnside approves the plan, then it will go to General Meade and maybe all the way to Grant.

Anyway, the mine is under way, unofficially, because we cannot proceed without approval and the right tools. The men and I chafe with impatience. Bill Cabot—I promoted him to sergeant again this week—

did a fine thing at the groundbreaking. He christened
the mine for Jack. I will write his widow about that. I
hope it will show her what we thought of him.

Cabot remains smitten with you, awed by how politely you corrected him when he misquoted that
Shakespeare sonnet. He tells me I am too young and
untutored for you, that you need a more worldly and
mature man. He admits that his wife and eight children
are a slight impediment, but nothing true love cannot
overcome.

I am rambling, I know, to keep from grieving for
Jack. It is a great comfort, the value of which I cannot
put into words, that I can share my pain with you and
write honestly about this horrible war. I remember how
you chided me for trying to protect you from the truth.
You said you could not be of help to me if I treated you
as if you were a maiden who would faint at a drop of
blood. I want you to know that you are a great help,
allowing me to write of the bad as well as the good.

Jack O'Brien, bless him, saved my life when I had no
will to live, and you, my dear Anne, saved my sanity by
giving me reason to live.

> Love and devotion forever,
> Henry

"How well do you know General Burnside?" Potter asked as he
and Pleasants guided their horses along a narrow trail a mile
behind the lines.

"I don't know him at all, sir, beyond shaking his hand at
official functions."

Pleasants gritted his teeth and clutched the reins as his horse,
whom he refused to name, reared its head. He hated to ride. A
horse could suddenly take it into its mind, assuming horses had
minds, and Pleasants was none too sure about that proposition,
to charge into the trees or wherever it chose, leaving the rider

to hang on until the horse grew tired of the game. Pleasants would rather be in a mine any day.

"You should get along well with Burnside," Potter said. "Everyone does, at least everyone subordinate to him. He's a decent sort, and that's a rarity among our generals, as I'm sure you know. He's a likable, simple, honest soldier trying to do his best and not always succeeding. That's not always his fault. He's had more than his share of bad luck. He's a modest man, not out for personal glory at the expense of others. He doesn't think he's Napoleon."

Pleasants grunted and tried to shift to a more comfortable position in the saddle, knowing he'd be sore for hours. He agreed with Potter's assessment of the corps commander, but from what he'd heard, there was another side to Burnside as well. The man had good reason for not thinking he was Napoleon. He could be obstinate and indecisive and was given to brooding fits of anxiety. Sometimes, it was said, he shirked responsibility and did not have the mental capacity to handle a large command. One of Meade's staff officers said of Burnside that few men had risen so high on so slight a foundation.

Pleasants knew the story—who in the Army of the Potomac did not?—of Burnside's reaction when President Lincoln gave him the army to command back in 1862. Burnside said he was not big enough for the job. When he finally accepted the appointment, after twice turning it down, he did so with tears in his eyes.

That was a switch, Pleasants thought. Most generals overestimated their abilities. Either Burnside was selling himself short or he had a realistic picture of what he was, and was not, capable of doing.

Burnside had demonstrated the latter at Fredericksburg, one of the great tragedies of the war, and in most of his other commands. He seemed to have a talent for bringing about defeat. At Fredericksburg, he had persisted in ordering his men across a four-hundred-yard open field, in wave after wave, against a rebel force four deep, safe behind a stone wall. It was a killing ground, no more and no less, and by the time a merciful dusk settled over the field, more than 12,600 Union troops had been struck down. Burnside proved he was not a quitter, but at what cost! To many, the price was obscene. The general had broken down and wept.

Pleasants and his Forty-Eighth Pennsylvania saw the carnage the day after the battle. The regiment was part of the more than 100,000 Union troops massed at Fredericksburg who had not been sent up the sloping plain of Marye's Heights. They had groused at the time, eager for battle. Those were still the glory days. When a truce was called so that the wounded could be retrieved and the dead buried, Pleasants and his men realized how lucky they had been.

He heard many men curse Burnside that day. They said the general wanted to continue the battle, to send the entire Ninth Corps against the stone wall in a charge he would lead himself. His division commanders argued against it. They called it crazy and told him he was the only man in the army who thought he had a chance in hell of succeeding.

Burnside didn't push it, but more than a month later he tried to move his army around Lee's flank seven miles south of Fredericksburg, only to fail again, this time beaten by nature. No sooner had the army set out than it was beset by shrieking winds and a deluge of rain and sleet that continued for three days. Few men had seen such a furious storm. It stopped the army as completely as any Confederate force ever could.

Artillery, caissons, quartermaster wagons, ambulances, cavalry, and infantry bogged down in mud up to axles and hips. Horses and mules sank out of sight and cannon could be spotted only by the muzzles protruding from the oozing dark muck. Guns normally hauled by six horses would not budge, even when twelve were hitched to them. As many as three hundred men tugging on ropes could inch a cannon only a few yards, and when the men stopped pulling, they had to throw fence rails under the cannon to keep it from disappearing.

By the third day, Burnside's men were giddy with fatigue and misery and they broke out laughing at their ridiculous plight and at the leader who put them there. The rebs laughed, too, watching them founder in the mud. Confederate soldiers shouted advice and erected signs pointing the way to Richmond. But the Southerners never fired on their enemies. They were having too good a time and the Union troops were too pitiful to take advantage of them.

Finally, even the stubborn Burnside realized that the situation was hopeless, and he ordered his men to turn around, but it proved as impossible to go backward as forward. Some died where they stood, others wandered away and went home, and more succumbed to pneumonia. They called it Burnside's Mud March, and it did nothing to improve his reputation.

They made camp north of Fredericksburg. The Second Corps, commanded by Gen. Edwin Sumner, "Bull" to his men because of his booming voice and because a musket ball had once bounced off his head without doing any apparent damage, held a review, hoping to raise morale. Burnside was invited to participate. As he and Sumner and their staffs, resplendent in dress uniforms, rode up and down the lines of troops—shoes polished and brass gleaming—they waited for the cheering to start. But the generals were greeted with silence, with a dull and sullen anger that reached out from the ranks.

Sumner was embarrassed and outraged. A cheer was their due. He instructed his chief of staff to make sure the men did what military etiquette required. The order was passed from officer to officer. Up and down the silent lines, division, brigade, and regimental commanders and their aides raced on horseback, swinging their hats and sabers in the air, calling for three cheers for the general.

Not a sound was heard save the plaintive calls of the officers. A few brave souls jeered and hooted, but not a man cheered. Old Burnside, forlorn and lost, and Bull Sumner, choleric with rage, rode off the field in the worst howl of silence they had ever heard. The troops had expressed their feelings about the man who left half their number at Marye's Heights.

Humiliated, despairing, beaten, Burnside gave the President a list of officers whom he said had failed him at Fredericksburg. Either they would have to be relieved, he told Lincoln, or he would go. Abe Lincoln told Burnside that he would be the one to go, this time to the Department of the Ohio, away from the fighting, where it was assumed he could do no more harm.

Burnside arrested a prominent Northern dissenter there, slapped him in jail on a charge of treason, and tried to suppress a Chicago newspaper that was defending the man. Howls of protest erupted throughout the Northern states over this intrusion of the army into the rights of free men. There were no cheers for Burnside in Ohio, and before he could do more damage on the political front, he was dispatched to Grant's command, to fight in Tennessee, and eventually given back his Ninth Corps. His immediate superior was George Meade, who had been a mere division commander when Burnside led the Army of the Potomac. And now fate, chance, and geography had placed Burnside opposite Cemetery Hill, the most important point in the rebel line of defense. He wanted desperately for *his* troops to breach that line. The war was winding down and there would be few opportunities to vindicate his past mistakes, to finish his career on a note of glory and to hear the cheers of his men once more.

"General Burnside," Potter said. "May I present Lieutenant Colonel Pleasants of the Forty-Eighth Pennsylvania Volunteers."

Burnside pushed himself out of his camp chair and extended his hand across a map-covered table.

"So," he said, "you're the man who's going to help us put an end to this war."

"I hope so, sir."

"Please, gentlemen, make yourselves comfortable. As comfortable as one can in this dreadful heat."

The tent flap was closed and the air was humid, close, and musty. Moths and gnats fluttered about a lantern that sat precariously on the corner of the desk. Burnside mopped his brow with a silk bandanna and lighted a half-smoked cigar. The smoke climbed to the peaked ceiling of the white canvas tent and spread along it, looking for a way out. Burnside glanced up for a moment and brushed the bugs away from his face.

He had an impressive mien, a dignified air, a friendly face. He could have been a county judge or a minor official of a bank or railroad. His brown hair was parted neatly and those bushy, awe-inspiring whiskers that descended from his ears seemed to puff out his cheeks. His short jacket, belted over a tubby figure, looked as if it could stand to be let out a little. Overall, Pleasants decided, Burnside had an open, honest, unassuming face.

Pleasants leaned back in his chair, wishing he could unhook his tight collar as Potter presented the plan to tunnel under Cemetery Hill. Potter gave a detailed briefing, to the point, omitting nothing of importance. Pleasants realized that he could not have spoken better himself or with any greater enthusiasm. Clearly, the mine project had Potter's unqualified endorsement.

"It sounds pretty impressive," Burnside said, "on paper. But so far as I can remember from my student days at the Academy, no tunnel of this length has ever been attempted. Is that not correct?"

"That's true, General," Potter replied, "but just because such a tunnel has never been attempted does not mean it cannot be done. I believe that Colonel Pleasants is the perfect man to do this job. We are fortunate to have someone of his experience to put in charge. He has dug many mines, longer and deeper than this one, under more difficult conditions.

"It seems to me, sir, that if tunnels can be run in the coal regions of Pennsylvania, they can also be run in the clay of Virginia. Above all, the most compelling argument for this project is that the Confederate fort on Cemetery Hill is the major obstacle between us and Petersburg. If Colonel Pleasants and his men can destroy it, a quick assault on the heels of the explosion will carry us through the rebel defenses.

"Every day we wait gives the rebels time to strengthen those defenses, while our men grow weaker. As you know, General, the Ninth Corps has lost a thousand men in the trenches and morale is low. Colonel Pleasants and his men are willing and eager to undertake the job. I think it's worth a try."

Burnside puffed on his cigar and studied the ceiling. Slowly, he began to nod his head. He lowered his gaze to Potter and Pleasants and sighed wearily, a man who had gone too long without sleep.

"What you say about the troops is absolutely true. They are dispirited. I have never seen men so . . ."

He waved his cigar vaguely in the air and looked around as if searching for someone to finish his thought. Or perhaps he could not bring himself to finish it because he *had* seen men so dispirited before. At Fredericksburg.

"We will never be able to take the Confederate fortifications, not even with an army twice this size, not even with fresh troops who were not ground down at Spotsylvania and the Wilderness and Cold Harbor. The firepower and the nature of their defensive positions is overwhelming."

Burnside pounded the rickety desk.

"But we cannot remain here, being picked off one by one. We've got to take some initiative or we will be here all summer and President Lincoln will lose the election to that damned"— he cleared his throat and gave his subordinates a weak, apologetic smile—"General McClellan, who will sign a peace treaty with the Confederates. All we have fought and died for will count for nothing. By God, we cannot have that! Pleasants, you are offering a way to avoid that calamitous outcome. As far as I am concerned, you have my blessing and full support."

Pleasants grinned in exultation. He wanted to jump up, pump Burnside's hand, and rush back to tell his men the news. But the general was not finished. He brushed some gnats away and rubbed his hand across his weary eyes.

"You both must realize, however, that I do not have the last word in this matter."

Bitterness edged its way into Burnside's voice and his eyes narrowed and seemed to lose their focus.

"Final authorization for you to dig the tunnel and for me to mount the assault that would follow the explosion rests with

General Meade. I will present your plan to him in writing, and I will press for it most earnestly. I hope, Colonel Pleasants, that you are as good as General Potter says. We are not mining coal here, you know."

"No, sir," Pleasants said, relieved finally to be able to speak. "But we will be digging the same type of tunnel I have engineered before and my men have dug all their working lives. Believe me, General Burnside, if you give us the tools, we'll dig a hole to China for you."

"Cemetery Hill will be quite far enough. If you succeed in blowing up their fort, my Ninth Corps will be in Petersburg before the day is out."

"Sir," Potter said, "I beg the honor of having the Second Division spearhead the assault."

Burnside chuckled but shook his head.

"I appreciate your spirit, Potter, but all three of my divisions that have been in the line these past weeks are too drained. We need fresh troops to lead the attack. The rest of you will follow."

"Do you mean to allow General Ferraro's men to lead?" Potter asked. "The black troops?"

"Yes. I know they are untested in battle, and, of course, are of inferior intelligence compared with white troops, but they are well trained and as eager to fight as any soldiers I've seen. The colored troops have all got something to prove. The outfits that have been in combat have shown they're as good as any white soldiers. Most generals won't give their coloreds the chance, but I intend to. I think they'll tear into those rebs with their bare hands. They deserve the opportunity to earn themselves a little glory in this war. Can you picture them in our victory parade down Pennsylvania Avenue in Washington? That would be a fitting end to this catastrophe, wouldn't it, gentlemen?"

Burnside puffed greedily on his cigar, wrapping himself in a sheath of smoke that gradually edged up toward the ceiling. He looked at the maps on his desk and when he spoke again, he lowered his voice to a whisper.

"If only General Meade will agree to this plan. That is the sticking point. You may not realize it, but I have only the most tenuous relationship with Meade. Of course, that has been true with all my superiors in this war."

Burnside's voice became fainter and he closed his eyes. He could have been talking to himself.

"Antietam," he muttered, as if it was a loathsome place a person dare not mention aloud, a ghost too evil to be summoned. "That bridge." Another ghost, the arched stone bridge across Antietam Creek, now called Burnside's Bridge. His men had run the gauntlet of fire to cross it, suffering heavy losses, even though it did not have to be crossed. McClellan had ordered him to take the bridge and reach the other side. Burnside had become so obsessed with the bridge that he never discovered that his men could have forded the stream at several other points with little opposition.

"My men took that bridge, you know," Burnside said without looking at either man.

Pleasants glanced at Potter, both of them uncomfortable with the situation. Burnside was admitting them to that most secret place where he kept his darkest memories.

"Yes, we took the bridge," Burnside continued, "and pushed the Confederates from the heights beyond it."

He glanced at them and seemed surprised that they were still there. He held up a hand and brought his thumb and index finger together, almost touching.

"That close, gentlemen. We were that close to crushing Lee's army and ending the war. All we needed was reinforcements and ammunition. I begged General McClellan, but he refused. There was nothing I could do but pull my men back. If I had not, they would have been slaughtered. The chance of a lifetime lost because McClellan would not support me."

Burnside dropped his cigar and stomped it out with his boot. He leaned forward, placing his elbows on the desk. The faraway look in his eyes disappeared.

"I tell you this story, gentlemen, so that you will not raise your hopes. I lost a chance to end the war at Antietam because my superior refused to support me. Now, thanks to you, I have another opportunity to end the war. Once again, it will depend on whether my superior, General Meade in this case, chooses to support me. We cannot succeed without it."

Another awkward moment of silence lingered in the tent with the odor of leftover cigar smoke. All three men watched a moth circle the lantern before landing on the maps on Burnside's desk. Burnside raised his hand slowly and brought it crashing down, but the moth fluttered away unhurt. Burnside looked scornfully at his palm.

"There you have it, gentlemen. I shall forward General Potter's dispatch to General Meade, adding my full endorsement. We shall see what that is worth."

He studied Pleasants, gauging the younger man's tenacity, his endurance, his resolve. Pleasants returned the general's gaze, trying to make the same judgments. Neither man blinked or looked away. If it was a test of wills the general wanted, Pleasants was determined to pass.

"You truly believe you can do this, Colonel? There is no doubt or reservation in your mind?"

"Not a one, General. As I said, if I get the tools and supplies, you'll have a tunnel beneath that fort ready to blow in a few weeks' time."

Burnside nodded and smiled ruefully, as if to remind them that he had heard such assurances before, only to be disappointed. He stood and held out his hand to Pleasants.

"You have my authorization to begin work while we wait to hear from General Meade. There is no harm starting. You can always shut it down if the project is not approved."

"What do you think our chances are, sir?"

Burnside shrugged.

"Do you know General Meade, Colonel?"

"No, sir. I've never met him."

"I will not speak ill of a superior, but he can be difficult. He is a man of high temper. I have not a clue about how he will react. I assume he is as frustrated with this trench warfare as we are. I can assure you, however, that if we obtain his approval and we fail—you with your mine or me with my assault—we will never get another chance to do anything. Anything at all. Failure will go very hard on us, Colonel, very hard indeed."

Burnside buried his face in his upturned hands after Pleasants and Potter left. Despite the enervating heat, he felt a chill. He wondered if it was a premonition, something to do with Cemetery Hill, with what might be the last chance to remove from his name the stain of Fredericksburg.

He raised his head and looked around the tent. It was furnished sparsely: a cot against one wall; four camp chairs, battered and worn with use, staggered around the desk; and there, hanging from the far tent pole, his sword and hat, its gold tassel threadbare and stingy, a stark emblem of his profession—a profession he had never wanted.

He did not think he had ever liked the army, not with the kind of lover's passion he saw in so many men. His love for the army, if it had ever existed, had grown cold and stale with familiarity, routine, and boredom. Burnside had once been too ambitious to settle willingly for such a life, but when he tried to leave it, he had failed. Perhaps that was when he set the pattern for failure that marked most of the years to follow.

Burnside thought of what he might have made of his life if circumstances had been different. His memories reached back to his boyhood home in Liberty, Indiana, and the wealth, comfort, and serenity provided by his father's successful law practice. A life of affluence, position, indulgence, and high hopes for young Burnside and his six brothers and sisters. The older ones were lucky, already launched on their careers and marriages by the time their father lost everything. The others were too young to register the change, but poor Ambrose, as his mother called him, was caught by the reversal of fortune just when he was ready to embark on his own. Only now, there was no money to help him.

He took whatever job he could find—store clerk, postmaster, apprentice to a tailor—but his father wanted more for him and, in truth, so did he. The free education offered at the

Military Academy at West Point, New York, was his only path out of the bleak circumstances he faced.

He studied, he worked, he was popular, and he graduated eighteenth in a class of thirty-eight, in 1847, during the Mexican War. He chose the artillery and was sent to Vera Cruz, but aboard the Ohio River steamer heading south, he lost all his money gambling. In Mexico City, he gambled and lost again, playing cards so ineptly that he owed his next six months' salary. Some said he played cards the way he later fought battles, by raising the stakes every time he was dealt a poor hand, betting again and again despite mounting losses until his last dollar was gone. He was saved from disgrace and forced resignation this time by the kindly intervention of a senior officer who loaned him the cash to pay off his debts.

He was sent to New Mexico in 1849 to fight Apaches, under the command of Braxton Bragg. In his first skirmish, he charged a band of Apache warriors twice the size of his command, killing eighteen, capturing nine, and running off the rest. In 1851, he was ordered to traverse twelve hundred miles of wilderness to deliver dispatches to Washington. Accompanied by only three men—including his Negro servant, Robert—he made the hazardous ride in seventeen days, pursued by a party of Indians. A good soldier, Burnside found garrison life dull. The occasional spurt of action was a welcome antidote to the routine of peacetime army life, but such excitement was rare.

Burnside grew restless. He wanted more from life. He hoped marriage would provide him the satisfaction denied him in his career. While stationed in Kentucky, he fell in love with a woman who first accepted his proposal but then said no, firmly and loudly, at the altar. Not long after that he married a woman from Providence, Rhode Island.

Eventually, Burnside turned his ambition toward inventions, working on a breech-loading rapid-fire rifle that could fire faster, more accurately, and at a greater range than anything the army had. He saw it as his chance to leave the military and become a successful businessman. He took the design to the War Department. They studied it and tested it and agreed that his gun was far superior to anything they had seen. They offered him a contract to manufacture the rifle in quantity.

In 1853, Burnside resigned his commission. With his savings and money borrowed from wealthy Rhode Island citizens— friends of his wife's family, the ones who did not say no—he built a factory to manufacture his rifle. The War Department changed its mind. There would be no contract, no orders, and no money to finance the operation or repay creditors. Broken, despairing, and bankrupt, Burnside sold everything, including his patent, his uniform, and his sword.

But he still had friends. George McClellan, who had left the army to become vice president of the Illinois Central Railroad, gave Burnside a job as a cashier. Burnside lived frugally and by 1860 repaid his debts. He worked his way up to treasurer of the railroad. The stain against his name was wiped clean.

He could not ignore his country when it was imperiled. He felt an obligation to defend the Union and the War Department that had broken its word and reduced him to penury. He joined the Rhode Island militia, and after Bull Run, where he commanded a brigade, he was given the job of seizing Confederate shipping and forts along the North Carolina coast. His men called him Old Burny with affection, for he was always poking around in the mess shacks and the food stores, making sure they were well provisioned. He ran a good campaign and achieved a high reputation in the military and with the public and a promotion to major general.

Lincoln tapped Burnside to lead the Army of the Potomac. It would have been better had Lincoln accepted Burnside's own judgment that he was not the man for the job, but Lincoln learned that lesson the hard way as Burnside suffered one embarrassment after another.

He was determined it not happen again. The war was ending; there would be few more chances for glory. Would this mine Pleasants planned to dig restore Burnside's luster or would it be added to the string of defeats to be studied by future generations of West Point cadets?

* * *

Burnside snapped open his pocket watch and waited for Robert to bring supper, beef and potatoes again. It was a measure of the man, and of the impact of his failures, that he no longer trusted anyone else, not his staff and subordinates, and certainly not his superiors, Meade and Grant. They had disappointed him too many times.

Burnside recognized that there was something terribly sad about it all. He felt it day and night in his bones. He had no one to confide in but old Robert, his black servant from the Indian fighting days in New Mexico. Every night of the campaign at Petersburg, with tent flaps closed against the outside world, Ambrose Burnside, major general, commander of fifteen thousand troops, shared a meal and bared his soul to an aging, semiliterate former slave.

Stan Michnik beat his fist against the wall of the tunnel, gouging loose clods of dirt and clay.

"Cas," he cried. "Cas!"

It was nearly dusk; the tunnel was growing dark. Shadows and dim light and Stan's fears, as well as a half bottle of commissary whiskey, combined to people the facing with demons and ghosts from an earlier mine, the Number Four, which had collapsed, killing his friend and two others. Taking Stan's soul, just as his father had said it would.

Stan was unused to drinking. Every Sunday, his father had harped on the evils of drink after he staggered from his bed, clasping his head in his hands and moaning about Saturday night out with the boys. But Stan was looking for courage, for something to help him face the mine, and he offered half a month's pay for the contraband bottle. He carried it as gently as his firstborn son down the passageway from the trench to the railway cut.

Stan stood outside the mine entrance for a long time before forcing himself to go inside. He took a single step, then another, steadying himself on the rough-hewn logs that lined the walls. He glanced back over his shoulder toward the reassuring daylight.

The first swig of whiskey tasted awful. His breath came hard and fast and he coughed in pain. Bobby Lee said the stuff tasted like a mixture of bark juice, tar water, turpentine, brown sugar, lamp oil, and alcohol. Stan didn't care, as long as it quieted the demons and the fears. For two days, he had worked with the men to break open the hillside and burrow five feet inside. He could not do any more. At night, he could not sleep. All day, he heard his father's voice: "You will dig, boy." Stan screamed in his mind, telling the old man that he could not. But the voice would not be stopped.

Stan forced more raw whiskey down his throat. It burned less with each swallow. He took a few more unsteady steps into the shaft and slumped to the wood-plank floor, drawing up his knees. He reached out with one hand and fingered the soil. It felt cold and clammy, like a corpse. "Cas," he sobbed, and he pulled his hand back.

He drank from the bottle again and choked and retched, spraying whiskey on his hands, dribbling down his shirt. He was past caring. He was back in the Pennsylvania coal mine, watching the ceiling collapse on his friend. He called out his name and clawed at the earth, splaying his fingers like the tines of a rake, scratching deep furrows in the dirt.

Suddenly, his hand brushed against the thin interlacing root structure of a scrub bush. Stan gasped. He closed his eyes, tracing the brittle roots with his fingers, imagining the skeletal bones of a human hand. He pulled at them with superhuman strength, but they snapped, one by one. Stan fell back, sobbing.

He did not hear the stomp of heavy shoes on the floor planks.

"Jesus Christ, you dumb Polack," Bobby Lee roared. "What in the name of God are you doing?"

He reached for the whiskey bottle. Stan grabbed his wrist.

"No," he pleaded. "Don't take it. I need it."

"That's the last thing you need. Let go, Stan."

Tears rolled down Stan's cheeks. He mumbled something incoherent, released Lee's wrist, and lunged, butting him in the chest with his bowed head, knocking him against the wall. The bottle slipped from Lee's hand and fell, unbroken, leaking its contents onto the wooden planks.

"Don't do this, Stan," Lee said quietly. "Don't make things worse."

Stan growled and charged at Bobby Lee again, but Lee stepped aside nimbly. Stan crashed into the tunnel's sloping wall, smashing his forehead on the rough bark surface. Blood oozed down over his eyes. He wiped it away with the back of his hand and looked around for Lee. He lashed out with a ham-handed fist as solid as rock, but his aim was awry. He swung off balance and collapsed against Lee, his weight carrying them both to the floor. Lee shoved Stan aside and pinned his arms.

"What the hell is going on?" Pleasants shouted, stomping down the tunnel.

Bobby Lee released Stan and stood up. Stan rose to his hands and knees, then collapsed like a wet sack of flour.

"I asked what the hell is going on."

"It's nothing, Colonel," Lee said.

"Nothing! The two men I depend on the most to dig this mine are at each other's throats and one of them obviously drunk, and you tell me it's nothing?"

Lee placed his hand on Pleasants's shoulder and guided him outside. Pleasants did not protest.

"Let it be, Henry," he said quietly. "I'll handle it. Stan will be all right."

"And if he isn't?" Pleasants asked.

"Then I'll find somebody to replace him. Look, you put me in charge of the tunnel. You said I would be superintendent, just like at home. Don't you go playing mine owner on me and tell me how to do my job. Now how did your meeting go with Burnside?"

"He's agreeable, but final approval is up to Meade."

"And who after that? God?"

"Grant first, then God."

"That could take weeks," Lee said.

"Tomorrow, actually," Pleasants said. "Burnside said to

keep digging while we wait for Meade. Potter will send men to relieve our regiment in the trenches tomorrow morning. We can make camp here along the cut."

"Just like home," Lee said with a smile. "Living next to the mine."

"And in company-owned tents," Pleasants added. "What did you do about straightening the axes?"

The army's curved pickaxes were fine for breaking up the earth at one's feet but awkward to use hunched over inside a tunnel, striking at the wall. Miners' axes had straight flukes.

"I found a blacksmith with an artillery battery who had nothing to do," Lee said. "He'll fix them for us. All we need now is the timber."

"Potter said the army will supply logs and boards once Meade gives his authorization. Until then, we can dismantle the abandoned railway bridge a few miles down this cut and have enough wood for the next few days."

"And when that runs out?"

"We'll find more—just don't ask me how. There's one more thing. With Jack gone, there's a captain's slot vacant. You're it."

"I hate like hell to get it that way."

"I know, Bobby," Pleasants said, "but that's how we all got our rank, because some poor bastard got killed or wounded. Someone else has to be moved up to replace you as first lieutenant."

"Who do you have in mind?"

"Young Atwood."

"Atwood? A mine owner's son?" Lee said. "A goddamn rich kid college boy who never worked a day in his life!"

"Who did not have to join up in the first place," Pleasants interrupted, "and whose father had enough pull to get him a staff job in Washington. Instead, Atwood volunteered as a private and pulled his weight with the best of them. He's a good soldier. You've ridden him hard since he joined the outfit. Hasn't he proved himself to you by now?"

Lee nodded reluctantly.

"Yeah, I guess he has."

"He can't help it if his father owns the mines," Pleasants said. "I want you to be the one to tell him about his promotion and I want you to give him your lieutenant's insignia. It will mean a lot to him. He thinks the world of you."

"You want me to pin it on him, too?" Lee grumbled.

"Not a bad idea. You might kiss him on both cheeks like the French do. Now go get Michnik straightened out. I want to see him working tomorrow."

"He will be," Lee said, "or he's going to be one sorry soldier."

There was just enough daylight left for Pleasants to make his way toward the campfires of the Fourth Division, United States Colored Troops. He wanted to talk to Lieutenant Ezra Boyce, one of the white officers serving with the division. He knew the twenty-six-year-old Boyce slightly from Pottsville, where he clerked for one of the mine companies. He had served on the town council for two terms. Pleasants had voted for him.

When the Forty-Eighth Pennsylvania was formed, Boyce was among the first to enlist. He was a dependable soldier who pestered Pleasants for a commission. He was frank about his reasons—being an officer would help him in his postwar political career. Boyce's ambition was a seat in the United States Senate, and a good war record would be an asset.

Pleasants did not fault him for his motivation. Many men wanted commissions for baser reasons. Pleasants believed that Boyce would make a good officer, but during the long period when the Forty-Eighth was out of action, Pleasants had no slots open for him. A year ago, the army offered commissions to men who could pass the stiff requirements to serve with black troops. The training was more demanding than for officers in white units—it was assumed that black soldiers needed better-trained leaders—and many an ambitious, or idealistic, soldier like Boyce took advantage of the opportunity.

Pleasants had not seen him for almost a year, but Boyce had written occasionally to let him know of his progress, and,

Pleasants suspected, to make sure he would get Pleasants's vote after the war. When Burnside said he planned to use the black division to spearhead the assault on Petersburg, Pleasants decided to call on Boyce. The lieutenant would tell him whether his men were good enough and confident enough to take Cemetery Hill. They looked sharp on the drill field, but Pleasants knew that did not always translate into a cold, ruthless fighting ability.

Pleasants could dig the mine, blow up the rebel fort, and leave a huge gap in the enemy lines, a gap Robert E. Lee would plug as fast as humanly possible. Pleasants figured that Union troops would have, at best, a half hour to exploit the opening he would give them, to pour through the breach unopposed and move on Petersburg. The success or failure of Pleasants's plan depended on the quality and aggressiveness of the division leading the attack. If the black division was awarded the honor, they had better be damn good.

"Halt!" a voice boomed from the darkness. "Who goes there?"

Pleasants stopped in his tracks. He did not want to be shot by some trigger-happy guard.

"Colonel Pleasants, Forty-Eighth Pennsylvania. I've come to see Lieutenant Boyce."

"Advance and be recognized."

The accent was Deep South, so heavy that Pleasants had trouble understanding the words. He took a few hesitant steps forward, straining in the growing darkness to see the guard, who appeared from behind a row of overgrown bushes. Even then, Pleasants could not distinguish the man's features, but his shiny bayonet was clear enough. It was pointed at Pleasants's stomach. He repeated his name and that of Boyce.

"Yes, sir, I heard you the first time. If you will kindly stay where you are. Corporal of the guard!"

The two men faced each other in silence. In the background came the sounds of a sad Negro spiritual.

> My army cross over,
> My army cross over.
> Oh, Pharaoh's army drownded.
> My army cross over.

Pleasants was struck by the aptness of the words. Were they prophetic? Was it an omen? That was why he had come here, to find out if that army could cross over.

> We'll cross the mighty river,
> My army cross over.
> We'll cross the River Jordan,
> My army cross over;
> We'll cross the danger water,
> My army cross over.

The voices faded away. A burly corporal of the guard crashed through the underbrush and peered at Pleasants.

"Sir," the corporal said, "do you have business with the Fourth Division?"

Pleasants identified himself again and said he wanted to see Boyce.

"If you will point me in the right direction, Corporal," he added, "I'll be on my way."

"I'll escort you, Colonel," the corporal said. "Begging your pardon, sir, but we don't allow folks to wander about on their own."

"Do you think I might be a spy, Corporal?"

"I'm not saying that, Colonel, but if you are, I don't want to be the one who let you in."

The corporal did not lead the way but stayed instead at Pleasants's side, with the barrel of his carbine cradled in the crook of his arm. Pleasants was impressed. This was right out of the manual. If these colored troops could fight as well as they did guard duty, then the rebs were surely in for trouble. Most units stationed behind the lines grew lazy, quickly abandoning the military practices they had learned when they joined up, discarding procedure like the winter overcoats they no longer needed. Camps were often left unguarded and a rebel spy or a scrounger from another unit could walk in and help himself.

The Fourth Division's camp was a model army post. The tents were laid out in orderly rows, the paths bordered with small stones and logs painted white. The site was neater and cleaner than many towns Pleasants had seen. The troops were well fed and clothed, at a time when some Union units still looked more like vagabonds than soldiers. The black troops sat around their camp fires, boiling coffee and cooking food, the aroma of which was foreign to Pleasants. He quickly took their measure. Their morale and spirit and their belief in themselves were apparent in scores of small ways, which Pleasants noticed as soon as he walked among them.

"Colonel Pleasants!"

A stocky man with a grinning florid face, who would have looked more at home in a smoke-filled club room, enfolded Pleasants's hand in both of his. Boyce's features were almost comical, all flashing teeth and protruding ears and laughing eyes, with curly black hair that sprouted from his head. In the flickering light of the camp fires, the animated lines of his face appeared exaggerated, making him look, to Pleasants, like a caricature, a political cartoon from the newspapers.

"Good to see you again, sir."

"Good to see you, Boyce."

"Here, sit down, Colonel Pleasants," Boyce said, gesturing to the camp chairs in front of his tent. "Coffee? Grits and beans? We've got some terrific apple pie tonight."

Pleasants shook his head and Boyce beamed at him with the smile of a man who's got a secret he's bursting to tell.

"Funny you should show up this evening, Colonel. I've been thinking about you and the boys of the Forty-Eighth. How's that tunnel of yours coming along?"

"How did you know about the tunnel?" Pleasants snapped.

"I'm a politician, remember? Information is my stock-in-trade. It's food and drink to me."

Pleasants groaned. If Boyce knew about the tunnel, how long

before the Confederates learned of it? Before they started sinking countershafts to find it and blow it up? He leaned back in his chair and told Boyce about the mine and the plan to assault the rebel fort and march on to Petersburg.

"Don't tell me," Boyce said. "Let me guess. General Burnside wants the Fourth Division to lead the assault and you've come to find out if I think the men can do it."

Pleasants laughed.

"You're going to be President some day, Ezra," he said.

"Could be," Boyce said. "And being in on the final charge of the war, the one that breaks the back of the Confederacy, would not hurt my chances any. Rest easy, Colonel. I'm here to tell you there's no finer outfit in the whole United States Army than the Fourth Division. If they can't carry that hill, then it can't be done."

Boyce glanced around and lowered his voice, though it was not easy for him to restrain his natural exuberance.

"Let me tell you about these men, Colonel. You know why I joined them—idealism, altruism, love of the black man had nothing to do with it. It was the only way I could get a commission. Call it cynical, say I was using the coloreds for my own purposes—it's all true. But, by God, Colonel, they've made a believer out of me. And you know well enough that there's not much I believe in beyond the perfidious nature of my political opponents and my own ability to get people to vote for me. But I have to tell you . . ."

He paused to shake his head in wonder.

"I honestly, truly believe in these men, in their basic decency and, more to your point, in their fighting ability. Now, I know they've not been tested in battle, but every other unit of colored troops that has fought has done so with distinction, and they're begging for the chance to do it.

"They want to be able to say they earned their freedom by fighting for it themselves. Liberty is not an abstraction to them. It's real."

Boyce leaped out of his chair and paced back and forth in front of Pleasants like a perpetual-motion machine. His hands moved as fast as his mouth, rising and falling and sparring with each other. He was in his element, out on the hustings pleading for votes.

"Most of the time, the blacks are in the rear guarding wagon trains, building defenses, unloading ships, and that makes them feel ashamed. Ashamed that so few people have confidence in them, embarrassed that they cannot fight to become freedmen. It's heartbreaking to me to see how hard they train and drill, only to end up working behind the lines as stevedores.

"They are fanatical about training, and they learn faster than any soldiers I've ever seen. Not just the manual of arms but company and battalion and regimental drills, as well. They're damn complicated, all that wheel right by fours and wheel left by something else. My men learned them in a fraction of the time it took us in the Forty-Eighth. All the black units compete to see who's best. When's the last time you saw white troops do that?"

Boyce fell back in his chair with so much force that Pleasants thought he would topple over. His hands continued to gesticulate and he crossed his legs, beating a tattoo in the air with his shoe. Pleasants was growing nervous from watching him. The man was a whirligig.

"Another thing about these men, Colonel. We have no discipline problems at all. There is virtually no desertion and never has been, not even after that colossal miscarriage of justice—the execution we had the other day. I saw you and O'Brien, God rest his soul, watching from the hillside.

"The coloreds don't get drunk, they don't disobey orders, and they don't sass their officers. They never complain, not even when they found out that their pay was less than what white soldiers get. Take it from me, Colonel, General Burnside won't find any better troops than the Fourth Division to lead the way into Petersburg."

"What about their officers?" Pleasants asked.

"With few exceptions, they are the most competent, committed, and dedicated men I've seen, and I immodestly include myself. We white officers serving with colored outfits go to war with a penalty hanging over our heads. We know that if the rebels capture us, we're dead. They will kill us on the spot for inciting servile insurrection. That's how the Confederate congress worded their monstrous law. 'Any white officer of a black unit shall be put to death if captured.' And they've done it, too. I'm damn proud of the fact that not one of our officers resigned when we heard about the death sentence.

"As for me, Colonel, well, you know I'm not given to talking a lot about myself."

Pleasants chuckled.

"But I'd lead these men into hell itself. And if hell is up there on Cemetery Hill, then we'll clean it out faster than any other outfit you can name. And if that doesn't get your vote, Colonel, then I don't know what will."

5

IT took four men to carry the black snub-nosed cast-iron 5.8-inch Coehorn mortar. And two more to carry four of its seventeen-pound shrapnel-filled shells and enough powder to send them twelve hundred yards into the Union lines. The six-man Confederate mortar team stepped carefully over the scarred landscape south of the earthen fort, feeling their way in the darkness to find a new site from which to fire four more shells. It was 2:30 in the morning. They fired twenty shells every night, four at a time, before moving on, before Yankee gunners zeroed in and sent their own mortar and cannon shells in retaliation.

The team had moved about 150 feet from the last position when their leader, a rail-thin corporal from Tennessee, stopped. He didn't have to issue orders. The men knew what to do. They set the three-hundred-pound mortar on the ground, settled down around it, and fell asleep, oblivious to the continuous noise of shelling from both sides that rarely stopped for more than a few minutes throughout the night. They were entitled to a break before the next volley and had acquired the knack of never sleeping more than an hour at a time. After fifty minutes, the corporal snapped awake and kicked and prodded the others into action. They moved like automatons through the drill, the aiming and firing procedure, leveling the mortar and loading the powder and shell.

The corporal glanced toward the Union lines, scratched his

scraggly beard, and determined the angle of fire, more on the basis of a hunch than anything else. He elevated the stubby tube four more degrees, grasped the square iron base in both hands, and shifted it a few inches to the left. His men figured that he was taking deliberate aim at a specific part of the Yankee line, an illusion he never bothered to correct. In reality, it was, like so much in war, a random choice. It was too dark to zero in on a particular target, and the chance of hitting it on the first shot, before the Yanks could run for their bombproof shelter, was slim.

He understood the mortar team's purpose. It was the same for his counterparts on the Yankee side, to harass, to keep one another awake and fearful, and occasionally to maim or kill. Nuisance fire. A waste of time, he thought, but it was his job and he did it without thinking.

"Let her rip," he ordered.

The shell with its sparkling fuse burst from the short tube. The corporal ignored the deafening roar. His eyes did not follow the shell's graceful trajectory. Once it left the gun, the men had no further interest in it. They applied themselves to firing three more shells and moving on so they could grab another hour's sleep. The corporal shifted the mortar's base a tick to the left for each shell so they would land in a straight line twenty feet apart. Then the team hefted the gun and trudged off.

The four flame-colored stars fired from the Coehorn mortar arced over the desolate area between the lines of trenches, part of a fireworks display that crisscrossed the night sky. Here and there, soldiers watched them. Those who could see that none of the shells was heading their way admired the beauty of the display. Others tensed and cowered in their trenches. They flattened themselves and clung to the earth or ran for the haven of a bombproof.

In the shallow ditches in advance of the trenches, pickets of both sides lay awake all night. In one, Paul Atwood took deep breaths to control his pounding heartbeat and his fear. He had been working to master that fear ever since he'd joined up. His men thought he was brave. He squirmed deeper into the hole, sure that now, or tomorrow, or next week, they would find him out.

Back in the Union line, Stan Michnik shivered in his trench. He rubbed his eyes and blinked at the fuzzy lights. His head pounded from the cheap whiskey and he wondered whether he could force himself to go back into the mine when morning came.

Stan gazed groggily at the red smudges overhead, wishing that one of the shells would find him and obliterate the dawn, wiping out the images of the mine, the sight of Cas's hand, the sound of his father's voice saying, "You will dig, boy." He prayed for it.

The first of the four mortar shells aimed by the corporal from Tennessee caused a jarring explosion on the chevaux-de-frise in front of the Union trenches. Wood, dirt, clay, and steel projectiles chewed the defenses to bits. They would have to be rebuilt by the Twelfth New Jersey when they replaced Pleasants's miners on the line. Debris rained down on the bomb-proofs, jarring Bill Cabot out of a sound sleep. He glanced up at the roof, glad to see it was intact, and rolled over and went back to sleep. Henry Pleasants did not stir, but his hand tightened on the small silver-framed daguerreotype of Anne Shaw. Bobby Lee continued to snore, undisturbed by the explosion.

The second and third shells exploded near the trench at the northern end of the First Division's position, General Ledlie's command. Most of the soldiers slept through the bombardment. One man awoke and wondered whether the rebs weren't getting a mite too close, but he held that thought only briefly. The fourth mortar shell fell into his trench. Seven soldiers never woke up again. Only two of them could be identified. There was not enough left of the others to bury.

The eighth man in the trench bolted upright when a headless, legless torso plopped across his chest, spattering him with blood, tissue, and splinters of bone. He screamed. Pvt. Wolfgang "Dutch" Streisser, twenty-six years old, one of the 200,000 German-born troops serving with the Union Army, shoved the mutilated remains away, jumped up, and ran shrieking down the zigzag line of trenches.

Others tried to stop him, but Streisser was a huge, powerful man, mad with terror, and he knocked them over with ease. He kept on going until he reached one of the deep-pit passageways that led to the rear. He turned so abruptly that he smashed into the corner where the passage met the trench and tore out a chunk of the wall. In his panic, he did not hear the singing, as General Ledlie and two of his staff officers gaily slurred the words of the popular hit "Katy Darling."

They had had a fine time, drinking and frolicking aboard the *Lucky Lady*, a floating pleasure palace, a side-wheeled steamer berthed at the City Point docks, a dock that should have been used for unloading supplies. The *Lucky Lady* supplied the finest array of food and wine available south of Washington's Willard's Hotel, along with an elegant casino. A choice selection of ladies, it was rumored, was also available for a price, a fee guaranteed to ensure that the clientele was restricted to full colonels and above. James H. Ledlie, brigadier general, Army of the Potomac, was one of the best customers.

The general bawled out a bawdy verse to "Katy Darling" and shook himself free of the two colonels who were holding him upright, guiding him through the passageway to his bombproof shelter. As his voice strained for a high note to end a particularly raunchy lyric, he glanced behind him to make sure his companions appreciated his wit. Wolfgang Streisser, head down, running full tilt from the gruesome sight in his trench, rounded a bend in the narrow passageway and collided with the happy general. They collapsed in a tangle of arms and legs, guttural German curses and high-pitched American yelps.

"Rebs!" Ledlie shouted, fighting off his attacker. "They've broken through the line."

He groped for his revolver but could not find it. The two colonels, slightly less inebriated than their leader, pulled Streisser away and pinioned him against the dirt wall.

"He's not a reb, sir. He's a deserter. He was running away."

Ledlie hauled himself up and brushed off his jacket. He looked at Streisser with contempt.

"Nothing I hate worse than a coward," he said loudly. "What's your name, soldier?"

Streisser mumbled something in German, too distraught to realize what he was saying or who this officer was.

"Aha, you're one of those damn Dutchmen," Ledlie said. "Dirty foreigners are all cowards. All right, boyo, it's the barrel for you."

At 7:00 that morning, with the sun already promising another scorching day, a cheer rang out from the rebel line opposite Ledlie's trenches and the Confederate soldiers put down their guns.

On the Union side, Henry Pleasants and Bobby Lee were standing outside their bombproof, waiting for the arrival of the Twelfth New Jersey Regiment that would replace them in the line.

"What's Ledlie up to now?" Pleasants asked.

From where they stood, they could see uphill to Ledlie's trenches without having to climb on the firing ledges.

"Oh Christ," Lee said. "Some poor guy's getting the barrel treatment."

Pleasants looked up, spotted the barrel balanced precariously atop the Union parapet, and shook his head in anger.

"That bastard," he said, meaning Ledlie, the only general in the Army of the Potomac known to resort to this barbaric form of punishment.

Three Union soldiers climbed on the parapet, dragging a fourth man by the arms.

"I feel sorry for him, whatever he's done," Pleasants said.

"Yeah," Lee said. "I'd rather be horsewhipped than go through that."

The guards tied Wolfgang Streisser's hands behind his back and hooked a large placard around his neck. The single word COWARD was painted on it in bold strokes. He was sobbing as he was led to the barrel. Although the soldiers were gentle and tried to calm him, Streisser dug in his heels and tried to pull back.

"Come on, soldier," one of them said. "We're just doing our jobs. Don't make it any worse. The rebs see you acting like this, they'll shoot you down for sure."

Another held him by the shoulders and looked him in the eyes.

"You're a soldier," he said. "Act like one."

"Ya, ya," Streisser said. "I am a soldier."

"All you have to do is stay up here for a few hours and then it'll be all over. Okay?"

"Okay."

Streisser smiled at the man and took a deep breath. He mumbled a prayer in German and climbed up on the barrel, determined to stand there at attention like a good soldier.

The barrel was none too steady. Unless Streisser remained still in the center of the lid, the barrel would tip and he would fall. If he pitched backward, the drop to the bottom of the trench was about twelve feet. If he fell forward, he would roll down the embankment. With his hands tied, he would not be able to break the fall.

If he fell, another half hour would be added to his four-hour sentence. And if he stayed motionless in the baking sun, he still faced the terror of being shot at. The Confederates found it great sport to shoot holes through the barrel and to send bullets whizzing past the victim's ear to see whether he would lose his balance. They could set the barrel rocking by striking one of its iron bands, or shoot enough holes in it to cause it to crumble. No one ever shot the prisoner outright, unless he was a nigger, of course.

The Southern soldiers jeered at Streisser and started taking potshots. A lot of good-natured yelling and laughing issued from the rebel side until Yankee sharpshooters began to pick off those who, in their exuberance, got careless. Far down the rebel line, about seventy-five yards from the earthen fort, Caleb Caffee trained his telescopic sight on Wolfgang Streisser and laughed when he saw the German wince and duck his head as if he could dodge the bullets zinging past his ears.

Tears rolled down Streisser's cheeks.

"You'll be calling for your mama next," Caffee sneered.

A few holes had been punctured in the wooden barrel staves and Caffee saw at least two dents in the iron hoops. He wondered whether he could get off a good shot at this distance—about one thousand yards, he estimated—and decided that the barrel was about at the limit of his range. He was sure he could hit it, but unless he could place the bullet precisely where his eye willed it, then it was a poor shot and a waste of good ammunition.

Caffee took careful aim at the top iron band, a little off to one side. If he could strike the barrel there, he might cause it to teeter. There was some sport to that, like hitting a rabbit without damaging its good eating parts. He squeezed the trigger and saw the bullet strike an inch below the band. Just as he thought—he was too far for a decent shot. He moved the scope back up to trace the man's face and saw his lips move.

"Prayer ain't gonna do you no good," Caffee said, and he shifted the sight slightly to the right and squeezed off another round. Streisser's head jerked aside and Caffee laughed out loud.

"Not bad," he muttered. "Maybe I can have me some fun, after all."

But he was in no hurry. He would wait a while until the others lost interest. Already the gunfire was dying down. That way, he would know for sure whether the shot was really his. Then, too, the longer he waited, the more confident the soldier would be that he could keep his balance on the barrel.

Caffee reached into his knapsack and pulled out a quarter loaf of buckwheat bread and a crock of apple butter. With his penknife, he cut a slice of the bread, slathered it with thick waves of the fruity mixture, and gobbled it down before the food's rightful owner could claim it. He laughed at the thought and licked the excess from his fingers. The rightful owner, that snobbish son-of-a-bitch lieutenant from Charleston, was dead.

He finished off a second slice of bread and glanced across the field at the Union soldier on the barrel. Nobody was shooting at him anymore. They had tired of the game. Caleb focused the Whitworth's telescopic sight on Streisser's face. The damn fool was smiling.

Wolfgang Streisser told himself over and over that he was a soldier, and he forced himself to stand straight and tall and still. Gradually, his fear left him, replaced by a sense of pride. He could take it. He was going to live through this. A voice called up to him from the trench below.

"How you doing up there, Dutch?"

It was his platoon sergeant.

"I am okay," Dutch said.

"Well, no wonder," the sergeant said. "Hell, you got the safest spot in the whole damn line. Nobody's shooting at you. They're sure pelting us good down here. Tell you what. When you're finished, I'll get up on that there barrel. I could use the rest. Okay?"

"Okay," Streisser said, laughing aloud at the thought.

Caleb Caffee was livid. The Yank was laughing at him. He focused the cross hairs on Streisser's forehead and when the grinning German turned his way, Caffee pulled the trigger and watched his target explode. Streisser's body tumbled backward into the trench.

"Goddamn it!" Pleasants said. "Somebody shot the poor bastard." Anger twisted a knot in his stomach. Another stupid, wasted death. Just like poor Jack O'Brien.

He glanced around the trench and vowed he would never live in such a place again. This was no way to fight a war, sitting in your own filth in the merciless sun, being shot at and shelled day and night. Pleasants knew that if the assault that would be launched when he blew up Cemetery Hill failed, he and his men, and the whole Army of the Potomac, would be condemned to those miles of trenches until they starved the rebels out—and there was little chance of that happening with the railroads still running through Petersburg—or until McClellan won the election in November and negotiated a settlement with the Confederates.

"We're going to bore a hole right under that hillside and blow it away," Pleasants said, "and the Ninth Corps is going to sweep through like the flood from a broken dam and then we'll all go home."

"Sounds like a good idea to me," Lee said.

"Did the morning shift get started?"

"Yeah."

"And Stan?"

"He's the foreman," Lee said. "He was on the job at dawn with his pickax on his shoulder."

"It's a wonder he could stand up after all that whiskey."

"We had a little talk, Stan and me."

"You still think he'll be all right?"

"He'll be fine," Lee snapped. "I told you that."

Pleasants smiled and patted Lee's shoulder.

"Now don't go getting mulish on me, Bobby. We mine owners care about the welfare of our workers. We just want them to be happy."

"Don't get me started on mine owners," Lee said. "Thanks to you, I've got to go see Atwood and tell him about his promotion. When you win the war and I go back to the mines, that kid's gonna be my boss."

"Maybe he'll be better than his old man."

"Don't count on it. Mine owners are all alike."

"Well, I'll leave you to it," Pleasants said, turning away. "I've got to see General Potter. I need to borrow two wagons to haul the lumber from that abandoned railway bridge. I want a cavalry escort, too. That bridge is five miles behind our lines and there have been reports of guerrilla bands on the loose."

Bobby Lee shoved his hands in his pockets and shuffled down the trench. A minié ball whistled overhead and the drawn-out shriek of a rebel shell filled the air. He looked at the sky and scowled, daring the projectile to come anywhere near him. It fell obediently behind the trench line. He saw one of his soldiers peek through a gun slit.

"Get down from there, you dumb bastard," Lee shouted.

The boy jumped down and smiled an apology.

"I just wanted a last look, sir, before we leave."

"Be the last look you had at anything."

Lee glared at the half dozen men of his company nearby. All had broad grins on their faces.

"I swear, I don't know what you fellows would do without me looking out for you."

"Yes, Mother," one said.

"Don't get me riled up, if you know what's good for you."

"No, sir, Captain Lee, sir," they barked in unison.

They snapped to attention and gave the smartest parade-ground salute he had seen in some time. The soldiers had been nudging one another and jumping to attention in his presence all morning, ever since he showed up wearing his new captain's bars. Lee was pleased, but he scowled at them, anyway. He had his reputation to preserve.

"The captain's wish is our command, sir."

"Does the captain need his boots polished, sir?"

"What the captain needs," Lee said, "is some real soldiers instead of you sorry misfits. No wonder we haven't won the war. Take your gear and head for the new camp—if you think you can find your way there without a map."

They saluted again and scampered off like schoolboys playing hooky. Lee smiled and walked on to the next bombproof. He stooped to enter and saw Paul Atwood stretched out on the floor, sound asleep after a twenty-four-hour stint on picket duty. Lee squatted beside him and studied his face for a moment. He was a handsome boy with an aquiline nose, high cheekbones, a strong jaw, and wavy brown hair. He was so attractive that the men had teased him and called him "Pauline" before they saw how well he acquitted himself from his first hour in battle.

Atwood had had a tough time, what with his good looks, his quiet and polite manners, and the handicap of being the son of the most hated mine owner in Pottsville. Two years at Harvard did not count well with the men, either, not in an outfit in which most, Bobby Lee among them, had not finished high school.

Lee made Atwood's life miserable from the beginning, chewing him out for flaws he was willing to overlook in other men, demanding extra duty, and taunting him so recklessly that the boy once broke down in tears. Pleasants ordered Bobby Lee to stop, to give Atwood a chance to prove his worth. But Lee hated him because of who his father was. It gnawed at his guts to give Atwood a commission. Deep down, Lee knew that Pleasants was right—the boy deserved it—but Lee could not be generous enough to admit that he had been wrong.

He reached over and shook Atwood's shoulder.

"Wake up, kid."

Atwood flinched at the sound of Lee's voice. He came awake with the look of a frightened deer. He sat up at attention and blinked at Lee, wondering what he had done wrong this time.

"Did I forget something, Lieutenant Lee?"

"Yeah," Lee said, pointing to his shoulder straps. "You forgot to call me captain."

"I'm sorry, sir. I didn't know. Congratulations, Captain Lee."

Atwood started to extend his hand. It was an automatic, gentlemanly reaction, but he stopped, unsure whether to complete the gesture. He started to withdraw his hand when Bobby Lee grinned. Atwood was dumbfounded. In three years, Lee had never smiled at him except in malice.

"What's the matter," Lee asked, "can't you shake hands?"

"Uh, no. I mean, yes, sir," Atwood said, pushing his hand forward again, half-expecting to have it bitten. "Congratulations again, sir."

Lee clasped his hand. He reached into his pocket and tossed out a pair of patches, his first lieutenant's insignia.

"Same to you, kid," Lee said. "Only now that you've been promoted, maybe I'll have to stop calling you 'kid.' "

"Promoted, sir?"

"Yeah. Colonel Pleasants's idea, but I want you to know

that, well, the fact is, I support it a hundred percent. You deserve it, kid."

Atwood fingered the shoulder-strap insignia as if they were precious gems and stared at Lee with awe. Lee was embarrassed and looked away.

"Those are mine," he finally said, breaking the awkward silence. "I thought you might like, well, maybe they'll bring you luck. Anyway, I survived the last year and a half wearing them."

"I appreciate that, sir, more than I can say."

Lee wished he was someplace else, anywhere, and with anyone but this nice-looking, decent young man who symbolized everything Lee despised—privilege, property, power, and indifference toward those who labored under the earth to produce the fortune Atwood would inherit. Still, none of that was the kid's fault, Bobby Lee reminded himself, and he knew it was time to make amends.

"Look," Lee said. "I guess this won't come as any great surprise, but I suppose I've been pretty hard on you."

He paused, hoping that Atwood would say something to help him out, but the lieutenant just looked at him, expectantly and eagerly, waiting to hear that Bobby Lee, the toughest man in the outfit next to Colonel Pleasants, had finally accepted him as a soldier.

"Maybe I was too hard on you."

"Well, sir, I was pretty green. I didn't know much about being a soldier, but I watched you and tried to do the same."

"Yeah, well," Lee said with a wave of his hand as though shooing away a fly. "Whatever you did, it worked. You're a damn fine soldier and a good officer. If I was unfair to you, I'm sorry."

"Thank you, sir, but if you don't mind my saying so, I figured you weren't going after me so much as after my father."

Lee chuckled self-consciously.

"Him, and that coat of yours with the fur collar," Lee said.

"Coat, sir?"

"It must have been ten years ago, just before Christmas. I

was coming off the shift with my crew. We were miserable and shaking from the cold and your old man announced that he was closing the mine down for two weeks because business was bad. There we were, Christmas coming and no money for food, much less presents for our kids. The wind was blowing through those flimsy houses we lived in and we had to smuggle out lumps of coal to heat them because your old man wouldn't give us any, or even sell it to us.

"Anyway, we were coming out of the mine and you and he were standing near the office shack watching us, you all gussied up in a gray wool coat with a big fur collar. It probably cost more than I made in a year. My kids stuffed newspapers in their shoes to cover up the holes, and there you were, looking down on us like we were vermin. Your old man never allowed us a place to wash off like some mine owners do, and I hated you for looking so clean and neat in that coat. Of course, you were just a boy and didn't know any better."

Bobby Lee paused and stared at the dirt floor as though it were a mirror in which he could see himself. Silence filled the bombproof. The rifle fire and the shelling sounded far away.

"I'm not like my father," Atwood said quietly, his voice hardening like steel. "And I never will be. I've learned a lot in the army and it's changed me. I'll inherit those mines, but I won't run them like he does. You're right about the way he looks down on miners. But I've lived with the men of the Forty-Eighth. I know what they're like. Things will change when I take over the mines."

Lee shook his head and raised a hand to interrupt Atwood.

"No, kid. I know you mean well, but when this war's over, you'll go back up the hill and after a while you'll look down on us the same way your old man does. No, the only chance we have for things to change is for the miners to organize, to form a union of workers and shut down the mines by refusing to work until our demands are met. That will give us the power to force changes, to make our lives decent."

"You make it sound like a war, the workers against the owners."

"It always has been," Lee said, "except that we were powerless. We'll have to fight you to claim our share of that power and it will be bloody and awful before it's over. But that's the way it has to be."

"So we'll always be enemies," Atwood said.

"We always have been. Some things never change."

"Captain Lee, I'm going to prove you wrong. My miners won't have to organize. I can build new homes and schools. And I can pay higher wages."

Lee looked at Atwood wistfully.

"That's a nice dream, kid," he said. "Who knows? Maybe it will work out. But right now, we've got a new mine to dig, so get off your behind and take your men down to the new camp at the railway cut. And be quick about it. You may be a first lieutenant now, but you still work for me."

Lee smiled.

"I'm the mine owner here."

"Yes, sir, Captain Lee," Atwood said, and he followed him out of the bombproof.

"Claptrap and nonsense!"

Gen. George Gordon Meade slammed Burnside's dispatch down with a massive hand as though he was squashing a cockroach. He twisted the heel of his hand on top of the papers, grinding them into the desk and glaring at them with contempt.

"Claptrap and nonsense," he repeated, his voice carrying beyond the confines of the big white headquarters tent. "That's all there is to it."

He glanced toward the open tent fly and bellowed for his aide, Col. Theodore Lyman, the staff officer he trusted more than anyone else. Lyman embodied everything Meade aspired to, the perfect gentleman, patrician of birth, noble of bearing. "If there is any reputation I aspire to," Meade was fond of saying, "it is that of a gentleman."

"Lyman, get in here."

Lyman had been expecting the call ever since he had handed Meade the dispatch about the mine. Having read it, and knowing Meade's opinion of Burnside, he had been waiting for the inevitable explosion. He placed his wineglass gently on the linen-covered mess table—dwelling in a tent was no reason to abandon a gracious lifestyle—and looked around the luncheon table at the rest of the staff. Fourteen in all, it was a small group for the commander of the Army of the Potomac. It reflected Meade's compulsive attention to detail. "If you want something done right," he liked to say, "you have to do it yourself."

The other officers were relieved that they had not been called. Most of them would rather face the Confederates than General Meade's towering rages. They lived in constant anxiety, never knowing who would be the next target of his ungovernable wrath. The troops called him an old snapping turtle, and he looked like one, with oversize glasses magnifying his bulging eyes.

He could be savage as a wounded grizzly and was as likely to cuss out an officer, a stable boy, or a courier bringing bad news, or even good news. Charles Dana, assistant to Secretary of War Stanton, had been discussing Meade with his boss just a few days ago. Lyman had been waiting in the outer office and overheard every word.

"I do not think Meade has a friend in the whole army," Dana said. "No man approaches him without being insulted in one way or another, and his own staff officers do not dare speak to him unless first spoken to, for fear of either sneers or curses."

Stanton agreed, adding that Meade didn't seem to want any friends. Dana suggested that Meade be relieved, not only for his irascibility but also for his failings as a leader, first at Gettysburg and now at Petersburg. "He has to go," declared the unctuous and influential Dana. Stanton mumbled something in reply, but Lyman did not catch it.

Lyman dabbed at the corners of his mouth with his damask napkin, rose from his chair, and straightened his jacket. He cast a glance over his shoes and brass buttons. General Meade prized neatness.

"Once more into the lion's den," a major said. "Any last-minute changes in your will in case you don't return?"

Lyman smiled and headed for the general's tent, ignoring the chief of artillery, who was telling the others, "Lyman doesn't have to worry. He always comes back." The rest of the staff, professional soldiers all, were jealous of the special relationship between Meade and Lyman, a friendship established nearly fifteen years ago when Meade was building lighthouses in Florida and Lyman joined his camp as an amateur naturalist.

Lyman had spent the first two years of the war traveling in Europe. When he returned to Boston, he wrote to Meade, offering to serve as an unpaid aide-de-camp, a position for which Lyman assumed, correctly, that his social graces would be valued. Meade replied promptly, urging him to come, noting that he would have to supply his own horse and servant and secure a commission from the Massachusetts militia. Within the week, Lyman was on his way south with a wardrobe of fitted uniforms and the rank of colonel.

He approached Meade's tent, careful to stay on the path, away from the watered and manicured lawn that surrounded it, an oasis in the sea of sunburned grass that stretched to a grove of trees. He glanced at Meade's headquarters flag hanging limply in the still, sultry air. The huge swallow-tailed banner of magenta showed a golden wreath encircling a gold eagle. Lyman thought it was pretentious, and he chuckled to himself, recalling General Grant's first sight of the flag flapping royally in a brisk breeze. The general of all the armies, who flew no headquarters flag himself, had stared at it, bemused, before asking his aide whether he had wandered into the wrong century. "Is Imperial Caesar about here?" Grant had quipped.

"Render therefore unto Caesar the things which are Caesar's," Lyman reminded himself as he entered Meade's tent and saluted. Meade gestured for him to sit down.

"Have you read this?"

"Yes, sir."

"What do you think of it?"

Lyman knew better than to offer his opinion. He knew that Meade thought poorly of Burnside and, by extension, of any plan Burnside submitted. Lyman did not think the mine was such a bad idea. Nothing else was working. Why not try it? But he knew he could not counter Meade's prejudice against anything associated with Burnside.

"I'm not sure it's a sound idea," Lyman said smoothly.

"You're just being polite," Meade said in his low, bland voice. "I know how you shy away from criticizing others. An admirable quality, but one I cannot afford in my position."

The color of anger rose in Meade's face, broken only by the wide lenses of his spectacles. Although tall and imposing in a carefully tailored uniform, Meade appeared dour, more like a scholar than a general, with a hooked nose, piercing eyes, and a full brown beard. His hair showed flecks of gray, and he looked older than his forty-nine years. Lines of worry, even pain, streaked his face and creases flared alongside his nose. Pouches sagged beneath his eyes. He wore high cavalry boots, shined to the brilliance of glass, and his decorations and buttons were equally dazzling.

"Who is this fellow Pleasants?" Meade asked, flicking a long rim of ash from his cigar. "Some demented dreamer or a glory hound?"

"I don't know, sir. I've never heard of him. According to General Burnside, he's some kind of coal-mining engineer."

"Engineer?" Meade snorted. "You don't need engineers to dig coal mines. All you need is a strong back. He was probably a mine foreman before the war and now he's a lieutenant colonel. That's the way in these volunteer regiments, handing out commissions to anybody, promoting them out of proportion to their ability and their background."

"General Burnside speaks highly of him, sir," Lyman ventured.

Meade laughed.

"Poor old Burnside. He's easily impressed by any harebrained schemer who promises a quick end to this war."

He pointed his cigar at Lyman and winked hugely behind his outsize lenses.

"Anything that might help people forget Fredericksburg. Old Burny is so gullible, always looking for a miracle. He ought to know that miners don't win wars. You can't go under the Confederate trenches and you can't go over them, though Burnside did use one of those fool observation balloons at Fredericksburg. Lot of good that did him."

Meade leaned back in his camp chair and Lyman tensed when the wood cracked under the strain. Toppling over would not improve the general's disposition.

"I don't have to tell you what I think of Burnside," Meade said before proceeding to tell him precisely that, and not for the first time.

"I like Burnside. He has always been considerate of me, even when I served under him. But at the same time, I feel sorry for him because the poor fellow does not know what he is about."

He paused for a moment and shut his eyes. Lyman imagined that he was trying to remember his set speech about Burnside. So far, his recall had been almost perfect. It made Lyman feel as if he was grading a recitation and that Meade was aiming for a perfect score.

"Don't misunderstand me," Meade continued. "The man has positive qualities. He is determined, although some call that obstinacy, and he has a great deal of nerve. No one faults his bravery. But he has proven that he lacks a sufficient quantity of judgment. Just look at this fool thing he endorses."

With two fingers, Meade picked up Burnside's dispatch and dropped it as if it was a piece of trash.

"Then there is the larger issue. I do not believe, and never have, that General Burnside has sufficient mental capacity to be a corps commander."

It was at this point in the narrative that Lyman always asked the obvious question, but only to himself. If Burnside was not fit to command one of Meade's corps, then why didn't Meade relieve him?

"You're wondering why I keep him on," Meade said on cue. "The fact is that few men are fit for a command of that size. None of his division commanders could take over, certainly not that fool Ledlie. And no one in my other corps is up to the job, so Burnside stays by default."

Lyman knew there was another reason, one Meade never articulated. Meade himself was under as much of a cloud as commander of the Army of the Potomac as Burnside had been previously, and was in a similar danger of being relieved. Meade knew that if he dismissed Burnside for incompetence, that might make it easier for General Grant to fire him.

Meade picked up Burnside's papers and thrust them at Lyman.

"Burnside gave this man Pleasants permission to proceed and now he wants my approval. He's not going to get it. Write him a letter rejecting the plan, but don't make him feel like a complete idiot for endorsing it."

Lyman started to reach for the dispatch and hesitated.

"You don't agree?" Meade said, surprised. "Do you think this mine idea has merit?"

"No, sir, I don't, but I would suggest that you not be too hasty in rejecting it."

"Why the hell not?"

"Because, sir, General Grant has been pressuring you to push your troops forward, to break through the enemy lines. We both know that the thing cannot be done, given the strength of the rebel defenses and the deplorable physical condition and morale of our men."

"I know all that," Meade said testily, "and so does Grant. He's under pressure from Washington for a breakthrough and he's passing the buck to me because he does not have any better idea. What's your point?"

"My point, sir, is that this mining operation, however foolhardy it may appear, would permit you to report that you are exploring an option. You would be able to tell General Grant that you have under way a plan to break through the lines. Since this mine will take several weeks to complete, you could consider that a grace period during which alternative operations might present themselves. Therefore, I see little to be gained by refusing to allow Burnside's project to continue."

Meade smiled. His enlarged eyes sparkled.

"Good, Lyman. Yes, I like that. Grant could not continue to

accuse me of failing to take action when I have a scheme already in place."

"Exactly, sir."

"It would silence those who want to see me fired. You don't relieve a commander who is showing initiative and who might have the means at hand to bring about a breakthrough."

Meade narrowed his eyes and frowned, studying his aide closely.

"You've just come back from Washington. Do you know something I don't? Did you hear anything at the War Department about them replacing me?"

The fear in Meade's voice troubled Lyman. He liked Meade and did not want to see him hurt, and, selfishly, he did not want to lose his own position at the center of power.

"There are always rumors in Washington," Lyman said.

"Tell me what you heard," Meade demanded.

Lyman reported the conversation in Secretary of War Stanton's office. The color drained from Meade's face. It was his worst nightmare, to be cast out as a failure for the events following Gettysburg. To be written about in history books as the man who let the chance to end the war slip away with the retreating Confederate wagons. Meade had survived a congressional hearing and vicious newspaper attacks, but he knew he was not yet absolved. He needed a victory, certainly as much as Burnside did, to make people forget Gettysburg, to erase the stain against his name.

Meade bit his lip and dabbed at his forehead with his handkerchief. He brushed through the sheaf of papers on his desk. That damn fool mine could be a way out for him. At least it would delay any plan to dismiss him until a better idea, a more realistic one, came along. He stood up abruptly. Lyman jumped to his feet.

"You're right," Meade said. "I will not reject Burnside's plan. Get hold of my engineering officer, Major Dunne, and tell him to talk to this Pleasants and see what he makes of the business. Tell him to find out if there is any merit at all to the man and his project. I want a complete report and a recommendation on whether this thing will work. Meanwhile, I must see General Grant."

Meade reached for his slouch hat with the conical crown and turned-down brim, a hat so distinctive in shape that his men could spot him a half a mile away. He clapped it on his head.

"Do you wish me to accompany you, sir?"

"No, Lyman, this is a social call. I will sound Grant out on these confounded rumors from Washington. It's high time I knew where I stood with him, whether he is for me or against me."

Meade mounted his horse and rode slowly away from his camp, shadowed by a twenty-man cavalry escort. Grant's headquarters at City Point was eight miles away, and the ride gave Meade time to brood about his sorry state.

His reputation, his pride, honor, and family name were under attack. His career, one he had never wanted, and his position as commander of the Army of the Potomac, which he had tried to decline, were in jeopardy. It was almost a year ago that the job had been thrust upon him—June 28, 1863. At three o'clock in the morning, he had been awakened in his tent near Frederick City, Maryland, by a courier from General Halleck, Lincoln's military adviser and chief of staff.

Meade smiled as the memory expanded in his mind. When he saw the staff officer from Washington, his first thought had been that the man had been sent to arrest him. The courier showed Meade the orders. He was to replace Joe Hooker as commander of the Army of the Potomac. Fighting Joe had replaced Burnside after the debacle at Fredericksburg and had managed to remain in command for five months. Meade declined for the same reason Burnside had—he did not believe he had the ability to command the army—but Halleck and Stanton and, finally, Lincoln had been adamant. The Army of the Potomac was Meade's, and, like it or not, he inherited an army committed to tactical maneuvers already under way. In five days, the army, now Meade's army, would be fighting a major battle in Pennsylvania, at a town called Gettysburg.

It became the Union's greatest victory of the war, but it marked for Meade the beginning of a controversy, one responsible for the recurring rumors that he was about to be fired. Within days after the battle, before all the dead were buried, it began with an angry message from General Halleck: The President was dissatisfied that Robert E. Lee's army had escaped, had been allowed to retreat unhindered, to cross the rain-swollen Potomac River with a wagon train of wounded that stretched seventeen miles back into Maryland. Why hadn't Meade attacked the column? The President demanded to know.

Meade thought his army was too exhausted from three days of heavy fighting to risk another engagement. The Union soldiers needed rest and resupply and reorganization, a chance to recover from the loss of 23,000 men. Lincoln, and the rest of the country, if one believed the newspapers, thought otherwise. Meade took offense at Halleck's telegram and wired back at once, asking to be relieved of command. He had performed to the best of his ability, he said, and had been censured undeservedly.

The accusations, charges, rumors, and innuendos had not ceased in the eleven months since Gettysburg, and Meade was widely believed to be as great a disappointment as Burnside, Hooker, and all the other Union generals who had preceded him. Meade was the man who let Lee escape. Meade was the man who could have ended the war but failed.

Meade let his horse stop to nibble the grass in the shade of a maple tree and thought about his mother's shock when he stayed in the army. She said it was not the best career for him, and she had been right. Meade's horse ambled back onto the trail, but he didn't notice. He was three thousand miles and nearly fifty years away.

Meade's memory led him back to Cádiz, Spain, though he had never been able to summon up his own images of his birthplace. His recollections were of stories told and retold by his mother. Through her words, Spain became an idyllic place in her son's life. Meade's father had slipped his old-line Philadelphia family traces fifteen years before to become a successful businessman abroad, but when young George was two, the family returned home, where the boy, the second son of ten children, was later enrolled in private school. He was thirteen when his father died, reducing their circumstances to what one sibling described as genteel poverty.

His older brother attended the Naval Academy in Annapolis, and when it was George's turn for an education, his mother insisted on the Military Academy at West Point. It was free, but, more important, it was a school for gentlemen. He went dutifully, and although he was not an outstanding cadet, neither was he a dunce, finishing nineteenth in a class of fifty-six. He knew long before graduation, however, that an army career would not suit him. He was too ambitious to settle for a succession of dreary army posts and low pay.

He thought of resigning his commission right after graduation, spending his three-month leave working as a surveyor for the Long Island Railroad. But when his leave ended, he found that he could not relinquish the permanent job the army offered. Sent to join his regiment at Tampa, Florida, in January of 1836, to fight in the Seminole Indian War, he endured only four months of the enervating tropical climate before being declared physically unfit to serve in the field.

Reassigned to duty in Washington, Meade resigned seven months later and took a series of temporary contract jobs as a civilian surveyor for the War Department. For several years, he helped fix the boundary lines between the United States and the Republic of Texas in the south and the British provinces to the north. Between jobs, he returned to his mother's home in Washington, relying on her social connections and his charm and intelligence—he had not yet become ill-tempered and irascible—to enter the highest social and political circles.

In 1840, Meade married the daughter of a Pennsylvania senator, yet even with this new political connection, he was unable to find permanent employment. To make matters worse, Congress decided to stop contracting with civilians for survey work, turning that responsibility over to the army's Corps of Topographical Engineers. Faced with the loss of his livelihood, he used the influence of another senator, his brother-in-law, to get back into the army. His job was to build lighthouses, first in Delaware Bay and then along the Florida coast.

Abandoning his dream of success in the business world, Meade settled into the life of an army engineer with its low pay and slow promotions. He did not make captain for fourteen years, and he became increasingly bitter about the path his life had taken. In a reflective mood on the eve of his thirtieth birthday, he wrote to his wife.

What a dream has the last ten years been to me since I left West Point. What a waste of time and energy! I tremble sometimes when I think what I might have been, and then remember what I am. But, alas, it is useless to speculate on what is past. It is the better part now to make the most of a bad bargain, and put the best face on it.

But it became increasingly difficult for Meade to do so. Anger and irritability deepened apace with the age lines on his face. His mother considered him a failure. The future held little beyond the dreary prospect of repeating the years that had passed, more surveying, more lighthouses, and periodic visits to his beloved wife and three children.

The war saved him, as it rescued many others. Overnight, he became a brigadier general, given command of a brigade of Pennsylvania volunteers. Flags flew, crowds cheered, and pulses raced. At last, at long last, the army offered him the opportunity to be something. At first, Meade's outfit was put to work constructing defensive positions around the capital city. Then came active campaigning, serving under every commander of the Army of the Potomac until he received that appointment himself. He fought at Mechanicsville, Second Bull Run, South Mountain, Antietam, and Chancellorsville, winning a good reputation.

As the luster drained from Fighting Joe Hooker, word reached Meade that he was being considered to command the mighty Army of the Potomac. He protested, perhaps too much, in letters to his wife that he had no desire for the job. He was pleased that other officers talked of the possibility and declared their willingness to serve under him, but no, surely it would not happen. The habit of failure was too long in him, dreams too long thwarted, ambitions too long frustrated.

He got the prized command, only to be labeled by Halleck a laggard who needed spurring at Gettysburg. And since then, nothing but acrimony, criticism, and condemnation in the newspapers, the halls of Congress, and behind his back in his own headquarters.

It was small consolation to be still in command eleven months after Gettysburg. The verbal sniping never ceased, nor did the rumors that he was about to be relieved. They were as persistent today as when they began, when his nostrils were full of the smell of death in that small Pennsylvania town whose name he had come to hate.

Yes, Meade remained in command, although few seemed to recognize it anymore. Not since March 3, more than three months ago, when U. S. Grant, newly named commander of all the armies, decided that he could not stand Washington and would move to the field instead, with Meade's Army of the Potomac. Meade's army became known throughout the North as Grant's army, and every victory—Spotsylvania, the Wilderness, Cold Harbor—was touted in the newspapers as another laurel for Grant. Meade was lucky if his own name was even mentioned. He had become Grant's shadow, his executive officer, carrying out the Old Man's orders. Meade felt belittled, degraded, shamed. It was another sign that he was considered incapable of command.

He reached a small stream and paused long enough to let his horse drink, then crossed to the frenetic world of City Point. Noise and movement, vitality and power assailed him from all directions. Surely, he thought, nothing could stop an army the likes of this one. And yet it had been stopped, unable to advance so much as a yard. There was nothing he could do about it. Grant would continue to make the decisions for Meade, to issue orders to Meade's army, and Meade would carry them out. Unless, of course, Grant relieved him.

But not now, dear God, he did not want to be relieved now, not so close to the end. He wanted to stay, even in Grant's shadow, for the Southern surrender and the victory parades and the promotions and medals and glory and his place in history books. Meade had never known fear in battle, but he knew it now. He could fail again, and all that might prevent it, or at least delay it, was some crazy idea to dig a tunnel under the earth, which stood not a chance in hell of succeeding.

6

"YOU going to dig the mine all by yourself, Stan?" Pleasants asked.

The other men of the day shift were on their break, but Stan Michnik refused to leave the mine even for twenty minutes. He was afraid that if he left, he would not be able to force himself to enter it again. He hacked like a machine at the clay and dirt facing.

Pleasants started to repeat the question.

"I heard you the first time," Stan shouted, not bothering to turn around. "Just get the hell out of here and leave me alone."

Pleasants stood beyond the arc of the swinging pickax and watched great clumps of earth shatter under the impact. Stan was stripped to the waist. Rivulets of dirt-stained sweat rolled down his broad back. His muscles flexed and rippled with each motion and he grunted every time the sharp fluke of the ax bit into the tunnel wall. He reminded Pleasants of a punch-drunk prizefighter who continues to batter a helpless opponent against the ropes.

The ax bit deep again, striking a rock with a heavy metallic twang. Stan braced his foot against the wall and pulled the ax free. He wiped his forehead with the back of his hand and let the ax rest at his side. For a moment, the only sound was his breathing as he sucked in huge gasps of air. He sensed that someone was still behind him.

"Dammit, man. I told you to leave me alone."

He whirled around, spied Pleasants, and groaned.

"Oh, jeez, I'm sorry, Colonel. I didn't know it was you."

"That's okay, Stan. How are the retooled axes working out? They do the job?"

Michnik hefted his ax.

"They work great, Colonel. They've got a good balance and a good heft."

"The men making the supports, are they doing it right?"

Stan clapped a hand against one of the log supports that formed the wall and tried to move it.

"Solid as a rock, Colonel. And not a nail in any of them. They fit as snug as a log cabin. Our only problem is getting the dirt out. It's not bad yet since we're only about twelve feet in, but soon we're going to need a wheelbarrow or two. So far, the men are filling up empty sandbags and we've got a couple of those wooden boxes the hardtack comes in. But they really get heavy and they don't have any handles. It's hard dragging them out of the tunnel. By the time we reach a hundred feet or so, we'll have most of the regiment trudging back and forth carrying dirt."

"I've already requested wheelbarrows, Stan. Is there anything else you need?"

"No, sir."

"Well, I've got a surprise for you and the men," Pleasants said. "I sent Cabot off this morning to get six cases of whiskey."

Stan felt his stomach heave.

"Starting today, every man gets a drink when he comes off his shift."

Stan took a deep breath and swallowed.

"The fellows will appreciate that. As for me, Colonel, I'm on the wagon. I'll never touch another drop of whiskey the rest of my life."

"Well, I'm sure you won't have any trouble finding somebody to drink your share," Pleasants said as he headed for the mine entrance.

Stan watched Pleasants disappear into the bright pitiless sun that flooded the opening of the mine shaft. His head still felt like a vein of coal under assault by a dozen pickaxes. He crossed himself and whispered another prayer to Saint Piron, the patron saint of miners.

He repeated the vows he had made during the night, when he lay in his trench watching the red-fused mortar shells trace lines over his head. He had made a bargain with God, his mother's God. No more drinking or gambling. He'd see to it that his children went to church every Sunday and he'd even go to confession. In return, God would get him through this mine. Just five hundred feet or so, and then Stan would never go under the earth again.

He reached up and gently touched the log over his head. Closing his eyes, he listened for the sounds of strain in the wood but heard nothing. He glanced back toward the entrance and felt his heart race, wondering what it would be like when he was two hundred, three hundred, or four hundred feet in. He shuddered like a wet dog shaking itself dry and turned back to the dirt facing. He hefted the pickax over his shoulder and began tearing at the earth again, knowing that every foot, every yard he scraped away brought him that much closer to the end of this underground hell.

He hacked away as he heard the other men on the day shift coming back from their break. They were laughing, and it reminded Stan of Bobby Lee's reaction when he'd told him what he was going to do if God kept His part of the bargain. Lee had been standing over him when he awakened that morning, pointing to his new rank and grinning.

"The army must really be hard up for captains," Stan said. "What are you here for, to make sure I get to work on time?"

"To make sure you get to work at all. The condition you were in last night, I didn't think you'd be up for two days, much less ready to dig."

"I can dig rings around anybody else and you know it, but this is my last mine."

"What are you going to do, retire?"

"I'm not going to tell you. You'd laugh."

"Come on, Stan, you know me better than that. I might say

it's the dumbest fool thing I ever heard, but I wouldn't laugh."

Stan looked around. He didn't want anyone else to hear.

"I've won more than six hundred dollars gambling since I joined up, and with the four-hundred-dollar reenlistment bonus, I figure I'm rich. I'm planning to take the wife and kids and go out west."

"What are you going to do, be a cowboy?"

"A farmer."

Lee stared at him for a moment and burst out laughing.

"That's the dumbest fool thing I ever heard. What do you know about farming?"

"What's to know? You drop seeds in the ground, the rain falls, the sun shines, your crops get big, and you cut them down and sell them. You're out in the sunshine and fresh air all day long."

"And in the snow and ice," Lee said, "with tornadoes and locusts and dust storms and hail and lightning and crop diseases and Indians. Stan, there are Apaches and Cheyennes out west. They kill people like you. They shoot arrows in them and roast them over fires and tie them over anthills and take their scalps."

Lee leaned closer to Stan.

"If there's anything Apaches hate worse than farmers, it's Polacks. I swear, Stan, I think that whiskey got to your brain."

He wandered down the trench, muttering about Polish farmers and leaving a trail of laughter behind him.

After Pleasants left Stan in the mine, he went to Second Division headquarters to meet with General Potter. When he returned, he found Bobby Lee waiting for him.

"How did the meeting go with Potter?" Lee asked.

"He agreed to the wagons to haul lumber from the railway bridge but not to the cavalry escort. Couldn't spare them, he said."

"Hah," Lee scoffed. "The cavalry never does anything but prance around and look pretty. You hear the one about the general in Sherman's command who offered a reward for a dead cavalryman, blue or gray? He's gonna have a long wait. A dead cavalryman is about the rarest sight of all in this war. Any word from Meade?"

"No. Potter said he's very busy."

"And we're not, I suppose. We could have this tunnel dug before Meade makes up his mind."

"Ours is not to reason why," Pleasants said.

"Yeah. Just dig and die. When do we get the wagons?"

"They're on their way now. Put Atwood in charge of a sixty-man detail and send Sergeant Ross with him. He used to build bridges before the war. If he can put them up, he should know how to tear them down. I want the men ready to leave as soon as the wagons arrive. We need every piece of wood from that bridge. There's only enough lumber on hand for maybe ten more feet.

"Potter gave me the location of an abandoned sawmill, too. When the crew's finished with the bridge, send them there for whatever wood they can find."

Lee nodded.

"Did you tell Atwood about his promotion?"

"Yeah."

"And you gave him your insignia?" Pleasants asked.

"Yeah," Bobby Lee said. "The kid thinks that when he takes over the mines, we'll all be one big happy family. He swears he won't be like his old man."

"Maybe he'll surprise you," Pleasants said.

Lee started to object but stopped when he spotted a wagon approaching from City Point, trailing a cloud of dust.

"Must be Cabot with the whiskey," he said. "He's really making time."

"There won't be a bottle left unbroken at that speed," Pleasants said. "What the hell's the matter with him?"

As the wagon got closer, they could distinguish only two men, the soldiers Cabot had taken with him. The driver tugged on the reins and the horses, lathered with sweat, eyes bulging, came to a stop in front of the tunnel entrance. Both men were bloodied and their shirts were torn.

"Where's Sergeant Cabot?" Pleasants asked. "What happened?"

"Sergeant's in the Bullpen, sir."

"What's he doing in the stockade?"

"Provost guard arrested him, sir. He put up a good fight, the sergeant did. Must have been a dozen of them. They beat the hell out of us, sir."

"Goddamn turkey drivers," Lee said.

"What did they arrest him for?" Pleasants asked.

"Well, sir," the driver said, "first there was impersonating an officer."

"Oh boy," Pleasants said. "What rank was he this time?"

"Captain, sir. One of the police recognized him and grabbed his jacket and saw the sergeant's stripes on his shirt."

"What other charges?"

"Unauthorized possession of intoxicating spirits."

"He had my written authorization."

"Yes, sir. One of the guards read it and tore it up right in front of us. He said they was gonna have themselves a party, and they took all our whiskey. That's when Sergeant Cabot got mad and tried to stop them. The provost sergeant shoved him and Sergeant Cabot hit him."

"He hit him?" Pleasants said.

"Yes, sir, right on the nose. The police ganged up on him and beat him good. When we tried to help him, they started on us. Sir, they could lock him up and throw away the key with all those charges."

"Like hell they will. You two go back to the division hospital and get tended to. I'll deal with the provost guard."

He turned to Bobby Lee.

"I want ten of the meanest-looking men we've got."

"The day shift," Lee said.

"Get them, and tell them to bring clubs and axes. We've got to get Cabot out of there before they kill him. And I want the whiskey back, too. I paid for it myself."

Lee rounded up Stan and the day shift, told them what had happened, and asked for volunteers. The entire crew, shirtless and caked with grime and dirt, grabbed clubs and axes and jumped on the wagon. They looked as if they were ready to tear the stockade down board by board.

Pleasants picked out a short wooden club from the junk lumber pile, whacked at the air a few times, and climbed up on the wagon. Bobby Lee found a stout stick and clambered up next to him.

Pleasants drove as if possessed. The men clung to the sides of the wagon as it bounced over the rough road to City Point. Foot soldiers and cavalry leapt out of the way of that raucous crew of roustabouts and the wild-eyed officer at the reins, cursing like a teamster. For all his speed, Pleasants drove with consummate skill, never slacking off or swerving from the road.

At a crossroad, Pleasants spied an officer on horseback followed by a squad of cavalry. The officer wore a slouched hat with a high conical crown and turned-down brim, and sat his horse exceedingly well. The man glanced at the wagon racing toward him and continued at his stately pace into the intersection, confident that the wagon would stop.

"Out of the way, you damn fool!" Pleasants roared.

Bobby Lee shook his club at the man as the wagon rushed by, missing him by a few feet. The officer's horse reared, but he quickly brought it under control. The golden aura of dust that settled over him brought on a fit of coughing.

"You know who that was?" Pleasants said.

"Nope."

"Our boss."

"Abe Lincoln?"

"No, you idiot. General Meade."

"Oh sweet Jesus," Bobby Lee said.

The commander of Meade's cavalry escort raced to the general's side.

"Are you all right, sir?"

"No, Captain, I am not all right," Meade snapped, blinking behind his huge glasses.

"Do you want me to go after them, sir?"

Meade cocked one eye at the fast-moving ball of dust in the wagon's wake and shook his head.

"Don't bother. Perhaps they have good reason for their speed."

"They were dirty and out of uniform, sir, and were carrying clubs and axes. They looked like coal miners."

"Coal miners, eh?" Meade said. "Could you see the rank of the driver?"

"Lieutenant colonel, sir. I heard a rumor about coal miners in the Ninth Corps digging a tunnel under the rebel lines. Do you suppose that was them, sir?"

"I would not be surprised," Meade said.

"Wonder where they were going so fast," the captain said, more to himself than to Meade.

"I'm not sure I want to know," Meade said. Burnside's miners, he thought. And he expects to win the war with men like that!

The guard on duty outside the Bullpen looked alarmed when Pleasants brought the wagon crunching to a halt not five feet from him. A gang of grimy cutthroats descended, waving clubs and axes, yelling like jackanapes. As Pleasants and Lee approached, the guard brought his rifle to present arms. He thought the colonel looked mad as a hatter.

Pleasants ignored the guard and threw open the door. Lee and the others followed him inside. Surprise, distaste, and fear registered successively in the eyes of a captain, a sergeant, and a private who occupied the office.

The provost guards stood to attention.

"William Lawrence Cabot," Pleasants snapped. "You've got him. I want him back. Now."

"I'm sorry, sir," the captain said. "I can't do that. Serious charges have been made against him—impersonating an officer and—"

Pleasants shut him up with an abrupt wave of his hand.

"Have the papers been drawn up?"

"Yes, sir," the captain said, gesturing to the desk occupied by the private. "The clerk is making a copy now."

"So they have not gone beyond this office?"

"No, sir, but as soon as—"

"Let me see them," Pleasants said, striding over to the desk. He picked up the papers and stuffed them in his shirt.

"You can't do that, Colonel. That's against regulations."

"Who made these charges?"

"Sergeant Joslin, sir," the captain said, indicating a jowly, heavyset man who looked a bit less the bully than he had a few moments ago.

"So," Pleasants said, "you're the bastard who stole my whiskey. My men are none too pleased about that, Sergeant."

He pointed to two of his men.

"Take the private out for a little stroll. And be nice to him, unless he gives you trouble."

The captain sputtered and stuttered, not knowing how to handle this challenge to his authority.

"Corporal," Pleasants said to Stan. "I think the rest of you want to have a talk with Sergeant Joslin, don't you?"

"I'm not going anywhere with these goons," Joslin said.

Stan and the others took his arms, lifted him off his feet, and smoothly led him outside.

"You'll be court-martialed for this, Colonel."

Pleasants whacked his club on the captain's desk. The man jumped, and so did Bobby Lee.

"Sit down, Captain," Pleasants ordered. "Let's get a few things straight. What went on here today will not go beyond this room. You will not file any report, not in writing or orally."

"But Sergeant Joslin will make his charges again," the captain protested, "and I'll have no choice but to forward them."

"I think you will find that Sergeant Joslin is about to experience a memory lapse, so there will be no charges against Sergeant Cabot to forward. And there will be no charges against me or my men. If they found out you reported these events, there's no telling what they might do."

"Are you threatening me, sir?"

"Yes," Pleasants said.

"Oh."

"I guess we know where we stand, then. We'll be taking our whiskey back, too. Any questions?"

"No, sir."

"Good. Now let's go get Cabot."

The captain reached in his desk drawer, pulled out a ring of keys, and led Pleasants and Lee through a metal door to the cells. Cabot was in the first cell, lying on his back on a cot, one arm over his eyes.

"Get up, Sergeant Cabot," Pleasants said. "We're taking you home."

"What kept you, sir?" Cabot said. "I was getting lonely."

Cabot looked awful. His face was puffy and bruised, stained with dried blood. His clothes were torn and he poked carefully at his ample stomach.

"How do you feel?" Pleasants asked.

"Not too well, Colonel. I may need considerable rest."

"Well, we'll drop you at the hospital if you promise not to get into trouble again."

"I promise, sir."

"Why do I find that hard to believe, Sergeant? Or should it be corporal again?"

"Corporals take longer to recover, sir. Sergeants, on the other hand, bounce back in a day or two and keep their colonels from drowning in paperwork."

"I take your point, Sergeant."

General Meade brushed the dust from his uniform and cursed under his breath about Burnside's coal miners.

"Those damn fool miners of Burnside's! God help us if we have to depend on them to win this war. Dig a tunnel under Cemetery Hill and blow it up. Claptrap. And nonsense," he muttered.

He took a few more ineffectual swipes at his jacket and urged his horse up the hill to Grant's headquarters. He closed his eyes and bowed his head in silent prayer for God to safeguard his name and reputation, and when he opened them, he had reached the top of the hill. Grant was in his usual place, slouched in his camp chair under the tent flap, deep in conversation with his keeper, John Rawlins. The same uncharitable thoughts that arose whenever he saw Grant crossed Meade's mind again.

There was no apparent trace of breeding or gentility about the man. He lacked the grace, manners, bearing, even the gait of a gentleman. He looked to be a shabby, down-at-the-heels, out-of-luck shopkeeper. Not at all what, in Meade's opinion, the commanding general of all the Union armies should look like. Meade had heard that Grant did not even own a sword.

Meade dismounted and tied his horse to a hitching post but remained out of earshot, waiting for Grant to summon him. He took off his hat and wiped the sweatband with his handkerchief. What he wouldn't give for some cooling rain, even a cloud, to break the grip of the relentless sun. He fed his horse a piece of carrot. A military band started playing not far away. Meade loved music. He closed his eyes and hummed along to "Annie Laurie," then "Come Where My Love Lies Dreaming," thinking about his first meeting with Grant three months ago.

A band had been playing then, too, and Meade had commented on how stirring the music was.

"Never did have an ear for music," Grant said. "Matter of fact, I can only recognize two tunes. One's 'Yankee Doodle' and the other isn't."

Meade had not been prepared to like Grant. He had known him slightly in the years before the war, but their social and career paths seldom crossed. He had heard the stories about Grant's drinking and his poverty, but Meade, like everyone else in the North, also knew about Grant's indomitable energy and tenacity in the fighting in the West. Like a mountain lion with his prey, Grant grabbed hold of the enemy by the throat and never let go.

At their first meeting, Meade expected to be relieved of

command. Surely, Grant would want one of his own people to command the Army of the Potomac—Sherman perhaps. So Meade offered to step aside and serve in whatever other capacity Grant chose for him. Grant was touched and told Meade he wanted him to stay on. The two men, so different in temperament and style, had gotten along well. It had been a promising beginning.

By the end of June, Meade accepted the fact that the Army of the Potomac was not his anymore. Once Grant moved out of Washington and into the field, he made most of the decisions and got the credit. Meade became a figurehead. Meade clung to the hope that there might be a chance for glory yet, if he got the right breaks, if he saw an opportunity and seized it. But if the rumors from Washington were true and he was relieved of command, then George Gordon Meade would once again curse the day he had joined the army.

"You're not bringing him whiskey, are you?"

Meade was startled from his reverie by Rawlins's peremptory tone, and he turned toward Grant's chief of staff, feeling offended by the question.

"No, I am not," he said.

"Somebody gave him a drink the other day while I was away," Rawlins said. "I never did find out who it was."

"It certainly was not me."

Rawlins stared at Meade for a moment with a doubtful look.

"You can see him now," Rawlins said, "but don't wear him out. He hasn't been sleeping much lately."

Meade approached Grant and saluted. Grant took a fresh cigar from his pocket, held it up to the brim of his hat to return the salute, and gestured to an empty chair.

"Sit yourself down, General," he said.

His fingers worked his mechanical lighter, an ugly contraption of flint and steel with a coil of oiled wick.

"Very useful on windy days," he said as the wick took fire.

He puffed contentedly for a few seconds, looked at the glowing tip, and chuckled.

"Rawlins was telling me about that fellow who takes photographs, Mathew Brady. Ever met him?"

"Yes, sir. A few times."

Grant shook his head.

"Fellow can't see worth a darn. Lafayette Baker, the President's secret service man, seems to think Brady is in cahoots with some Wall Street brokers to help them make more money out of this war. He says Brady is sending coded telegrams to his New York City workshop asking for certain assistants by name. The real messages tell about a military success or defeat in the field, something that can affect the stock and gold markets. I'm told that traders who get this kind of information before anyone else stand to make quite a lot of money."

Grant drew on his cigar and sighed.

"Men dying all around us and other men making a profit on it. Hardly seems fair. Well, that's neither here nor there. What can I do for you?"

"Sir, it's these confounded rumors that reach me from different quarters saying that I am to be relieved of command of the Army of the Potomac. I would like to know, General, if there is any substance to those rumors. If I am to be relieved, I would rather get it over with and not have the prospect hanging over my head."

Grant nodded and puffed reflectively, revealing nothing in the expression on his face.

"I understand your concern," he told Meade, "and I would like nothing better than to put your mind at rest. There are indeed rumors, and they come from many sources."

"Is Mr. Dana one of those sources?" Meade asked, blurting out the first name that came to mind.

"Oh, yes, he is not one of your admirers," Grant said, recalling the vitriolic way Stanton's assistant described Meade as weak, timid, and puerile. Other critics included members of Congress, and some of Meade's own staff.

Grant chuckled.

"I'll tell you who your latest critic is. Horace Greeley."

Meade snorted in disgust. Greeley, the powerful owner and

editor of the influential *New York Herald*, was no friend of the Lincoln administration or anyone who served it.

"When Greeley urged me to replace you," Grant said, "I told him that any time I wanted the advice of a newspaper fellow to help select my generals, I would call on him. That's the way I feel about anyone—cabinet officer, general, congressman, I don't care who—who presumes to tell me how to choose my officers. And when I decide to relieve someone of command, then, by God, I go ahead and do it. I don't let the man wither on the vine."

"That's good to know, sir," Meade said. "May I take it, then, that you have no plan to relieve me at present?"

"You may indeed."

Meade felt giddy with relief but tried not to show it. He merely nodded.

"Let me tell you," Grant said, "what I told Secretary of War Stanton last month when I recommended your name and Sherman's for promotion to major general in the regular army. I said that, in my opinion, the two of you were the most fit officers for large commands. Whether these promotions are granted is, of course, out of my hands, but I would hardly make such a recommendation for someone I intended to relieve."

Meade was almost unable to believe what he had heard. To be in the same category as Sherman, Grant's favorite, was a prize he had scarcely hoped for.

Grant did not tell Meade that the staff had opposed the recommendation, arguing that Meade was so hotheaded, no one could get along with him. They argued that Meade should be fired, or at least bypassed in the command structure, with Grant taking over the Army of the Potomac, a situation that, in truth, already existed.

The present system, Grant's staff insisted, where Grant's orders filtered down through Meade's headquarters, was cumbersome and time-consuming. The force and vigor of Grant's directives were lost by the time they reached corps and division levels. Meade was often slow and inept in executing Grant's orders. Having two commanders on the scene was growing awkward and self-defeating.

But, Grant insisted, there was no alternative. He could not command all the Union armies and assume active control of the Army of the Potomac as well. He needed someone like Meade to handle the myriad daily details of such a large force.

Grant admitted to himself, as he listened to Meade thank him for the vote of confidence, that Meade had not handled his forces well in the initial assaults at Petersburg. Meade lacked the killer instinct, that single quality Grant prized most in a general officer. Sherman had it, and Phil Sheridan, the cavalry commander, and that young fellow Custer for all his foppery and glory seeking had it, too.

But Meade did not. He was too cautious and conservative, unwilling to take great risks for great gains. If Grant had been at Gettysburg, he would have hounded Lee day and night, chasing him all the way to Richmond and picking the army's carcass clean. That was not Meade's style, but for now there was nobody else available for Meade's job. Meade would have to stay, at least as long as Grant stayed, a point never far from his thoughts.

"You know, General," Grant said, "you are not the only one with enemies in high places. There are those calling for my dismissal, too. Some reporter just the other day described the march from the Wilderness as Grant's Funeral March. I'm being called a butcher again, pilloried for keeping the army bogged down in these trenches for so long."

His cigar had gone out. He worked a flame in his mechanical lighter and surrounded himself with a cloud of smoke.

"Perhaps we will both be relieved if we cannot move out soon. We have tried flanking movements, but they have been unsuccessful. I am uncertain what course to take next.

"I would like to send troops south and west of Petersburg," Grant continued, "to cut off the railway lines and starve the rebels out, but this awful heat makes it difficult for large-scale troop movements, particularly with cavalry. The countryside is dry as dust. There's no water for troops on the move. The creeks and streams are dry and the men have to dig deep to reach well water. We must suspend all such movements until we get some rain. Lord knows when that will be."

Grant looked off into the distance, in the direction of the trenches.

"Sometimes I wonder whether we have the rebels treed or if it's the other way around. I know we have the advantage in numbers of men and supplies, and we are getting reinforcements while the Confederates are not. But they've still got plenty, so long as they remain behind their defensive works. We learned at Cold Harbor that the defense has the advantage in trench warfare and that superior numbers don't count for much. Even a mediocre division well dug in can beat back a crack corps, and that corps will take more casualties trying to take a trench than a division will in defending it."

Meade nodded his head and struck a match to light a cigar. The match went out and he tried another and another before one took hold. He waved away Grant's offer of his mechanical lighter. Meade did not trust newfangled gadgets.

Grant leaned forward in his chair and tugged on his beard.

"As I see it, we have only two choices and neither one's very good. One would be a flanking operation to cut off the rail lines, similar to the one that failed but with a force of at least one corps. But that would weaken our defenses here and Lee could take advantage of that and attack our line at its weakest point."

Meade feared that kind of operation.

"There's another problem with that, General," Meade said. "We would be dividing our army and perhaps allowing Lee to get in between, leaving one part out in the open. Also, we would still have the water problem. Until we get substantial rain, the flanking force would not be able to find enough water to live on."

"You're right on both counts, of course," Grant conceded, "which leaves the second choice. A massive assault on a narrow portion of Lee's defenses. Strip the line as much as we dare and attack in force at one point in the Confederate line."

Grant raised a hand to forestall the objection he knew Meade would make.

"I know," he said. "If it failed, the rest of our line would be ripe for the picking. Lee is capable of a quick counterattack. And we would suffer horrendous losses in either case. The newspapers would again be full of casualty lists. That is why we cannot attempt another frontal assault. The price is too high. We will have to wait for the rains and try a flanking maneuver. Unless you have a better idea?"

Meade hesitated, taking a moment to organize his thoughts. He did not want to give the impression that he endorsed Burnside's tunnel idea, but it seemed like an opportune moment to bring it up. Personally, he knew it was nonsense, a damn fool idea that could not possibly succeed.

"There is another possibility, sir," Meade said, "one I've been giving some thought to over the last day or so. Burnside has some coal miners in his Second Division, opposite Cemetery Hill. They seem to think they can dig a tunnel under the Confederate fort on the hill and blow it up. Burnside could send the Ninth Corps through the opening. He says he could be in Petersburg in less than half an hour."

"Hmm," Grant said without enthusiasm. "Awful long hole to dig. A project like that could take weeks. There would have to be a gigantic explosion to destroy enough of the fortifications to make a difference."

He clapped the arms of his chair in annoyance.

"Still, I suppose there's no harm in letting them try. It would give the troops something to do. At Vicksburg, I set my men to digging canals with the crazy idea of rechanneling the course of the Mississippi River."

Grant laughed aloud at the memory.

"I never thought it had a chance in hell of succeeding, but it gave the men a goal. Terrific for morale. Even the soldiers who weren't digging felt better because they thought something big was going on. This crazy tunnel of Burnside's could do the same thing."

"That was my feeling, too, General. I don't have a lot of faith in the idea, but I do agree with you that it is worth pursuing. I've sent my engineering officer to assess their progress."

"You mean they've already started?"

"Yes, sir. Burnside told them to proceed before he contacted me. He's very keen on it. I would not be surprised if he has his bags packed, ready to move into Petersburg to celebrate another brilliant victory for his Ninth Corps."

"Old Burny," Grant said with a smile. "He does sometimes get carried away with his enthusiasms. Still, a general's morale needs a lift, too. Let me know what your engineering officer says. I don't promise to plan any big campaign around this mine, but I will certainly mention it to the War Department. Can't have Mr. Stanton thinking we're just sitting down here doing nothing, waiting for a miracle to happen."

James Carrothers Dunne was tall, angular, and spare, a blue stick figure of an officer. His nose was long and sharp and he peered over it with a look of disapproval, as if everything he saw was out of order. His small beady blue eyes darted like tiny bugs looking for a place to light, and his mouth, topped by an almost invisible line of mustache, turned down at the corners. Nothing was ever quite good enough for Major Dunne.

He sat on his horse, frowning at the disarray of the miners' camp, the bits of logs and odd pieces of lumber littering the ground. His frown deepened as he watched the grimy shirtless men emerging from the mine entrance, hauling sandbags and boxes of dirt. They emptied the containers in a far corner of the railway cut before scurrying back for more. Dunne shook his head at the haphazard rows of tents that stretched far down the cut.

The place looked like a camp for refugees, not soldiers in the United States Army. He mentally corrected himself. The Forty-Eighth Pennsylvania was a volunteer regiment, not regular army, but the same standards of order and discipline were supposed to apply. He knew he would not care for this Colonel Pleasants. Obviously the man had never read an army manual and took no pride in his camp.

Major Dunne dismounted, plucked a piece of lint from his sleeve, and examined it a moment, wondering where it came from. He let it fall, stepping back so it would not catch on his trousers.

A guard slouched against the wall at the tunnel opening, smoking a pipe. If one of my men looked like that, Dunne thought, I'd have him up on report.

The guard, a thin, round-shouldered, bespectacled man of about thirty, eyed the major and listlessly brought his rifle up to present arms.

"Afternoon, Major," he drawled.

"Take that pipe out of your mouth, soldier!"

The guard leaned his rifle against the wall, knocked the tobacco out of his pipe, and stuffed it in his pocket.

"You're not supposed to smoke on guard duty, soldier."

The man picked up his rifle and stared at the major.

"Well?" Dunne asked.

"Well what, sir?"

"Don't you have anything to say for yourself?"

"I learned a long time ago that it don't pay to say much of anything to officers. Sir."

"You're a sorry, insolent excuse for a soldier," Dunne snapped.

He turned away and started to enter the mine.

"You can't go in there, Major," the guard said.

"General Meade ordered me to inspect this mine."

"My orders are to let nobody in."

"And my orders require me to go in," Dunne said. "What do you intend to do about it?"

"Well, sir, I'll either have to bash you in the head or shoot you. Of the two, I'd rather shoot. It's awful hard to get blood and brains off my rifle butt."

"Where's your commanding officer?" Dunne demanded.

"He's not here."

Dunne was furious. He watched with disdain as a wagon pulled up, disgorging a cargo of roughnecks carrying cases of whiskey. Whiskey! A lieutenant colonel and a captain looked on. They were all whooping and laughing.

A crowd gathered around the wagon and cheered. The colonel stood up and announced that they had recaptured the whiskey and saved Sergeant Cabot.

"How many provost guards did you shoot?" someone yelled.

"Didn't have to," the colonel said, "but we sure put the fear of God and the Forty-Eighth in them. They won't mess with us again."

This is a mob, Dunne thought, not an army.

He walked up to Pleasants and saluted, surprised to receive a smart salute in return.

"Colonel Pleasants?"

"Yes."

"I am Major Dunne, General Meade's engineering officer. The general asked me to look at your mine."

"Delighted to see you, Major. Let me show you what we've done."

"Your guard threatened to shoot me when I tried to enter the tunnel."

Pleasants laughed, which irritated Dunne.

"He was just following my orders, Major. We don't want sightseers interfering with our work. It's a good thing you didn't force the issue. He probably would have done it."

Pleasants led Dunne into the mine, pointing out, as one professional to another, how the heavy shoring timbers were set in place, how far the men had managed to dig without having proper equipment, and the substance of the clay and soil they were encountering. It appeared rough and crude to Dunne. He had never dug a mine, but he had graduated second in his class at West Point, which qualified him to join the elite Army Engineers. He had served ten years without ever entering a mine, although he had written the army manual for engineering troops, which was the standard textbook on constructing everything from mines to bridges. In his book, mines did not look so primitive. Pleasants seemed proud of his tunnel, leading Dunne to speculate about the man's training.

"Where did you study engineering, Colonel?" Dunne asked when they got outside. He busied himself brushing off the grains of dirt that had attached themselves to his uniform.

"I learned it on the job," Pleasants said, "working for a railroad."

"Ah," Dunne said, raising his eyebrows. "I studied engineering at West Point. I taught there and wrote the army's engineering manual."

"Yes, I've read the section on mines. It's very thorough."

"Thank you," Dunne said.

"I was impressed," Pleasants continued, "with the list of equipment you prescribed for a mine like this. It is almost identical with the one I compiled and gave to General Burnside. Have you seen it?"

"I have," Dunne said.

"We can keep improvising if we have to," Pleasants said, trying to keep his temper in check, "but we'll do a better job if we have the tools. I particularly need a theodolite and the miners' bellows. Do you have access to those items on my list?"

"Certainly. We have everything I described in my manual."

"When can we get them?" Pleasants asked.

"General Meade has not decided whether to approve this project. That is why I am here, to evaluate its probable success."

"What do you think are our chances of success?"

"Frankly, next to none," Dunne said with a small, tight smile of disdain. "No army in the history of warfare has ever dug a five-hundred-foot tunnel. If it was possible, army engineers would have done it a long time ago. The longest military tunnel was completed by the English at the siege of Delhi, and that was less than four hundred feet. There is no way to ventilate such a long tunnel except by digging air shafts at regular intervals. You cannot do that beyond our own forward trenches. The rebels would see you digging.

"Also, it is likely that a tunnel of this length will collapse and kill everyone in it. Finally, should you reach enemy territory, they would hear you at work, sink countershafts, and drop explosives on your men. No, Colonel, it cannot be done."

Satisfied, Dunne looked at Pleasants like a professor who has just shown a student the error of his ways.

"How many tunnels have you dug, Major?"

"None, but I have made a thorough study and consider myself an expert on the subject. One does not have to dig to understand the principles, and the dangers, involved."

"Well, Major, I'm not quite the expert you claim to be, but I have successfully planned, supervised, and dug more than two dozen mines and tunnels, including one through four thousand feet of solid rock. I've never lost a man or failed to complete a project. If a tunnel is sufficiently shored, the chances of collapse are minimal, short of having the bad fortune of breaching an underground stream. As far as the enemy hearing us thirty feet above, that's why the support beams and planks are cut to precise lengths outside the mine and notched to fit, so that no hammering is necessary inside.

"As for proper ventilation, I grant you that this is a problem for which I've not yet found a solution. If you will provide us with a miners' bellows, we can go at least seventy-five feet before having to find some other means of getting fresh air in and the stale toxic air out. I have no doubt that the problem can be solved."

"I applaud your optimism, Colonel, but I fail to share it. In my view, the project is unworkable. That is what I shall tell General Meade."

"While you're about it," Pleasants said as calmly as he could, "you might remind the general of one thing. If we dig this mine and blow up Cemetery Hill, the gap in the enemy line, if properly exploited, could lead to the end of the war. Fifteen minutes, Major, or half an hour at most, and the Army of the Potomac could be in Petersburg. That's a prize worth going for.

"Let us try to dig this mine. If we can't, I'll be the first to admit that you were right. But what do you and General Meade have to lose by letting us go on? We're the only ones at risk here and it's a risk we gladly take. It costs the army nothing but some equipment you're probably not using anyway. I don't ask you to believe in this project. All I ask is that you give us the chance to prove it one way or the other. Don't shut us down when we've hardly begun."

"You're very persuasive, Colonel," Dunne said smoothly, "but you have not changed my mind. However, I grant you the possible value of the mine, if it could be dug, and I take your point that there is little to be lost beyond the lives of your men. I tell you, though, the thing cannot be done. Any trained engineer could see that. Good day, Colonel."

Dunne saluted, mounted his horse, and rode away, leaving Pleasants with an overpowering urge to smash something.

"You arrogant son of a bitch," he said aloud. "The Forty-Eighth is going to dig the longest, safest, most beautiful mine in the history of warfare. And you can write that up in your army manual and choke on it!"

7

———≺◦≻———

THE first bullet tore a hole through the crown of Paul Atwood's hat. For a second, he was too stunned to move. He
remained motionless on his horse, staring at the wooden railroad bridge that spanned the gully.

"Take cover!" he yelled over his shoulder.

The words spilled out automatically, reflexively, even before
the thought came to him. His sixty-man detail jumped into a
shallow ditch that paralleled the gully, about fifteen feet behind
it. Atwood heard more shots from beyond the bridge and spied
specks of gray smoke rising from the tangled undergrowth. He
spun his horse around and raced back to the ditch.

"Spread out," he ordered.

The men had bunched up in the ditch near their wagons and
the single railroad track. Atwood reined in his horse at the edge
of the ditch, his back to the enemy, making an effort to control
his fear, trying not to spur the horse to leap over the ditch and
ride for the safety of the woods a half mile away.

Shots rang out around him as his troops settled in and began
to return the rebel fire. A few urged the lieutenant to take
cover. They liked him well enough, but they did not appreciate
the stupid chances he took. Too brave for his own good, they
said.

Sgt. Nathan Ross, forty years old, "Pops" to the men, raised
his head and called out to Atwood.

"Maybe you oughta take cover, Lieutenant," he said, wondering how one person could be so rich and so smart and so handsome, and so lacking in common sense.

Atwood nodded gratefully at Ross and dismounted, amazed that his heart had not burst from its furious pounding. He hitched the horse to a wagon and forced himself to walk, calm and upright, to join his men in the ditch. The sergeant cast a dubious glance over him, relieved to see him in one piece.

"Go back where you came from, you no-good Yankees," a Southern voice called from the other side. "This is our bridge and we aim to keep it."

"Can you tell how many there are?" Atwood asked.

"Probably no more than a dozen, sir," Ross said, "but that's more than enough to keep us pinned down. There's no way we can cross that bridge in daylight. There's not a speck of cover. They'd pick us off before we advanced five feet. The bridge looks to be a good seventy-five feet across and the gully's too steep to traverse. I'd say we've got a problem here, Lieutenant."

A fresh wave of shots whipped over their heads. So far, no one on either side had been hit. It was a draw, but the Confederates held the high cards.

"We've got to take the bridge," Atwood said, not eager to return to Bobby Lee and report that he had failed in his mission. He pulled a white linen handkerchief from his pocket.

"I'm going to talk to them."

"To the rebs?" Ross asked, twisting around to look at young Atwood. "Begging your pardon, sir, but I don't think that's a good idea. They may not shoot you down, but there's no way you'll talk them into letting us have the bridge. You've got no leverage."

"Nevertheless, I'm going to try. Give me your bayonet."

Ross sighed and shook his head. Atwood tied the handkerchief to the tip of the bayonet and waved it back and forth over his head. A bullet struck the bayonet, knocking it out of Atwood's hand. He retrieved it and waved it a few more times until the rebel fire slowed, then stopped.

"I'm coming with you, sir."

"No, Sergeant, you stay here. No point in both of us getting killed. Besides, you're the only one who knows how to disman- tle a bridge."

"It's not ours to dismantle, and it's not going to be unless we get some artillery and blast the rebels out. Why don't you order up a couple of fieldpieces?"

"It would take too long," Atwood said, knowing that the real reason was that he did not want to admit to Bobby Lee that he needed help.

Atwood unbuckled his holster and handed it to Ross.

"This won't take long," he said.

He clambered out of the ditch, hoping he was right in think- ing that no one would shoot a man carrying a white flag. He had once seen a scared, green Union soldier shoot at a reb carrying a flag of truce and he hoped these Confederates were seasoned veterans. He glanced down at his men.

"Fingers off the triggers, boys. Let's not give them any reason to open fire."

He took a deep breath and started for the bridge, shoulders squared, back stiff, marching as smartly as if on parade. His eyes scanned the bushes on the far side of the gully. He counted fourteen rifle barrels tracking him as he reached the end of the bridge. His boots thudded on the wooden planks, the only sound he was aware of except for his own breathing.

Atwood felt naked. There was no cover, no place to hide. The gully was maybe fifty feet deep. He would break his neck if he jumped or fell.

Halfway across the bridge, an image of the coat with the fur collar sprang to mind. He had forgotten about the coat until Bobby Lee described it. "It probably cost more than I made in a year," Lee had said. Atwood pushed the memory from his mind.

A Confederate corporal rose up from behind a bush and ambled out on the bridge to meet him. Atwood was shocked by the man's appearance. Surely, he belonged in a hospital. Bare- foot, as most rebs were, his uniform was nothing more than dirty rags, worn to shreds in spots. His hair and beard were long and unkempt. He looked like a walking skeleton. Atwood could count the ribs beneath his open shirt. He moved slowly, as if every step exacted a toll, and Atwood hurried across so the pitiful man would not have to walk so far.

"You fixing to surrender, Lieutenant?" the Confederate soldier asked, raising his arm in a sloppy salute.

"No, Corporal."

"Then you might as well turn around and skedaddle on back to wherever you came from. You're sure as hell not gonna cross this bridge. My orders are to keep you Yankees on the other side and that's what I aim to do or die trying."

"I don't want to cross the bridge."

"You don't?" the corporal asked, raking his fingers through his beard as though trying to find something in it.

"Nope. We want to tear it down. All we want is the wood. I've got a proposition for you."

"What kind of proposition?"

"Your job is to keep us from crossing the bridge. Mine is to tear it down. Now if you let me get on with it, then I'll be doing your job for you. Nobody's going to cross the bridge if there is no bridge. I'm offering a way out for both of us."

The corporal rooted around in his beard and cocked his head to one side as he studied Atwood. He raised a bony hand and gestured to the two Union wagons.

"You got any coffee over there?"

"We've got lots of coffee."

"I mean real coffee, the kind you make from coffee beans."

"Real coffee," Atwood said, smiling for the first time. "And fresh beef, ham, bacon, sugar, and salt. Beans and hardtack. I think maybe there's a couple of apple pies, too."

The corporal licked his cracked lips and swallowed hard. His eyes seemed to glaze over as he stared at the wagons.

"You and your men are welcome to have some supper with us," Atwood said. "We've got more than enough."

"Lieutenant, you just bought yourself a bridge."

* * *

My Dearest Anne,

I write in haste as General Burnside has asked to see me this morning. General Meade's engineering officer, Major Dunne, who has never dug a tunnel in his life, told me that, one, I did not know what I was talking about; two, I had no proper training as an engineer since I had not attended West Point; and, three, I was fixing to kill my men through suffocation or a cave-in or because the rebels would discover it and blow it up. He told me the mine cannot be dug.

I am sorry I have not written since Jack O'Brien's death, but I have become obsessed with this tunnel. My impatience grows as each day passes without hearing of General Meade's decision. And I still have not solved the ventilation problem. How much longer will it take for the army to reach a decision? Perhaps General Burnside knows something and that is why he has sent for me. I can only hope it is good news. It will be a terrible blow to morale if we have to suspend the operation.

As for your letter, I am at a loss. I have read it so many times that the paper has begun to tear at the creases. Are you trying to frighten me off? Are you hoping that what you said about being so different from Sallie, about wanting a different kind of life than what my marriage to her was like, will cause me to change my mind about wanting to marry you?

Pleasants dipped his pen in the inkwell without looking and tipped over the tiny bottle, spilling its contents onto the floor. He cursed and watched the black ink sink into the dry earth, carrying with it all the words he had planned to write. He wondered if he had knocked it over on purpose, to free him of the burden of responding to Anne's letter.

The task had kept him awake most of the night, although, if he was to admit the truth, it was the ventilation problem that most occupied his mind. If he could not figure out how to exhaust the stale air from the tunnel, then the project was finished, even if Meade did decide to support it. Already the miners were having trouble breathing. They could not go much farther.

Anne's letter added to his confusion and frustration. It interfered with his work and made him angry with her for that. Sallie had never intruded on his work. She believed that his world was outside and hers was at home and that neither should interfere with the domain of the other. But Anne was not going to be content with that. It was this so-called modern woman business again. She wanted more from a marriage. Pleasants wasn't sure what she wanted, and he did not know whether he could give it.

He snatched up his unfinished letter, tore it in half, and shoved it in his pants pocket to join the one he had begun last night. The tunnel under Cemetery Hill had to be his only commitment right now. There wasn't room for Anne Shaw, too.

His hand moved unbidden to his shirt pocket and patted the small framed photograph. He started to take it out but forced himself to stop, feeling again that unreasoning anger toward her. A wife was supposed to help her husband, not get in his way!

Bobby Lee pushed aside the tent flap. Pleasants scowled at him.

"What do you want?" he snapped.

"My, my," Lee said. "The colonel has certainly been in a nasty mood since he got a letter from his sweetheart."

"Do you have something constructive to say?"

Lee lowered himself into a camp chair. He smiled at Pleasants and shook his head.

"Ah, young love," he said, picking up the empty inkwell and replacing it on Pleasants's desk. "Do you want to talk about it?"

"No, I do not want to talk about it. I thought you were looking for a place to dig an air shaft."

Pleasants had sent Lee out to explore the terrain between the mine entrance and the forward trenches, hoping to locate a spot where a shaft could be sunk beside the mine. If a fire was kept going at the base of the shaft, it would draw the stale air out of the tunnel and fresh air in from the entrance, enabling the men to dig the mine another seventy-five feet. Beyond that, Pleasants would have to devise some other means of ventilation.

"I found a spot," Lee said, "about eighty feet in from the entrance, in the old second line of trenches. The rebs won't be able to see us digging, and the dirt can be disposed of right there."

"What are you waiting for?" Pleasants said. "Get it started."

"I already did, boss. There are four guys out there cussing me up and down, grumbling about having to dig a thirty-foot hole. Another crew's cutting four-foot planks to line the walls like a chimney, just like you ordered. It should be done tomorrow."

"You're sure you took careful measurements so the shaft will come out at the mine? It's got to be within two feet for the fire to create the proper draft."

"It will be," Lee said. "And by the way, there's a general out there looking at your mine. He's either Burnside or a damn good imposter."

General Burnside stood alone a respectful distance from the mine entrance, watching the men carry out boxes of dirt. He looked lonely without a cavalry escort or even an aide. His horse waited obediently behind him, gently nudging him in the back, as though he, too, was lonely.

"Sorry I wasn't here to greet you, General," Pleasants said, giving a smart salute. "I thought I was supposed to meet you at headquarters."

"I decided to come see for myself how your project is progressing."

To Pleasants, he seemed terribly sad, worn out, like a man who had trouble sleeping.

"How are you, Pleasants?" the general asked with an almost embarrassing degree of solicitude in his voice. When he shook Pleasants's hand, he held it a moment too long, as though starved for human contact. Pleasants sensed that Burnside had brought bad news but did not want to tell him right away.

"I'm all right, sir," Pleasants said.

"And the mine? How is it going?"

"We've dug more than seventy-five feet but have had to slow down because we need the miners' bellows I requested. The air is stale up at the facing, so the men can work only in half-hour shifts. I'm having a perpendicular shaft dug that should help for a while."

Burnside nodded. Two soldiers coming out of the mine tripped and stumbled, dropping a hardtack box full of dirt.

"Those boxes look heavy," he said.

"Yes, sir, they are. As you can see, I've had those poles attached to the sides so two men can carry them like a stretcher. But the height of the tunnel is only five feet. The men have to walk hunched over. It's a tiring job. When we get wheelbarrows, it will be a lot easier."

Burnside's face took on a pained expression. He glanced away from Pleasants and mumbled something in a voice so low that Pleasants had to ask him to repeat it.

"I said, there will not be any wheelbarrows. Or anything else."

Pleasants clenched his fists and silently cursed that arrogant bastard Dunne. He took a deep breath to compose himself. It would do no good to take his anger out on General Burnside.

"That was General Meade's decision, sir?"

Burnside nodded. He came to attention and confronted Pleasants squarely, ready to do his duty.

"I am sorry, Colonel Pleasants," he said formally, "but General Meade, acting on the recommendation of Major Dunne, has concluded that this thing cannot be done. He said, and I quote, that it is all claptrap and nonsense. A mine of this length has never been excavated in a military operation and cannot possibly succeed.

"Further, Major Dunne is convinced that your men will suffocate for lack of proper ventilation or be crushed by falling earth. Also, it is likely that the enemy will discover the mine and act to thwart the plan. General Meade refuses to take responsibility for the deaths likely to ensue from your operation and he does not grant his approval."

"Damn!" Pleasants said, then remembered whom he was addressing. "Sorry, sir," he added quickly.

"That's all right, Colonel. I feel just as angry and helpless as you do."

Burnside sagged again, no longer a soldier at attention but a tired old man.

"I had a heated argument with Meade. We could probably be heard all the way to City Point. But he was not favorably disposed toward the project from the outset, and Major Dunne's denunciation of it—ridicule, really—bolstered his view."

Pleasants glanced toward the tunnel and read the sign—THE JOHN FRANCIS O'BRIEN MINE. The men would have to seal it off, destroy all their work, all the dreams and hopes of ending the war.

"Let me ask you a question, Colonel," Burnside said. "Please be as honest as you can in your answer."

"Yes, sir."

"Is it possible that you could complete this tunnel under the rebel fortifications at Cemetery Hill without the tools and equipment you requested? General Meade will not provide so much as a shovel or a piece of wood. He has warned his engineers to safeguard the equipment so you cannot obtain anything, shall we say, informally. I have no such equipment at my disposal—if I did, you would have it. Can you manage on your own?"

Pleasants looked curiously at Burnside, wondering what sort of game the general was playing.

"Yes, sir," he answered. "We could do it. We've improvised so far and we're almost one-fifth the distance to the Confederate fort. We've scrounged shovels, pickaxes, drills, and saws. We've had the axes shaped to fit our needs. We dismantled an old railway bridge for timber and we have crews working the abandoned sawmill and cutting down trees."

Pleasants glanced around at the relays of men hauling out the dirt.

"Yes, sir," he repeated. "The Forty-Eighth can do it, though it may take a week or so longer. But there are a few things I can't do on my own. I've got to have a theodolite to measure our direction and calculate precisely when to stop. Otherwise, we won't know if we're under the fort."

"I can get a theodolite from a civilian engineer I know in Washington," Burnside said. "What else?"

"Powder, sir. Twelve thousand pounds. Without it, there's no point in tunneling under the fort."

"Powder I can get," Burnside said. "As a corps commander, I am entitled to requisition all I need."

"We also need electrical wire, at least five hundred feet, to set off the powder, and a galvanic battery to supply the spark."

"That is more difficult, but I will see what I can do."

Burnside placed his hand on Pleasants's shoulder and led him away, out of hearing of the soldiers at the mine.

"I know I asked you before, but I am compelled to do so again. Are you certain, beyond any doubt, that you can dig a tunnel of this length?"

"Yes, sir," Pleasants said without a moment's hesitation, at the same time wondering how in the hell he was going to ventilate it.

"No doubts, Colonel? No reservations?"

"None. But forgive me, sir, why are you asking when General Meade has rejected the plan? We can't disobey his orders."

Burnside's mouth gave a broad smile and his eyes glittered. Suddenly, he looked ten years younger.

"No, Colonel, we cannot disobey the commanding general of the Army of the Potomac. I would not consider such a thing. Nor would you. We are soldiers. We do as we are told. Now General Meade may have disapproved of the project, but he did not order it stopped. He did not say close it down, stop digging, and fill in the tunnel. Nor did he say yes, proceed, you have my endorsement. What he said was that he does not grant his approval. That is not the same as ordering it to stop.

"It's the old army game, Colonel," Burnside continued. "Meade plays it well. I've done the same thing myself. He is shifting the responsibility to me. If the operation is successful, he will say that after pointing out the dangers involved, he did not forbid the work, thereby indirectly claiming credit for its success. If it fails, he is covered equally well, for he can say he did not approve and that the blame for the failure rests with me because I elected to continue despite his warnings."

"Then we can keep digging, sir?" Pleasants asked, not caring about the army politics involved.

"We keep digging, Colonel. I am gambling my reputation. In a few weeks, when I tell General Meade that you have dug the mine and that I have a fresh, trained division ready to exploit the gap you will create in the Confederate line, General Meade and General Grant will have no choice but to give their approval. They are so desperate to break through the line that they will have to accede. My Ninth Corps will march into Petersburg and this dreadful conflict will come to a close."

Burnside shook Pleasants's hand and nimbly mounted his horse.

"I am going to see General Ferraro now to tell him the good news. His colored troops will lead the assault. I predict that tonight those boys of his will be dancing in the streets."

Burnside's expression turned serious.

"I am counting on you, Colonel. Don't let me down."

"I won't, sir," Pleasants said.

"Well?" Bobby Lee demanded. "What did he say? Did Meade give his permission, or do we have to shoot the old bastard?"

"Not exactly," Pleasants said.

"What the hell kind of answer is that? Yes or no? Tell me what's going on. I've been standing over there trying to eavesdrop and I couldn't hear a thing."

Pleasants laughed and led Lee off toward his tent, explaining Burnside's proposal.

"I'll be damned," Lee said. "Burnside's a shrewd old fox."

"Yes, but not half as shrewd as we have to be to get fresh air in the mine. How can we sink more air shafts down there?"

"The only place left to dig is in the forward trenches," Lee said, "but that's no more than thirty feet beyond the present shaft. It won't help all that much more. It's the next four hundred feet we have to worry about. The rebs would see our men digging and pick them off. Even if we dug only at night, the rebs would see a line of holes aimed at them and figure out what's going on."

"That much, I already know," Pleasants said. "What I need is a solution, not a restatement of the problem."

Pleasants bent down to enter his tent. Shouts from the mine entrance startled him.

"Colonel! Come quick!"

Two men staggered out of the mine, dragging a third between them. Stan Michnik stumbled out after them, carrying another miner in his arms like a baby. Behind him, three more men dragged themselves out, coughing and retching.

"What happened?" Pleasants yelled.

"They started passing out," Stan said. "We can't go back in there, Colonel. The air's too bad. It's poison."

Stan fell to his hands and knees. He tried to get up and collapsed on the ground. For all its strength, his body refused to move. The others, too, lay where they fell, gasping for air.

Pleasants went from man to man, grabbing their wrists to check for heartbeats. Other soldiers gathered around, bringing water and fanning the stricken men with their handkerchiefs. Sergeant Watkins ambled up with a bottle of whiskey and a tin cup.

"Does this count as the end of a shift, Colonel?"

Acting against Bobby Lee's advice, and to the amazement of everyone else in the Forty-Eighth Pennsylvania, Pleasants had appointed Watkins custodian of the whiskey. He knew that Watkins had a drinking problem, but he also knew the sergeant to be a man of integrity on the job. Watkins had been pestering him for some part in the mine.

"I would remind the colonel," Watkins had said with dignity, "that this operation was my idea. I am too old to dig and haul dirt, but there must be some other assignment the colonel can arrange."

He was pleased with the job of guarding the whiskey supply and doled out the precise amount due each man at the end of a shift with fastidiousness and fairness.

"Yes, Sergeant," Pleasants told him. "This counts as the end of a shift. In view of the hardships these men have labored under, a double ration would not be out of order."

Watkins raised the single black line of eyebrow that overshadowed his eyes like an awning and frowned but performed his duty like the good soldier he was. The suffering men revived quickly at the prospect and lined up in order of rank, Corporal Michnik first. Pleasants was surprised because he had always declined his ration before.

Stan took the tin cup in both hands, inhaled the pungent aroma, and looked as if he might be sick again. His hands shook as he raised the cup to his lips. He had been spared today. If he had not recognized the early signs of the poisonous air and hustled the men out of the tunnel, they all might have died. God was keeping His part of the pact; now Stan had to keep his.

"No thank you, Sergeant," he said, returning the cup to Watkins. "I don't drink and this is no time to start."

"It certainly is not," Watkins agreed. "No time is good, but there's them that don't know that. I admire a man who stands away from evil temptation. Next!"

Pleasants took Bobby Lee aside.

"Okay," he said, "that's enough. Shut the mine down for now. Nobody goes in the tunnel until the ventilation shaft is sunk. Set crews to work through the night. I want it completed and the fire going by morning so we can send the men back in."

"I'll get on it," Lee said, "but, like I told you before, that's only good for another thirty feet or so, one day's digging. After that, the air will get bad again."

"Then I'd better figure out a way to have fresh air for the full five hundred feet, or we'll be out of business."

* * *

Pleasants sat in his tent, brooding over the top-view sketch he had made of the mine, each thin line straight and true, drawn with a draftsman's precision. He studied the black-lined square representing the ventilation shaft his men were now digging and wondered where he could sink more shafts to connect with the mine.

He unrolled his United States Army topographical map of the Petersburg battlefield. Jagged lines indicated the trenches, the long ugly scars in the earth in which Union soldiers lived and died. His eyes roamed from the abandoned railway cut 110 feet behind the Union trenches where he now sat in his tent to the empty landscape bordered by the rebel trenches. It was a short distance to walk or run but a long way to burrow under the earth like a mole, with nowhere to pop up for air. He traced with a forefinger the lines of Confederate trenches and followed the contour lines up the slope of Cemetery Hill, capped by a tiny square representing the looming presence of the earthen fort, the only obstacle to victory, to peace, and to his new life with Anne Shaw.

Then he remembered her perplexing letter. He pulled it out of his pocket, unfolded it carefully, and placed it on top of the drawings and the map. Instantly, his resentment returned. Her modern ideas were interfering with his work. Clearly, that was not what a wife was supposed to do. He picked up the six pages of heavy buff-colored stationery filled with her graceful hand-writing and shuffled them. He turned the letter over and over in his hands, like a specimen of rock he was examining from all sides.

"Is the colonel in?" Sergeant Cabot asked from the open tent flap. "Or would he rather not be disturbed?"

"The colonel would rather not be disturbed but, yes, he is in. Is the sergeant here to add to his burdens?"

"Oh, no, sir," Cabot said. He entered the tent and placed a sheaf of papers on Pleasants's desk. "Quite the contrary, sir. I am here to relieve you of your burdens. The colonel knows that I live to serve."

Pleasants understood his part in this ritual. It was to sign each of the papers Cabot placed before him, preferably without looking at them or asking questions. He performed this chore every day with morning reports, sick-call lists, status reports, leave requests, and supply requisitions. He sometimes shuddered to think what else. He figured he was better off not knowing.

"It's just the usual, sir," Cabot said. "Nothing to worry about."

"I don't worry, Sergeant. I will swear under oath at your trial that you forged my signature."

"A healthy attitude, sir."

"How is your health, Sergeant? You look a little better than when we found you in the stockade."

"I think I will live, sir, though it was touch and go for awhile."

Pleasants signed the last paper and gestured to the camp chair next to his desk.

"Sit down a minute."

"A problem, sir?" Cabot asked, his eyes darting to the pile of papers.

"Yes, a problem. You."

"Me, sir?"

"You, sir."

Pleasants stroked his goatee and stared at Cabot.

"I can explain, sir."

"This is serious, Bill. I want your word of honor—no more impersonating an officer. This time, we were able to help you. We were lucky, but the provost guards are angry and will be looking for a chance to get back at you. If they catch you breaking any rule, they'll shoot you and claim you were resisting arrest. There won't be a damn thing I can do about that. Am I making myself clear?"

"Yes, sir."

"Good. I don't want to have to concoct some story for your wife about how bravely you met the enemy and went to your death."

"She wouldn't believe that anyway, sir. She knows me too well."

"Do I have your word that your days as an officer are over, at least for the time being?"

"Yes, sir, you have my word. I believe I have learned my lesson."

"I hope so. I'd be lost without you."

"I know, sir, and I want to thank you and the men for rescuing me. I appreciate that more than I can say."

"It was the whiskey," Pleasants said.

"Sir?"

"We came to get the whiskey. You were an afterthought."

"Yes, sir. A question of priorities. I understand."

Cabot smiled and gestured to the letter in Pleasants's hand. "I can't help noticing that you have heard from our Miss Anne. Please tell the dear child that her prayers rescued me from death's door and that I am still available if she changes her mind."

Pleasants escorted Cabot out of the tent and watched him climb into the driver's seat of the regimental wagon, clutching his file of papers, the fuel of a modern army. He rode off to division headquarters, no doubt to swap and scrounge, to pick up whatever was not nailed down. Pleasants absentmindedly rolled up Anne's letter to form a tube. Raising it to one eye like a telescope, he followed Cabot until the wagon was out of sight. He turned and trained the tube on the mine entrance, forcing his mind back to the ventilation problem.

He went back inside and studied the top-view drawing. He put the stiff paper tube to his lips and blew across the edge to make a whistling sound. Resting his arm on the edge of the desk, he noticed that the air rushing through the rolled-up letter felt cool on his skin. Pleasants shifted the paper and blew straight down the tube. The hairs on his forearm rose in the breeze.

"By God, that's it!" he said.

He gently flattened Anne's letter, placed it in his pocket, and picked up his pen. He drew two parallel lines beginning outside the tunnel and running the length of it and a single line across the tunnel between the entrance and the air shaft. He laughed aloud, so uproariously that a squad of men passing by were startled and wondered what was wrong with the colonel.

Pleasants summoned Bobby Lee.

"It's so simple," he said.

"What is?" Lee asked.

"Can you build a square wooden duct eight inches on each side?"

"Sure. My carpenters can do that easily."

"It has to be airtight at the seams."

"They can caulk it with putty or pitch. How long do you want it?"

"As long as the tunnel. That's what, eighty feet now? It will have to be extended as the rest of the tunnel is excavated. We'll have to keep up with the digging on a day-to-day basis."

"Easy enough," Lee said. "Anything else?"

"An airtight canvas door that can be opened to allow the men to go back and forth. When it is closed, it must seal off the tunnel between the air shaft and the mine entrance."

"That's no problem, either. You want to tell me what this is all about?"

Pleasants showed him the drawing, stabbing a finger at the base of the air shaft.

"A fire is kept going here around the clock. It creates a draft that draws the stale air out of the tunnel and sucks it up the chimney. With the airtight canvas door closed, a vacuum will be created in the mine. The vacuum will draw in fresh air from the outside through this wooden duct on the floor of the tunnel. Air will be constantly circulating, drawn in and sucked out so long as the fire is going and the door closed. What do you think?"

"It's brilliant," Lee said. "I've never heard of anything like this before."

"There isn't anything like it because it's never been done before. You know what this means, Bobby?"

"It means we've got ourselves a five-hundred-foot mine."

"Right. The Forty-Eighth Pennsylvania is back in business."

Henry Pleasants dreamed about his dead wife, Sallie, something he had not done since he had met Anne Shaw. A little after four o'clock in the morning, he bolted upright in his narrow cot. The air was clammy and still and his body was covered with a fine layer of sweat. He splashed water on his hot face and wandered outside. The night was quiet save for muffled snores from the rows of tents that made up the Forty-Eighth Pennsylvania's home in the railway cut.

He clasped his hands behind his back and ambled away from his tent, past the entrance to the mine. The guard jumped to his feet. He had probably been sleeping, Pleasants thought, but he couldn't prove it. No matter. They were as safe from the enemy as if they were back in Pottsville.

Their camp was surrounded by the Union Army, including the black troops of the Fourth Division stationed to the rear. Pleasants was sure their guards did not sleep at night. He reminded himself to call on Ezra Boyce to find out how the coloreds felt about leading the assault.

He had heard them last night, singing in the distance, joyful, hand-clapping, foot-stomping, pulse-racing songs of jubilation. The whole operation depended on them. If they failed, the white divisions coming on behind them—weaker and with low morale—would likely fail, too. Then Pleasants's mine and the Forty-Eighth Pennsylvania would be minor footnotes in history, if that.

Pleasants wandered over to the far side of the railway cut and sat down, leaning back into the mounded, crusted earth to make it fit his shape. With his knees drawn up and his arms resting atop them, he looked across at the dark hole of the mine and the dim, faint blurs of white that were the regiment's tents. They looked like an army of ghosts standing at attention.

He closed his eyes and saw in his own inner darkness another ghostly, shrouded figure: Sallie, as she appeared in his dream, arms outstretched toward him, imploring him to come to her.

She looked so alive, her long auburn hair undone, and she wore the white silk sleeping gown he had bought in Philadelphia for her twenty-first birthday. Her last birthday. She had been buried in that gown.

Her lips moved and she appeared anxious, concerned for him. Strangely, her features were indistinct. As in his waking memories of her, Pleasants had trouble picturing her precisely. The face he once thought he would never forget had, like a photograph, faded with time.

He strained to hear her words. She became agitated and moved closer, but still he could not hear her. He called her name and groped through a dense fog, trying to reach something that was not there. Only her voice remained, until it, too, disappeared and she was once again lost to him. He sensed that her spirit would never come again, that he would never know what she so desperately wanted to tell him.

He opened his eyes and recalled her final words before she died, before she became the ghost in his dreams. As she lay delirious on their sweat-soaked bed, crying in pain, Pleasants had held her hand tightly, as if he could keep her from slipping away. She had no strength left to return his grasp.

"Promise you won't leave me," she whispered.

"I'm here," he said. "I'll always be here."

Tears formed in her eyes and he felt a slight pressure, a gentle squeeze of her hand.

"I won't be here when you get back," she said. Her head fell to one side and she was gone, leaving him with that enigmatic message.

"I'll always be here," he said aloud in the abandoned railway cut near Petersburg, Virginia, wiping tears from his eyes. He felt unbearably sad and alone. He glanced toward the mine again, reassured to see a human figure, the guard, staring at him. The story will be all over camp by sunup, Pleasants thought. The colonel was wandering about in the night talking to himself.

He stood up and forced himself to saunter back to his tent, waving briskly to the guard.

"Too hot to sleep," he said to the man.

"Know what you mean, Colonel. Having the same trouble myself," the guard said, cackling as if he had said the funniest thing in the world.

Pleasants walked on, envying the man's untroubled attitude, until he remembered who the guard was. Six months ago, his two daughters had died of scarlet fever. He threatened to kill himself when he got the news. Pleasants gave him a month's leave, in defiance of regulations, which allowed hardship leave only for officers. He stayed away three months, and Pleasants pretended not to notice that Cabot kept him on the roll. Cabot was sure the man would return when he was ready, and one day he did. Neither he nor Pleasants had ever spoken of it.

Pleasants entered his tent, lighted a candle, and read Anne's letter again, skimming the first page about Jack O'Brien and the sadness she felt over his death.

> I mourn for him, as I mourn for so many, North and South. The list of those killed seems never to end. They were all so young, with shining faces and bright eyes and dreams of glory. It is terrible for those of us left behind, for we shall remember and mourn them the rest of our lives and regret the promise their lives held, now never to be fulfilled.
>
> So many women I know have lost fiancés and husbands, the young men who were their future, the men who were to give their lives meaning and purpose and fulfillment, for women are not allowed these things on their own.
>
> Now these women are alone, left to fend for themselves in a world that is crumbling around them. After the war, there will not be enough men left in the North or South to give these women a second chance at life. They are condemned to loneliness in a society that offers no outlets for their talents and hopes and dreams, save marriage.
>
> They are sad, withering flowers, destined to dry up

and fade like the blossoms on our magnolia tree that
was struck by lightning last week. The flowers turned
brown and dropped off. The tree is dead. Next winter,
the ice will snap off the branches. I feel like the war has
killed it, too, and all that it meant to me.

Pleasants and Anne had often sat hand in hand beneath the
magnolia tree. Her father had planted it, a cutting from his
mother's plantation, the day Anne was born. On a white
wrought-iron bench at the base of the tree, she had told him
how much time she had spent there in solitude, reading the
books her father gave her and spinning her dreams.

The only cross words that had passed between them were
under the magnolia tree. Anne did not want to wait until after
the war to get married.

"I intend to be your wife, Henry Pleasants," she had said,
"and the sooner I am, the happier we will both be. And that's
all there is to it. If you go off and get yourself killed or meet
somebody else, I'll never forgive you. Or myself."

"You're too young to be left a widow. I can't do that to
you," he'd replied.

"The choice isn't only yours. I have a stake in this, too.
Sometimes you men act like you're the only people in the
world and that you always know best. What gives you the right
to decide that I would be happier as an old maid who never had
the chance to express her love than as a widow, maybe with
your child? At least I would have my memories!"

Pleasants was adamant. He would not marry her until the war
was over. He thought about her magnolia tree and what a loss
it must have been to her. Maybe she had been right. Maybe he
should have married her and taken his happiness where he
could find it rather than waiting. Then he remembered something else Anne had written and he ran his finger down the
second page of her letter until he found it.

I wish you had not been so stubborn. If you showed up
on my doorstep today, I believe I would not take no for

an answer. But there are times when I get to feeling low and tell myself that maybe it is best to wait, to give you more time to understand what you are getting yourself into. I have told you that I cannot be the kind of wife your Sallie was.

Dear Henry, my love for you is tinged with jealousy over the inequities in life between men and women. You have so many opportunities to become whatever you wish to become. As a woman, these things are closed to me. I can be wife, mother, hostess, but that is all I am allowed. You know I want more than that.

If I were a man, I could be a soldier, but as a woman my duty is to sit at home and wait and worry. Boys my age can enlist, but we women are hardly allowed off the front porch. It is so unfair. We are fighting a war to free the Negro slaves, but no one is fighting to free women, the slaves of a patriarchal society. No wonder so many succumb to nervous flutters and swoons and take to patent medicines as we grow older.

My daddy did not teach me to be a shrinking violet, to join the ladies after dinner for gossip while the men discuss business and politics and the ways of the world. I intend to be part of every aspect of your life. You build things that are important. The railroad tunnels you designed carry thousands of people and tons of freight and they will stand a hundred years from now. The coal mines you engineered provide fuel for factories and homes and contribute to the economic growth of the entire nation. The mine you are now digging at Petersburg may end this terrible war and save thousands of lives.

Women also have the ability to do great things. All we need is a chance. I am intelligent. I am capable of learning anything you can. I want to work with you, behind the scenes if that is how it must be. I can help. I can make a contribution, not only to you but to the world.

My darling, I hope and pray that you will consider this seriously. I tried to tell you my feelings when we were together, but perhaps you did not believe me. Or perhaps I did not state my views forcefully enough. Perhaps you were humoring me, thinking this was a phase I would outgrow.

It is not easy to write these thoughts because I know I risk losing you by speaking so openly and boldly. I can no more imagine life without you than I can imagine the sun not rising every morning. But I must be honest with you, for both our sakes. I do have confidence that you will understand and accept me for what I am, the person who loves you more than anyone else can and who will be, if not always the perfect wife, still the best friend and partner you could ever hope to have.

Your loving and devoted Anne

Pleasants placed the letter on his desk, covered it with his hand, and sighed loudly. Women live in their own little world, his father had taught him. They have their place and are nice to be around, but one doesn't take them seriously. Wives ran the household and reared the children. What was so wrong about that? That was the way of things, and it was not about to change in his lifetime. Still, he loved her, and perhaps his love was stronger for having loved before. He owed her an answer, one way or the other.

He took a fresh sheet of writing paper from his footlocker and placed it on the desk. His pen dipped into the inkwell automatically and hovered above the paper. Outside, a drum-roll announced reveille and he heard the camp begin to spring to life. He put the pen down and stood. There was so much work to do—the air shaft, the ventilation duct, the digging. He had to get the theodolite from Burnside and take measurements.

Pleasants placed the stationery and Anne's letter in his foot-locker and closed it, feeling immensely relieved. He would deal with it some other time. Maybe tomorrow.

8

GENERAL Grant ran a nicotine-stained finger over the map, tracing the line of the Shenandoah Valley northeast toward the Potomac River. He grunted and puffed on his cigar furiously, sheathing his head in a halo of smoke. His finger tapped at the meandering line of the Potomac where it met the town of Harper's Ferry, then raced southeast the forty miles to Washington City.

"So you think that's what General Lee is up to, sir?" asked his aide, Horace Porter. "Attacking Washington while the bulk of his army is tied up here at Petersburg?"

Grant took another pull on his cigar, his fifteenth of the day. And it was only 3:30 in the afternoon, Porter noted.

"Wouldn't put it past him," Grant said, his forefinger pressing on Washington. "He's taken crazier chances than that."

"And gotten away with them," Porter added.

"Yes," Grant said, "but I don't think that was his intention when he sent old Jubal Early up the valley. I think he was trying to compel me to attack him here, head-on, like we did at Cold Harbor. He knows I hate to weaken my forces by sending units off hither and yon, chasing after every enemy column raising a trail of dust somewhere."

Grant chuckled and shook off a pile of cigar ash that had fallen on his sleeve.

"The more I think about it, the more certain I am that's what Lee had in mind, that I'd come charging across these open fields believing my action would force him to recall Early. Of course, we would take heavy casualties in the process and Lee would live to fight another day. I'll wager he's one disappointed general right now."

"You think because the plan did not work, he's now ordered Early to keep on going and to menace Washington?" Porter asked.

"That's how I see it. You know how those people in Washington are, Mr. Lincoln excepted. It does not take much to threaten them. A whiff of powder in the distance and they're all for moving the capital to Maine. You've seen the telegrams from Halleck, each more frantic than the one before. Each one bolstering the rumored size of the Confederate force. Now it's up to thirty thousand troops, but we know he cannot have more than ten thousand with him."

Grant shuffled through a pile of telegrams.

"I'll grant you that ten thousand troops can do a lot of damage on the north side of the Potomac. We don't have many troops to stop them with between Harper's Ferry and the capital. A few militia units that are not worth much. The only real force we had was Franz Sigel's outfit and they got beaten badly near Harper's Ferry. And that other general—the one Halleck fired twice?"

"Lew Wallace, sir. I think he's more interested in writing books than leading soldiers."

"Well, right now, Wallace and his motley force are all we have there, now that Early's in Maryland tearing up bridges. He's also forcing towns to pay ransom or he'll burn them down. He got twenty thousand dollars from Hagerstown alone. He's moving too fast to suit me."

Grant pondered the map, considering his options.

"What's the date?" he asked Porter.

"July the eighth, sir."

"That force we sent out two days ago should arrive in Washington later today or tomorrow morning."

Grant had dispatched a division from the Sixth Corps, plus all of Sheridan's cavalrymen who no longer had horses—nine thousand men in all—to join General Wallace's shaky command.

"They may not be enough to protect Washington," Grant said. "Send a wire to Halleck to inform him that I will send the rest of the Sixth Corps."

"All three divisions, sir?" Porter asked.

"As much as I hate to do it, yes. When is the Nineteenth Corps expected to reach Fortress Monroe at Norfolk?"

"Any day, sir."

The Nineteenth, veterans all, was on its way from New Orleans by ocean steamer, eventually to join Grant at Petersburg, significantly increasing the size of his command. Their arrival would have given him the flexibility to plan large-scale flanking maneuvers without weakening the trench lines.

"Send a telegram to Norfolk ordering the Nineteenth to Washington as soon as they disembark. By God, if two corps of crack troops and four thousand of Sheridan's cavalry cannot stop Early, then we don't deserve to win."

"That still leaves us stalemated here."

"Afraid so," Grant said, nodding wearily and taking another hungry puff on his cigar. "All we can do is remain in the trenches and hope Lee will be foolish enough to attack and get mangled in the process, like we did at Cold Harbor. That's not likely, though. I expect we've both learned our lessons about frontal assaults on well-defended positions. With neither side willing to attack and neither of us with troops to spare for a flanking maneuver, we sit here twiddling our thumbs, losing more men to random shelling for no gain. I tell you, Colonel, it is frustrating."

Yesterday, Grant had received a fresh batch of newspapers from New York and Washington. The reporters castigated him for sticking in the trenches and not carrying the war to the rebels more aggressively. Some journalists suggested that a new commander was needed. An editorial writer said, "If this one refuses to move, then let us find one who will."

"What about that mine, sir," Porter interrupted, "the one in the Ninth Corps area?"

"Is that thing still being talked about?" Grant asked, surprised.

"More than that. Colonel Lyman, General Meade's aide, told me that the tunnel already extends beyond our forward trench line."

Grant snorted and shook his head.

"When Burnside gets a bee in his bonnet, he never lets up. The last I heard, Meade told me that his engineering officer called the idea ridiculous. He said it could not be done. We'd end up with a lot of dead miners when the thing collapsed or suffocated them."

"Sir, from what Colonel Lyman told me, there have been no fatalities. What's more, General Burnside has the colored division training for the big breakthrough when the miners blow up the fort on Cemetery Hill."

"The colored troops!" Grant said. "The whole thing gets more bizarre. I don't put any stock in it. I tell you, Colonel, we are not going to win this war by digging a hole. If I thought it stood half a chance, I'd get a shovel and join them myself."

General Meade's staff sat outside around the mess table, wilting in the afternoon heat. Neither a breeze nor a cloud tempered the hot sun. The men paused in their conversation to listen to the angry voices emanating from the general's tent.

"That fool mine again?" one asked Theodore Lyman, who was finishing a glass of lemonade.

"Yes," he said. "Burnside seems to talk of nothing else. He thinks he is going to win the war with those ragamuffin miners of his."

The officers fell silent, straining to hear the exchange between Burnside and Meade. They could distinguish few words, but there was no mistaking Meade's anger. A new crop of rumors had reached him from Washington. Stanton's assistant, Dana, was persisting in his crusade to get Meade relieved of command. Grant's assurances that Meade would remain in his job were no longer as calming as they had been several days ago.

Inside Meade's tent, beneath the limp imperial pennant, the

two generals faced each other across Meade's desk. Both remained seated but leaned forward combatively, elbows on the table, whiskers bristling and eyes flashing, with Meade's like two great lumps of coal.

"Do you mean to say that you are still flogging that dead horse?" Meade hissed.

"If you are referring, General, to the mine that will end this bloody war, the answer is yes. I am proceeding despite your lack of endorsement and failure to provide assistance."

"I sent you Major Dunne's report. You know the thing cannot be done. That is why I do not endorse or approve it."

"Colonel Pleasants says it can be done and he is busy doing it."

"Who, I ask you, General, is better informed?" Meade said. "A West Point engineer who has written the standard book on military engineering or a coal miner with no training and few credentials?"

"I believe Colonel Pleasants," Burnside answered. "If he says it can be done, my money is on him."

"Then you will lose your bet. Dunne insists that the miners will be asphyxiated before they go a hundred feet, far short of the five hundred feet required to reach the Confederate fort."

Burnside leaned back and folded his arms across his chest, his scowl becoming a smug smile.

"As of today, General, the mine has progressed more than two hundred feet."

Meade blanched. His bespectacled eyes blinked and he gripped the edge of the table as though to upend it.

"That cannot be," he said.

"It is so. Colonel Pleasants has devised a technique for providing fresh air to the mine for its full length. A new method that is nowhere discussed in Dunne's manual."

"I do not credit that this coal miner person could resolve a problem our chief engineer says cannot be solved. I shall send Dunne over to examine it."

"Colonel Pleasants will be most pleased to demonstrate, sir."

Meade was doubtful, even defensive. He did not like to be contradicted.

"That still does not alter the situation," he told Burnside. "The tunnel could collapse or the rebels could blow it up. I will not order you to suspend this foolhardy operation—it is in your sector and you have the right to try it—but I reiterate that you do this entirely on your own. My command will still not provide any tools or supplies. So far as I am concerned, that would be a waste."

Meade pulled a sheet of paper from his jacket pocket and slapped it on the desk.

"And that includes your request for twelve thousand pounds of powder. It is denied."

"Sir, as a corps commander I am entitled to—"

Meade hit the table again.

"You are entitled to what I decide you need to hold your portion of the line. You are asking for twice the normal corps requirement for a month! Further, you cannot have five hundred feet of wire and the galvanic battery my quartermaster says you have been trying to obtain through unorthodox and irregular channels. You will not persist in that attempt. Is that understood?"

Burnside took a deep breath to control his anger.

"Perfectly understood, sir. May I put a hypothetical question to you?"

"Yes, yes," Meade said impatiently.

"Suppose, General," Burnside said quietly, "for argument's sake, that the mine can be completed. Will you refuse us the chance to blow up the enemy's fortifications?"

Meade knew that the newspapers, the congressional Committee on the Conduct of the War, and all of his many other critics would ride that wagon hard. Headlines formed in his mind: MEADE REFUSES CHANCE TO DESTROY REBEL DEFENSES.

"No, of course not," he told Burnside, forcing a note of amiability into his voice. "The day you tell me that the tunnel has been dug, I will supply all the powder and fuse you need.

I would not thwart an opportunity to inflict such damage on the enemy."

"Then it follows, sir," Burnside said, "that you would wish to exploit the gap in the enemy line that my explosion will create? And you will permit me to send my corps through it? And supply two additional corps to support the movement and ensure its success?"

Meade felt sandbagged. He had stepped neatly into Burnside's trap. He could not allow one and withhold permission for the other or his critics would be snapping at his throat again.

"Well . . ." he said, drawing out the word to play for time. "I don't know about two additional corps. That would significantly weaken our line in the event of a counterattack. But I suppose I would not object to your making a little demonstration with your own troops, so long as you pulled back before the rebels regrouped and hit you on your flanks."

"The rebels will not have time to regroup, General. They will be in such disarray from the explosion that the sight of my men pouring through the breach before the dust settles will panic them. I tell you, sir, it will be a rout. My Ninth Corps will be in Petersburg before the hour is up."

"I think you expect too much of your men," Meade said. "After all this time in the trenches, their condition is not sound. They are as played out as the other corps and have lost their aggressive edge. The men are used to the shelter of the trenches. I am no longer certain we can rouse them for a massive assault."

"I have a fresh division to spearhead the assault," Burnside countered. "Troops who have not been in the trenches and who are training daily in maneuvers designed to exploit the situation."

"Ah yes," Meade said with a chuckle. "I do not share your faith in the colored troops. I doubt they have the mental capacity to grasp the intricacies of movement required in an operation of this size."

Burnside started to protest, but Meade held up his hand and continued.

"I also do not share your faith in the Fourth Division's commanding officer, General Ferraro. The man was a dancing master before the war! An Italian! His father barely speaks a word of English. I suppose he is better than Ledlie, but that is not saying much."

"General Ferraro is eager and willing," Burnside said. "He knows this is a chance to prove himself as a division commander."

"Hmm," Meade said. "Well, it is your operation and your prerogative to select the officers and the troops. However, I remain unconvinced that the coloreds will prove adequate, and I am equally unconvinced of the wisdom of the whole idea, but you're free to proceed—for now."

"Thank you, sir," Burnside said. "One more thing. If this is to be my operation, I think it should be left to me to decide how to conduct it. I believe I should have complete command of the assault."

Meade stiffened. His hands tightened into fists and a crimson hue rose on his neck, inching its way up across his face. His eyes popped and his thinning hair seemed to bristle. Burnside knew he had gone too far.

"General Burnside," Meade said. "You have exceeded your authority, sir. You have presumed too much. Should it be determined to employ the army under my command in any offensive operations at the front, I alone shall exercise the prerogative of my position to direct and control them. I stand ready to receive any suggestions a subordinate commander thinks it proper to make, but the final authority is mine."

Meade had worked himself up to a high point of irritability and he lashed out with glee, seizing the opportunity to get even with Burnside for entrapping him.

"Make no mistake, General Burnside," Meade continued, "I am in command of the Army of the Potomac and every soldier in it. For you to suggest that an offensive operation can best succeed if I step aside and relinquish my authority to you implies a lack of confidence in my ability to lead my army. Was that your intent?"

Meade glared at his subordinate commander, enjoying the man's discomfort. Burnside sat at attention, his hands folded in his lap like a chastened schoolboy. It was time to eat crow, to apologize for something he had neither said nor intended, and he framed his reply carefully, as though dictating a letter that would enter the army's endless files and remain there for future historians to read. If Burnside had to grovel, he would do so expertly.

"Perhaps I spoke in haste, General, and in my excitement exercised a poor choice of words. I assure you, sir, in all candor, that I never dreamt of implying a lack of confidence in your ability to do all that is necessary in any movement that may be undertaken by my corps in your army. Were you personally to direct such an attack as I have in mind from my line, I would express nothing but confidence in the outcome. I would serve in my subordinate capacity with cheerfulness, as I have done since you assumed command of the Army of the Potomac."

Meade smiled politely. Go ahead and squirm, he thought.

Burnside paused to clear his throat, collect his thoughts, and ponder how much more was required to appease Meade. Go ahead and gloat, you arrogant bastard, he thought. The tables will turn soon enough and you will be lucky to get command of a regiment in Colorado by the time I'm finished with you.

"It is hardly necessary for me to say, sir," Burnside continued, "that I have had the utmost faith in your ability to handle troops throughout my acquaintance with you. My duty to my country, and to you, forbids that I should presume to embarrass you by suggesting an authority I do not possess. The Army of the Potomac is indeed yours to command, as am I. If I gave any impression to the contrary, I apologize. Believe me, sir, no slight was intended."

Meade thrust his head forward in a tight little bow. Spoken like a politician, he thought.

Burnside bowed slightly more. If that does not appeal to your vanity, he thought, I don't know what will.

"No slight taken, General," Meade said heartily, "now that you have explained yourself. Consider the incident forgotten."

"Very kind of you, sir," Burnside said. "I had best return to my headquarters. So much planning to do. So many details to work out."

"The price of leadership," Meade bantered, rising to his feet. "I wish you well in your operation, even if I do not share your faith in it." It does not stand a chance in hell, he thought, and when it fails, I will see that your days in my army are numbered.

"I think you will be surprised and pleased with the results, sir," Burnside said. When I get to Petersburg, he thought, I will tell every reporter I can find how you tried to block me. I'll see you hounded out of the army with a greater stain than Gettysburg.

"Good day, General," Burnside said.

"Good day to you, General," Meade replied.

Both men smiled, each relishing the imminent downfall of the other.

The following morning at 5:00 A.M., reveille sounded the length of the Union trenches and in every encampment behind the lines. Drums rolled, fifes trilled, and trumpets resounded, as each unit had its own favorite instrument for waking up its men. In the First Division portion of the line, General Ledlie sounded the call with his sixty-piece band, waking up the Confederates as well.

In the trenches previously occupied by the Forty-Eighth Pennsylvania, Colonel Pleasants stretched, yawned, and hauled himself upright, stiff from a night on a blanket on the hard ground. He sniffed the air and watched the men of his replacement, the Twelfth New Jersey, boil their coffee and prepare breakfast. The sergeant detailed to help him brought a steaming cup of coffee and three pieces of hardtack.

"I checked for worms and weevils, sir. Hardly any in this batch."

"Thank you, Sergeant Weaver."

The man glanced at the large brass object at Pleasants's feet, some kind of telescope set on a platform with three adjustable feet and gears and knobs of varying sizes.

"If you don't mind my asking, sir, what do you call that thing?"

"It's a theodolite, Sergeant. Surveyors use it to lay out a road or a bridge."

"Or a tunnel under the reb trenches, sir?"

"That too, Sergeant."

"Why do you have to use it from three different places?"

"It's called triangulation. You take three readings—the angles here on these graduated circles—from three different sites, all aimed at the same spot. Then you can calculate the precise direction to that spot and determine its distance from the tunnel entrance. We wouldn't want to end up with our tunnel off to one side of the rebel fort or twenty feet shy of it."

"No, sir, but couldn't you just use a map? Setting that shiny gadget out on top of the parapet is like putting up a sign to the reb sharpshooters saying, Here I am."

"Believe me, Sergeant, if there were some other way I would surely do it, but I have no choice."

"I wouldn't want to lose you, sir. The captain says you're my responsibility while you're here. If you get shot, he's going to be awful mad."

"I won't feel too good about it myself," Pleasants said, "but with the help of you and your men, it should go all right. I'll be taking these readings with the rising sun behind me. That may put off the aim of any sharpshooters looking this way. I'll have the blanket over me, as well."

"Yes, sir," Sergeant Weaver said doubtfully.

Pleasants glanced at the top of the parapet high above his head, dimly outlined in the predawn light. For an instant, he had the sickening sensation that he was seeing the wall of his grave. He looked at the firing ledge and the box he had placed on it in order to raise himself to sufficient height to see over the parapet. His legs felt like rubber. He sat down and forced himself to look away, telling himself he could do this thing, he could climb on the box, balance the theodolite on the rim, adjust the legs until the bubble showed it was level, and calmly take his readings. He could jump down and run to the next site, with Sergeant Weaver carrying the box, and climb up on it and take his measurements all over again. And do it once more. Ten minutes in all, he reminded himself.

His fear of being exposed to enemy sharpshooters had led him to write to Anne Shaw last night. He could not bear the thought of dying without answering her letter, without assuring her that her modern ideas had not altered his desire to marry her, even if he was not so convinced himself.

He told her about the odious Major Dunne and about Burnside's decision to support the tunnel in the face of Meade's disapproval. He wrote about the ventilation duct and reported that the men had excavated 250 feet, halfway to the rebel fort. He wrote easily, describing Cabot's arrest and rescue from the provost guards and Atwood's escapade at the railroad bridge, inviting rebel soldiers to supper.

> Young Atwood and his men and the rebs had a grand time trading war stories and getting drunk on Confederate corn liquor and United States Army commissary whiskey.
>
> All the men worked together dismantling the bridge. They said their good-byes with tears in their eyes. It's a strange war sometimes. As far as his men are concerned, Lieutenant Atwood walks on water. His detail is now working at a sawmill a few miles away, keeping us supplied with timber.

Pleasants paused, realizing that he could not postpone the inevitable. And so he did something he never thought he could do—he lied. He told Anne that her letter changed nothing between them. He hoped his words would comfort her, but they brought little reassurance to him. One day, he would have to decide how he truly felt. But not now, not today, not with the parapet looming over him, its features taking on clarity in the gray light with the sun about to rise.

Caleb Caffee hated sunrise. It made him feel vulnerable, ineffective, and lonely. With the sun in his eyes, he did not have as clear a shot at his target as he would later in the day. Worse, with the bright sun shining on him like a lighthouse beacon, reflecting off the lens of his telescopic sight, Yankee sharpshooters had a clear shot at him.

Mornings also brought the sounds of camaraderie as the soldiers set to a new day. They were at their most cheerful, laughing and joking, not yet wilted and soured by the heat and danger and boredom of another day in the trenches. The easy sociability reminded Caffee that he was an outcast in his own army.

He ate his meager breakfast of hardtack alone, hunkered down in his lair, a shallow depression behind a bramble bush at the base of the brown wall of the earthen fort. The smells of food and the noises of fellowship welled up around him. He did his best to ignore them.

"Who needs them," Caffee muttered, focusing his sight on a gun slit in the Union line. He settled down to wait for some bored or overeager Yankee to peer through to see what the new day looked like on his side. He noticed again that column of smoke rising from the second line of enemy trenches. He was curious about that. He had seen it for several days now. Not that smoke was unusual—Yankees were forever boiling up coffee and frying food over open fires. But cooking fires never lasted long. This fire sent up a line of smoke all day long. It never went out. He wondered whether it continued at night and what the Yankees were up to. Caffee burrowed a little deeper in the earth as the first bloodred hint of the sun appeared over the Union trenches.

"It's time, Sergeant," Pleasants said. He grabbed his blanket and the theodolite and headed for the box on the firing step.

"You heard the colonel," Sergeant Weaver yelled to his eight-man detail. "Get those caps off and spread out."

The men hooked their blue caps on the ends of their bayonets and spaced themselves two feet apart.

"Ready, sir?" he asked Pleasants.

Pleasants nodded, took a deep breath, and climbed up on the box. Simultaneously, the eight soldiers raised their rifles over their heads so that the caps peeked above the parapet. Within seconds, rebel bullets whined over the trench, a few striking the caps and pinging as they spun off the hard steel of the bayonets. It was an old game played out of boredom by men on both sides. They liked to bet on whose cap received the most bullet holes. Sharpshooters knew it was sport—there were no heads inside those caps—but many of them fired just as eagerly as if they had clear shots at human targets.

Pleasants manhandled the heavy theodolite onto the dirt parapet, camouflaging it with the blanket. He stretched the blanket to cover his head, leaving an opening large enough to focus the telescope on a bramble bush at the base of the Confederate fort. He went through the motions mechanically, narrowing his mind to the numbers that indicated the angles, scratching them rapidly on a tiny piece of paper. He felt snug and secure inside his blanket cocoon.

A fusillade of rebel bullets stirred the morning air like a swarm of bees, but he paid no attention. His fear vanished the moment he set to work, limiting his world to vernier readings in minutes and seconds of arc. Nothing to it, he thought, making one last quick check to verify the readings. He felt a tug on the blanket. A tiny patch of light appeared beside his right eye, a bullet hole. Pleasants assured himself it was only a stray, that no one was aiming at him.

"Okay, let's go," he called.

He jumped off the box and Sergeant Weaver reached for it. They ran down the trench to the second of the three sites.

Caleb Caffee did not bother to take a second glance at the array of Union caps bobbing over the parapet. He thought it was a stupid game, a waste of good ammunition and a risk of giving away your position for no gain. Sure enough, a sharpshooter below him on the hill cried out in pain. Damn fool should have known better, Caffee thought, and he zeroed back in on his chosen target.

"Okay, boys, caps up," Weaver ordered.

Pleasants climbed on the box and retreated into his work and the rewarding feeling of a precision instrument in his skilled hands. A fresh round of bullets searched out the blue caps. He worked faster this time, more sure of himself and of his survival. He turned the blanket around so he could not see the bullet hole and wondered why he had been so fearful. It was all a matter of control and confidence, he thought as he scribbled down his angles and numbers.

Caffee's curiosity was piqued by the second set of Yankee caps bobbing up and down. Usually when a bunch of boys decided to sport around with their caps, others along the line joined in. This was different. There was something funny about it. It was too neat, too orderly, with the same number of hats evenly spaced. The Yanks were up to something.

He swung his rifle barrel toward the caps and focused his sight, squinting against the sun. He took in the caps and adjusted the sight slightly to the left. There, on top of the parapet, a brown lump and a glimpse of glass set in a brass rim. A telescope! Some Yankee bastard's spying on us! Caffee lined up his cross hairs on a point just above the lens and started to squeeze the trigger. The flash of glass was gone. The parapet was bare.

Caffee cursed and released his finger from the trigger. He turned his rifle sight back to the gun slit, tore off a piece of moldy bread, and chewed slowly, simmering over his missed opportunity to get an officer.

One more, Pleasants thought as he followed the sergeant to the last site. The fear and weakness in his legs had returned. He told himself that the worst was over—two down and one to go—but his muscles and his pounding heart did not believe it.

"Off your duffs, boys," Weaver shouted as he placed the box on the firing ledge. "Get those caps in the air."

Pleasants jumped on the box and almost dropped the theodolite. He grabbed it before it fell into the trench. Shots echoed to his right and the soldiers laughed as their caps were shredded by rebel bullets, but Pleasants barely heard them. His fingers twirled the adjusting knobs as he leveled the instrument, making the bubble swing over to the center of its glass tube. He focused the lens and tugged the blanket around him.

Caleb Caffee snorted and swung his rifle toward the line of blue caps outlined against the new dawn. He saw it again, the tiny glass eye peering at him. He acted faster this time, squeezing off a round before he had the sight fully focused. A hole appeared in what he recognized as an army blanket.

Pleasants saw a puff of smoke come from the bramble bush at the base of the Confederate fort. He cursed and ducked his head and felt the bullet whiz past his ear. He straightened up, and instantly another sharpshooter's round plowed the air where the blanket and his head had been.

"Jesus, Colonel," Sergeant Weaver said. "Some reb's got you in his sights. Get down from there."

"I'm not finished yet," Pleasants said.

He read off more numbers and wrote them down quickly. A third bullet whipped through the blanket.

"Goddamn sun," Caffee roared, his eyes burning from squinting into the brightness.

He rubbed his closed lids until tears came. When he opened his eyes, everything was blurred, the trench line, the blanket, the glass eye atop the parapet, staring at him, mocking him. He trained his gun sight on it, tracking it as it started to move.

"Done," Pleasants said.

He whipped the blanket off his head and jumped down, dragging the theodolite off the parapet.

"Got you now, you bastard," Caffee said as he fired.

The bullet struck the brass instrument as Pleasants hauled it down. He gaped in surprise when he saw the dent where the round had hit and ricocheted off. He barked a short laugh and turned to show Sergeant Weaver. The man had a puzzled expression on his face. His hands were moving over his chest, exploring it. Blood ran through his fingers. His body swayed and he looked up at Pleasants as his eyes glazed over.

"And I was worried about *you* getting hit," he whimpered.

He was dead before Pleasants could reach him.

The last person Henry Pleasants wanted to see when he returned to the camp at the railway cut was Major Dunne. The engineering officer appeared to have ensnared Bobby Lee and Bill Cabot within his web, but not for long. Lee, looking more fierce and pugnacious than usual, took a step toward Dunne, shouting and jabbing a finger in the man's face until he was forced to retreat. Lee stormed off into the mine. When Dunne spotted Pleasants, he beckoned with a manicured hand and started toward him, Cabot trailing reluctantly behind.

Cabot spotted blood on Pleasants's shirt.

"Are you hurt, Colonel?"

"I'm all right," Pleasants said. "This is someone else's blood."

Relief spread over Cabot's face.

"Did you get your readings, sir?" he asked.

Pleasants nodded. He removed the blanket from the damaged theodolite and handed them to Cabot.

"Put these in my tent, please."

"Yes, sir," Cabot said. "May I bring the colonel a clean shirt?"

Pleasants shook his head and turned to Dunne. The major was laughing.

"Something funny, Major?"

"That antique," Dunne said, pointing at the theodolite. "It belongs in a museum. You used that thing to take your measurements?"

"I didn't have much choice, since you refused to supply a better one."

"We have a new Taylor repeating model with two micrometer microscopes mounted opposite each other. It gives much more precise readings than yours. We train our enlisted men to take the actual readings. It's a pedestrian job anyone can learn. I never do it myself anymore. Haven't in years."

"I find it useful to keep my hand in," Pleasants said, "even for the most ordinary of tasks. It makes me a better engineer."

Dunne snorted contemptuously, until he saw real anger on Pleasants's face. He changed the subject.

"That man of yours," he said. "Captain Lee. He was insubordinate."

"He usually is," Pleasants said. "On a good day, he's merely rude, but I'm sure you did not come all this way just to criticize my officers, Major. What can I do for you?"

"General Meade heard from General Burnside that your tunnel has gone some two hundred feet. I'm sure he's got it wrong. I find the figure hard to believe."

"It is wrong," Pleasants said with a smile. "The tunnel's length exceeds two hundred fifty feet. We have excavated halfway to Cemetery Hill."

"You solved the ventilation problem?" Dunne said, his face mirroring his disbelief.

Pleasants nodded.

"How did you do that? It isn't possible to ventilate a tunnel that long without sinking at least three air shafts. To do that, you would have had to dig two of them beyond our trench line in sight of the enemy."

"Would you like to see how it was done?"

"You mean, go back in the mine?" Dunne asked, glancing at his immaculate uniform. "Perhaps you could describe it for me."

"I think you should see this for yourself," Pleasants said. "Come on."

Pleasants walked toward the mine entrance at a brisk pace. He glanced over his shoulder and saw Dunne remove his jacket, fold it neatly in regulation style, and place it and his cap on a pile of boards. If he could have left his trousers and boots without losing his dignity, Pleasants thought, he probably would have.

Dunne caught up with Pleasants, stooped to enter the mine, and was immediately flattened against the rough timbered walls by two men carrying out a box of dirt.

"If we had wheelbarrows," Pleasants reminded him, "the men would not have to work so hard. Two hundred fifty feet is a hell of a long way to haul those crates."

"I see you've managed to obtain plenty of lumber and logs," Dunne said.

"Only because I've got sixty men working twelve hours a day at an abandoned sawmill. If the army had supported this project—if you had supported it—it would have gone faster and smoother."

Dunne scowled.

"How many cave-ins have you had, Colonel?"

"None," Pleasants said. "Look how solid the ceiling and walls are. With the floor, they form a unitary load-bearing frame. It would take a lot of pressure to break through. Right now, we've encountered a seepage problem. Water is coming through the ceiling farther down, so we've reinforced the side braces and tops."

"What is this wooden pipe?" Dunne said, examining the duct that ran along the left edge of the floor.

"Part of the ventilation system. That duct reaches from the outside all the way to the end of the mine, and it's extended daily to keep up with each day's digging. It's our source of fresh air."

"What draws the air in?"

"I'll show you," Pleasants said.

He unfastened the canvas door and gestured for Dunne to go through. He showed the major the air shaft that intersected the tunnel and the fire burning on the open grate, explaining how the stale air was drawn up the chimney, leaving a vacuum behind that sucked fresh air through the wooden pipe.

Dunne was speechless. He gaped at the fire and the duct and stared down the length of the tunnel, a distance so great, he could not see the end.

"This is brilliant, Colonel. Crude and simple to be sure, certainly nothing elegant, but brilliant nonetheless. This could change the nature of tunneling operations. Using this system, there's no limit to the length a mine could be dug."

Dunne paused to shake his head.

"I can't imagine why I haven't come across this. I certainly would have put it in my manual. Who designed it? A German engineer?"

"I designed it," Pleasants said. Seldom had so few words given him such immense satisfaction.

"Yes, yes, but based on whose work?" Dunne snapped. "Where did you get the idea?"

"It is my idea, Major Dunne. As far as I know, the system has never been tried before. I would be happy to grant you permission to describe it in your manual. You can say that it was used to build the longest military mine in the history of warfare, a feat the experts said could not be done."

Stan Michnik glanced warily at the ceiling of the mine, made the sign of the cross, and said another prayer. He felt uneasy, finding it more difficult every day to work in the mine. First, it was the canvas door that made him feel trapped when it sealed behind him. Before, he had been able to look over his shoulder and see a pinprick of light from the entrance, connecting him with the outside, making him feel safe. Now, it was gone; when Stan glanced toward the outside, he saw nothing but eerie flickering candles every twenty feet, converging to blackness.

Now there was a new worry, that he would drown in an oozing sea of mud. Three days ago, water began to seep from overhead and the situation was getting worse. Chunks of wet dirt had been falling on the miners. The water soaked them through as it continued to drip down. Today, the floor, where they braced themselves to heave their axes against the facing, had become slippery, and the wooden frames were beginning to sink into the muck.

Pleasants ordered the beams reinforced, but he knew it was only a matter of time before they passed what had to be an underground stream. If the miners broke through to it, they could drown. If they came too close, the ceiling near the facing might buckle before they erected the next frame of logs.

"Dirt's piling up," Jacob Dodson told Stan, putting down his pickax.

Dodson was Stan's neighbor back home in Pottsville. They had never been particularly close, but they had become friends in the army. Stan had chosen Jacob for his partner on the day shift. Jacob was huge and husky and could swing an ax almost as hard as Stan. The dirt carriers had to work faster for them than for any other pair because they made the dirt fly.

Stan and Jacob stepped back from the facing and motioned for their four-man crew to shovel out the dirt.

"Already?" one said. "We just got back from dumping the last load."

Stan and Jacob moved a few feet back to the water barrel and took turns drinking from the metal dipper. The crew piled the loose dirt and mud into two hardtack boxes. When the crates were full to overflowing, they hefted them with a chorus of mock moans and began the long walk down the tunnel. Stan looked after them with envy and saw Bobby Lee coming through.

"Might have known I'd catch you loafing," Lee said. "How's the leak?"

"It's like standing in the rain," Stan said, "and it's getting worse."

Lee ran his fingers along the low ceiling and down one wall. Dodson went back to work at the facing. With his second ax blow, the farthest ceiling beam snapped. A cascade of mud and water followed, burying him instantly.

"Get out!" Lee yelled. He grabbed Stan's shoulder and tried to pull him away.

Stan shook himself free, tearing at the mudslide with his hands. Cracks resounded from the adjoining logs.

"Shore them up," he shouted.

Lee grabbed a log and braced it under the last ceiling timber, which was already bowing and ready to snap. He piled additional logs beneath the neighboring timbers. The first two support beams cracked under the strain and the ceiling collapsed to within two feet of the floor, cutting Stan off from Bobby Lee.

Entrapped in a tiny tomb, Stan was almost overwhelmed by a feeling of panic, which brought with it memories of the last cave-in, when he had abandoned his friend Cas. Again he saw a hand reaching for him, only this time it was Jacob Dodson's.

Stan tore at the earth, screaming Jacob's name. Each stroke of his splayed fingers seemed to occur in slow motion. As his eyes adapted to the darkness, he grasped the twitching hand. It closed tightly on his own.

"He's alive!" Stan shouted.

"Hurry up, Stan," Lee said. "I'm running out of logs."

Pleasants stopped in midsentence when he heard the cracking timbers, the worst sound a miner could hear. The four dirt carriers came tearing down the tunnel toward him and Dunne, who suddenly looked pale in the candlelight.

"Cave-in!"

"Who's up there?" Pleasants asked.

"Captain Lee, sir, and Stan and Jacob."

"Get the second shift in with shovels and extra logs. Move!"

"Want to see what a cave-in looks like?" Pleasants said to Dunne.

"If it's all the same to you," Dunne said, backing away, "I'd only be in the way."

He started to run, but Pleasants caught him by the shoulder and spun him around. Dunne's eyes widened and rolled back, staring at the ceiling as if expecting it to collapse.

"The whole thing's not going," Pleasants said. "The problem is just at the facing where the water's coming in. We're safe here."

"Yes, sir," Dunne said, though he clearly did not believe it.

"This will not stop us," Pleasants said. "Do you understand me, Major?"

Dunne nodded, unable to speak.

"We'll have this cleared and shored up before the day is out. You tell that to General Meade. You tell him that in ten days, no more, we'll be underneath Cemetery Hill. You got that?"

Dunne nodded again. Pleasants released him and gave him a little shove toward the entrance.

"Hurry, Stan," Lee said. "I'm down to the last log."

Stan pawed through the mud, tugging on Dodson's arm.

"I've got him," Stan shouted as the unconscious man's shoulder and head burst free.

Stan shivered. He imagined water and mud forcing their way into his mouth and nose. He wanted to scream, but his father's voice echoed off the walls. "You will dig, boy. You will tear and scratch and claw at this earth until you die."

He took a deep breath and pulled on Dodson's arm. The wall of mud began to crumble, falling to pieces at his feet. He grabbed Dodson around the waist and laid him gently on the ground.

"Pull him through, Bobby," he said.

Lee took hold of Dodson's arms and tugged the body under the low ceiling. He pumped the chest to force in air. Stan crawled through the opening and knelt beside Dodson, taking his hand.

"Will he make it?" Stan asked.

"He'll live," Lee said.

Pleasants came running down the tunnel.

"Let's get him out of here," he said.

Bobby Lee hoisted Dodson on his back.

"Are you all right, Stan?" Pleasants asked.

Stan glanced at the cave-in, crossed himself, and nodded.

"Yes, sir, but we lost about five feet."

"Don't worry. We'll fix it. This mine's not going to beat us."

9

PLEASANTS, Bobby Lee, and Stan Michnik took the men of the second shift back into the tunnel. The miners set to work with a furious energy, as though the fallen mud and snapped timbers were their enemies.

They hauled broken beams and loads of dirt down the tunnel. Outside, carpenters and their assistants fabricated heavy wooden frames. More than a dozen men scurried back and forth, carrying frames and logs inside and bringing out boxes full of mud. Not a whine or complaint was heard. They were angry at the mine—it had injured one of their own and set back their schedule. They had to show the mine who was boss.

At the facing, there was a problem. One boss too many. Pleasants had pitched in with a shovel and was tossing dirt behind him as fast as he could dig, but it was not fast enough for some.

"Let me do that, sir," a nineteen-year-old private said, taking the shovel out of Pleasants's hand. "That's my job, Colonel."

Pleasants looked around, feeling helpless without something to do with his hands. He walked over to where Lee was directing three men who were positioning reinforcing logs.

"Shouldn't you put two layers there?" Pleasants asked.

Lee scowled, ignoring Pleasants, and went on with his work. Pleasants stepped back to survey the progress.

"A little more to the left," he said.

Bobby Lee placed his hand on Pleasants's shoulder and led him out of earshot.

"Look, Henry, I've fixed more cave-ins than you've ever seen and I know what the hell I'm doing. There's only room for one boss in here, so why don't you go do something else."

Pleasants opened his mouth to tell Lee that this was his goddamn mine, but Lee smiled at him.

"Just a subtle suggestion, sir," he said.

"You're about as subtle as a pickax, Bobby," Pleasants said. "You're lucky I'm so good-natured."

"We all appreciate that, sir. Don't trip on your way out."

"We're open for business again," Bobby Lee said as he entered Pleasants's tent.

"That was fast." He checked his pocket watch. "A little over two hours."

Lee dropped into a camp chair, pulled out a handkerchief, and wiped his face.

"It went a lot faster once we got the brass out of the way," he said. "No hard feelings?"

"No more than usual," Pleasants said.

He tilted back in his chair and shook his head over Lee's appearance. Bobby was so covered with mud from head to foot that it was hard to tell his uniform was blue.

Lee rubbed his mud-stained hands over his bald head, leaving two dark streaks.

"The new ceiling's holding," he said, "and I don't see how anything could collapse it, not as thick as we've made it. We dug in a few feet more and got past the stream that was overhead. It will continue to seep where the cave-in was, but the dirt beyond it is dry. The day shift is back at work with a vengeance, trying to make up the lost time."

"Stan, too?" Pleasants asked.

"Yeah," Lee said, chuckling. "He and another guy got into an argument about which shift was best. They decided to settle it with a bet. A month's wages to the shift that digs the farthest from tomorrow morning until the mine is finished. They elected you referee, to keep track of who's ahead. The guys are gonna dig their hearts out now."

"Good," Pleasants said.

He waved a hand at the pages of calculations littering his desk, the result of his morning's work with the theodolite.

"According to my measurements, the total distance to the Confederate fort is five hundred eleven feet. We need to raise the daily quota from twenty-five to thirty-five feet. If we can dig that much every day, we'll finish in seven days. Another five for the laterals—that's seventy-five feet more—and then we'll be ready to place the powder. Do you think the men can do that?"

"Unless we hit solid rock or get flooded out," Lee said. "Nothing else would stop them now that there's serious money riding on it."

He stood up and stretched his arms over his head, causing lumps of drying mud to drop from his uniform.

"You're getting dirt all over my dirt floor," Pleasants complained.

"War is hell," Lee said, brushing himself off. "One other thing. There's trouble at the sawmill."

"What's the problem?"

"It's Billy Satcher. He's giving Atwood a hard time."

Satcher, two hundred pounds, six feet four, was the most hated soldier in the regiment. A logger before the war, an illiterate, foulmouthed bully at the best of times, he became sadistic and cruel when drunk. He had already beaten several men.

Bobby Lee was the only man Satcher feared, knowing that Lee could take him easily in a fight. Pleasants would have court-martialed Satcher long ago, but General Potter, the division commander, rejected the request on the grounds that Satcher, for all his faults, was a good soldier. He never shirked his duty in combat and, when sober, was a tireless worker. Pleasants had agreed when Lee assigned him to Atwood's sixty-man bridge-dismantling detail, the outfit now working at the sawmill.

"What's Satcher done?" Pleasants said.

"Nothing yet. It's what he might do that worries me. Sergeant Ross stopped me on my way over here."

"I thought Ross was with Atwood at the sawmill."

"He's on his way back now. He came in with one of the timber wagons to report to me. You know Ross, he's kind of an old lady. He keeps tabs on everything, knows all the gossip. If he say's there's trouble, I believe him. It seems that Atwood has found himself a girlfriend, a woman with a twelve-year-old son. They live in a cabin not far from the sawmill. Atwood goes off to see her every evening.

"Sergeant Ross followed him a couple of times—to see if the lieutenant was all right, he explained. He said the woman is a stunner and is crazy about Atwood. Doesn't that beat all? The only people I ever see are you and Stan and the same bunch of filthy miners I used to see every day at home. And the rich mine owner's kid finds a beautiful girl!

"Anyway, yesterday Ross saw that he was not the only one following Atwood and the woman. Satcher was there, too, and later bragged to some of the guys that he was going to have himself a woman. Said if anybody tried to stop him, he'd kill him. So I think I'd better go over there and have a little talk with Satcher."

"Sounds like a good idea," Pleasants said. "But Bobby, take a bath first."

"Is that an order, Colonel?"

"I think it is."

"You're worse than my wife."

Atwood watched the shadows of the trees lengthen on the parched ground. Another half hour before he could leave. He was impatient to be with Mary Elizabeth again. He checked his pocket watch, wondering why the wagon had not returned from delivering the wood to the mine. The men were due back with food supplies and casks of water. It was not the wagon or the food he missed. It was Sergeant Ross, who, uncharacteristically, had ridden off with them that morning. Ross was a comfort, a man Atwood could count on. If Ross didn't get back soon, Atwood wasn't sure he should leave his post, the noisy clearing in the woods with its heady smell of fresh-cut timber and pine resin, its cooking fires, its scattering of conical white tents.

Suppose something happened and neither he nor Ross was there to deal with it? Colonel Pleasants would be furious. Pleasants and Lee believed in him. He couldn't let them down. But Mary Elizabeth needed him, too. She would be waiting in their own tiny clearing amid the trees, fresh from her bath in the pond he had built, damming a stream with packed earth and logs.

It was on the third evening after he built the dam, for his own use, that he heard someone singing when he approached. He slithered noiselessly through the underbrush and watched, spellbound, as a woman splashed, soaped herself, and rinsed off in the cool clear water, rising, sputtering, laughing. She stepped out onto the spongy grass and dried herself with a thin towel. After she left, he undressed and slipped into the water, pretending that she was with him.

Two evenings more he watched her, entranced, and later, when she called out to him while he was bathing, he was startled.

"If you can watch me," she said, "then I reckon it's all right to watch you." She had spoken as calmly and easily as if they were sitting in his mother's parlor, having been properly introduced. Atwood had never met anyone like her.

Mary Elizabeth had long black hair and skin the color of mahogany from working outdoors in the fields. Her face to him was exotic, like a painting in a museum, and her laugh was deep and rich. He savored her delight when she showed him a well-thumbed book of poems she had found and he read them aloud to her and explained their meaning. And the rest—the private times—they proved he was a man, after all. He felt obsessed, besotted, drunk with desire. He had never imagined such ecstasy was possible.

Her husband had been dead almost two years, she said, killed at Antietam. She had felt nothing for him. Except for her son, Nat, she was alone. Her father and older brother had been lost at Gettysburg and her mother had died of heartbreak soon

after. Three months ago, Yankees had burned out their Shenandoah farm and killed the cows, chickens, and goats, leaving
little but charred timbers and ruined fields.

Mary Elizabeth took the boy and a shotgun and set out on
foot for North Carolina, where an uncle lived. They came
across a deserted cabin near Petersburg and there they stayed,
living on turnips and potatoes left in the fields, and the rabbits
and squirrels Nat shot. And in the evenings, she would meet
Paul Atwood, who brought food and love and hope for the
future.

She knew it would not last. He talked about marrying her
and taking her home to Pennsylvania, but she knew he couldn't
do it. One day, he would return to his world and his people and
there would be no place for her.

Mary Elizabeth did not blame Paul for the death of her
family, the destruction of the South and of her life. Like floods
and droughts, war was God's work. She knew he was a kind,
decent man, even though he was a Yankee, and she would
always love him and be grateful to him. But their time together
would pass like a fairy tale. In real life, people like Mary Elizabeth never lived happily ever after.

Atwood heard the wagon returning long before he saw it, a
trick of the topography that projected sounds far ahead of
sights. He took a quick look around the camp, confident that
all would be well in Sergeant Ross's hands, and strode off into
the woods. A few soldiers saw him leave. They nudged one
another and cracked a joke or two about the lieutenant, but the
remarks were meant kindly.

Billy Satcher watched, too, his eyes narrowed to slits, until
Atwood had disappeared among the trees. Satcher was in no
hurry. Let the lieutenant and his woman have their fun first,
then he would show her what a real man was like. In the
meantime, he had some serious drinking to do, to get in the
mood.

Satcher sat down under a tree at the perimeter of the camp,
leaned back, and closed his eyes. He opened one eye when the

wagon rolled into camp. Ross detailed a squad to unload the wagon and distribute the mail. He asked about Atwood and was told that the lieutenant had already left. He looked around the clearing and spotted Satcher asleep under a tree. Good. That meant things would be quiet tonight. Tomorrow, Bobby Lee would arrive to deal with Satcher.

"I don't want this to end," Atwood said. "You must marry me. I can't bear the thought of living without you."

He kissed Mary Elizabeth once more and rolled over on his back beside her, his hand reaching for hers.

"We agreed, Paul darling. There isn't any point to talking about it. Let's thank our lucky stars for the time we've got, but that's all we can have. Lord knows, it's more happiness than most people get in a lifetime."

"It's so unfair."

"Hush," she whispered.

She leaned over and placed a finger on his lips and kissed him chastely on his forehead.

"I don't need lessons in what's fair and what's unfair in this life," Mary Elizabeth said. "I learned long ago there's very little that's fair, at least for my kind. Now I won't have this beautiful night spoiled. You're a sweet man, Paul Atwood, and I love you more than life itself, but I swear sometimes you do talk too much."

Atwood smiled and closed his eyes, listening to the night sounds of the moonlit forest. He moved closer to her so their bodies touched and breathed deeply of her scent. There was so much he wanted to say, words he had rehearsed while he waited for the afternoon shadows to lengthen. He told himself there was no reason why their relationship could not continue forever.

That was how he felt when he was with her. It was different during the day, when doubts assailed him. What would his parents say? His friends? They might be polite to her face, but they would snicker about her lack of education, her accent, her age and background. She would know that she did not fit into his world.

Mary Elizabeth bolted upright and screamed. Paul followed her terrified gaze and saw Billy Satcher emerge from a clump of trees. He leered at them and took a swig from a whiskey bottle. In his other hand, he carried a club.

They jumped to their feet. Paul pushed Mary Elizabeth behind him, shielding her from Satcher's sight. Their clothing, neatly folded, lay on the ground beside the pond, about ten feet away, along with Atwood's service revolver in its leather holster.

"Don't even think of going for your gun, college boy," Satcher said. "You'd never make it in time."

"Get out of here, Satcher, or you'll be in serious trouble."

Satcher laughed and stepped closer. He tossed the bottle away and slapped the club against his open palm.

"What are you gonna do, put me on report? I'm real scared, Lieutenant. Now you be a good boy and run off and leave us alone."

Atwood sprang to his right, hoping to reach the gun. Satcher bellowed and charged, waving the club. Paul felt an explosion beside his ear, and he tripped and fell. Waves of noise and dizziness closed over him; a fearsome pain roared inside his head. He looked up through a haze, like peering through spectacles that were too thick.

Satcher struck again, hitting him across the forehead. Blood spurted over Atwood's eyes, blinding him. He rolled on his side and curled into a ball, hearing the swish as Satcher's club beat the ground inches from his skull. Distorted sounds came to him. Mary Elizabeth was screaming.

He forced himself to his knees and tried to stand, but his legs collapsed under him. He sensed footsteps and raised his arms to protect his head. He heard a noise like a shot, and when pain seared him from forearm to shoulder, he knew it had been the sound of his bones snapping.

"You killed him," Mary Elizabeth said, her voice reaching Paul as if in slow motion.

"Yeah," Satcher said. "He's dead."

Atwood's pain disappeared and a great peace overcame him, a feeling of serenity. A bright golden light revealed his mother and beloved grandmother, and Paul knew he was safe. He was five years old, playing on the lawn with his puppy. So this is what it's like to die, he thought, and he drifted away, oblivious to the woman's cries.

It's like a carnival, Pleasants thought, as the guard walked with him through the camp of the Fourth Division, United States Colored Troops. The faces of the black soldiers glistened with sweat in the stagnant night air as they sang and swayed beside the scores of camp fires. This guard was tall and imposing, and more talkative than the last one. He regaled Pleasants with stories about their daily training and how rapidly they were learning the drill.

"Corporal Mutesa, sir," he announced, explaining that he had changed his name when he heard about Lincoln's Emancipation Proclamation. "It's an African name, Colonel, the name of a great statesman and king. It seemed proper to discard my slave name when I was no longer a slave."

The light from a score of camp fires glittered in his eyes. He smiled at Pleasants and gestured toward Cemetery Hill.

"Just over yonder, on the other side of that hill, is where I was a slave before I ran away eight years ago. The abolitionists in Boston, they took me in and taught me to read and write and to dress proper. They got me a job clerking in a store and then Mr. Lincoln set me free. Of course, I was already free, but he made it legal.

"Then the army gave me a uniform and a gun and these two stripes of a corporal. They made me a warrior and sent me here to Petersburg so I can set free my mama and my brothers and sisters. It's a miracle is what it is, sir, being picked to lead this charge, to be the division that ends the war. That's the kind of thing you don't even dare pray for because you can't believe it could ever come true. But here it is, coming true."

"Are all the men as pleased about leading the assault as you are?" Pleasants asked.

"Pleased ain't the half of it, Colonel," Mutesa said. "This is the best thing that ever happened to us. To be chosen over all those white soldiers? That's an honor we never thought would come our way. All we've been allowed to do is guard wagon trains, dig ditches, and haul boxes from one place to another. After a while of doing that, you come to think the army don't have any trust in you. They're saying you're good enough to wear the uniform and carry a gun but not good enough to use it."

Mutesa stopped and turned to face Pleasants.

"We know we're good enough, sir, and we work hard like they order us to. We behave ourselves and we don't break the rules and we keep our uniforms and guns clean and we wait. We keep asking ourselves, How long, oh Lord, how long do we have to wait to prove that we can fight and die as good as any white men? We know the white soldiers don't like us or trust us. We know they call us names. Not all of them, sir, don't get me wrong. But we can tell from the looks we get.

"Now we got our chance. They'll see that we follow the same flag and we will follow it so long as there's a single man left to hold it up to the breeze of heaven. We feel freedom in our bones, Colonel, and we're willing to fight for it. We mean to earn it."

The corporal stopped suddenly and straightened to attention, looking embarrassed.

"Beg pardon, sir. I shouldn't have gone on like I did and take up the colonel's time. I get carried away with the glory of it all. I'll get you over to Major Boyce right away."

"Did you say Major Boyce?" Pleasants asked.

"Yes, sir. Got promoted last week and we're all mighty happy about it. He's a good officer, Major Boyce, and there ain't nothing we wouldn't do for him."

Mutesa grinned and lowered his voice to share a secret with Pleasants.

"But he sure can talk a lot, sir. He's got more words in him than any preacher."

Pleasants chuckled.

"Yes, sir, he sure can talk," the corporal repeated.

He stopped at the last in a row of tents and pointed to Boyce up ahead, standing amid a circle of officers. Boyce's hands fluttered like nervous birds and he seemed to hop from one foot to the other as he shifted his weight. The words rolled off his tongue like bullets from a cavalryman's rapid-firing Sharp's rifle.

"Lord, there he is at it again," Mutesa said. "Anybody'd think he was trying to sell snake oil. No disrespect intended, sir. We'd follow him anywhere—and some of us might even buy that snake oil from him. I'll leave you here, Colonel, and wish you a pleasant evening."

"Thank you, Corporal. I envy you. You'll be going home any day now. And by the way, you're not a bad talker yourself."

Mutesa laughed and snapped a salute. Pleasants returned it and strode over to where Boyce was holding his audience like a Fourth of July orator in the town square. As Pleasants approached, Boyce looked up and grinned.

"Colonel Pleasants," he said. "Good to see you, sir."

Boyce turned to the other officers.

"This is the man I was telling you about, the one who's making this operation possible. The best mining engineer and regimental commander in the business, Colonel Henry Pleasants, from Pottsville, home of the next United States senator from the great Commonwealth of Pennsylvania, namely me."

He winked at Pleasants.

"See you gents later. Mustn't keep a colonel waiting."

He saluted Pleasants, gripped his extended hand in both of his own, and pumped it hard.

"Congratulations on your promotion, Major," Pleasants said.

"Thank you, sir. It's all due to your mine. If not for that, there'd be no assault planned and the Fourth Division would not have this opportunity to march to everlasting glory. Of course, not everyone is enthusiastic about everlasting glory. When we received word that we were to lead the attack, my immediate superior decided that he was urgently needed at home and resigned within the hour. The regiment needed a new commander and I was available."

"Did any of the men desert?"

"Nary a one, Colonel. I've never seen soldiers so overjoyed at the prospect of going into battle. Why, some of them dragged themselves out of the hospital so they wouldn't miss out. It's all they talk about, how they'll smash through the rebel lines and move into Petersburg and march down Pennsylvania Avenue in Washington at the head of the Army of the Potomac's victory parade. They believe they're God's chosen instrument to end this war."

Boyce fell uncharacteristically silent for a moment. He looked slowly around the campsite.

"Who knows?" he said quietly. "Maybe they are God's chosen instrument. Here they sit, the people this whole damn war is about—if not for slavery, there'd have been no Fort Sumter or any of it—and wouldn't it be splendid if they brought it to an end?"

He gazed off into the darkness and up at the star-spotted sky. Pleasants said nothing, not wanting to intrude on Boyce's thoughts.

Boyce clapped his hands and broke the spell.

"Come back to my tent, Colonel. I want to show you something."

He bounded off at a furious pace, waving to a man here, nodding there, asking after another's health, joking and carrying on a conversation with Pleasants about the high spirits of his men.

"You can probably hear them singing every night. Have you noticed the change? No more hymns and sad ballads. Now it's rollicking camptown meeting songs that a body can't keep still for. There's lots of foot stomping and hand clapping and hallelujah shouting. I don't see how they have the energy for it as hard as they train all day, but the singing goes on for hours.

"They made up a new one the night they found out about the assault. They do something they call studying. They sit around the fires at night thinking. It's almost eerie to watch them sitting so quiet and still. It means they're studying their new situation, whether it's good or bad, confusing or pleasing, and they're trying to figure out what it means to them.

"Then somebody puts his thoughts into words. The others listen, and if they don't like it, the song trails off and dies. But if they think it reflects their mood and their feelings, then one by one they'll join in, adding verses to the tune. Pretty soon, you've got four thousand voices pouring out their souls. I swear, it's one of the most moving things I've ever witnessed.

"Well, they made up a new song to express how they feel about being chosen to spearhead the attack. It's got two main lines. After that, they improvise, but they always return to the same lines to begin a new verse."

Boyce stopped and stared at Pleasants for a moment before reciting the lines in a low voice.

> We look like men a-marching on;
> We look like men o'war.

"That's what they feel they are now," Boyce said. "Not slaves, not stevedores, not guards, not objects of derision, but men o'war. And they're standing ten feet tall. They know that because of what they'll do here, they and their people will truly be free at last."

Both men were silent until they reached Boyce's tent.

"Look at this, Colonel," Boyce said. "One of my men made it."

Pleasants bent down to examine the model. Measuring four feet square, it showed to scale the battlefield sculpted from earth, neatly framed with whitewashed twigs. Tiny colored flags mounted on sticks dotted the miniature terrain and painted arrows pointed the way to the rebel lines, forming intricate angular patterns. Boyce popped into his tent and emerged with a long carved stick.

"Here are our forward trenches," he lectured, stabbing at the model with his pointer. "Over here are the rebel trenches, and up the slope is the fort your mine will destroy. Each flag represents a unit of the Fourth Division. The blue circles are brigades, the white triangles are regiments, black squares for companies, and green rectangles for platoons. Every soldier in the division, from General Ferraro on down, has seen this, and each knows where his unit is to go and what maneuvers it has to follow."

Boyce waved his pointer in the air like a band conductor keeping time.

"Every man can recite the battle plan from memory." He aimed his stick at the Union trenches. "Here's how it starts. Our two brigades form up just behind our trenches, double columns closed in mass in a line half a mile long. The instant your mine explodes, they start for the gap in the rebel trenches. As soon as the lead regiments of both brigades cross the enemy line, they execute by the right companies on the right into line, wheel, and by the left companies on the left into line, wheel. They advance down the trenches on each side of the gap. We expect any rebs left alive to have abandoned the trenches by then.

"The rest of the regiments advance past the fort and to the crest of the hill. The three other divisions of the Ninth Corps should be on our heels, and they'll fan out right and left to widen the breach in the Confederate line. We march down the far side of Cemetery Hill and into Petersburg and that's that.

"We've practiced the maneuvers every day, and we'll keep on practicing until the day of the assault. Not much more than twenty minutes from start to finish, Colonel, and I think we can shave another two minutes off that."

Boyce planted the pointer like a giant flagpole at the crest of Cemetery Hill and nodded his head in approval.

"Would you like to meet General Ferraro, sir?" he asked Pleasants. "His tent's just across the way."

Without waiting for an answer or even looking to see whether Pleasants was following, Boyce stalked off, talking volubly over his shoulder.

"The general wants to meet you, sir. He told me that the next time the man who's digging the mine comes by, I was to bring him over. Did you hear the story about the whiskey?"

"No," Pleasants said, hurrying to catch up with Boyce, who seemed to be carrying on at least two conversations at the same time, greeting everyone who crossed his path.

"It happened at Antietam. Ferraro was a colonel, commanding a brigade in the Ninth Corps. You know the story about Burnside's Bridge?"

"Yes," Pleasants said, recalling the stricken look on Burnside's face when he had described it to him and Potter.

"Two of Ferraro's regiments were supposed to cross first, the Fifty-First New York and the Fifty-First Pennsylvania. They were waiting in a line about a hundred yards behind the bridge, a bit reluctant to move forward. Who could blame them? The rebs had it covered—every inch of the bridge and the approach. Nobody could make it through.

"Ferraro rode up, assessed the situation, and made a little speech to goad them on. 'It is General Burnside's request,' he said, 'that the two Fifty-Firsts take that bridge. Will you do it?' The men looked at one another and at the bridge and some Pennsylvania corporal called out, 'If we make it, Colonel, will you give us back our whiskey?' Ferraro had suspended their whiskey ration because they were heavy drinkers who often got into trouble.

"Ferraro sputtered a bit and laughed. 'Yes, by God, you'll have it,' he said. They took the bridge, but not many men came back. Ferraro apparently forgot his promise. About a week later, they turned out for a ceremony at which Ferraro was to receive his brigadier's star, a reward for the actions of the two Fifty-Firsts at the bridge.

"There's the new general in his dress uniform on his horse in front of the brigade. One of the Pennsylvanians yells, 'How about that whiskey?' Ferraro doesn't miss a beat. He grins and shouts back, 'You'll get it.' The next morning, he sends over a keg and he has them in the palm of his hand from then on."

"Why did he take a black division?" Pleasants asked, aware that all the officers were volunteers.

"He'll tell you," Boyce said. "He loves to talk about it. In fact, he just loves to talk. I've never seen a man who can talk so much."

Pleasants stifled the urge to laugh. He asked how the black troops liked Ferraro.

"They'd walk through fire for him, sir. He can do no wrong. And he's good with them. He's with the men every chance he gets and makes sure they're well fed. You know how important that is for morale. He turns out for maneuvers, spurring them on, encouraging them, setting the example. You couldn't ask for a better commander. Only—"

"Only what?"

"Well," Boyce said, "I may be wrong, but I think maybe he's drinking a bit more than he used to."

"A lot of officers drink," Pleasants said, "generals among them. It's a tough job. You've heard the stories about General Grant."

"Yes, sir, but General Grant doesn't have to be out front leading four thousand black soldiers who depend on him. It's true that the men know what's expected of them, but you have to remember that not so long ago most of them were slaves. They're not used to taking initiative. They're used to taking orders, to doing what the master tells them. Here, General Ferraro is master, father, and God, all wrapped up in one. If he lets them down, if he's not there to say, 'Follow me, boys,' then I fear the outcome."

"Well, there he is, sir, sitting in his rocking chair. He takes it with him wherever he goes."

Pleasants looked ahead to see, amid a protective cluster of officers, a short, trim, handsome man with black hair and a bold, sweeping mustache. The staff seemed at ease with Ferraro, respectful, but not cowed, more like a group of students gathered around a favorite teacher.

Ferraro waved to Boyce, rose, and walked toward them, bouncing on the balls of his feet. His graceful walk reminded Pleasants that the general had been a dancing master before the war.

"Sir," Boyce said, "I have the honor to present Colonel Henry Pleasants of the Forty-Eighth Pennsylvania Volunteers."

"Delighted to meet you, Colonel," Ferraro said, returning Pleasants's salute and extending his hand. "Boyce has told me a lot about you. In fact, he hardly ever stops talking about you."

"A pleasure to meet you, sir," Pleasants said. "In my experience, Major Boyce hardly ever stops talking about anything."

Ferraro exploded in laughter, draped his arm around Pleasants's shoulder, and led them over to his tent. He introduced Pleasants to the staff and reclaimed his place in his rocker, beaming at Boyce like a proud father.

"Major Boyce promises me that when he is elected President, which we all know is only a matter of time, he will appoint me ambassador to Italy."

He twirled his glorious mustache and winked at Pleasants, building up speed in his rocking chair like a child in a swing.

"Tell me, Colonel, how is your tunnel?"

"My men are working three shifts around the clock, sir. They should finish in no more than twelve days."

"You hear that, boys?" Ferraro said. "In two weeks, this war could be over. This was your idea, Colonel, to tunnel under the rebel lines?"

"No, sir. One of my men suggested it."

"Now there's a good officer," Ferraro said to his staff. "He gives credit where it's due and doesn't try to hog it all himself."

"My men are doing all the hard work, sir," Pleasants added. "I just tell them where to dig and how far to go."

"Let's not carry modesty too far, Colonel. We both know that soldiers are only as good as their commanding officer. You give them leadership and inspiration, set an example, provide the tools and equipment and sufficient food and—"

"And whiskey, sir?" Pleasants asked.

Ferraro stopped his rocking chair, pounded the arms, and guffawed so loudly that his face turned red.

"Yes, by God, whiskey, too. But you know, that only works with white troops. My men of the Fourth Division don't seem to drink. They are the most serious, dedicated soldiers I have ever commanded. Perhaps this war is more personal for them. After all, it is their freedom that is at stake."

He started to rock again, urging the chair into ever-wider arcs.

"I had my pick of several white divisions, but I chose the Fourth. Do you know why?"

Good-natured groans rose from his officers. Ferraro smiled and waggled a finger at them as if they were wayward children.

"My officers have heard my immigrant stories once too often, Colonel. All right, men, off you go," he said with a sweep of his hand. "Don't stay out too late."

When they had gone, Ferraro looked intently at Pleasants and Boyce, stroking his mustache.

"Pleasants," he said, "and Boyce," pronouncing the names with exaggerated emphasis. "Two fine, upstanding American names. As a child, I envied boys with such names. I dreamt of changing my own. It is terrible for a child to grow up hating his name and what he is.

"What I was, gentlemen, was the only child around with a foreign-sounding name, an immigrant father who could not speak English, and a mother who took in washing. We lived in a shack on the wrong side of town and belonged to the wrong church. It was, as the moralists like to say, a character-building experience.

"All of which is a roundabout way of saying that I can identify with the colored race more easily than most people because I know what it is like to face prejudice and discrimination. To be called names and have doors slammed in your face."

"If I may say so, sir," Pleasants interjected, "the door with the star on it opened up for you."

"Quite right, Colonel, and that is the beauty of this great

country. If you persevere, you can kick in some of those doors. I stand in awe of this brigadier's star. For an immigrant boy to rise so high is a miracle, the American miracle. That is why I fight to preserve this Union, and why I fight for the black man, so that one day he, too, can kick open some of those doors and be let in. I am grateful to you, Colonel. Your mine will give us the chance to open doors."

In the background, a dozen voices rose in song. Slowly, from many quarters, others joined them until a chorus four thousand strong filled the night air, the words climbing skyward with the smoke from the camp fires.

> We look like men a-marching on;
> We look like men o'war.

"Listen, gentlemen," Ferraro said. "Just listen to that. I cannot wait to lead these men into battle. Nothing on God's green earth can stop us."

Pleasants studied the general's handsome dark face in the glow of the firelight. Ferraro's eyes were misty and had taken on a reverential glow. Pleasants read pride in those eyes. But the longer he looked, the more certain he became that he saw something else. It was doubt, perhaps fear. Gen. Edward Ferraro, it seemed to Pleasants, was not nearly so sure of his men, or himself, as he claimed.

10

ATWOOD slowly regained consciousness and took stock of his situation. He got to his feet, staggered to the edge of the pond, and dunked his head into the pool of water. He tried to wipe the dried blood from his face, carefully fingering the crusts around his broken nose. His left arm hung broken and useless. One eye was swollen shut. He blinked the other to bring the trees into focus. Stiff and aching with pain, he fumbled with his clothing. The gun still rested on top of the neat pile.

He moved quietly. The hulking figure of Billy Satcher, apparently asleep, lay on the far side of the clearing. Mary Elizabeth's clothes were scattered about, but there was no sign of her.

He took out his pocket watch and squinted to see the time: 6:30 in the morning. His head felt as if it was clamped in a vise. The throbbing made him almost too dizzy to stand. He pulled on pants and shoes but could not tie the laces. With his one good hand, he fastened some of the buttons of his shirt and tried to buckle his holster, but the pain nearly made him cry out. He stuffed the gun into the waistband of his trousers and crawled over to a tree, hauling himself upright. He leaned against it, taking deep breaths to regain his balance, trying not to think about what Satcher had done to Mary Elizabeth.

Keeping an eye on Satcher, Atwood forced himself to move, stumbling from one tree to the next, telling himself he would grow steadier. But by the time he had circled the clearing to get behind the sleeping figure, he felt no stronger. Sweat covered his body. He was panting and just as weak as when he had started out.

Atwood braced his back against a stout tree and reached for his gun. His hand was trembling, too shaky to aim properly. He tucked his elbow tightly against his side, but still the gun shook. He took aim at Satcher's broad back and saw that the man's shirt was ripped in parallel lines. Claw marks were visible on his bare skin. Tears welled up in Atwood's eyes and he rubbed them away with his sleeve.

"Wake up, Satcher," he growled.

The man rolled over and stared at him.

"I must be slipping," Satcher said, shaking his head to clear it of sleep and drink. "I could have sworn you were dead, college boy. As many times as I hit you, you got no right to be alive."

"Where is she?" Atwood asked as Satcher rose to his feet. "What have you done with her?"

Satcher grinned. He reached down and scratched his groin.

"What didn't I do with her is more like it," he said.

"Did you kill her?"

Satcher looked offended.

"Hell no, Lieutenant. I don't go around killing women. What kind of man do you take me for?"

He jerked a thumb over his shoulder and yawned.

"She ran off somewheres. I figure she's long gone from here by now."

He stared at Atwood's shaking gun and laughed.

"You don't look too steady with that thing, college boy."

"I'm going to kill you," Atwood said.

"Hell, Lieutenant, you wouldn't shoot me. You're not the type. You don't have the guts. Your kind lives by rules and fair play and justice and all that crap. You could no more shoot an unarmed man in cold blood than fly to the moon."

Satcher stretched and yawned again and put his hands in his pockets.

"I'll make it easy for you, college boy," he said. "I'm gonna turn around and walk away and keep on walking. It's time for me to get out of the army. I've had enough of this war. All this commotion over a bunch of niggers nobody up north wants anything to do with, anyway."

He gave Atwood a jaunty salute.

"If you find what's-her-name, tell her I hope to see her again someday."

Atwood raised his arm, took aim, and pulled the trigger. Satcher fell to his knees, his mouth open in disbelief. His hands rose to his chest, the fingers clawing at the bloody wound. Atwood watched dispassionately. He felt no remorse, no guilt, and no satisfaction.

"Help me, Lieutenant," Satcher cried, reaching out a hand. "Do something."

Atwood zeroed in on the bloody hole in Satcher's chest and calmly pulled the trigger again and again until the gun was empty. Satcher sprawled on his back, his legs apart and twitching. Atwood's gun dropped from his hand and he slid to the ground, resting his back against the tree. He watched until the twitching legs became motionless, then he passed out.

Bobby Lee and Sergeant Ross were bending over him, gently examining his shoulder.

"It's okay, kid," Lee said. "We'll get you to the hospital."

Atwood moaned.

"Where's the girl?" Lee asked.

"He hurt her," Atwood whimpered. "I've got to find her before you arrest me."

"Arrest you for what?"

"I killed Billy Satcher, sir. I murdered him."

Lee shook his head and gestured for Ross to check on Satcher's body.

"Is he dead?"

"As a doornail," Ross said, "and good riddance. Somebody should have done that a long time ago."

Lee buttoned Atwood's shirt and tied his shoes, a kindness that made the lieutenant want to cry. He turned his head away.

"Where does your girl live?" Lee said.

"A cabin about a mile south."

"All right. If you're strong enough to ride, we'll take you there. As for Satcher, well, it didn't happen. Do you understand? Satcher's deserted. Isn't that the way you see it, Sergeant?"

"Yes sir."

They hoisted Atwood to his feet and walked him over to Lee's horse. Ross leaned over to make a step of his back and Lee helped Atwood up into the saddle. He picked up the reins and led the way across the clearing.

Nat Puckett, at twelve a scrawny image of his mother, sat beside her bed and placed a damp rag on her hot forehead. He didn't know what else to do for her. Mary Elizabeth moaned and her body shook in a terrible spasm. In her delirium, she had been crying out.

When she had stumbled into the cabin, he hardly recognized her. She was naked, her body covered with cuts and purpling bruises. Three front teeth were missing and one eye was black and swollen. Nat led her to the bed and covered her with the thin blanket. He did not think she would ever be beautiful again. He sat with her, stroking her hand, telling her that everything would be all right, although he didn't think anything would ever be all right again for as long as he lived.

She had been so happy with that nice Yankee officer she had told him about, the one who brought food when she met him in the evenings. She talked about how safe she felt with him. But he was a Yankee and he must be the one who had done this terrible thing.

Nat knew that Yankees were the devil incarnate. That's what the preacher said on Sunday mornings, and though Nat did not know what *incarnate* meant, he knew about the devil. It was God's will that the devil be stamped out without mercy. His mother had talked about forgiveness, but the boy believed in the preacher's vengeful God, the God of the flaming sword who said the Yankees would roast in hell for all eternity.

The Yankees took his daddy and his granddaddy and every man in the valley. Then they took the valley itself, slaughtering the animals and torching the houses and barns and granaries and haystacks, turning the sky black with smoke.

Mary Elizabeth shuddered and opened her eyes. She bolted upright, looked around the cabin, and clutched at Nat's hand.

"We've got to get away," she said, her voice small and panicky. "He'll find us here and kill us both."

"How are you doing, Lieutenant?" Bobby Lee asked. "You want to rest a bit?"

"No, sir," Atwood said.

He was barely hanging on. His head and shoulders drooped and his good hand draped loosely over the pommel. Lee led the horse slowly. Ross followed with his own horse, refusing Lee's entreaties to mount up. A sergeant does not ride while a captain walks, and nothing Lee could say would make him change his mind.

Atwood forced himself to look ahead, to examine the narrow, winding trail, matching the scene with the one in his memory from the evening he had followed Mary Elizabeth to her cabin. He had wanted to know where she lived, and he had seen her cross a clearing and enter a long ramshackle dwelling. Part of the roof was bowed. The lopsided stone chimney tilted like a tired old man. A boy sat on the broken front steps, resting his chin in his upraised hand. His face brightened when he spotted Mary Elizabeth. A good-looking lad, Atwood thought, but with the gaunt look of a growing child who was not getting enough to eat.

Atwood saw the boy run to her and wrap his arms around her waist, clinging to her as if he'd never expected her to return. She hugged him and showed him the food Atwood had given her. They linked arms and went inside, leaving him with an ache of loneliness, a yearning to run to them, embrace them, become part of their lives. But he didn't. He slipped back down the trail, haunted by the vision of what might be, if only he had the courage.

He shook his head to erase the memory. A spasm of pain gripped his body.

"There's a clearing up ahead," Lee said. "Is that the place?"

Atwood stared at the leaning chimney and nodded. His breath quickened and he felt a jab of fear that the cabin would be empty, that she and the boy had fled and he would never see her again.

"Okay," Lee said. "Let's go."

"No," Atwood said. "I'll go by myself."

He brought his leg slowly over the saddle and slid to the ground, leaning against the horse to catch his breath.

"Let us help you up to the door," Lee said.

"No, sir. I have to do this myself."

Mary Elizabeth lay back against the pillow, hands tight over her aching stomach. She had taken only a couple of bites of bread and a sip of coffee before the gnawing cramps hit her. She waved away the food Nat was holding out to her.

"Later," she whispered.

Nat took the bread and the coffee cup over to the table and set them down. Through the open door, he glimpsed a man in a blue uniform heading toward the cabin.

"Mama! He's coming!"

Atwood spotted a flash of movement inside the cabin. He was overjoyed to think that Mary Elizabeth was still there.

"Mary Elizabeth!" he yelled, stumbling toward the open door.

Mary Elizabeth opened her eyes. She thought she heard Paul's voice but knew it couldn't be. He was dead. She burrowed under the blanket and curled up in a ball. Footsteps resounded on the porch. She screamed.

"Mary Elizabeth," Atwood called again.

He grabbed the door frame and hauled himself inside.

"Paul!" she cried.

A shotgun blast drowned out her words. A gigantic red splotch ripped Atwood's chest and he fell to the floor.

"I got him, Mama," Nat shouted. "He won't hurt you no more."

Bobby Lee roared with rage when he heard the gun go off. He ran to the cabin, stepped over Atwood's body, and aimed his revolver at the boy. Mary Elizabeth stepped between them and gripped Lee's sleeve.

"For God's sake, don't. He's all I have left. He was trying to protect me."

Lee glared at the confused boy. Ross came up behind him.

"Put the gun away, Captain," he said quietly. "There's been enough killing for one day."

Lee did as he was told. He knelt down, smoothed Atwood's hair, and closed the eyes. For an instant, he saw a dignified little boy standing on a Pennsylvania hillside, wearing a coat with a fur collar.

"He was going to make things better," Lee said.

Henry Pleasants felt like the Pied Piper of Hamelin as he led the men of the night shift out of the mine at precisely seven o'clock in the morning. The miners followed him past an impatient Stan Michnik and his day crew. The instant the last man came out, Stan crossed himself and led his miners in at a run. This changing of the guard was now a ritual, and it had become necessary to avoid further bloodshed.

The wager about which shift could dig the fastest was causing trouble. The men were not above trying to increase the odds for their team. One effective way to do so was to stay several minutes after the shift ended—every extra foot counted—and claim that the pocket watches of the incoming shift must be wrong. Soon the men of the entering shift were setting their watches ahead and starting to dig at the facing before their time. That only had to happen once for fists to fly.

Pleasants settled the matter. His watch became the official timepiece for shift changes. He ordered the new shift to remain outside the mine until the old shift had emerged.

When the last of Stan's men disappeared into the tunnel, Pleasants turned to a board nailed up beside the entrance. A crowd gathered, as it did three times every day, for nearly everyone in the regiment had placed a bet on the outcome. Pleasants took a damp rag from Sergeant Cabot and wiped off the number for the total length dug to date, chalking in the new figure of 326 feet. He wrote the score for the night shift, to an assortment of groans and cheers. The night shift remained in third place in the competition, eight feet behind the first-place afternoon shift. Stan's day shift was second and gaining, now only four and a half feet behind the leader.

Cabot pursed his lips and grumbled that he was losing his shirt on Stan.

"You, too?" Pleasants said. "I didn't know you were a betting man."

"A small wager, Colonel, to show my solidarity with the men. It is good to encourage them in their labors."

"If they had any more encouragement, they'd kill one another," Pleasants said. "The betting has speeded up the work, but it's a damn nuisance for me without Bobby Lee here."

He cast a sideward glance at Lee's tent, the only one with the flap closed in the face of another searing day. Pleasants wondered how long it would take for Lee to stop grieving. He had shut himself in three days ago when he returned with Atwood's body. Looking as bleak and despondent as a moonless night, Lee had snapped to attention when he saw Pleasants.

"Permission to get blind stinking drunk for three days, sir," Lee said.

Pleasants hesitated, but he knew Bobby Lee would get drunk anyway, permission or no.

"Permission not recommended," he said, "but granted. Only for three days. I need you to keep the miners from each other's throats."

"Thank you, sir," Lee said. "I shall return."

He saluted, shuffled off to his tent, and closed the flap behind him. No one had seen him since.

"He'll be all right, Colonel," Cabot said, following Pleasants's gaze. "Captain Lee is very resilient."

When Pleasants did not answer, Cabot decided that he needed cheering up.

"Have you heard the latest rumor about General Meade, sir?" Cabot said.

"No, but I have the feeling I'm going to."

"Well, sir, it seems that General Hancock visited Meade yesterday and told him that he had heard from a reliable, highly placed source, whom he refused to identify, that Meade was about to be removed as commander of the Army of the Potomac. What's more, Hancock would be the one to replace him. He also told Meade that General Grant opposed the change but would be overruled by the War Department.

"You can see the implications," Cabot continued. "If the change of command was made despite Grant's opposition, it would mean that Grant has lost his standing in Washington, most notably his support from Mr. Lincoln. It also suggests that someone—again the President comes to mind—wants to shake up the entire command structure, perhaps in the hope of ending our stalemate here at Petersburg."

Cabot folded his arms over his chest and grinned in appreciation of the brilliance of his analysis, as pleased as if he had hoodwinked a supply officer out of oysters and champagne.

Pleasants shook his head in exasperation.

"Hell, Bill, we've been hearing rumors that Meade would be relieved ever since we joined the Army of the Potomac. Every week, a new story makes the rounds and Meade's still here."

"Yes, sir, I know, but this one may have greater credibility because of its source. Hancock has never been one to spread rumors or push himself for higher command. He's one of our staunchest and most reliable commanders."

Pleasants nodded. That was true enough. Winfield Scott Hancock was as solid as they came. Wounded at Gettysburg repulsing Pickett's charge, he refused to leave the battlefield as long as a rebel could be seen upright. While lying on his stretcher, he dictated a note to Meade, urging an immediate counterattack while the Confederates were reeling from their failed assault. He continued to urge Meade to attack, and when

Lee took his beaten army south, Hancock tried to persuade Meade to chase him.

Hancock was a fighter. His men called him Hancock the Superb for his aggressive spirit and his appearance, for everyone considered him the handsomest general in all the Union army. He was no spreader of idle gossip, Pleasants agreed. Maybe this time the rumors about Meade were true.

"If Meade is finally going," Pleasants said, "I wish he'd go soon. He and that Major Dunne of his have done nothing but obstruct us. Maybe Hancock will be more supportive. Of course, we're already beyond the rebel trenches as it is. Five more days, maybe four, and we'll be under the Cemetery Hill fort. Even if there is a change of command, it probably won't happen soon enough to make a difference to us. Still, I'd like to see the old bastard get his comeuppance."

The old bastard was, at that moment, glaring at General Grant, who sighed at the sight of Meade's red face and popping eyes.

"I demand to know, sir," Meade said, "if I am to be replaced by General Hancock. I have the right to be told to my face. You owe me that much."

"Now, now, General, let's try to calm down. Please have a seat. Would you like a glass of lemonade? It's a salve for the nerves on such a miserably hot day."

Meade yanked the camp chair back from the little table under the tent fly and sat down heavily.

"I do not want lemonade, General," he barked, "and I cannot calm down when I learn from one of my subordinates that I am about to be relieved."

Grant glanced up at the sagging canvas flap as if to say, Why me, God, why me? But he lowered his eyes and smiled at Meade with the benign look of a teacher dealing with an obstreperous pupil whom he wished would go away.

"I thought we laid that issue to rest," Grant said. "I told you before that I have the utmost confidence in you. Nothing has caused me to change my opinion. I have no plans to relieve you of your command."

"That's not what General Hancock says," Meade replied, his tone accusing.

"Is Hancock privy to thoughts of mine of which I am unaware?" Grant said. "Have I decided to relieve you and don't know it?"

"No, sir. Hancock did not say that you plan to relieve me."

"I am relieved to hear that," said Grant, pleased with his little joke. "But if I am not to relieve you, who is?"

"Washington." Meade swept his arm in a northerly direction as though to smite the hated city. "Over your opposition."

"I see," Grant said, feeling a stab of apprehension at Meade's verbalization of his worst fear, that Stanton or even Lincoln was about to meddle in his affairs and try to run the army. Grant silently cursed the rebel trenches that had stopped his lightning warfare, wondering whether they would halt his career, as well.

"I think you had better tell me exactly what General Hancock said."

Meade did just that, echoing the rumor that Cabot was telling Pleasants. When Meade finished his breathless recital, Grant contemplated his cigar, thankful that it had gone dead. Relighting it gave him time to compose himself. To Meade's annoyance, Grant took his time working the mechanical lighter and puffing out clouds of smoke. Meade crossed and uncrossed his legs and beat one booted foot in the air. He pursed his lips and stared at Grant through narrowed eyelids.

"Well now," Grant said, "that's a yarn I hadn't heard before. I don't believe there's the slightest substance to it."

He raised his voice to project a confidence he did not feel.

"I would have been consulted if such a major command change was being considered for the Army of the Potomac. Mr. Lincoln and Mr. Stanton have always been straightforward with me and have never, to my knowledge, operated behind my back. Further, I am proud to say that neither man has ever interfered with my running of the army."

At least not yet, Grant thought. But maybe things were

changing as the presidential election drew near and the pressure for a victory deepened.

"So you see why I cannot put any faith in this rumor," Grant finished.

He waited for Meade to indicate his agreement with a word or a nod, but Meade's face remained rigid with anger. He continued to stare at Grant expectantly while Grant shopped around in his mind for some plausible explanation for the rumor, anything to send Meade away mollified. Grant nodded his head, pulled on his chin whiskers, and examined the end of his cigar for whatever wisdom it contained.

"Ah," he said, smiling. "I'll wager this rumor arose because of the troops we sent to Washington to deal with Jubal Early. Your Sixth Corps, and the Nineteenth, which was to be yours as soon as it came up from New Orleans."

Grant slapped one knee and flicked a long ash across the other.

"Of course that's it," he said. "By the way, did you hear what happened to Mr. Lincoln yesterday when he went to see Early's men in action?"

Grant continued without pause, not wanting to give Meade the chance to object.

"Old Jube gave the folks in Washington a scare, coming within thirteen miles of the White House. The Confederates were so close, the congressmen could hear the sound of cannon fire. You know congressmen talk a good game of war, but most of them don't want to be anywhere near it."

Grant watched Meade seethe as he tried to control his anger, a sight that almost made Grant chuckle as he deliberately drew out his story. Let Meade stew, Grant thought—might do him some good. Do me some good, anyway.

"So there were Early's men bearing down on Fort Stevens below Silver Spring. They had the gall to loot the wine cellar at Francis Blair's country home. Drank it dry, I'm told. A tragic loss. And they burned his son's house—Montgomery Blair, the postmaster general.

"It looked like Seventh Street—the road to town—was theirs

for the taking because all we had guarding the capital was a bunch of convalescents dragged out of the hospitals, some militia and National Guard outfits, artillerymen from the local forts, and quartermaster troops who exchanged their pens for rifles, probably the first time they had shouldered arms.

"It did not look good until the men of your Sixth Corps arrived. There was no way Early could get past them. And then Mr. Lincoln came out. I guess he wanted to see what a battle was all about.

"Your General Wright did kind of a dumb thing. I suppose he was just being polite, but he invited old Abe up on the parapet with him and there Lincoln stood, the tallest figure around for miles and certainly the only one wearing a frock coat and stovepipe hat. Kinda conspicuous standing there. The rebs must have thought so, too, for they sent a lot of bullets his way. Didn't seem to bother him, according to what I heard. Lincoln stood his ground calm as could be, like he was watching a parade, and never flinched or ducked, not even when an officer next to him was killed.

"General Wright was beside himself with worry that he would go down in history as the man who got the President shot. Try as he might, he could not persuade Lincoln to take cover. Old Abe seemed to be enjoying himself. Taking fire from the rebels probably beat dealing with Congress. Then that bright young captain from the Sixth, the writer's son, Oliver Wendell Holmes, Jr., he got into the act. He claims he didn't recognize the President, but that hardly seems credible. He shouted, 'Get down, you damn fool, before you get shot.' "

Grant laughed heartily, watching to see whether the tale defused Meade's anger, but the dour expression did not change.

"The President seemed amused by Holmes's remark but remained where he was. Poor General Wright was apoplectic. He could stand it no longer and told the President that if he did not take cover, he would order up a squad of soldiers to remove him by force. This amused Lincoln even more, but he finally agreed to step off the parapet."

Grant chuckled again, but Meade's scowl deepened. He thrust his face into the aura of Grant's cigar smoke, which obediently parted like the Red Sea.

"What has this to do with the rumor that I am to be relieved of command?" Meade demanded.

"Well now, I'm getting to that," Grant drawled, "if you'll just be patient. Early's gone off now, back to the Shenandoah with the Sixth close behind him, and the Nineteenth Corps will join the pursuit. That's two whole corps we have up north, too big a force for Wright to command. I'll bet some people with nothing better to do put two and two together and decided that a force that size needs an experienced army commander. And who's the nearest army commander? Why, George Meade, of course. If Grant sends him north to take charge, the only one with enough experience to replace him is Hancock. That's how your rumor started, General. Idle talk and speculation to fill up the day. I surely have no such plans."

Meade nodded ponderously.

"I would be willing at any time to turn over the Army of the Potomac to General Hancock and to wish him joy at his promotion."

"Spoken like the generous person you are," Grant said. "Now let's have no more talk of your being relieved."

"Do you really think that's how the rumor got started?" Meade asked.

"Absolutely," Grant said. "If I was a drinking man, I'd wager a bottle of the best on it."

Grant worked a flame from his mechanical lighter and seared the end of his cigar.

"There's something else we can conclude from all this," Grant said. "We are not likely to get the Sixth or Nineteenth corps back any time soon. We've seen before how the Shenandoah swallows up whole armies and runs them ragged. This means we're in worse shape than before, with some ten thousand men gone. Lee's gamble with Early was successful after all because it compelled me to reduce the size of my force here and it also kept reinforcements from reaching us. Lee has effectively reduced our fighting capability."

"Where does that leave us?" Meade asked.

"Just where Lee wants us. Up a tree, where we can't do much but take potshots at him. Unless—"

"Unless what, sir?"

"Whatever happened to that mine of Burnside's? Are his people still digging?"

"Yes, sir," Meade said. "Contrary to all expectations, they appear to be making progress. They are already beyond the Confederate trench line. However, Major Dunne, my engineering officer, still does not believe they can tunnel the full five hundred feet to get under the Confederate fort. There is too great a danger of cave-ins or discovery by the rebels.

"Further, it seems ridiculous to think they could stuff enough powder down that hole to blow up the hillside and create a gap in the enemy lines wide enough for Burnside's corps. I put no stock in it, but in an effort to be open-minded, I've directed Major Dunne to take another look. I've also asked my staff to determine whether there is a second line of trenches beyond the rebel fort. If there is, that would keep our troops from reaching Petersburg, even if the mine was successful."

"I don't put much stock in it, either," Grant said, "but we don't have any other options at the moment. We may try to make some use of it. We have to do something to keep Washington happy or there will be rumors about both of us being relieved. And this time, they might be true."

"Captain Robert E. Lee reporting for duty, sir."

Pleasants returned Bobby Lee's salute. Lee's eyes were bloodshot and puffy, with dark bags slung under them. His body drooped as though he was about to faint.

"You look awful," Pleasants told him.

"Thank you, sir. I appreciate that."

"How do you feel?"

"How do you think I feel?"

"Worse than you look?"

"That about sums it up. Now, do we still have a mine, or has the operation ground to a halt with you in charge for the last three days?"

"We managed to stumble along in your absence. The men are approaching the four-hundred-foot mark."

He led Lee to the scoreboard. Lee whistled softly.

"That's good. You don't need me, after all. I could go on leave."

"You've been on leave, Bobby, and I'm tired of keeping the men on each shift from one another's throats. It's your turn."

"Stan must be mighty unhappy," Lee said, "being three feet behind."

He glanced at the mine entrance and rubbed his bald head. "I suppose I have to go in there and check up on things."

"If you can find your way," Pleasants said.

"Colonel Pleasants!"

It was one of Stan Michnik's day-shift miners.

"What is it? Another cave-in?" Pleasants asked.

"No, sir. We've struck marl."

"Marl?" Lee said slowly, as though he could not comprehend the word.

"It's a deposit consisting chiefly of clay mixed with calcium carbonate," Pleasants explained, tapping his head to indicate that Lee was being dim-witted.

"I know what marl is," Lee snapped, "but I never expected to find it here. We can't dig past that."

"What a ray of sunshine you are today, Captain," Pleasants said. "Let's go see how bad it is."

"Corporal Michnik's none too happy, sir," the miner said. "He swears we'll lose the bet for sure. He says God is punishing him for making the wager. That's why the marl showed up on his shift."

"He's probably right," Pleasants said.

When they reached the facing, they found the miners milling around, muttering and dejected. A few men toyed with blobs of the thick puttylike substance, which hardened when exposed to air, sculpting crude figures from it. Stan mumbled to himself and hacked at the facing, heaving his pickax with all his strength. He barely dented the chalky white seam that rose from the floor nearly to the ceiling. Each time his ax struck the marl, Stan had to use both hands to free it.

"Hold up a minute, Stan," Pleasants said. "Let me take a look."

"Nothing to see but marl, Colonel," Stan said, reluctantly backing out of the way. "It's costing us time."

Pleasants ran his hands over the facing and pinched off pieces of marl, rolling them in his fingers to determine the consistency. Bobby Lee did the same.

"I've seen worse," Pleasants said. "At least it doesn't go all the way to the top."

"We don't know how thick the deposit is, sir," Stan said. "I've seen veins of marl twenty-five feet across."

"I've seen some only five feet across," Pleasants countered. "We won't know the thickness until we get through it, and by then it won't matter."

He stepped away from the facing and studied it.

"It will be slow going, but I'm guessing the vein slopes downward. Here's what we'll do. Because the terrain inclines toward the fort, we can start to angle the tunnel up at this point. I'll check my measurements and maps to make sure, but for now you start digging at an angle of ten degrees. No more."

"What about our bet, Colonel?" Stan said. "We come out on the short end. My men will be lucky to do ten feet today."

"The competition stops until we pass the marl, then we'll start keeping score again. Fair enough?"

Stan thought for a moment and nodded. He heaved his pickax over his shoulder and waved to his men.

"Break's over," he said.

"You coming back?" Pleasants asked Bobby Lee.

"Nope," he said. "I'll stay here and spell Stan. Do me good to break up some marl."

Major Dunne had a knack for arriving at the mine at inopportune times. There he was, staring contemptuously at the wooden scoreboard. He brushed a speck of imaginary dust from the front of his immaculate jacket and sniffed as if the board emitted some foul odor. Pleasants returned his brisk salute.

"Sorry, Major," he said. "There's no cave-in for you this time."

"I see you've struck marl," Dunne said with a self-satisfied air, gesturing at the ball of hardened putty Pleasants had forgotten he was carrying. Pleasants cast it aside and shrugged.

"Nothing we can't handle. The men are working their way through it. Miners are used to marl."

"It will put you behind schedule," Dunne said, gesturing toward the scoreboard. "Your daily progress, which I admit appears impressive, will be considerably slowed."

"The men are angling the tunnel away from the vein," Pleasants said. "Are you a betting man, Major?"

"No, sir," Dunne said. "I never gamble."

"Too bad. I was willing to wager fifty dollars that we reach the fort in three or four days. Add another three days to dig the two laterals. So, a week at the most and we're finished."

"We shall see, sir," Dunne said. "I will inform General Meade about the delay."

"You might also inform the general that we need our powder, fuses, and galvanic battery within ten days. There's no point in finishing the tunnel if it sits empty while Meade makes up his mind."

"General Meade will make his decision in due course, Colonel. As to the powder, I have made preliminary calculations. Your estimate of twelve thousand pounds is excessive."

"Excessive!" Pleasants roared. "Take a look at that goddamn hill, Major. That's a hell of a lot of earth to move. If we're only out to jolt the rebels a little, there's no reason for this whole operation. We're not setting off a tremor. We want a volcanic eruption! We want to blow the top off Cemetery Hill and leave nothing standing for a hundred feet."

"I'm aware of that, Colonel," Dunne said, "and in my judgment you do not need twelve thousand pounds of powder to accomplish your mission."

"Your judgment," Pleasants sneered. "In your judgment, the mine could never exceed eighty feet. In your judgment, the miners would suffocate. In your judgment, the men would die in a massive cave-in or the rebels would discover the tunnel and blow us all up. In my judgment, your judgment stinks. And now you judge that we don't need twelve thousand pounds of powder? What are you trying to do? Save it for the next war?"

"Sir," Dunne said, bracing himself the way he had been taught at the Military Academy, "I resent being addressed in that tone of voice."

"Don't push me, Major," Pleasants said. "I'm not regular army and I don't play by your rules. I'll do whatever is necessary to complete the mine and get enough powder down there to do the job and put an end to this war. Your job is to supply that powder."

"As you pointed out, Colonel, we have at least ten days before you need the powder. Indeed, by then the argument over the amount may well be academic."

"Meaning?" Pleasants asked.

"Meaning, sir, that regardless of your progress to date, your mine is not yet finished. A lot can happen in that time. There is another complication you do not know about. General Meade is concerned that the Confederates have a second line of trenches beyond the fort, between the crest of Cemetery Hill and Petersburg."

"I've seen no evidence of that," Pleasants said.

"You wouldn't from this distance, Colonel. It makes sense, however, that they would have established a backup defensive line. The general's staff is analyzing the situation. If a secondary line exists, then General Burnside's troops would be unable to break through, regardless of how much of the hill you destroyed."

Dunne smiled again and rocked back on his heels. Pleasants knew he was gloating, enjoying foretelling the failure of the operation.

"I do believe," Pleasants said, "that you would rather see the mine fail than win the war. You told Meade the mine could not be dug, and it must be embarrassing for you to report our progress. I think you would do anything to keep us from succeeding, just to assuage your own vanity."

"That's unfair, Colonel, and libelous. If you carry that accusation further, I shall press charges against you."

"If you persist in obstructing us, Major, you might meet with an accident in my mine."

Rebel sharpshooter Caleb Caffee placed his ear against the ground, closed his eyes, and listened to the quiet spreading over the battlefield. He lay in a shallow depression midway between the fort and the Confederate trenches. He had fired twice that morning and hit both targets, each time burrowing in his ditch to avoid return fire, the fusillade of bullets aimed at his position.

He fell asleep in the hot sun and awakened around noon, his mind adrift in the scary state between dreaming and consciousness, momentarily unsure whether he was alive or dead. Lately, he had been wondering whether his luck was about to run out, fearing that a Yankee bullet or shell or mortar round had his name on it.

He shook his head to clear it, sure that he still heard voices, the sounds he had first detected last night. He was convinced that somewhere below him, in the dark bowels of the earth, the wretched Yankees were tunneling. There was no mistaking the thunk of steel biting into clay or the steady, monotonous rhythm. They were working fast, obviously digging around the clock.

Caffee squirmed at the idea of people he could not see, targets he could not stalk or capture in his gun sight. They were as safe from his Whitworth as if they were a thousand miles away, as if they were the hunters and he the prey. He knew nothing of military history or tactics, engineering or coal mining, but he knew as sure as he knew his own name what the Yankees were doing. They were digging a tunnel, and when it got beneath the fort, they would pack it with powder, set the fuse, and blow the Confederates to bits.

It's just like those Yankees to fight unfair, Caffee thought. It was cowardly to blow up a man when he thinks he's safe, down in a trench or sheltered behind fortress walls, when he's sleeping and thinks nothing can touch him.

He checked the position of the sun. It hung directly overhead. He ticked off on his fingers the number of hours before he could leave his hiding place, grunting with annoyance when he got to seven. If he tried to leave the shelter of his ditch now, he would surely die, cut down by a sharpshooter's bullet. He debated whether to tell someone about the tunnel and decided that he should try, though he had no idea what could be done to stop it.

Caffee dreaded talking to the snooty lieutenant, the one who had given him the Whitworth and told him to stay away. The man probably wouldn't believe him. He'd laugh and accuse him of imagining things. He'd tell the others and they'd all laugh at him. Then they'll die laughing, Caffee thought, and it'd be no more than they deserve.

He splayed both hands on the ground, trying to sense the sounds through his fingertips. His stomach heaved at the thought of the earth opening its jaws and swallowing him whole.

11

GENERAL Robert E. Lee glanced at the members of his staff with a mixture of fondness and forbearance, the way a family patriarch, which he was to the whole of the Confederate States, might view his sometimes-unruly children. He said nothing. Anyone who did not know him would think he was asleep, sitting in his camp chair with his eyes half-closed beneath the canvas fly of his headquarters tent. The staff knew better. The Tycoon, as they called him in occasional irreverent moods, was listening to every word—weighing, judging, remembering— and reaching a decision on how to deal with the latest rumor; namely, that the Yankees were tunneling beneath them.

At fifty-seven, Lee still looked like the Marble Model, the appellation West Point cadets had bestowed on him twelve years ago when he had been Superintendent of the Military Academy. Back when Cadet James Ewell Brown Stuart was Mrs. Lee's pet, and when Lee had to dismiss another favorite— Little Jimmy Whistler—who was not cut out for the army. It was said he'd gone to England and become a painter. Lee cut a majestic figure, with a full beard, almost all white now, and hair fluffed over his ears, but he looked tired and careworn. The stifling heat was hard on him, draining his remaining energy.

He made no sartorial concessions to the weather. He dressed as a gentleman in dark blue trousers, high black boots polished to a mirror shine, and a gray double-breasted jacket open at the collar to reveal a black bow tie and white linen shirt. The three stars of his rank formed a wreath on his collar. Outfitted to perfection in every detail, he sat as though perched on a chintz settee in the cool parlor of his wife's elegant home in Arlington instead of on the front lawn of a house of fading grandeur in Petersburg, where he resided in the same leaky, battered tent he had called home since 1861.

The house itself, Violet Bank, was set in a grove of trees north of the Appomattox River, close by the Richmond-Petersburg Turnpike. It was owned by an elderly lady, an invalid like Lee's wife, who kept Lee and the staff supplied with gifts of food, which Lee, to the dismay of his aides, dispatched to nearby hospitals. In a rare moment of self-indulgence, he had once tried a tureen of delicious calf's head soup her servant had brought out to him. Usually, Lee ate sparingly, passing up meat in favor of hard moldy biscuits. His only other culinary luxury was one egg a day, dutifully deposited on his cot by his pet hen.

The argument around Lee grew heated, the words darting about him like the pesky mosquitoes that came to life in the early evening.

"It is patently ridiculous," said Lee's aide, Maj. Walter Taylor. "No one can dig so long a tunnel. It has never been achieved in the entire history of warfare."

"I agree," said Col. Robert Chilton, the titular chief of staff—Lee preferred to do that job himself. "The distance is between four hundred and five hundred feet. They would require a series of fresh air shafts, and we've seen no sign of them. Without them, the miners would suffocate."

"If they were not killed in a cave-in first," added a major. "And where would they hide the dirt from such a tunnel? How did this tale get started, anyway?"

"Several sources," Taylor said. "Some of our men in the trenches claim to hear the sounds of digging and even voices."

"From under the earth?"

"That's what they say," Taylor replied. "Others say the Yankees told them. We all know that in the quieter parts of the line there is considerable fraternization at night to barter tobacco for food and coffee. Apparently, the Yankees are bragging about a mine and how they'll blow us to kingdom come."

"We've all heard the stories," Chilton said, "but only the newest recruits could believe them. The veterans tease the new boys, saying that Yankee troops will rise up out of the ground in the middle of the night. Scares them half to death, I shouldn't wonder."

"It would scare me, too," another aide said, "if I had not studied engineering at the Academy under Major James C. Dunne. He's on Meade's staff now. If anybody proposed a tunnel of that length, you can bet he disabused them of the notion pretty quick. There's no better engineer than Dunne. He taught us that you cannot dig a military mine that long. The thing simply cannot be done, and that's that."

Chilton turned to Lee and everyone fell silent.

"General," Chilton said with a slight bow of his head. "You have been an engineer most of your career. What do you think? Could the Yankees be digging a tunnel, or is this so much poppycock and nonsense?"

Lee paused before replying. He almost always did. The long periods of reflection lent substance to his alleged oracular powers. The men sat on the edges of their camp chairs, waiting as though expecting the voice of God Almighty.

"Colonel," Lee drawled, "my engineering years were limited to bridges and fortifications. I have never been involved with a tunnel or mine, but from what little I know about them, I would say that these stories are the product of an overactive imagination."

He paused again, gathering strength to continue.

"I knew Major Dunne and would be inclined to accept his judgment. He was one of the brightest engineers I ever met. What a shame he is on the other side."

"Sir, then you do not believe we have to lie awake at night listening for voices from down below?" asked Taylor.

Taylor was a favorite of the general's and could get away with the occasional flash of lightheartedness. Lee smiled and slowly shook his head.

"I do not think we should let it interfere with our sleep."

He ran his hand over his chin whiskers to smooth them.

"Still, I would not discount any sort of treachery or skulduggery on the part of those people. They are capable of violating all standards of acceptable conduct in war or peace and will use any mean, evil, dishonest, or unfair trick they can concoct. They are morally capable of such an action, no matter how much reprobation it might bring.

"We must always expect the worst from those people and so, while I believe these rumors are, as you put it, Colonel, poppycock, we cannot afford to ignore them. It does not hurt to err on the side of caution. Let us dig some shafts to probe for this alleged tunnel."

"Yes, sir," Chilton said. "Should we dig all along the trench line or only opposite Burnside's Ninth Corps, where these stories originated?"

"Dig along the entire line but concentrate on General Burnside's front. Pay particular attention to the approaches to our forts. And dig only at night. We would not want those people to see what we are doing or to think that we give serious attention to idle rumors. The digging will give our men something to do. They might surprise us and find something."

Lee permitted himself a chuckle.

"It would be quite a surprise to those people, too—if they really are down there."

A portly, balding, middle-aged man wearing a snug white linen suit emerged from the guest-quarters tent hidden among the trees. He waddled over to General Lee. His name was Francis Lawley, a correspondent for *The Times* of London, who had been with Lee long enough to gain not only his respect but his friendship, as well. Lawley was one of the few people to whom Lee could unburden himself and reveal his feelings about the war's progress.

Lawley had been in England for several months and had only recently returned, running the blockade on a fast packet into Wilmington, North Carolina, under the guns of the federal blockading fleet. A gifted raconteur, a superb teller of tall tales, he kept the general and his staff entertained with stories of London life and his travels throughout the Empire.

Lee brightened when he saw Lawley, and the staff unobtrusively slipped away to give the two men their privacy. The general and the journalist greeted each other formally, as was their way. Lawley sank down heavily in the camp chair next to Lee's and accepted a glass of lemonade proffered by Perry, Lee's loyal Negro servant.

Lee told Lawley about the rumors of a mine. The Englishman waved his glass in a gesture of dismissal.

"Four hundred feet," he said emphatically. "The British army has never succeeded in digging a military mine longer than four hundred feet."

That settled it. If the Royal Engineers could not do it, clearly the thing could not be done.

"General," Lawley said, "if I may say so, you are looking much more tired than on my last visit."

"Oh, I am that, Mr. Lawley," Lee said. "I am sorely tired. I have never been so tired in all my life. I long for peace and rest and an end to this terrible war."

"It is not going well for you, is it, my friend?" Lawley said, a blunt statement that Lee would not have tolerated from anyone else.

"No," Lee said. "It is not going well at all. I say this to you as I would to none of my countrymen. It is a mere question of time."

"As bad as all that?" Lawley asked.

"As bad as all that, and worse. Have you seen the poor condition of my men?"

"Yes, General. I have ventured forward into the trenches."

"Then you know how starved and exhausted they are. How they swelter in this heat. How they are picked off one by one by sharpshooters and mortars and shells. How deplorable their lives are. They have a new name for themselves—God bless them, they say it with pride. They call themselves Lee's Miserables, a parody on the novel by that Frenchman."

"Les Misérables," Lawley said in his terrible schoolboy

French. "By Victor Hugo. That shows they have a lot of spirit left."

"That is all they have left, Mr. Lawley. We are running out of everything else an army needs to fight a war."

"Is there truly no hope, General? You have worked miracles before."

"Only God can work miracles," the intensely religious Lee reminded the atheist Lawley. "And He seems to have deserted us."

Lee sighed and gazed into the distance. His face brightened as he recalled his recent ploy.

"With God's help, General Early came close to working a miracle while you were away. It did not accomplish all I had hoped, but it had an unintended benefit that will give us time to hang on here. I sent General Early out of the Shenandoah, across the Potomac into Maryland."

Lawley thought Lee suddenly looked ten years younger, talking about the daring chance he had taken with Early's force. This was the Lee of old—before Gettysburg demonstrated his vincibility, before bogging down in the Petersburg trenches, which was no kind of war for a man of bold and swift movement.

"Early's men took several towns in Maryland and exacted ransom in return for pledging not to burn them down. I am not altogether certain I can countenance such behavior—it smacks of piracy—but I did not admonish General Early.

"He swung around to attack Washington City from the north. I never expected him to capture it, of course, but I did expect the action would force Grant's hand here at Petersburg."

Lee shook his head and glanced east to Cemetery Hill, the comforting presence, the bulwark that was keeping those people at bay.

"I do not have much respect for Grant, as you know, neither as a strategist nor a tactician. There is also the matter of his past, but I suppose that is neither here nor there. His only talent and strategy, it seems to me, consists of accumulating overwhelming numbers of men, artillery, horses, and supplies, all of which are abundant in the North, and applying them en masse to wear us down and wear us out. Those people can replace every man they lose with four or five more, while we are lucky to scrape up ten recruits for every two hundred lost.

"Grant hammers away and that is all he does. There is no finesse, no genius to his method. Even on the march from the Rapidan, his sole tactic was stolid and consistent flanking to my right. Those who were with him at the Academy tell me he was not a very apt pupil."

Lee shook his head as though awakening from a deep sleep.

"But I was talking about General Early's foray to Washington," he reminded Lawley. "My plan was to force Grant to attack my forces here, knowing how repugnant it is to him to divide his force. I had hoped that he would react to Early's maneuver by mounting a full-scale attack on my line in the belief that it would compel me to recall Early to strengthen my defenses.

"It would have been another Cold Harbor, a failed assault with horrendous casualties that would dampen the ardor of the Northern civilians and their political leaders. There is, as you know, a good deal of war weariness in the North. They do not have the intestinal fortitude to lose so many more of their men and to see this war drag on indefinitely. That, Mr. Lawley, is our only hope."

Lee paused to take another sip of lemonade. He waved Perry away when he approached with the pitcher.

"Our only hope," Lee repeated, "is to hold out here, maintaining the stalemate, denying Grant any victory until the federal election in November. If we still hold this line, Mr. Lincoln will lose and General McClellan's peace party will sue for a settlement that will allow us to continue as separate nations.

"But I digress again. Early got within ten miles of the capital, creating quite a panic. Unfortunately, he sacked the country home of Francis Preston Blair. I am genuinely sorry about that. Mr. Blair always treated me with respect and courtesy. It was he who offered me command of the Union army and the rank of major general back in April of '61. I was but a colonel at the time."

Lee became lost in reverie for a moment, revisiting the opulent library in Blair's town house, opposite the President's White House. Lee had rejected Blair's offer, albeit sadly, because it meant turning his back on the United States. He did not believe in secession, he told Blair, and if it was in his power, he would free every Southern slave if it would bring peace, but he could not take up arms against his beloved Virginia.

Lee had walked from Blair's house to the office of the general in chief, the aging, ailing Winfield Scott, Old Fuss and Feathers, hero of the War of 1812. The Duke of Wellington had once called him the greatest living soldier. Lee informed Scott of his decision. The old man sighed. "Lee," he said, "you have made the greatest mistake of your life, but I feared it would be so."

Lee shifted in his camp chair and studied the nearly empty lemonade glass as if it were a crystal ball in which he saw the future, or the past.

"Of course, General Early was beaten back at Silver Spring," Lee said. "That was, as I said, to be expected. What I had not expected was that Grant would take an entire corps out of his line and send it north, and divert the corps that was on its way to him from New Orleans. This is the unintended benefit I spoke of earlier. Those forces will not be returned to him anytime soon. They will have to shadow Early to make sure he does not strike for Washington again. That represents perhaps thirty thousand troops that Grant will not have available to him.

"That is the good news," Lee said. "The bad news is that we remain locked in this grim stalemate in the trenches. Grant has me effectively trapped, for I can do nothing but stave him off. Neither of us can afford to attack the other, and I lack sufficient troops to attempt a flanking maneuver. As long as we remain here, he is in a position to inflict more damage than I can."

Lawley put down his glass and wagged a finger in the air, asking permission to intrude on Lee's thoughts. The general nodded.

"I would remind you, sir, that you have Grant trapped just as effectively as he has you. He can do little but hammer at your powerful fortifications. Grant cannot beat you here because he cannot break through your defenses."

"Let us pray that he cannot burrow under them like a mole."

"Impossible, General," Lawley said with a dismissive sweep of his hand. "The thing simply cannot be done."

"One more foot, Stan," Pleasants said, rolling up his measuring tape. "That will do it."

Stan said a silent prayer of thanks to God for allowing him to reach the end of the tunnel. God had heard his prayers and calmed the terror that gripped him every time he entered the mine.

"The rest of you guys get back," Stan said to his crew.

He wanted to complete the job himself, to be the one who hacked away the final inches of a tunnel they had driven more than five hundred feet into the earth. He sliced away with his pickax, taking clean, bold strokes out of the dark earth. They had left an eight-foot vein of marl behind them and had been angling the mine upward ever since, digging more each day than any man thought possible.

Since they'd broken through the marl, a transformation had taken hold of every miner. It was as if they were possessed, driven to see the project through and to set a new speed record in doing it. At first, it had been for the wager, the prize of the money and the satisfaction of being the best. Fellow miners on other shifts became enemies, challengers to be beaten at any cost.

The closer they came to the end, the more winning took on a new meaning. The goal was no longer to beat one another but to best the devil that was the mine. In some mysterious fashion, the miners became one. Fights and taunts ceased; hostility no longer divided Pleasants's men into warring camps.

Pleasants and Bobby Lee no longer had to escort each shift out of the mine before allowing the next one in. When the miners mobbed the scoreboard at the end of each shift, the numbers they cheered were not for their own shift but the total length of the mine, how far they had taken it together.

Pleasants watched Stan tear away the final layers of earth. He gazed at the ceiling, wishing he had the power to see through those thirty feet of dirt to know whether his calculations were correct, to be certain he was directly beneath the rebel fort on Cemetery Hill.

Stan scratched at one last clump of soil and stepped back from the facing. He turned to look at the miners crowding the tunnel, waiting for this moment. Even Bill Cabot, who had never set foot in the mine before, had joined them. No one spoke or laughed. All the men stared somberly at the smooth facing.

Stan was disappointed. After all the work, the steady, driving work, the fear and the obstacles and the anticipation, he felt no elation, no sense of victory. He looked around again and knew the others felt the same way. They had won, they had beaten the devil of the mine this time, but they were destined to keep on digging for as long as they lived. This was just one more mine.

Pleasants sensed their mood and shared it, but he wanted the men to appreciate their accomplishment.

"This is not just any mine," he said quietly. "This may be the most important mine we will ever dig. Remember this date well, July 17, 1864, because someday you will tell your grandchildren what you did here and how you helped end this war. I am proud of each and every one of you.

"You labored, you improvised, and you built one of the finest mines I've ever seen. And you did so in record time, against all odds and the predictions of experts who insisted it could not be done. Well, the Forty-Eighth Pennsylvania did it. We still have to dig the two laterals, but the mine itself, the John Francis O'Brien Mine, is herewith finished, and it's one for the record books."

Pleasants stepped aside and gestured to the crew holding the notched planks and logs.

"Let's seal off the facing now," he said, "while I determine who won the bet."

He took a pencil and a small black notebook from his shirt pocket and began figuring. The first shift set to work, placing the protective wall at the facing. Stan and Bobby Lee examined the dirt in the last five-foot sections on either side, where the laterals for the powder were to be dug.

"Okay to get started, Colonel?" Stan asked, picking up his ax and glaring at the wall. He was in a hurry. All they had left to dig was thirty-seven feet on each side, with galleries cut along the shafts where the powder would be placed. Then Stan intended to leave the tunnel—all tunnels—for good.

"In a minute, Stan," Pleasants said. He put away his pencil and shrugged. "It's a tie," he announced. "The night shift is last by four feet, but the first and second shifts dug the same amount. Congratulations."

Stan and the second-shift foreman looked at each other and shrugged.

"Colonel," Stan said, "if it's all the same to you, we called off the bet day before yesterday. We figured whoever lost would be out a month's pay and that means a lot to our wives and kids. It didn't seem right. We're all friends here. We don't want to take food off anybody's plate."

"You all agree with this?" Pleasants asked the other foremen. They nodded.

"For what it's worth," Pleasants said, "I think you did the right thing."

Bobby Lee looked bemused.

"What do you think, Captain?" Pleasants said. "You're the mine superintendent."

Lee glanced at the miners and dirt carriers and shook his head.

"I think they're a regular bunch of goddamn princes, Colonel, no doubt about it. It brings tears to my eyes to see so much goodness about."

He put his hands on his hips and glowered at them.

"Now get the hell back to work," he said.

"That's more like it," Lee said to Pleasants as they started the long walk back to the entrance. "We're almost home free."

"Don't get carried away," Pleasants said. "A lot can happen yet."

Trouble came the next morning in the person of Maj. James C. Dunne. One look at his tight, superior smile told Pleasants that Dunne was not the bearer of good news. The engineer greeted Pleasants formally, officiously, with more than a trace of scorn in his voice. Pleasants controlled his anger, inviting Dunne into his tent and waving him to a camp chair. He outranked Dunne, but as chief engineer of the Army of the Potomac and the man Meade relied on for information about the tunnel, Dunne held all the cards. And he knew it.

"A message from General Meade, sir," Dunne said. "I notice that your scoreboard has been removed. What's the reason for that?"

"The tunnel is complete, Major. We finished yesterday—a record five hundred eleven feet. I'm sure you will want to inform General Meade of our achievement."

Pleasants smiled, enjoying the look of discomfort on Dunne's face.

"Of course, sir, although I believe your men have the two laterals to dig."

"The left one is almost finished and the right one is about halfway done. Three or four days to dig the storage galleries in both laterals to hold the twelve thousand pounds of powder I requisitioned and it will be ready for action. I hope General Meade will also be ready."

"We shall have to see, sir," Dunne said. "We have detected a problem that will upset your timetable."

"That doesn't surprise me," Pleasants muttered.

"The rebels know about your tunnel."

Pleasants was stunned. He maintained a bland face, but his hands gripped the arms of his chair so tightly that his knuckles bleached white.

"How do we know they know?" he managed to ask.

"Some Confederate deserters came over to our side last night. They said they were tired of fighting a losing war and that they did not want to get blown up in their sleep by the mine the Yankees were digging. They were taken to General Meade, who questioned them about it. They reported rumors of a mine up and down the line for days, but nobody in command took it seriously because they said it was impossible to dig so long a tunnel."

"They must all have read your manual, Major," Pleasants said. "Congratulations. But this indicates that the rebels don't know for certain about the tunnel. They merely suspect one."

"There's more. The deserters said that orders came down yesterday from General Lee to dig shafts along the front line, particularly around the forts. They started work last night and positioned men in the holes today to listen for sounds of tunneling."

"How deep are the holes?"

"We asked them that, but they said they didn't know. General Meade is concerned that if the rebels dig deep enough they will discover the tunnel and capture your men before an alarm can be raised. They could also send troops back through the tunnel to create havoc behind our lines."

Dunne stood up and straightened his cuffs, examining his sleeves for dust.

"General Meade wants you to stop digging immediately. You are to station men at the end of the tunnel tonight to listen for sounds of the rebels digging. If your men hear nothing, you may resume operations in the morning."

Pleasants sighed and nodded his head.

"I hate to lose the time, Major, but I agree. If the rebels are digging close by, they could hear my men in the laterals. I'll close it down for now."

"Now about your request for the powder. That is General Meade's decision. It is out of my hands."

"I'm sure you advised him of your view that my request was excessive," Pleasants said.

"That is my job, sir, to advise the general on all matters

involving engineering. I would be shirking my duty if I did not offer my best judgment. And I still say you do not need twelve thousand pounds. Good day, sir."

Stan and his crew were annoyed about being ordered to quit in the middle of the morning. The men complained about missing their ration of whiskey, but old Sergeant Watkins, keeper of the supply, was adamant.

"Colonel's rule is a dram of whiskey for a day's work. Three hours don't count as a day's work in my book."

"How about a thimbleful?" one man asked.

"Open a bottle and just let us have a whiff," another teased.

"A rule's a rule," Watkins said, folding his arms across his chest. "Without rules and colonels to make 'em and sergeants to carry 'em out, the army would be in chaos."

Pleasants took refuge in his tent, his mood alternating between rage and despair, between the belief that the tunnel was doomed and the hope that all would be well. He told himself that there were five miles of front where the Confederates could dig. The chance of their coming down on his tunnel was laughably small, but Pleasants was not laughing. When Cabot bounded in with the day's quota of papers to be signed, Pleasants berated him about something so inconsequential that he immediately felt ashamed.

"I take it the colonel is having a bad day," Cabot said.

"The colonel is indeed having a bad day," Pleasants said, "but it's not your fault. I'm sorry, Bill."

"I am relieved to hear that, sir," Cabot said.

He hastily gathered up the papers before Pleasants had a chance to examine what he was signing.

"I'll leave you to wallow in your misery, sir."

Pleasants chuckled, but the good humor did not last. He lapsed into gloom as soon as Cabot left the tent. The thought that the Forty-Eighth Pennsylvania had dug so far, only to be discovered when they were nearly finished, tormented him. He pictured the pointed end of a pickax breaking through the ceiling, revealing Stan and his shift. The rebels would drop powder charges and blow them up.

He spread out his pages of calculations and rechecked them, praying that he had not made a mistake that would lead them off course. The results were the same. He stacked the pages neatly on his desk and vowed to trust his own judgment. He centered a sheet of writing paper and started a letter to Anne Shaw.

She had not replied to his last letter, in which he had tried to persuade her, and himself, that her ambitions did not disturb him. He was still uncertain about his feelings and he wondered whether she had believed him. The night they became engaged, he promised never to lie to her. He thought he had broken that promise in his letter.

He tore up the paper after writing a single sentence and slumped in his chair. He told himself what he already knew. If he wanted to marry Anne Shaw, he had to accept her for what she was. Could he do that? He didn't know.

By the time the sun set, Pleasants was seething. When Bobby Lee and Stan Michnik reported in later that night, he was curt to them both. He led them to the mine, escorting them inside, past the flickering candles that cast dim pools of light against the walls. They stopped at the far end, beneath the rebel fort, and reviewed the plan. Pleasants and Bobby Lee would take the laterals; Stan would remain at the facing. They would lie on the ground, listening for the slightest sound. If the rebels found them, they would fight their way out. Pleasants would act as rear guard.

"Stay awake and alert," he told them, "and for God's sake, be quiet."

Pleasants turned and walked briskly down the left lateral, his hand automatically checking the braces, walls, and ceiling for signs of strain and seepage. The latter was a new worry clouding Pleasants's mind. Soon they would be stuffing the galleries with powder. If it got wet, it would be useless.

He lay on his side at the far end, where the flooring had not yet been placed, and put his ear to the ground, squirming in the dirt to find a comfortable position. He concentrated on the task at hand, forcing everything else from his mind—Anne Shaw, Dunne, the Confederates. Minutes dragged by. Exhausted, he dozed off, awakening with a jerk. He bolted upright and cursed, hoping Stan and Bobby Lee were awake. He took out his pocket watch and positioned it on the floor so he could see the hands and focus on their movement. Occasionally, the earth rumbled as a shell exploded overhead, but Pleasants heard little else, certainly not the rhythmic cadence of rebel troops swinging pickaxes or wielding shovels.

Pleasants thought that a three-hour vigil would be sufficient. If they had not detected anything by then, they were not likely to. As he rose, moving stiffly, a bone in his knee cracked. It sounded like a hammer dropping on an anvil. He thought he heard Bobby Lee curse at the noise.

He joined the others at the facing.

"Did you hear anything?" he asked.

"Not a sound," Lee said.

"Me, either," Stan said. "Those rebs may be digging somewhere along the line, Colonel, but I'll guarantee you, none of them's digging here."

"Stan's right," Lee said. "They don't have an idea in hell where we are."

A half mile north of the fort, Caleb Caffee stumbled over the broken ground in the false light before dawn. He had walked as far from Cemetery Hill as he could get and remain in his assigned area, and he was determined not to return. He would go hungry if he had to, but if the Yankees blew up the fort, he was not going to be anywhere near it. Caffee had done his duty. He'd reported his suspicions to the lieutenant.

The officer had cackled and sneered and asked Caffee whether he often heard voices. Caffee stuck to his story. There were Yankees down there talking and digging and heading straight for the fort, and if the lieutenant didn't believe him, he deserved to be blown off the face of the earth.

The lieutenant walked off, shaking his head and laughing,

and Caffee was annoyed with himself for speaking out. But later that night, damned if the troops didn't start digging holes all along the line. The fool lieutenant must have believed him, after all.

"That's the sweetest sound I've heard in a long time, Colonel," Cabot said.

They glanced up at the sloping canvas roof of Pleasants's tent and listened to the steady drumming rain. All along the trench lines on both sides, soldiers awakened to an unusual sight. There was no scorching sun. The sky was filled with a thick layer of dark gray clouds scudding from west to east, bringing the first cooling breeze in more than two months.

The war came to a stop. Even the sharpshooters, North and South, were more interested in the change in weather than in bagging someone in the opposite set of trenches. Rebs and Yanks called out to one another and traded tobacco for soap. One reb offered his rifle.

Artillerymen and mortarmen lounged by their weapons, lying on the ground, waiting to soak up the cooling rain, only rising and firing when a zealous officer passed by to remind them they were still at war.

The first drops fell around 9:00, and by 9:30 the cheering soldiers could barely see from one trench to another. They shouted and hugged one another and climbed atop the parapets. Nobody fired. Caleb Caffee wanted to, but he did not dare unwrap his precious Whitworth from its India rubber poncho. He fumed at the sight of all those targets but eventually succumbed to the festive spirit. Other rebs climbed out of the holes they had been digging through the night and gave thanks to the rain that had released them from their tombs.

"I've never seen anything quite like it, sir," Cabot told Pleasants. "I was up in the First Division area when the rain started. You'd have thought it was Christmas morning the way the men were acting. General Ledlie had just ordered out his band. When the rain began, they took off, said the water would ruin the instruments. The general was hopping mad and threatened to court-martial the lot. He stood outside his bombproof screaming at them, and nobody paid the slightest attention."

Pleasants chuckled and glanced down at the water puddling its way across the dirt floor of his tent. It seemed to him that the flow was becoming deeper and faster.

"We waited for rain for so long," he said, "and I know the men are enjoying it, but I'm ready for it to let up. Soon it's going to do more harm than good. The ground is so dry, it can't absorb all this water. It's just building up on the surface. If it doesn't stop, we'll have to build an ark."

"You're right," Cabot said. "By the time I left the trenches, the officers were organizing work details. The men were trying to bail out with tin cans and drinking cups. They're digging culverts to try to drain the trenches, but the water is rising. Will the mine be all right?"

"Depends on how long the rain lasts. We're thirty feet below the surface. It would take three or four days of steady rain for water to seep down that far."

A commotion outside cut off his words. They looked out and saw a dozen soldiers in various states of undress, a few carrying towels and bars of soap, running toward the edge of the railway cut. Something long and dark was making its way toward the tents, wriggling in a fast-moving stream of water.

"Snake!"

A few men with guns started shooting.

"It *is* a snake," Pleasants said.

He and Cabot flattened themselves against the wall as the six-foot cottonmouth flowed into the tent. The snake wrapped itself around two legs of Pleasants's desk. A couple of soldiers followed, keeping up their fire, the bullets causing tiny eruptions in the water. Pleasants pulled out his revolver and fired, adding to the din, but he had no more luck than the others.

"Hold your fire, you stupid bastards!" Bobby Lee shouted.

He pushed his way through the tent flap.

"Anybody else shoots and I'll shoot back. Christ! You'd think the rebs were attacking. It's only a snake. The poor thing's a lot more scared of you than you are of him."

"I doubt that," Pleasants said, holstering his gun.

"Is it a rattlesnake?" Cabot asked.

"No," Lee said. He reached down and grabbed the snake by the tail. "Just a cottonmouth. Now stand back out of the way."

Quickly and deftly, Lee dragged the snake outside and flipped it through the air. It disappeared beyond the embankment.

"Rain brings them out," Lee said. "If you see any others, just do what I did."

"Sure," Pleasants said. "With my luck, I'd pick up the wrong end."

"You wouldn't worry about it for long," Lee said. He sank down in a camp chair and glowered at Pleasants and Cabot. "Couple of real heroes you are."

"I did not join the army to fight snakes, sir," Cabot said, peering outside. "If you will excuse me, Colonel, I am going to move my tent to higher ground."

Pleasants inspected the legs of his desk and started to sit down. He hoisted himself atop the desk instead.

"Everything all right in the mine?"

"It is now," Lee said. He ran his hands over his bald head, massaging his scalp. "I thought we might lose the left lateral. The rebs moved a battery of artillery over it during the night. When they started firing, it was like an earthquake. The tunnel shook and some timbers cracked and a lot of dirt came loose. Poor Stan was sure the devil would get him this time.

"Luckily the rebs stopped firing when the rain began. We were able to shore up everything and I've got a crew putting up an extra layer of supports. It may cost us a day or two, but it'll be fine. No damage to the main tunnel or the right lateral, but I'll put extra framing on the right side, too, in case they move the guns over there."

"There's a good side to this," Pleasants said. "As long as the rebel guns are overhead, they won't be digging any shafts there looking for us. They won't be digging at all as long as this rain keeps up. Assuming there are no more problems, how much longer before you're finished?"

"With galleries dug and extra shoring," Lee said, "we'll be ready for the powder in four days, five at most."

"Great," Pleasants said. "Now all we need is for Meade to get off his duff and decide when to make the assault."

"So it seems, General," said Meade, "that we were correct all along in not depending on Burnside's mine."

It was July 24, five days since the rain had started. The downpour lasted two days and nights, stopped for a day, and resumed, turning the camp into a sea of mud. Life in the trenches was worse than before, the soldiers living, sleeping, eating, and dying in mud. The sun, so oppressive for so long, was nowhere to be seen. No one had a dry uniform. Mildew sprouted on shoes and belts.

General Grant waved a hand overhead as another shower drummed atop his tent.

"We wanted rain desperately," he said, "but this is ridiculous. Wagons are bogged down; the cavalry cannot move. It's difficult even to walk."

He took his time lighting a fresh cigar. Meade peered out through the open tent flap toward City Point.

"The war has to go on, rain or no rain," Grant said, puffing up a storm of smoke. "You were talking about this mine business?"

"Yes, sir," Meade said. "It looks like we were right not to put any stock in the idea."

Grant chuckled.

"Yes, maybe we were right," he said, "but for the wrong reason. We thought it was a fool idea because our expert, your Major Dunne, said it was impossible. In fairness, it must be said that others agreed with his assessment, you and me among them. But that colonel in the Forty-Eighth Pennsylvania. What's his name?"

"Pleasants, sir," Meade replied unhappily.

"Turns out this Colonel Pleasants fellow is cleverer than the rest of us put together. He and his men deserve a lot of credit. To have dug the tunnel at all is quite a feat, and to have done so in three weeks is amazing. And now you tell me that everything is in readiness, awaiting only the powder and the lighting of the fuse to blow it up?"

"Yes, sir. General Burnside reported this morning that it was done. I don't think I have ever seen Burnside so excited. He says his colored troops are honed to a razor's edge and he is ready to follow them into Petersburg."

"Old Burny," Grant said. "I hate to dampen his enthusiasm, but if your new information is correct, then it will not be so easy to get into Petersburg."

"It will be impossible," Meade said. "The staff officer who conducted the investigation is certain there is a second line of defense beyond the fort. Even if the explosion of the mine demolished the Cemetery Hill fort, Burnside's troops would be stopped by the second line, with their flanks exposed to Confederate fire. They would be cut off and annihilated."

Grant reread the single-page report Meade had brought, pausing to read the conclusion aloud.

"I am compelled as a matter of judgment to state that the chances of success are not such as to make the attempt advisable."

He folded the paper and stuffed it in his jacket pocket.

"It would be a shame," Grant said, "to have done all that work on the mine for nothing. Maybe something can come of it yet. I have a plan to break this stalemate that might make use of the mine, but it cannot be implemented until we have a day or two of—"

He looked up. Meade followed his gaze. The rain had ceased its noisy tattoo on the canvas roof. Grant got up and peered outside as the sun broke through the cloud bank. He laughed so hard, he almost choked.

"By God," he said, "if I believed in omens, this would certainly count as one. I was about to say that my plan requires a day or two of sunshine to dry out the roads. Maybe we are about to get just that. I think you should alert Hancock's Second Corps and Sheridan's cavalry to be ready to move as soon as the ground hardens."

"Where do you propose to send them, sir?" Meade asked, recognizing that once again Grant was directing Meade's Army of the Potomac as though it was his own. Meade imagined the newspaper headlines: GRANT'S TROOPS ON THE MOVE AGAIN.

Grant traced a path on the map as he spoke.

"The men would cross the Appomattox below Petersburg here, march north and cross the James River here at Deep Bottom, where they would be in a position to threaten Richmond. While Hancock's infantry moves thus toward Richmond, Sheridan's cavalry would swing northwest and destroy the Virginia Central Railroad line.

"Who knows?" Grant added, tapping his finger at Richmond, "It is possible that this would so surprise the rebel troops defending Richmond that we could take the city. However, Hancock and Sheridan will have to decide that on their own. It will be enough if we can force Lee to take some troops out of his line here. That will leave him too weak to keep a permanent force in their second line of defense—if it exists. And a defense that is not manned is not much of a defense."

Grant smiled, moving his finger from Richmond back to Cemetery Hill.

"That would seem to be an ideal time to blow up the fort and send Burnside's troops through the gap. Maybe Old Burny was right about the fool mine. Maybe he can end the war in fifteen minutes."

12

PLEASANTS loosed a string of expletives that terrified the lieutenant. He waved the invoice in the young officer's face and pointed toward the line of fifteen mule-drawn wagons.

"Goddamn it, Lieutenant," he shouted, "it says here you've got only three hundred twenty kegs of powder at twenty-five pounds to the keg."

"That's right, sir," said the lieutenant, who looked no more than seventeen. He backed away until he felt one of the mules nudge him in the neck.

"That's not enough," Pleasants roared. "I need twelve thousand pounds. That's four hundred eighty kegs. You're short one hundred sixty. Did you lose them on the way?"

"No, sir," the lieutenant gulped. "That's what's written on the invoice and all I was given at City Point."

Sweat poured down the boy's face. Pleasants thought the lieutenant might cry.

"Sir, this is my first day here. I'm sorry if there's been a mistake, but it's not my fault. They told me at the dock to load three hundred twenty kegs of powder—that's eight thousand pounds, sir—"

"I know how much it is," Pleasants said.

"And I did that. I counted every one of those kegs as they came off the boat from Norfolk and I counted again when they were loaded on the wagons. God knows, sir, I don't want to make a mistake on my first day."

The lieutenant's expression suddenly changed. He decided he'd had enough of this crazy man yelling at him. He took a deep breath, looked Pleasants in the eye the way his father had taught him, and hoped his voice wouldn't break.

"Sir," he sputtered, "it's not my fault. I'm just doing my job. You're blaming me for it and it's . . . it's not fair!"

"Not fair?" Pleasants shouted.

"No, sir. I mean, yes, sir. Oh hell, sir, I don't know what I mean."

"Neither do I, Lieutenant," Pleasants said. "But you're right, it's not fair to blame you, and I apologize. I'll sign your invoice and get the wagons unloaded and you can be on your way."

Pleasants scribbled his signature on the form, handed it to the young officer, and looked around for Bobby Lee. He was waiting with nearly a hundred men in tow.

"It's only eight thousand pounds," Pleasants said.

"I heard," Lee said. "The rebs probably heard, too. It'll be in the Richmond papers tomorrow."

"It's not enough," Pleasants said.

"It will have to be, because that seems to be all we're likely to get."

Lee ordered the men to start unloading the powder kegs. The soldiers grumbled as they hefted the containers on their shoulders and stumbled toward the mine. At the entrance, they stopped to shift the barrels, wrapping their arms around them so they could hunch over to enter the five-foot-high tunnel. Five hundred feet was a long way to walk in that position, but they couldn't roll the barrels because of the noise.

Pleasants reached for one of the kegs himself. He felt so frustrated and angry that he wanted some activity to dissipate his energy. The last several days since finishing the mine had been an agony of waiting. The rebels had dug every night since the rain had stopped. Some of their shafts were so close that Pleasants's lookouts could hear them from inside the tunnel. So far, the mine remained undetected, but Pleasants was sure it was only a matter of time before a shovel blade broke through.

Every morning, he rode to Burnside's headquarters to ask whether today would be the day the powder arrived. Each time, Burnside sadly shook his head. The general was as frustrated as Pleasants. Daily, he bombarded Meade with requests for the powder, each one more urgent than the previous one, emphasizing the need for the full twelve thousand pounds rather than the smaller amount recommended by Dunne. Burnside never received an answer, not even when he called on Meade in person. The longer they delayed, the greater were the chances of the Confederates finding them out.

Burnside was convinced that Meade was deliberately delaying the operation. Meade had so often predicted the failure of the plan that he was doing everything he could to kill it. To support it now would be to admit he had been wrong.

Not even Meade's remark that Grant was now in favor of the planned assault reassured Burnside. The last chance of erasing the stain of Fredericksburg from his name was slipping away.

When Pleasants went to Burnside's headquarters, he was chagrined by the general's appearance. Burnside looked like a beaten man, one who had lost all hope and given up completely. Pleasants did not have the heart to tell him of a new problem. Water was definitely seeping into the mine. Once the troops set the powder in place, they could not wait long before igniting it and blowing up Cemetery Hill. It was painful to realize that Grant's decision to use the mine may have come too late.

Pleasants clutched his keg of powder and staggered into the left lateral. The barrel felt considerably heavier than twenty-five pounds. His arms seemed numb and lifeless; his back and shoulders ached from the long walk. Behind him, Bobby Lee panted and cursed.

"Damn it, Henry, that's why we have hired help, to do this hard work. We're supposed to lead and inspire."

"That's what we're doing," Pleasants said, reaching the end of the lateral and gratefully releasing the keg. "I'll bet Corporal Michnik feels inspired seeing us work like this."

"Not exactly, sir," Stan said. "I'm worried about the magazines." He pointed to one of eight large wooden boxes spaced evenly along the walls of both laterals. The work crews were pouring powder into them. The one at the end was nearly full.

"Feel this, sir," Stan said, placing his hand on the lower part of the magazine.

"It's damp," Pleasants said.

"They're all like that, sir, about a foot up from the ground." Pleasants muttered to himself.

"We'll have to stop," he said. "Pass the word back quietly. Stop bringing in more powder."

Bobby Lee spoke to the man behind him and the order passed through the chain of soldiers linking the end of Pleasants's lateral with the wagon train outside.

"There's only one thing to do," Pleasants said. "It means more work and more time lost, but we have no choice. We've got to raise these magazines off the floor by at least six inches."

"You're right," Lee said. "I'll get the carpenters to cut some supports. It's going to be one hell of a job lifting these things to slide the supports under them."

"What about the troughs, Colonel?" Stan asked, gesturing to the wooden gutters that connected the magazines and converged at the point where the laterals joined the main tunnel. These would also be filled with powder.

"They'll have to be raised, too," Pleasants said, "and I want them lined with canvas to help keep them dry."

"We'll work through the night," Stan promised. "I'm not complaining, sir, but the men won't be able to finish until sometime tomorrow."

"Can't be helped, Stan. We don't have the fuses or the battery, anyway. Even if the powder was in place and dry as a bone, we don't have anything to set it off with."

"What a way to fight a war," Lee said. "The people on your own side get in the way worse than the enemy. I look forward to going home where the only ones I have to fight are mine owners. At least they give you the tools to do the job."

"Colonel?"

Pleasants turned around and saw Bill Cabot bearing down on him, carefully sidling around the kegs of powder.

"What bad news do you bring, Sergeant?"

"It's good news, sir. There's a wagon outside with a delivery. The driver says it's sandbags and fuses."

"Only one wagon?"

"Yes, sir."

Pleasants glanced at Lee. Bobby shrugged.

"It isn't good news?" Cabot asked.

"Not if it's only one wagon."

There was only one wagon and no more on the way, not as far as the surly, unshaven driver knew. A veteran, he did not care whether there was one or twenty wagons or how raving mad the colonel got.

"I'm supposed to have eight thousand sandbags, Sergeant. That was what I requisitioned."

The driver yawned and read the number from the invoice a second time.

"Three thousand, Colonel. That's what's written here and that's what you get."

"They were supposed to be filled with sand or dirt," Pleasants said. "Not just flat, empty bags."

The sergeant shrugged and glanced around the railway cut.

"Looks to me like you got plenty of dirt here, Colonel. Looks to me like your men could fill up those bags with that dirt. Dirt's dirt. Makes no difference where it comes from."

"It makes a difference who fills them," Pleasants said, snatching the invoice from the driver's hand.

"Where's the galvanic battery?"

"I don't know nothing about no battery, Colonel. I load what they tell me to load, make sure it's the same as the invoice, and drive it where it goes. All that's on that paper is sandbags and a bag of some kind of wire."

"I hope they got that right," Pleasants said.

Bobby Lee climbed up into the wagon and opened the bag the driver was pointing to.

"Jesus H. Christ!" he roared.

"Now what?"

"This isn't electrical wire," Lee said. "It's ordinary blasting fuse, the stuff you put a match to."

Lee emptied the sack on top of the sandbags, slowly shaking his head in disbelief.

"How much did you order?"

"I asked for three pieces," Pleasants said, "each five hundred feet long."

"Well," Lee said, "there may be fifteen hundred feet in all, but it sure as hell is not in five-hundred-foot lengths."

He picked up a piece of wire and dangled it over the side of the wagon. It looked to be about twenty feet long.

"Are they all like that?" Pleasants asked.

"No," Lee said. "Some are longer, some shorter. Must be more than a hundred pieces. Somebody must have rounded up every piece of scrap fuse he could find and said let's give it to those dumb coal miners. Give 'em something else to do, splicing together a hundred pieces of wire and hoping to God they stay spliced when they put a match to it."

Lee threw the wire down and jumped off the wagon.

"I quit," he announced.

"You can't quit," Pleasants said. "I'm quitting first. That leaves you in charge."

"Like hell. Let's all quit and go home. Meade can blow up this thing and himself with it."

"And Major Dunne, too?" Pleasants asked, trying to keep his temper.

"No, let's shoot that bastard," Lee said. "An explosion's too good for the likes of him."

"They've put every obstacle in our path, Bobby, but we're not going to be stopped. Get a crew started on filling the sandbags. Put the night shift on these bits of fuses to make three five-hundred-foot lengths. The men'll get it done."

Lee stormed off, shouting at the work crews to assemble. Pleasants waited a moment, watching the driver toss the empty sandbags and bits of wire off the wagon. He turned away, disgusted, to find Cabot grinning at him, one hand held behind his back.

"What do you look so happy about?" Pleasants said.

"You look like you could do with some cheering up, Colonel."

"A perceptive observation, Sergeant, but it will take more than your smiling face to do it."

"How about this, sir?" Cabot said, whipping a thick cream-colored envelope from behind his back.

It was from Anne Shaw. Pleasants frowned and stuffed the letter in his pocket. He didn't need more bad news.

"You're not going to read it, sir?" Cabot said. "It's from our Miss Anne."

"I know who it's from. I don't have time right now."

"Is there something wrong, sir?"

"Yes, there's a hell of a lot wrong! Water's leaking on the powder; the rebs are searching for the tunnel; I've got three thousand empty sandbags, no electrical wire, no battery, a hundred scrap fuses, and a fiancée who keeps telling me she's a modern woman, whatever the hell that is."

"This is the first letter from Miss Anne in more than three weeks," Cabot said. "You have not written to her in a long time. You used to correspond at least once a week."

"What are you, my keeper?" Pleasants snarled.

"Yes, sir, in a sense I am. And Miss Anne's, too."

"You're playing mother again."

"Everyone needs a mother from time to time," Cabot said.

"I haven't seen mine since I was thirteen and I don't need one now. Let's just stick to business."

Cabot looked hurt. He pouted and chewed his lip, wondering how far he could push the colonel.

"All right," Pleasants said, sighing and taking Anne's letter from his pocket. "We will let the war grind to a halt while I read the letter. Will that make you happy?"

"Yes, sir," Cabot said. "But more important, it will make you happy."

It did not make Pleasants happy. Anne's letter began with a

rambling account of acquaintances killed or maimed in the war, friends who had gotten engaged to soldiers, and her mother's illness. The dead magnolia tree had been cut up for firewood and the stump pulled out by a team of horses. It was as though part of her life had been pulled up by the roots.

First my tree and then you. The two things in life I thought I could count on. Now one is dead and I am not certain of the other.

Pleasants turned away from Cabot and went to his tent, forcing himself to read on. Outside, Bobby Lee barked orders to the men and they complained good-naturedly in return. Pleasants smiled at the familiar sounds of a world he understood, a simple, straightforward arena of right and wrong with no ambiguity. Not like dealing with Miss Anne Shaw.

I must confess that I went to a dance Saturday night to escape my unhappiness. It did not work and I came home early, hating you and missing you and loving you all at once. I declare I must have been tetched in the head, as my sainted grandmother used to say, when I wrote to you about my place as your wife. I am not sorry about what I said—I meant every word—but I believe my timing was as wrong as could be. There you are, fighting a war and digging your mine. You must have scores of problems every day and I should not have presented you with another one. For that, I apologize.

It upset me greatly that I gave so little thought to how distracting my letter must have been. The other thing that upset me, Henry Pleasants, was your reply. It was condescending, patronizing, and peremptory. I am not at all sure that I believe your assurance that you love and accept me for what I am. I think you are very much in doubt about whether you can live with me, or even want to.

Pleasants sighed and stroked his beard, thinking that she was far wiser than her years.

> I am right about that, aren't I? You are no longer certain about our life together, the years we planned with such joy and excitement while sitting under my now dead and gone magnolia tree. You are not sure you can adjust to a marriage that would be so different from the one you shared with Sallie. You need not answer that. I know I am right.
>
> I also know that we cannot deal with this by letter. The only way it can be resolved is in person, when we have a chance to put forth our views and to argue with reason and emotion and passion, and whatever it takes to realize that we can work this out and that our love is strong enough to overcome your doubts.
>
> I warn you, Henry Pleasants, you will never find anyone who loves you as I do. I will love you even if you decide you cannot marry me. I will do what is expected of me as your wife but I will not deny who I am. Please come to me as soon as you can.

Pleasants skimmed the words again, trying to remember her voice, her touch, her eyes and hair. He took her photograph from his pocket and studied it, but she seemed like a person he had known long ago in another life, part of some dim and distant past. He folded the letter around the photograph, overwhelmed by confusion and doubt. His mind drifted back to his last dream of Sallie, when she came to him dressed in white, arms outstretched, trying to tell him something but fading away before he could reach her.

He got up, strode over to the tent flap, and looked out idly at his men at work—carpenters sawing supports for the powder magazines and troughs, soldiers filling up sandbags, others splicing the short lengths of fuse. From the mine entrance, Bobby Lee and Bill Cabot watched him, waiting for him, depending on him. The whole regiment needed him. He stuffed

Anne's letter and photograph into his pocket and headed for the mine.

General Grant wet the tip of his stubby pencil with his tongue and wrote a careful and precise message to the War Department in Washington.

"We have failed in what I hoped to accomplish—that is, to surprise the enemy and get onto their roads with the cavalry near to Richmond. I am yet in hopes of turning this diversion to account, so as to yield greater results than if the first object had been accomplished."

He passed the note to Meade, who read it quickly and handed it back. Grant gave it to an aide.

"Get that to the telegrapher at once."

"So," Meade said, "Hancock and Sheridan have failed."

"On the contrary," Grant said. "They have succeeded. It is true they were not able to capture Richmond, but that was hardly to be expected. Nor were they able to destroy the railroad lines. However, Lee reacted to the foray exactly as I had hoped."

Grant smiled and waved a piece of paper at Meade before stuffing it in a pocket.

"Lee has sent more than half his army north to protect Richmond. According to my information"—Grant tapped the pocket where he had placed the dispatch—"twenty-nine carloads of Confederate troops were sent north in the past twenty-four hours. That means Lee has only eighteen thousand soldiers here to man the five miles of his front. He is stretched very thin, General, very thin indeed, while we grow stronger. Hancock's corps is on its way back to us. For the moment, we have a tremendous advantage over the Confederates in numbers."

Grant tilted back in his chair and drew on his cigar, feeling pleased and confident.

"We must strike as soon as possible," he continued. "If we launch an assault before Lee's troops return, we can pierce his line and capture Petersburg. I need not remind you that once we do that, we cut off his supplies from Richmond. The capital would be isolated and Lee's army split in two. The war would be all but over."

Grant leaned forward, placed his elbows on the desk, and stabbed his finger on the map at Cemetery Hill.

"This is where we will attack."

"Using Burnside and his mine?" Meade asked.

"Yes. Tomorrow morning."

Meade had been dreading this moment.

"I am afraid the mine will not be ready, sir," he said.

"Why not? They have had plenty of time. This is the twenty-eighth. You told me four days ago the mine was finished. Why can't the explosion come in the morning?"

"There are problems, sir. It took longer than I expected for the powder to arrive from Norfolk. The fuses sent were not the right kind. Water is seeping into the mine and it may dampen the powder."

"That powder should have been here the day the mine was ready," Grant said. "Do you mean to tell me this operation could fail because of mistakes in shipping? There will be hell to pay for this, General."

"Major Dunne may have slipped up there, sir," Meade said.

"Major Dunne never believed in this mine," Grant snapped.

Meade wiped sweat from his forehead with his bandanna and tried to sound hopeful.

"General Burnside assures me, sir, that the powder will be in readiness some time tomorrow. We could schedule the assault before dawn the morning after, on the thirtieth."

"All right," Grant said. "That will have to do."

"I received good news this morning," Meade said. "It may increase our chances of success. It appears that there is no second line of defense behind the Confederate fort, after all."

"Then your initial report was wrong," Grant said. "So much for our so-called experts. Why should we believe this new assessment?"

"A signal tower was erected yesterday, sir, with a command-ing view of that portion of the Confederate defenses. It shows clearly that no second line exists. There is nothing beyond the Cemetery Hill fort to impede the progress of our troops. The way into Petersburg is clear."

"The city is ours for the taking," Grant said.

"So it appears, General," Meade said, "but only if the explosion destroys the fort and the trenches in front of it. We can only hope the blast will be powerful enough to accomplish that objective."

"Why should it not be?" Grant demanded. "They're stuffing the mine full of powder, aren't they?"

"Yes, sir," Meade said, mindful of how it would look if it became known that he had authorized only two-thirds of the requested powder supply. He felt faint, seeing his reputation disintegrate, and he paused to take a deep breath. The more hopeful Grant became about the success of the mine, the more angry he would be if it failed. And the more questions Meade would have to answer about the reasons for that failure.

"There is still the problem of water dampening the powder, and the chance that the rebels will find the tunnel."

"Quit being an old lady," Grant said. "There are dozens of things that can go wrong with any plan. We do the best we can to ensure success. If the explosion destroys the fort and Burnside's assault is mounted immediately and with vigor, then it cannot fail. Even if the mine does not detonate, the assault will commence at the appointed time, let us say three-thirty A.M. With Lee's defending force so depleted and with surprise on our side, our troops might yet succeed.

"You work out the details. I want every piece of artillery massed to the right and left of the point of assault. They are to launch an intensive barrage the instant the mine explodes. Burnside's troops must advance at the same moment. Any delay will allow Lee time to bring up troops from elsewhere on the line. The explosion should leave the rebels in disarray for as much as a quarter of a mile from the point of impact, but the survivors will rally unless we immediately overrun them."

Grant rose and continued to issue his orders. He paced back

and forth, jabbing his cigar in the air, trailing wispy spirals of smoke and falling ash.

"Before the attack, Burnside's troops must clear away the abatis and chevaux-de-frise and any other obstacles in front of his trenches so that his men can charge along the entire front. He must place engineering troops in the forefront of the assault to destroy whatever may be left of the rebel defenses. You must emphasize that the troops must not stop to gawk at the site of the explosion. They must push past it at the run. If they pursue this mission with vigor, they will be in Petersburg before the dust settles. Also, alert Warren and Ord to have their corps ready on Burnside's flanks to support the assault. Meade, this could be the major victory of the war. It all depends on this miner fellow—"

"Pleasants, sir."

"Pleasants, and on Burnside. At three-thirty the morning after next, the future of the nation will rest on them. And, I might add, our own careers, as well. If they succeed, history will remember us as the architects of a great victory. We both need that victory, General. Our detractors are circling, waiting for us to stumble again. This is our chance for redemption. We may not, either of us, get another chance. See that it works."

"This could be the biggest victory of the war, Colonel Pleasants," Burnside said. "Indeed, if it goes according to plan, it will be the final victory of the war and you will go down in history as its architect. You will be a national hero and get a brigadier's star at least."

"I'll settle for a leave, sir."

"You'll have that, too, in no more time than it takes me to sign the papers. You would return to Lexington to see your young lady?"

"Yes, sir," Pleasants said, wondering whether everybody in the Union army knew about him and Anne Shaw.

"No need to sound surprised, Colonel. One hears things in my position. I'm told Miss Shaw is the belle of Lexington."

Burnside smiled wistfully, remembering his first love, the one who had left him waiting at the altar.

"I hope you will make her your bride when you see her, Colonel. Take my advice. Nothing is gained by waiting. Marry the girl before she changes her mind."

"Yes, sir," Pleasants said automatically, shaken by the thought that he might see Anne in a matter of days. What would he say to her? He wiped her from his mind and turned his attention back to Burnside.

Burnside had appeared at Pleasants's tent at 8:30 that morning in a highly agitated state.

"Colonel," he said, his voice quaking, "General Meade has informed me that my attack on Cemetery Hill will be launched at three-thirty in the morning, with or without your explosion. Will the mine be ready?"

"It's ready now, General. We finished the preparations late last night. The sooner we blow it, the better. We heard the rebels digging all around us."

"You have no doubt that the explosion will level the fort and leave a gap for my troops? If not, then I am not optimistic about our chances of success. When you first came to me with the idea, you were confident it would work. As I recall, you guaranteed it. Do you still feel so certain?"

"Sir, I said then that if I got the tools and supplies I needed, the mine would work. As you know, General Meade gave us nothing, not so much as a single shovel. We overcame that and improvised—a tribute to my men. But, to be honest, I do not know if eight thousand pounds of powder is sufficient to level the fort, or if the spliced fuses will hold."

"I did what I could to obtain more powder and fuse," Burnside said, "but Meade would not budge in light of the recommendation of Major Dunne. Now that General Grant recognizes the value of your project, Meade is beside himself with worry. He even asked this morning whether he should send more powder."

"It's too late now, sir. Everything is packed and tamped down and ready to blow."

Burnside looked off into the distance and closed his eyes. Pleasants thought the general was offering a silent prayer.

"Meade intimated that his career, and Grant's, depends on your success."

"He should have thought of that earlier," Pleasants said bitterly, "when there was still time to help."

"You're right, of course," Burnside said, "and I'm sure he realizes that now. If it fails, I shall fail along with it—with Grant and Meade. The difference is that I, who supported the mine from the outset, will be held accountable. I shall be the scapegoat, the man who lost the chance to win the war, even though they were the ones responsible."

Burnside shook his head and smiled lamely.

"History, as I said, Colonel, is in the making here. It is victory or defeat. Next to that, the career of any one individual is insignificant. Unless you happen to be that individual."

He peered through the open tent flap toward the mine.

"Colonel, might I ask a favor? Would you show me the mine? I would like to see what all this commotion has been about."

"My pleasure, sir."

Pleasants led the portly Burnside past a large contingent of gawkers, curious about the general's presence. A few saluted, but, as was the way with most soldiers, the rest smiled and said, "Morning, General," as though he was anyone strolling through camp.

The tunnel was empty. The guards were instructed to admit only Pleasants, Bobby Lee, and Stan Michnik. The mine was dark and eerie because the candles had been removed—one could not permit open flames around four tons of powder. They had been replaced by glassed, kerosene-fed, bull's-eye lanterns spaced on the wall every thirty feet.

Pleasants explained the method of construction to Burnside, their voices muted, in part because the Confederates were overhead but also because the empty, silent vault inspired feelings of awe and reverence.

"The fuse," Pleasants said, pointing to the black wire snaking its way down the middle of the floor. Every several feet it bulged where the lengths had been spliced. Burnside knelt to examine one of the bulges.

"There are a lot of those splices, Colonel. What happens if one does not hold?"

"Then I have to come back inside, splice it again, and set another match to it."

"And get out before it reaches the powder."

"That would be nice, sir," Pleasants said.

They walked on in silence until they reached a mound of sandbags and logs that stretched from floor to ceiling, closing off the remainder of the shaft.

"Where is the powder?" Burnside asked.

"Forty feet on, where the tunnel ends. The powder is stored in eight wooden magazines, four in each of the side laterals, connected by wooden troughs full of powder. The troughs meet where the laterals join the main tunnel and that is where the other end of the fuse is."

"These logs and sandbags stretch from here to there?"

"Yes, sir. The sandbags will confine the explosion to the laterals so the force goes upward and does not come roaring down the tunnel where the energy would be dissipated. The bags are interspersed with logs to admit sufficient oxygen to strengthen the explosion."

"I'm impressed, Colonel," Burnside said, running a hand over the sandbags. "But what if the spliced fuse breaks between here and the end?"

"Then we're out of luck, sir. The only way to reach it is to dismantle this wall. It could take a whole day."

"I see," Burnside said soberly. "I don't know if you are a praying man, Colonel, but it would not hurt to call on some extra help."

"Yes, General. We need all the help we can get."

At eleven o'clock that morning, Burnside was facing a highly agitated Meade, who paced back and forth inside Burnside's tent.

"We've thought of everything," Meade said in a clipped, strident, uncharacteristically high-pitched voice. "Everything. It cannot fail. It cannot."

He stopped to glare at Burnside.

"By God, it has to work," he said before setting off again. "You should see the artillery I have massed to support you—one hundred forty-four guns, General—one hundred forty-four! We have eighty fieldpieces, eighteen giant ten-inch mortars, twenty-eight of the Coehorn mortars, and eighteen four-and-a-half-inch siege guns. They will pulverize the rebels! The crews are dug in and sighted where they can sweep over a half-mile swath of the enemy's line around the fort.

"Ord and Warren are ready to support you with all of their troops. As soon as you have seized Cemetery Hill, or whatever is left of it"—he gave a quick nervous laugh—"they will advance. Ord on your right, Warren on your left. You need have no worry about your flanks."

Meade broke his aggressive stride and dropped into a camp chair, rubbing his hands as though warming them.

"All depends on you, General. You must clear the fortifications in front of your trenches. You must have engineers in front of your troops to sweep away the enemy's abatis and chevaux-de-frise. You must not waste time having your attacking troops execute complicated formations.

"It could not be simpler," he continued to lecture Burnside. "You must rush for the hill and seize it immediately after the explosion. You must move with lightning speed. Vigor! Promptitude! Rapidity of execution! Those must be your watchwords."

Meade stared at Burnside, his eyes looming behind his oversize spectacles. His face was crimson and a nervous tic overtook his left eyelid.

"My Fourth Division, the colored troops, are prepared and eager, sir," Burnside said. "They plan a wondrous celebration when they take Petersburg tomorrow morning."

"Ah yes," Meade said. "The colored troops."

"I'm confident they won't let us down."

"The colored troops," Meade repeated. "There has been a change of plan, General, a change of plan. You cannot use the colored troops to spearhead the assault."

"Perhaps I did not hear you correctly, sir," Burnside said, unable to comprehend the news.

"You cannot use the colored troops," Meade said, "not at first. If you want to send them in after your other three divisions have attacked, that is up to you, but the coloreds cannot lead the assault."

Burnside slumped back, feeling faint and disoriented, as if laudanum was dulling his senses. He managed to utter only a single word.

"Why?"

"Why?" Meade shouted, jumping up to resume his furious pacing. "I will tell you why. First, you cannot trust black troops. They are unreliable. They are good only to perform the army's menial chores so that white troops can do the fighting. Second, this assault is a gamble. Your mine may not even explode. Or it may do little damage. The troops spearheading the assault could be slaughtered. It would be bad enough if a white division was wiped out, but think how it would look if we sent inexperienced black soldiers to their deaths. The abolitionists and the Radical Republicans and the newspapers would have our hides! They would say we had shoved the coloreds out front to get themselves killed because we did not care anything about them. It's a political decision. And it's final."

"But General," Burnside said, "my white divisions are in no condition to lead any kind of attack. They have been in the trenches under enemy fire for forty days and nights. As many as sixty a day are killed or wounded and many more are on sick call. The divisions are woefully understrength and the men have acquired a trench mentality. They have gotten in the habit of hiding, to shelter themselves from enemy fire. They are worn down from the privations of this stalemate, they have not trained for an assault, and their officers have not even examined the terrain."

Burnside reached out with both hands, beseeching Meade, seeing in his mind the slaughter of his corps.

"Good God, General, it is less than fourteen hours until we attack. There is no time to train these men. The black troops are fully trained. Their morale is exceptionally high. They are fresh, their ranks are full, and their spirits elated at the prospect of battle. Their officers know the terrain and what is expected of them. With respect, sir, it is madness to replace them at this hour. New troops could never learn the maneuvers I have worked out."

"That is precisely what I have been trying to emphasize," Meade shouted. "Do not waste time with your damned intricate maneuvers. They are not needed here. All the men have to do is rush the hill after the explosion, when the enemy is dazed and scattered, seize the fort, and march into Petersburg. Your white divisions need no training to do that. All they need do is get out of their trenches and advance."

"I am not certain they will leave the trenches, sir," Burnside argued. "They are used to being under cover. We cannot depend on them to attack, not in their debilitated condition."

Meade stood at attention, glowering at Burnside.

"If troops will not obey a direct order from their commanding general, then that officer should be replaced. That is my answer to you."

Burnside pushed himself out of his chair to confront Meade.

"Sir," he said shakily, "may I have your permission to present my argument to General Grant?"

Meade turned crimson, the tic in his eye flashing like a repeating rifle.

"No, sir, you may not have my permission to go to General Grant."

"Will you present my case to the general?" Burnside pleaded.

Meade studied Burnside for a moment and did not like what he saw. The man looked so distraught that he was capable of anything. He might go to Grant on his own. Meade would not have it said that he couldn't control his own officers.

"If you insist," Meade growled, "I will present my argument and yours. The final decision will be his. I will let you know."

Burnside received his answer at two o'clock. General Meade, pleased with himself and more calm and composed than he had been earlier, spoke briefly and to the point.

"General Grant agrees with my assessment of the situation. You will detail one of your white divisions to take the advance. If you choose to use the colored troops, they must bring up the rear, not moving forward until the three white divisions have done so. Is that clear?"

"Yes, sir," Burnside said, but Meade, who had not bothered to dismount from his horse to deliver the news, was already trotting off. He did not even wait for a salute.

Burnside stumbled back inside his tent and threw himself down on his cot. It was over. His career, his reputation, and his name would forever carry the onus of defeat and failure. He would be an object of derision and scorn once more, as he had been after Fredericksburg.

The assault would fail. Burnside could feel it in his bones. It would fail on a colossal, gigantic scale, one of the great debacles of the war. Failure repeated itself in his mind like the relentless beating of a drum, and he pressed his fingers to his temples to try to quell the noise.

A half hour later, Burnside roused himself and summoned two of his division commanders—Robert Potter of the Second Division, who had brought Pleasants to him originally and urged him to accept the miner's plan, and Orlando Wilcox of the Third Division. The officers saluted and sat down opposite Burnside's desk.

Burnside looked as white as his canvas tent. His hands shook, his voice faltered, and although he looked directly at them, they sensed that he was not wholly aware of their presence. He spoke hesitantly, rambling like a demoralized old man, talking more to himself than to them. Their shock deepened when he told them about the black troops.

"The assault is only twelve hours away," Potter said. "That

is not enough time to prepare another division to take the lead."

"None of our divisions is in shape for such an undertaking, General," Wilcox said. "The men are not up to it."

"I know," Burnside whispered, "but we have no choice. One of you must spearhead this assault."

Potter and Wilcox exchanged glances. Wilcox spoke first.

"Sir, General Ledlie should be here, too. He has the First Division."

"I thought perhaps one of you . . ."

Burnside's words trailed off and his head dropped forward as if he had fallen asleep.

Potter and Wilcox knew why Burnside had not summoned Ledlie. The man was a fool, a drunken, incompetent coward who should not be leading a company, much less a division. Nevertheless, he was a division commander and, much as they detested him, he was their equal in rank and responsibility. It was only proper that he be in attendance.

Wilcox argued the point again and finally Burnside nodded. He waved a hand in the air like a man past all caring, a man who had lost all control over his surroundings. Wilcox went outside to send word to General Ledlie. The three men waited in an awkward silence for half an hour, until Ledlie strode into the tent, playing the role of the conquering hero.

A dark-eyed, pudgy little man, thirty-two years old, Ledlie sported a flowing mustache and a showy uniform of his own design. He sat down, all smiles and light chatter, until Wilcox filled him in on the situation. Burnside was incapable of doing so.

"My God," Ledlie said. "Oh my God."

He turned as pale as Burnside and tugged so rapidly on his mustache that Potter thought he would pull it out by its roots. Clearly, Ledlie was terrified.

"Which of us is it to be?" he asked, his eyes darting between Potter and Wilcox.

"That is what we are here to determine," Burnside said, blinking in surprise as if he had just recognized Ledlie. He realized it was time to make his decision, to select the division to spearhead the assault. But Burnside knew he could not. He felt paralyzed; both his body and his brain were inert. Incoherent, unrelated thoughts filled his head.

"Which of us is it to be, sir?" Ledlie asked again.

"I was hoping," Burnside heard himself saying, "that one of you would volunteer."

A shrill cackle erupted from Ledlie. No one volunteered.

"I must confess," Burnside said, "that I cannot for the life of me see any reason to choose one division or one commander over the others."

Potter and Wilcox stared at each other, each thinking of at least a dozen reasons why Ledlie should not be chosen. They kept their thoughts to themselves and peered blankly at Burnside.

"I am frankly incapable of deciding," Burnside admitted finally. "We shall have to leave it to chance."

Potter and Wilcox were shocked, convinced that Burnside must be temporarily insane. They wanted to protest, but neither was able to do so. For the moment, they were as stupified as Burnside.

Burnside rose and walked outside, returning with three blades of grass protruding from his closed fist.

"One of these blades is shorter than the other two," he said.

He walked slowly from man to man, first Wilcox, then Potter, then Ledlie. The first two selected their blades of grass and withdrew them from Burnside's hand. They were identical in length. James H. Ledlie would lead the assault.

13

THE black sentry slumped listlessly against a tree. His rifle rested butt-first on the ground at his side and his hands were shoved deep in his pockets. It was around 7:30 in the evening, light enough for Pleasants to make out the expression on the man's face. He wondered why the soldier seemed so angry. Still, that was no reason to slouch in front of an officer. And it was odd to see such sloppiness in an outfit that prided itself on its appearance.

"Evening, Private," Pleasants said.

The guard shifted his back against the tree, took one hand out of his pocket, and raised it halfway to his cap.

"That's a sorry excuse for a salute, soldier," Pleasants snapped.

The man's eyes flashed with the hatred he might have reserved for the Confederates. He removed the other hand from his pocket, straightened up, and smartly touched the visor of his cap. Pleasants returned the salute.

"I'm here to see Major Boyce," Pleasants said.

The guard jerked a thumb over his shoulder.

"That way, sir," he mumbled.

"Shouldn't you summon the corporal of the guard to escort me?" Pleasants asked.

"You can find him easy enough," the man said. "He's white, like you."

Pleasants turned away, disgusted by the man's insolence. As

he approached the rows of tents, he was struck by the silence. No one was singing or laughing or talking aloud. There weren't even many camp fires.

Knots of men sprawled on the ground, many of them huddled in the growing darkness. The few low, desultory conversations Pleasants heard as he made his way through the camp ceased at his approach. He felt a thousand pairs of eyes watching him with sullen anger. A few soldiers spat on the ground as he passed. Others turned their backs, Corporal Mutesa among them.

Pleasants stopped to question the man who had been so talkative on his last visit to the Fourth Division's camp.

"What's going on, Corporal? What's wrong with everybody?"

Mutesa turned around slowly. He seemed to have shrunk in size. His shoulders drooped and he wouldn't meet Pleasants's eyes. He said nothing.

"What has happened here, Corporal?" Pleasants said.

The soldier raised his head, looking through Pleasants as if he was seeing something far away.

"We been betrayed, Colonel," Mutesa said quietly. "Betrayed. We ain't men o'war no more. The army says we're just dumb-ass niggers again, the way we always been. I guess some things never change."

He waved a hand limply toward the line of tents.

"Major Boyce'll tell you about it, sir. I haven't got the heart."

Mutesa moved away stiffly, head bowed, a man stripped of all hope, all dignity and pride.

Pleasants hurried on, anxious to see Ezra Boyce and get to the bottom of this. Clearly, these were not men preparing for battle, sharpening their bayonets, cleaning their rifles, downing coffee and joking nervously the way men do the night before they might die. This was a wake, a somber commemoration of death. They were acting like a defeated army.

He located Boyce's tent and saw that the camp fire had gone out. He peered inside, but it was too dark to see anything.

"Ezra?" he called.

"That you, Colonel Pleasants?"

"What is going on here? What's wrong with your men?"

A match flared in the darkness and shook as it was touched to a candle. Boyce sat up on the edge of his cot and rubbed his eyes. Pleasants sniffed, catching the aroma of whiskey. As his eyes adapted to the light, he noticed that Boyce was unshaven. His eyes were red and a dark stain ran down the front of his shirt. At his feet lay a half-empty bottle of commissary whiskey. Boyce had never been a drinking man, and as a politician he had always been careful about his appearance.

"You look awful," Pleasants said.

Boyce shrugged.

"You're a disgrace to your uniform. And so is everyone else in this camp. What's happened?"

"Goddamn it, Colonel, we have good reason. How do you expect us to feel after the way the army's treated us? It's a wonder the men haven't all deserted. I wouldn't blame them a bit if they did."

"What are you talking about?" Pleasants demanded.

Boyce stared at him and reached for the bottle.

"You mean you don't know?"

"If I knew, I wouldn't be asking you. Put that bottle down and tell me what the hell's going on."

Boyce did as he was told, propping the bottle against one leg of his cot.

"The Fourth Division, United States Colored Troops, will not be leading the attack on Cemetery Hill, sir! We will be bringing up the rear, sir, after the white soldiers have cleared the way and won the war and gotten the glory. It's the old story, Colonel. You can't trust the niggers. They're only good for digging latrines."

"Whose decision is this?" Pleasants asked.

"Meade's, with Grant's approval. I was with our division commander, General Ferraro, when Burnside came to tell him. You could tell that Burnside was devastated. After he left,

Ferraro took to the bottle and is probably a whole lot drunker than I am.

"You should have seen the men when we told them. The life went out of them. They weren't proud soldiers anymore, just a bunch of dumb niggers. Remember their song, 'We look like men a-marching on, we look like men o'war'? They sure don't look that way now, do they? They'll never sing that song again."

Pleasants sat down on the cot beside Boyce.

"You want a drink, sir?"

Pleasants shook his head.

"You said your men will bring up the rear?"

"That's right, sir. I suppose Meade and Grant figure that by the time Burnside's white divisions get to Petersburg, it will be safe enough to let the coloreds come along, to bury the dead and bring up supplies like pack mules."

"So who is to lead the assault?"

Boyce laughed and helped himself to another drink.

"The magnificent men of the elite First Division, sir."

"Ledlie!" Pleasants shouted.

"The fighting general himself, sir."

"I'll take that drink now, Major."

Ledlie's hand shook as he poured another round of cognac into a tumbler.

"A great honor," he said, taking a gulp.

He banged the heavy glass on his desk and glared at his two brigade commanders.

"A great honor," he repeated, "to be chosen over the other division commanders to lead this attack. Gentlemen, history will record what we do here. There will be glory enough for all."

A rebel shell exploded some distance away. Ledlie flinched, staring wide-eyed at the ceiling of his bombproof shelter, expecting it to collapse. His brigade commanders, Brig. Gen. William F. Bartlett and Col. Elisha G. Marshall, exchanged disgusted glances, each man knowing that he and his troops were slated for disaster, not glory, so long as Ledlie was in command. They were furious with Burnside for selecting his weakest division commander for this important assignment. They did not know the matter had been settled by a short blade of grass.

Neither commander had a hope in hell that the attack would succeed, even if the explosion wiped out a full half mile of rebel trenches, as Ledlie assured them it would. Their men were not up to the job. They had been in the line too long. They were too edgy and weary to charge the enemy with the vigor that would be needed. Bartlett and Marshall knew they would be lucky to get their men to leave the trenches, much less get them as far as Petersburg.

They had doubts about themselves, as well. Not about their courage, for that had been tested in battle, but both were new to their positions. Marshall had commanded the Second Brigade less than a week. Bartlett had taken over the First Brigade only two weeks before and he was worried about his ability to withstand combat now that he had lost his leg. The artificial limb pained him when he walked. Riding a horse was torture. Neither man had had sufficient time to get to know their officers and men. More important, both were unknown quantities to their subordinates. Accustomed to Ledlie's poor leadership, no one expected Bartlett and Marshall to be any better.

The two brigade commanders listened to Ledlie ramble on about glory and medals and his political aspirations. Unable to bear it any longer, Bartlett interrupted him.

"General, I am not certain the men are up to this. As you know, sir, they are in pretty rough shape."

"Nonsense!" Ledlie roared.

He waved his glass in the air, sloshing liquor over the side and wetting his sleeve.

"Finest soldiers in the goddamn Union army. I will not have them slandered. They will do whatever I ask. Think the world of me, they do. They'll follow me anywhere. I shall be out front leading them to Petersburg."

That would be a first, Bartlett thought. Ledlie never led his troops anywhere. Bartlett knew that Ledlie would remain in his bombproof while his men were dying on the hill.

"What are our orders, sir?" Marshall asked.

"Simplest thing in the world," Ledlie said. "As soon as the mine explodes, we advance at a run. That explosion will create one hell of a big hole in the ground, according to General Burnside, and that is where we head while the rebels are dazed and trying to dig themselves out."

He paused to take another drink and to open a map on his desk. He studied it for a long time, obviously lost, until Marshall pointed to Cemetery Hill and the rebel fort halfway to its peak.

"Right," Ledlie said. "That's where it is. And here's where we are," he added, running his shaky fingers along the black zigzag line of Union trenches.

"Right," he said again. "The Second Brigade goes first. Move forward to the crater left by the explosion and shift right to occupy the remains of the Confederate trenches. First Brigade occupies the rebel line left of the crater."

Ledlie grinned at his subordinates.

"That's all there is to it, gentlemen. Move up to the hole, take up defensive positions on both sides, and sit tight."

Marshall and Bartlett were dumbfounded. They had talked with General Ferraro, commander of the Fourth Division, and knew what his orders had been when his colored troops were scheduled to spearhead the assault. Rush beyond the crater to the crest of Cemetery Hill and on to Petersburg. And do it immediately, stopping for nothing. Now Ledlie was telling them to stop at the crater and dig in.

"I thought the object was to take Cemetery Hill," Bartlett said, "and advance on Petersburg."

Ledlie waved his glass in a dismissive gesture.

"That may be the overall objective, but it is not ours. After we secure the flanks of the crater, Potter and Wilcox will bring up their Second and Third divisions and fan out to our right and left to widen our defensive line at the crater. Then I think Burnside said Ferraro will bring up his colored boys, go through the crater, and see what they can do beyond it. Frankly, I did not pay much attention after Burnside told me what our objective was."

"Sir," Marshall said, "do you mean to say that we are not to move beyond the crater and the Confederate trench line? That we are to remain there and dig in?"

"That is exactly what I mean," Ledlie said. "Damn it! I made myself perfectly clear. We go as far as the site of the explosion and not a foot beyond. Cemetery Hill is not our concern. If it is to be taken, that is someone else's responsibility."

Ledlie rose unsteadily to his feet and dismissed them.

"Go get your men ready," he snapped, "and stop questioning my orders."

Marshall and Bartlett saluted and left the bombproof, walking in silence until they turned a corner of the trench out of sight of Ledlie's shelter.

"He's got it all wrong," Bartlett said. "Someone should have shot that man a long time ago."

They solemnly shook hands.

"God be with you and your men," Marshall said.

"And with you and yours," Bartlett replied, "but if there is a God, I do not think He is on the Union side tonight."

The night sky was clear. Around ten o'clock, a three-quarter waning moon rose in the east, casting a silvery light over the field of battle, quiet except for the occasional shells and mortar rounds arcing toward the trenches. Marshall and Bartlett summoned their regimental commanders and informed them that they, not the black division, would lead the assault. The officers were astounded at this sudden change of plans. Why had Burnside chosen them, the First Division, to be the shock troops, instead of the Second or Third, which were in better shape and had better commanders?

After the shock came anger and the knowledge that they were being sacrificed to free the niggers, while the black troops once more stayed safely in the rear. As the word filtered down from regiment to battalion to company to platoon and to the private soldiers, most reacted the same way. Let the niggers fight for their own freedom if they want it so much. It was damned unfair.

After the anger came despair and resignation, each man expecting certain death once he left the trenches. Some were sure they would die where they were when the mine went off. Rumors had spread for days that the mine was more dangerous than anybody said. If the least little thing went wrong, they would all be blown to hell.

Morale had reached bottom by eleven o'clock that night, when the First Division troops prepared to move a half mile to the rear. Replacing them on the line were the black troops of the Eighteenth Corps. The white soldiers jeered and taunted them.

The white regiments moved silently to the rear and lined up to fill their cartridge and cap boxes with powder and shot. Canteens were replenished with water and haversacks with three days' cooked rations. The officers held inspection, and it did not help the men's spirits to see that their lieutenants and captains were as downcast and discouraged as they were.

At 1:30 in the morning, after milling around for more than an hour, the division moved out. They secured their canteens and tin cups and bayonets, then marched down a narrow road through sweet-smelling piney woods to a new set of trenches. The men didn't know where they were. They felt disoriented, in an alien world, and were ordered to lie down and remain quiet.

The officers passed the word, whispering from man to man that the mine was set to detonate at 3:30, about an hour and a half away. The men of the First Division, Ninth Corps, Army of the Potomac, did what soldiers have always done—they waited to die.

"General Lee? Wake up, sir."

Col. Robert Chilton, the chief of staff, nudged Lee's shoulder. He hated to do it. The general needed sleep, but his standing orders were to be awakened if there was any portent of danger. The information Chilton had just received certainly qualified.

Lee awoke slowly, rubbing his eyes, and sat up on the edge of his cot.

"What is it?"

"Two things, sir. Hancock's corps is back in Petersburg."

"Already," Lee said. "That was a fast movement on his part. Now we must bring our men back as quickly as possible. What else?"

"We have reports of considerable movement on Burnside's portion of the Yankees' line. They might be preparing a surprise attack sometime during the night."

"What time is it?"

Chilton squinted at his pocket watch in the dim light of the candle he had carried into Lee's tent.

"A little past two o'clock, sir."

Lee sighed and absently smoothed his beard.

"I hate to do it, but we will have to alert the men on the line. It appears they will get no more sleep tonight. If those people are indeed planning an attack, then we will be ready for them. I earnestly hope those rumors about a mine are not true."

"We have dug and dug, sir," Chilton said, "and we have found no sign of a tunnel."

"Perhaps we did not dig deeply enough," Lee said. "Or maybe God does not want us to find it."

"Maybe our experts are correct, General, and there is no such thing as a mine."

Lee smiled at Chilton and prepared to go back to sleep.

"You summon me if the world blows up. I surely would not want to miss it."

"Wake up, soldier," the sergeant whispered, nudging Caleb Caffee none too gently in the back with his boot. Caffee bolted upright, snarled, and reached for his rifle.

"Hush up," the sergeant hissed. "You want them Yankees to know right where you are so they can drop a mortar round on you?"

"Hell, they're fast asleep," Caffee said. "Least they are if they got any sense. And so should we be. Whose harebrained idea is it to get us up?"

"Orders from General Lee himself. Seems the Yankees are up and about over yonder. The general thinks they might be making ready to attack."

The sergeant spoke with a sense of self-importance, as though Robert E. Lee had told him so in person.

"You stay sharp, you hear," he said, "and use that fancy rifle of yours if they come."

Caffee stood up and stretched and glanced at the sky.

"What time is it?"

"Don't know for sure," the sergeant said. "Maybe two-thirty, three o'clock."

Caffee looked at the outline of Cemetery Hill. Halfway up the hillside, the fort's blunt square walls were framed in moonlight. It was 150 yards away. Caffee was as far as he could get from it and remain in his sector, but it was still too damned close to suit him.

"If the Yankees come over tonight, that's where they'll come," Caffee said, gesturing to the fort, "after blowing the fort to smithereens."

The sergeant chuckled.

"Shoot, boy, they got no way to blow that up. There ain't no mine down there. Didn't you see all them holes we dug? If they were down there, we'd have found them for sure."

"Not if you didn't go deep enough."

"Hell, we dug down fifteen feet. Quit worrying. The devil himself couldn't dig a mine like that. Everybody says so. You stay awake now, you hear?"

After the sergeant had moved on, Caffee glanced again at the fort. He slid down into his shell hole and flattened himself against the earth. He clutched his Whitworth rifle as if it was a talisman that would keep him safe from all harm.

Burnside paced on a little knoll a quarter of a mile behind the Yankee trenches. Nearby, a tall redbrick chimney, known as

Taylor's chimney—all that remained of a fine home belonging to one William Taylor—loomed like a lone tree in the wilderness. Even in the moonlight, it stood out over the desolate terrain, visible for several miles. Burnside had moved his headquarters there shortly after 1:00 A.M. to be closer to the coming battle.

He pulled out his pocket watch and held it to catch the moonlight. He snapped it shut loudly, startling several of his staff, who waited a respectful distance away. It was three o'clock. In fifteen minutes, Pleasants would order the fuse lit, and in a half hour, the future of the war could be determined.

Burnside was highly agitated, tugging on his massive sideburns, puffing furiously on his cigar. He slapped his thigh repeatedly with his left hand while relentlessly pacing five steps in each direction. He paused before each about-face to stare at the outline of Cemetery Hill before dropping his gaze to take five more labored steps.

His mind changed directions as often as his feet, one moment resigned to abject failure, disgrace, and dismissal from the army, and the next moment planning, pleading, praying that there was a chance the thing might work. But how could it with Ledlie in command? Burnside watched the hill and hoped, ashamedly, that Pleasants's mine would not work. That might be his only salvation. Surely Meade would cancel the attack if there was no explosion.

Burnside shook his head and muttered a curse. He tried to picture the hillside obliterated, the rebel fortress gone, and the trenches deserted for a half mile. Even Ledlie might succeed under those conditions. There would be nothing to stop him. He could march his men to Petersburg as calmly as in a dress parade. If only he stayed sober. If only his men were not so inflicted with trench fever that they refused to advance. If only the rebels did not regroup too quickly.

If only he had not resorted to the luck of the draw. If only he had selected Potter or Wilcox instead of Ledlie. If only Cemetery Hill was in someone else's area. If only he had not persisted in sending his men against Marye's Heights at

Fredericksburg. If only McClellan had given him reinforcements at Antietam.

He turned his back on the hill and opened his watch again. It was ten minutes past three. Twenty minutes more and he would know. If only he had more time.

"Not much longer to wait now," General Grant said.

He closed the cover of his pocket watch and put it on his desk.

Meade grunted. He had been testy ever since he and his staff moved to Burnside's headquarters, a half mile behind Burnside's new camp. He and Grant were a full mile from the site of the explosion and could not even see Cemetery Hill. His aide, Colonel Lyman, had protested, saying that they ought to be closer to the front, within sight of the action. Meade retorted that a military commander does not have to see the battle. What he needs is instant and complete information. Meade had a telegraph link to Burnside's temporary headquarters and would learn of events in minutes. He could fire back orders just as rapidly.

"Communications, Lyman," Meade shouted. "That's the key to modern warfare. If a commander has good communications, he can run a battle from anywhere. Even Washington, God forbid."

"Yes, sir," a chastened Lyman said, and he retreated into the shadows with the rest of Meade's staff.

Then Grant showed up! Meade asked himself why. Would he never be permitted to operate on his own? Grant's amiability only heightened his anger. Meade was in no mood for idle chatter, not with his future riding on the next half hour. He was frantic with worry that all would go wrong. If so, he knew who would be blamed. Yes, he would get Burnside, sacking the man before the day was over, but Meade knew that his own position was threatened. It would not be Grant's army, as the newspapers persisted in calling the Army of the Potomac. If the operation failed, it would be Meade's army, and he would pay the price for the failure.

"Funny thing," Grant said, splitting the silence with the rasp of his mechanical lighter. "I was thinking how I never wanted to be a soldier. Never really liked the army. Of course, it turned out the army was the only thing I was ever good at. I sure hope it doesn't all end this morning. It would be hard going back to selling cordwood on a street corner."

Meade, for all his irritability, almost felt sorry for Grant. His voice sounded so sad, like a man who was finished and who saw no way out of his final predicament. Meade realized they were trapped in the same situation, and a rare feeling of empathy overtook him. He found himself echoing Grant's comments.

"I never wanted to be a soldier, either, General," Meade said, "but, like you, it turned out to be all I was good at, too. If you don't count building lighthouses."

"Only so many of those a man can build before he runs out of shoreline," Grant said, "but there will always be wars to fight. I guess we ended up in the right place, after all."

"Maybe so, sir," Meade said, "but I never thought I would be in a battle that depended on a bunch of coal miners."

"Nope," Grant said, chuckling. "They forgot to teach us that at the Academy. Still, if that fellow Pleasants has done his job right, he will do more damage than a thousand cannon and open a pathway to Petersburg. I guess Old Burny had something after all with this idea of his. He must be mighty happy about now."

"He will be if the mine explodes the way it's supposed to," Meade said.

"Won't we all," Grant said. "How did Burnside take the news about the colored troops?"

"He seemed upset."

"He'll get over it," Grant said. "Best not to trust the attack to the coloreds. Which division did he choose to replace them with?"

"I don't know, sir," Meade said. "That was his decision to make."

"Of course," Grant said. "Well, either Potter or Wilcox will do the job just fine, though I sure would hate to be depending on Ledlie to lead the attack."

"No chance of that, sir," Meade said. "Nobody in his right mind would choose Ledlie to spearhead anything."

Pleasants shoved a small tin box containing a dozen matches into his pocket. He buckled on his revolver and saber. He rarely wore the sword, only on ceremonial occasions, but he felt that this might be the most meaningful event of the war for him. He looked once more at Anne Shaw's photograph, daydreaming for a moment, wondering what the future held for them, if anything. But his mind kept returning to the mine, to its four tons of powder and all the precautions he had taken to keep it dry and to make sure all the splices were secure.

He sat down at the table in his tent, watching the flickering golden light of a single candle play over Anne's face. He set his open pocket watch next to the framed photograph, his eyes shifting from one to the other. All he really saw were logs and timbers, a snaking black fuse, a wall of sandbags. Mentally, he reviewed the construction procedures, the packing and tamping of the powder.

An hour ago, Pleasants had gone to the mine. Bobby Lee had asked to come, but Pleasants wanted to be by himself. He walked the length of the tunnel to the sandbags, ran his fingers over them, and examined the adjacent walls and ceiling in the pale light of the bull's-eye lantern. He listened for sounds of the rebels digging. He sniffed the air. There was dampness about— he could smell it and feel it—but the fuse was dry where it disappeared beneath the sandbag wall.

It was what Pleasants could not see that bothered him, the last hundred feet or so from the sandbags to the end of the tunnel and out to the laterals. Was it damp? Were the splices in the fuse intact? The only way to find out was to light the fuse. If it failed, if he failed, the war would drag on until November and Lincoln would surely lose the election if both sides remained mired in the Petersburg trenches. The thought nearly drove him crazy. If it did not work, he would blame himself.

Pleasants sighed as he watched the minute hand bisect the number two on his watch. Ten minutes past three. He rose, replaced the watch in his pants pocket, and blew out the candle. He stepped outside, only to retrace his steps, groping blindly on his desk until his fingers touched Anne's photograph. He squeezed it and thrust it in his jacket.

The entire regiment was waiting for him, filling the railway cut around the mine entrance. A soft murmur of voices, like the humming of bees, ceased as soon as he emerged from his tent. The sudden silence seemed ominous and overpowering. It was, Pleasants thought, as quiet as a tomb, as quiet as a five-hundred-foot tunnel crammed with wet powder and a broken fuse.

He knew the men were disappointed that they couldn't join the assault. A delegation led by Bill Cabot, an unlikely warrior at best, had approached Pleasants to ask whether they could participate. Pleasants spoke to General Potter, but he said no.

"I appreciate their zeal," Potter said, "but they have done enough already."

So the Forty-Eighth Pennsylvania would sit on the sidelines and miss the last fight of the war. As consolation, Pleasants asked Sergeant Watkins to distribute a double round of whiskey. Watkins clucked like an old hen and muttered about coddling the men, and by this morning, their desire to fight had diminished. They knew they were lucky to be seeing the end without losing any more of their number.

Bobby Lee joined Pleasants as he walked from his tent to the mine.

"Going in now?" Lee asked.

"Yeah," Pleasants said. "Time to find out if it works. You want to come along?"

"Yes, sir," Lee said.

"Colonel?"

Pleasants turned to see Stan Michnik, twisting his cap in his hands.

"You, too, Stan?"

"Yes, sir. I sure would like to be there when you light the fuse."

"Okay, come on."

Pleasants looked at the crowd, spied Sergeant Watkins, and waved him over.

"This was all your idea, Sergeant. You want to do the honors and light the fuse?"

"You mean go in there, sir? In the mine? In the dark? With all that powder? No sir. I didn't join this man's army to serve underground. If it's all the same to you, sir, I'll wait out here. Somebody's got to watch over the whiskey."

"And a fine job you've made of it, Sergeant."

Voices followed the three men through the night as they entered the mine.

"Good luck, sir."

"Hope she blows the rebs clear to hell."

"Hey, Colonel, don't forget a match!"

Pleasants led the way, holding a bull's-eye lantern. No one spoke until they had gone about fifty feet, when Stan gave voice to what they were thinking.

"It's funny, Colonel, I've never dug a mine before knowing it was going to be destroyed. I always believed that every mine I dug would last long after I was gone, as kind of a monument."

"I know what you mean, Stan," Pleasants said.

"Me, too," Bobby Lee added. "It doesn't seem right somehow."

"But remember," Pleasants said, "if this works, it will be the biggest monument any of us could ever hope to leave behind."

Stan nodded his head and reached out to pat one of the logs that braced the wall, his lips moving in a silent prayer.

"We did good work here," he whispered. "I'm proud of that."

When they reached the fuse, Pleasants knelt down to feel it.

"Dry," he announced. "At least at this end."

He took the tin box from his pocket and extracted a match, holding it between his fingers. He glanced at the others.

"All right," he said.

He struck the match on the side of the box and held it to the end of the fuse. It sputtered and sizzled like a piece of bacon dropped in a hot skillet, releasing an acrid burst of smoke. Pleasants, Lee, and Michnik watched, mesmerized, as the bright red glow moved along the length of the tunnel.

Pleasants checked his watch as they walked back toward the entrance.

"I give it twenty minutes," he said.

"Half that if the fuse is any damn good at all," Bobby Lee countered.

They quickened their pace and each in turn glanced over his shoulder for one last look at what they had done.

"The thing is not working, General," Meade said, furious. "It is already three-forty-five. The explosion is fifteen minutes overdue. Powder either ignites or it does not, and if it has not exploded by now, then it is not going to. I will telegraph Burnside to find out what the problem is."

Meade leapt from his chair, shouted for Lyman, and rattled off a message to Burnside.

"I want an answer immediately," Meade ordered.

"Damn fool thing," he said to Grant. "I knew we shouldn't count on it."

"Do you mean the telegraph?" Grant asked innocently, teasing Meade.

"No, sir," Meade said, failing to appreciate the joke and wondering whether Grant had taken to the bottle again. "I mean Burnside's mine."

"Don't give up on it yet," Grant said, though in his own mind he had done just that. "There could be several reasons for the delay."

"Suppose it doesn't work?" Meade demanded. "We have more than twenty thousand troops poised, ready to move the instant the hill blows up. They all expect to attack a shattered rebel line. What do we do if it is intact?"

Grant twisted in his chair and studied the sky to the east.

"It's still over an hour before dawn. We can afford to give the mine a little more time before making that decision."

The men of Ledlie's First Division cowered in their trenches, waiting for the earth to move and praying it would not bury them when it did. A few brave souls stood on the firing ledges to peer at the rebel fort, wanting to be the first to see it disappear in a mass of flame and smoke. Something to tell the folks at home about, if you lived long enough to get home.

By 4:00 A.M., the black sky on the eastern horizon was turning to gray and objects began to take on more definite shapes. As the sky gradually changed its hue, hope began to rise.

"Something's gone wrong with the mine," someone said.

"Shoulda gone off half an hour ago."

"Hell, if it hasn't exploded by now, it's not likely to."

"If the thing doesn't go off, neither do we. They won't send us charging across a field with the sun behind us and the rebs still in their trenches."

A few eyed their watches, willing the time to go faster. If they could hold out until dawn, until the rising sun removed all possibility of surprise and secrecy, then they would be safe. They could relax and boil up some coffee and a little bacon and get some sleep.

In the area beyond the railway cut, the soldiers of the Second and Third divisions also began to think they would survive the day. Some lighted fires and started coffee going. There was nothing like the smell of fresh coffee and a silent battlefield to make a man appreciate the new day.

Farther behind, the men of the Fourth Division, United States Colored Troops, finished their breakfast. Because they were not scheduled to join the assault until after all the white troops had gone in, they had been allowed to sleep until three o'clock. Each man had two pieces of hardtack with a slice of raw-fat salt pork between, washed down by strong black coffee. Ezra Boyce shared a treat with some of his fellow officers. His mother had sent two pounds of cucumber pickles. Nothing cut the fat of raw salt pork like a pickle. Maybe it was a good omen.

His men were still disappointed and angry at being replaced by a white division, but if the attack was not made, at least they would not feel they had been cheated out of the chance to win the final battle of the war, or suffer the humiliation of arriving on the scene after the victory had been secured, to pick up the casualties and dig ditches for graves.

Boyce felt sorry for Pleasants. All that work on that mine. Maybe he would get another chance to set it off. And maybe the next time it would work. But for Boyce, he would rather be a live politician than a dead hero with his name on a monument instead of on a ballot, where it belonged.

"It's those damn short fuses," Pleasants said to Bobby Lee.

They stood at the top of the railway cut, the men of the Forty-Eighth Pennsylvania arrayed behind them. Every man stared at the hill thinking of all the effort he had put into it for a month. It had come to nothing. A big shaft in the ground. Hell, there wasn't even any coal to take out of it.

"Could be the powder got wet," Stan said.

"Or it could be one section of fuse is just a little damp," Lee said. "Not wet enough to douse the flame but enough to slow it down. I've seen damp fuses that took twice as long to burn as dry ones."

"Colonel Pleasants, sir? Message from General Burnside."

A snappily dressed lieutenant handed Pleasants a telegram.

"The general says to tell you he received this from General Meade, sir, and he would like your answer."

Pleasants held the yellow sheet of paper close to his face and read the words aloud: "It is now one-quarter of an hour later than the time fixed for exploding the mine. Is there some difficulty?"

"I'd say there is," Pleasants remarked, "only now it's an hour later."

He turned to the messenger.

"Tell General Burnside the fuse has gone out. I'm going in to fix it."

The lieutenant repeated the message and left. Pleasants

scrambled down the embankment, followed by Stan and
Bobby Lee.

"I told you," Lee said, "the fuse could still be burning. The
whole thing could blow up any second."

"Well, there's no way we can know without going in there,"
Pleasants said. "Let me have your penknife."

Lee shook his head.

"No, Henry, you're trying to take over my job again. I'm the
mine superintendent. You may have figured out how to lay the
fuse, but I'm the one who put it down. I know every inch of it.
I can find the break and repair it a lot faster than you. Now
forget your damn pride and let me get on with my work."

Pleasants looked at him and nodded his head.

"All right, Bobby, go ahead. But if you get yourself killed in
there, you'll have to answer to me."

"Okay, boss," Lee said.

"And don't take all morning," Pleasants said.

Lee gave a nonchalant wave, shoved his hands in his pockets,
and kicked a small stone out of his path. He might have been
walking to the corner store. He turned and called back to
Pleasants.

"Marry Anne before she comes to her senses and changes
her mind," he said.

Stan ran to catch up with him.

"I'm coming with you," he said.

"You don't have to prove anything to me, you know," Lee
said.

"To me, either," Stan said, "not anymore. But I'm not letting you go in there by yourself. Besides, I've got ten extra feet
of fuse that might come in handy."

"It's four-thirty!" Meade shouted. "The sun will be up in
forty-five minutes."

Meade was fuming. He had not received a reply from Burnside. Fifteen minutes ago, he had sent another message, asking
where the general was. There had been no reply to that, either.

Grant chewed on the end of his cold cigar. He overheard one

of Meade's aides say that the mine was useless. The word stuck in his mind and for a moment he was a ten-year-old misfit leaving the schoolhouse, hearing the taunts of the other children. "Useless Ulysses!" cried the voices in his head. He turned on Meade as if he was one of his tormentors.

"Order the assault, General," Grant barked.

"But sir—"

"Do it now," Grant said. "We've got to try to salvage something from this mess."

"You heard the general," Meade said to an aide. "Order General Burnside to attack at once."

Burnside read Meade's telegram a second time. The paper trembled in his hand and he crumpled it, shoved it in his pocket, and covered his eyes with his hand. He slumped down in his chair, ignoring the stares of his staff, then glanced out at the rebel fort. He took out his pocket watch, but before he could open it, an aide announced the time.

"It is four-thirty-seven, sir."

Burnside's gaze wandered up the sloping hill to the crest and in his mind he saw the stone wall at the top of Marye's Heights at Fredericksburg, the solid sheet of flame from rebel rifles, the field of broken bodies in blue like a patchy carpet, and waves of troops, his troops, advancing, yelling, flags flying, never flinching as huge gaps were torn in their ranks. It was only with difficulty that he forced himself back to the present.

"General Meade has ordered me to launch the assault immediately," he told his staff.

"Sir," said Captain Scott, a junior aide, "without the mine, it will be a slaughter. It would be just like—"

Scott could not finish the sentence. He had been with Burnside at Fredericksburg, seeing everything the general saw. He still had nightmares about it.

"I cannot send these men to their death," Burnside said.

"You have your orders from General Meade, sir. You have no choice."

"Yes I do, Captain," Burnside said.

* * *

Bobby Lee whooped like a cowboy as he burst out of the mine with Stan close behind him. They ran to Pleasants, laughing and waving their arms.

"Ten minutes, Henry," Lee said. "No more. I guarantee it."

The three men climbed to the top of the embankment, Lee and Michnik competing to tell the story.

"The damn thing hadn't burned more than twenty feet when it went out."

"A splice broke just like somebody had yanked on both ends."

"Stan here brought extra fuse along."

"We fixed it and set it sputtering."

"And checked the fuse ahead for another thirty feet. Dry as can be."

"It's going to go, Henry, it's going to go," Lee shouted as he pummeled Pleasants on the back.

The troops began to echo their joy.

"By God, we did it!"

"The Forty-Eighth Pennsylvania Volunteers."

"Hah! A bunch of dumb coal miners, indeed."

"Nobody believed us."

"Said it couldn't be done."

"Wouldn't even give us a shovel."

Pleasants glanced at his watch. It was sixteen minutes before five o'clock on the morning of July 30 in the Year of Our Lord 1864.

14

THE ground heaved. It rippled and trembled and swayed. It rumbled deep and low like the peal of thunder in some far-off heaven. The rebel fortress and all the tons of earth around it began to bulge and rise out of the hillside. Slowly at first, almost leisurely, then faster until it split like the peak of a volcano and a fiery cauldron erupted.

A column of earth, smoke, and flame leapt two hundred feet in the air, all gray and black and rent with jagged red and yellow fire. At its summit, a black cloud spread like the cap of a giant mushroom. For an instant, it hung immobile in the sky, as if time itself had stopped, until, to the horror of thousands of spellbound spectators, a macabre rain of debris fell toward the ground: gun barrels, rocks, clods of dirt and clay as big as houses, artillery wheels, fluttering remnants of tents, shattered timbers—and men, and parts of men, arms, legs, heads, torsos, all burned black and lifeless.

Beneath the fiery mushroom cloud lay the bodies of 278 Confederate soldiers, blasted and broken, many buried alive. Nothing remained of the rebel fort. Its walls had been pulverized, atomized. In its place, a jagged crater had been ripped from the earth, a hole two hundred feet long, sixty feet wide, in places up to thirty feet deep.

While the debris was still falling, a shock wave of compressed air shot out from the center of the blast, setting the ground to trembling anew. It knocked men off their feet as if some huge hand had swatted each of them across the chest. With it came a dull, grinding roar that built and swelled to an eardrum-splitting clap. A ground fog of dust and smoke rolled with it, choking and blinding Ledlie's men in the forward trenches and everyone else up to a quarter of a mile behind. Men clamped hands over their ears, but the noise ground into their brains. Before it waned, other hands yanked the lanyards they had been gripping for more than an hour, releasing almost as a single burst a salvo of shells and mortar rounds from 144 pieces of Union artillery.

The massed firing of the guns produced billows of white smoke that filled the railway cut and the forward trenches, mixing with the gray-black dust and smoke from the mine explosion. The pale dawn light was eclipsed and suddenly the sky grew dark as midnight, a choking blackness that added to the terror of the soldiers on both sides.

In the Confederate trenches near the boiling column of smoke and fire, men panicked and ran to the rear, many of them struck down by falling rubble and Union artillery rounds. Not a living Confederate soldier remained in the trenches for two hundred yards on either side of the yawning crater. In a single blinding flash of flame and smoke, the Confederate line stood empty and defenseless for a quarter of a mile. The road to Petersburg lay open; the city was there for the taking.

On the Union side, Ledlie's troops believed they were safe, lulled into thinking that there would be no attack that day because the mine had failed for so long to explode. When the blast came, they were shocked into insensibility by its awesome power, and when the earth beneath their feet trembled and the log-lined walls of their trenches heaved and shook, some feared the sides would collapse and bury them alive. The ground quieted, but when they looked out, they saw a mountain of fire rising above them. Many of the Union soldiers panicked and ran for cover in the rear.

Officers and noncoms yelled for them to come back, but no commands could be heard above the din. Bartlett and Marshall had officers stationed in the deep-pit passageways and at intervals on the field behind the trenches. They drew their sidearms and fired in the air and at the fleeing men's feet. Two or three who refused to stop were shot dead.

"Get back where you belong," officers ordered, still unheard, but the sight of their pistols persuaded the frightened troops that they had a better chance of staying alive at the front.

"What the hell's going on?" Ledlie demanded, shouting from the entrance to his bombproof. "The mine went off, didn't it?"

"Yes, sir," Marshall said. "Didn't you hear it?"

"Heard some damn big noise, that's for sure," Ledlie said, eyeing in some confusion the column of smoke.

"What are you waiting for, Marshall? Your brigade is supposed to advance. Move them out."

"Forming up, sir," Marshall said. "We'll be going momentarily."

"About time," Ledlie groused.

"Aren't you coming, General?" Marshall asked.

"No," Ledlie said. "My job is here. Can't coordinate an attack on this scale unless I remain where I can be kept informed. I don't have the luxury of charging all over the place like you. Wish I did."

"Yes, sir," Marshall said as Ledlie disappeared in his shelter. He wondered how other division commanders in the Union army managed to lead their men from the front instead of the rear.

Marshall turned to confront his men, an anxious, milling mass whose organization into companies, platoons, and squads had been shattered by the numbers who had run away and been herded back, many to different parts of the line, finding themselves, as a consequence, packed in with strangers.

Marshall barked an order: "Second Brigade, move out!"

The men looked around as if they did not comprehend his words. Marshall started to repeat it when a major ran up to him, waving at the eight-foot forward trench wall.

"Sir! Where are the ladders?"

Marshall peered down the length of the trench and gasped as

if he had taken a bullet in the chest. He exhaled noisily. The men were laden with muskets and cartridge boxes and haversacks, and without ladders, none of them could scale the sheer log walls to get out of the trench. Someone somewhere along the chain of command had forgotten to bring up the ladders. Marshall hesitated, dumbfounded, as lost and confused as his men.

He glanced at his watch. Ten precious minutes had passed since the mine explosion. He had to move his men out before the Confederates regrouped. Petersburg might still be theirs, if only they could get out of the damn trench.

As far as Caleb Caffee was concerned, the Yankees could have Petersburg and all of Virginia with it. He ran to the rear through smoke so thick, he could not see an arm's length in front of him. He stumbled over timbers and broken cannon, fell into pits and tripped in shallow holes, glancing behind in terror. Caffee was certain that Satan himself was after him. He could hear the devil's screams, the moans of the wounded, the high-pitched shrieks of the shells, reflected and magnified by the acrid, choking smoke. Hell could not be any worse than this.

He had been knocked off his feet by the explosion, knocked down again by the shock wave, and when he tried to stand a third time, something struck him on the shoulder, covering him with a sticky gelatinous substance. It was a man's chest and head, the staring eyes burning like charcoal lumps, the oozing blood and brains spreading over him. For an instant, Caffee thought he recognized the face. Mercifully, his shell hole filled with smoke and hid the awful sight.

Almost unaware of his actions, Caffee climbed out of his pit and raced for the rear, and it was not until he covered nearly a hundred yards that he realized he had abandoned his Whitworth rifle, left it there for some Yankee son of a bitch to come along and claim.

* * *

"General Lee, sir!"

Taylor burst into the tent out of breath, hair disheveled, his fingers frantically buttoning his shirt. He waited, panting, embarrassed to appear so unkempt while Lee was already putting on his tunic.

"Yes, I heard it, Major. Was it an ammunition dump, or did those people manage to explode the mine everybody said could not be dug?"

Lee smiled and spoke slowly, both to quell his inner alarm and to calm Taylor. The aide fumbled with his collar button and took several deep breaths while Lee silently willed him to hurry.

"The mine, sir," Taylor blurted. "It's terrible, General. Half of Cemetery Hill has been blown away, the fort along with it. The Yankees opened up an artillery barrage at the same time. It looks like our defenses have been shattered for up to half a mile."

"How do you know the damage is so extensive?" Lee asked, knowing how quickly rumors spread in a catastrophe and how they usually were exaggerated.

"A chaplain of the Ninth Alabama was up on the crest of Cemetery Hill to watch the sunrise and, well, as he put it, sir, all hell broke loose. He's a bit earthy for a chaplain, but he seems to have kept his head."

Taylor flushed as he realized that he was babbling. Lee gestured for him to continue.

"The chaplain gave a good account, sir, until the smoke covered the field. He said that when he could no longer see the Union lines, he decided to come here and report. He said it was not the time for praying but for doing."

"Quite right," Lee said. "So, those people could be leaving their trenches and heading for the gap in our lines even while we are speaking?"

"I'm afraid so, sir."

"Have Traveller brought around. We've got to get up there. If we cannot close the gap, the war will be lost here and now."

Lee led the way out of his tent. An orderly was already

bringing up the horse, as gray as Lee's uniform. The horse had been called Jeff Davis before Lee paid two hundred dollars for him and changed his name to Traveller. Lee started to mount but held back when Francis Lawley, the London *Times* correspondent, approached, bedecked in a copious blue flannel nightgown, a stocking cap, and shiny high boots.

"What has happened, General?"

"It seems that your Royal Engineers are wrong, Mr. Lawley. It is possible to dig a mine longer than four hundred feet. Those people have done it and they have blown up a considerable portion of our front line. They are probably attacking us at this moment."

Lawley glanced toward the trenches and down at his outrageous garb.

"I had best get properly attired. It would not do to be taken prisoner in one's nightgown. How long before they arrive?"

"If they move with alacrity, they could have their breakfast here in half an hour."

"I cannot make out a thing now. Can you?" Meade asked.

"Nope," Grant said, smiling and lighting his cigar. "But it was the most beautiful sight I have ever seen. I have never witnessed so powerful an explosion. Perhaps no one ever has. Nobody could have survived it."

He reached over and clasped Meade's shoulder, a gesture so uncharacteristic of him, and so unwelcome to Meade, that both men instantly took a step away from each other.

"Yes, it was quite a sight to behold," Meade said stiffly.

"I never thought we would behold it," Grant said. "I gave up on that mine an hour ago."

"I gave up on it even earlier," Meade boasted.

Grant laughed.

"Hah! You never believed in it from the beginning. And now look. Somewhere in that mess, Old Burny's men must be out of their trenches and on their way to Petersburg. I wish the smoke would clear. I sure would like to see them moving up the rise. I tell you, General, we are on the verge of a great victory."

He paused to draw on his cigar and chuckled.

"To think I did not want to be a soldier. Right now, there is nothing I would rather be, not even President of the United States."

"If this succeeds," Meade said, "you could well be President someday."

Grant looked at him shrewdly and gave a slight nod of his head.

"In which case," he told Meade, "I would promote you to the highest rank the army has to offer. But first, Burnside's men must take that hill."

Burnside turned away from the mushroom cloud and the pall of dust that hid Cemetery Hill and wiped his eyes with his handkerchief. His staff pretended not to notice, but they had seen the tears the instant the fort exploded. The men took cover when the shock wave hit and when debris fell on the general's temporary command post, but Burnside did not flinch. He stood at attention, as if this was the proudest moment of his life.

"Can you see anything?" he called to Colonel Loring, his chief of staff, who was surveying with his telescope the base of the two-hundred-foot column of fire and smoke.

"Nothing yet, sir," Loring said, "but I am sure General Ledlie's men must be out of the trenches and on their way."

Loring was not sure at all, nor was anyone else on Burnside's staff. They were appalled that Burnside had chosen Ledlie to spearhead the assault and could not believe the general had selected the most inept of his division commanders for the job. But when they learned that Ledlie had been picked by drawing blades of grass, they understood. Burnside, explained those who had been with him at Fredericksburg, when faced with potential disaster, became incapable of coherent thought or action. Paralyzed, unable to make decisions, his training, instincts, experience, and wisdom failed him.

Burnside watched the clouds of smoke and saw in his mind's eye Ledlie's troops advancing at the run in a long blue line, sweeping up the shattered hillside and meeting no opposition. The rebels were all dead or on the run. He saw them reach the crest, the Second and Third divisions rolling up behind them, and heard their cheers before they disappeared down the far side, racing toward Petersburg. Not a single enemy soldier or cannon stood in their way. Soon Burnside would call for his horse and, with his staff riding in triumphant procession behind him, he would enter the city. He would order the colors hoisted, establish his headquarters, and await the accolades.

"Anything yet?" he asked Loring again, although he could see for himself that the forward trenches, fewer than five hundred yards distant, were covered by smoke.

Loring shook his head.

Burnside stared through the haze as if he could pierce it by willpower. His dreams of glory made him light-headed. Not even Ledlie could fail, given an opportunity like this one.

"Where is that bastard Dunne?" Pleasants shouted. "He was here a minute ago."

"Gone," Bobby Lee said. "I guess he couldn't stand it."

Dunne had appeared at Pleasants's side moments before the mine went off. Triumph was clear on his face.

"Still expecting it to blow up, Colonel?" Dunne asked. "It's a little late now."

"If you had given us the right kind of fuse in the first place," Pleasants said, "it would have exploded when it was supposed to."

"What's that old saying, Colonel? It's the poor workman who blames his tools."

"You never delivered the right tools, you no-good son of a bitch," Pleasants said. "You did everything you could to make sure we failed."

The major's reply was lost in the eruption that struck with such force that the men clung to one another to keep their balance. By the time they regained their footing, no one cared about Dunne. They were too intent on the spectacle of their own creation. The miners shouted and cheered like children,

pummeling one another in wild celebration. They huddled together, waiting for the smoke to clear, waiting to see the Union
troops leap from the trenches and advance on Cemetery Hill.

As the fog began to dissipate from the ground up in tiny but
expanding and contracting rifts, revealing a glimpse here and a
sighting there of the terrain leading to the trenches, Pleasants
shouted to Bobby Lee.

"The First Division must be halfway up the hill by now."

"How long since the explosion?" Stan asked.

"Twelve minutes," Cabot said, studying his watch.

"Then the troops should be approaching the peak," Pleasants said. "Once there, it's all over for the rebels."

A sudden breeze cleared the smoke and the miners could see
all the way to the crater and beyond. There were no Union
soldiers anywhere on Cemetery Hill.

"They're still in the trenches," Pleasants whispered, incredu-
lous. "They haven't moved out yet."

A lieutenant in Marshall's Second Brigade had the solution.

"Jab your bayonets into the logs, men," he yelled. "Like
this."

He grabbed rifles from two of his men, unclipped the bayonets, and plunged them into the trench wall, one at knee height,
the other at his shoulder. He beckoned to a soldier and showed
him how to climb the makeshift ladder. The soldier put one
foot on the lower bayonet, braced himself on the other, and
scrambled over the top.

"It's easy, Lieutenant," he said.

Up and down the line, the troops followed his example.
Other soldiers piled up sandbags to form crude steps. Here and
there a man climbed on his buddy's shoulders to go over the
top, then reached down for his rifle and gear.

Throughout the Second Brigade's portion of the line, men
clambered out of the trench, singly and in twos and threes, only
to gather and wait, uncertain of their orders. They felt vulnerable, expecting to be picked off by rebel sharpshooters. For men
who had spent two months under cover behind the safety of

eight-foot walls, it was damn frightening to be out in the open.

When the officers reached the top, they started to form the troops up two ranks deep in a line two hundred yards wide, the way they had been ordered to charge the hill. They stopped and looked across the field, confused. No one seemed to know what to do next. Marshall joined them, out of breath from climbing the steep sandbag stairs.

"Form up!" he shouted, and looked around in shock. "Oh my God. Is nothing to go right for us today?"

"Sir," a junior officer said, "how can we charge the hill with the defenses still in place?"

"I don't know, Captain," Marshall said.

He stared at the tangle of abatis and chevaux-de-frise that stretched in both directions. The men couldn't scale them. Dismantling them required axes and other tools, and precious time.

"Somebody fouled up," Marshall said. "This was all supposed to be cleared during the night by the engineers."

An officer down the line waved and called to him.

"Colonel? There's a gap here."

Marshall ran toward him and found an eight-foot hole in the defensive works, made to allow the nightly pickets to reach their forward observation posts.

"It's not much," Marshall said, "but it's all we have. Take the men through there."

Three or four soldiers at a time slipped through the opening. They stopped on the far side and looked back.

"Should we wait for everybody to come through and form up, sir?" the lieutenant asked.

"No," Marshall said, windmilling his arms to spur them on. "Get going and take the hill before the rebs have time to recover."

Marshall corralled the remainder of his brigade, more than eight hundred men, and directed them through the gap.

"Double-time!" he shouted. "Get up to that hole as quick as you can."

But the Union soldiers had lost whatever fighting spirit

might have existed before the mine exploded. They moved cautiously across the field, bent almost double to evade the bullets they were expecting. They scanned the terrain, looking for tiny puffs of flame and smoke from enemy rifles, listening for the rebel cannon, but the only sound they could distinguish was the steady roar of their own guns sending salvo after salvo over their heads.

"Spread out," the officers warned, but the men clustered in groups of three and four as they straggled in a wavering column toward the base of the hill, sure the rebs were out there somewhere. There was no massed charge, no momentum, no great surge of adrenaline to carry them forward.

Marshall's officers shouted themselves hoarse trying to get the men into line. Those were the orders and no one knew how to commence a charge any other way. The field manual said nothing about assaulting an enemy position in tiny groups strung out over a hundred yards.

As they neared the rebel lines, they saw that the Confederates' abatis and chevaux-de-frise, every bit as formidable as the Union's, were intact, impenetrable as a brick wall. Marshall groaned and cursed aloud. The same engineers who should have dismantled the Union's defenses were supposed to be out in front of the Second Brigade, chopping holes through the rebels' defensive fortifications. That outfit was nowhere to be seen.

Marshall glanced back toward his lines and saw Bartlett's First Brigade start through the gap in the defenses. Three more divisions were due to cross the field, and they would all face the same obstructions unless the engineers brought up their equipment in a hurry. He scribbled a note to Ledlie, requesting a company of engineers, and handed the paper to a runner. The boy headed for the Union side, making no effort to hide his relief. Marshall knew it was futile. Ledlie would not be sober enough by now to comprehend the need for engineers, but at least, Marshall thought, the gesture would cover him at a court-martial.

Ledlie denied the request.

"You tell Colonel Marshall that he does not need engineers. If there was a need, I would have sent them. It is my job to think of these things. His job is to get to the crater and dig in. And he'd better do it quickly."

Less than a minute after Marshall dispatched his message, the first of his men to reach the Confederate abatis found a six-foot opening where the fortifications had been leveled by the mine explosion. Slowly, they made their way through the space, not knowing what they would face on the other side. By the time a dozen were through the gap, they summoned up the nerve to peer over the rim of the crater and, to a man, they were struck dumb. Smoke rose from burning timbers and a pall of dust hovered close to the ground, which was littered with wreckage and more bodies than anyone wanted to count.

Some rebel soldiers were still alive, half-buried in the earth, their hands flailing at the air like drowning men. They screamed and moaned, as much in terror as in pain. Here and there, legs stuck up from the ground, wriggling and twitching like disembodied spirits. One soldier, his face so covered with muck that he could not see, was trying to haul himself out of the crater with his hands. The twin stumps of his missing legs left trails of blood behind him. An arm lay in the dirt, the hand clutching a rifle, its rope sling intertwined in the fingers.

The Union onlookers spoke in whispers, awed, stupefied, horrified. A brawny corporal from New Jersey crouched at the lip of the crater and peered beyond it up the hill where a single rebel cannon was firing a few ineffective rounds. Union artillery found the range and blasted it to pieces. Some distance north, too far to hit anything, a few Confederate soldiers stopped their retreat long enough to get off a couple of rounds in the general direction of the Yankee troops.

"Sounds like they're coming to life again," the corporal said to his squad. He glanced down into the crater. "I don't know about you boys, but the safest I've felt in this whole damn war was in my trench. Now here we are at the biggest, deepest trench anybody could ever hope to see."

He plunged down the sloping side of the pit, half-running,

half-sliding until he reached the bottom and loosed a yell of sheer exuberance. His buddies followed, and within minutes every Union soldier who crossed the gap in the Confederate lines did the most natural thing in the world—he followed the man ahead of him.

Some of the officers joined them. Others remained on the rim, trying to direct the newcomers toward the abandoned rebel trenches Ledlie had ordered them to occupy. Few men heeded them, and within ten minutes of reaching the crater, several hundred troops were milling around on the bottom, sight-seeing, as they called it.

The men busied themselves collecting souvenirs, rifles, swords, bits of uniforms, whatever they could find. A couple of artillerymen dug up two twelve-pound Napoleon cannon. They lugged them to the rim on the far side and set them up facing the crest of Cemetery Hill. If their job was to dig in, then they intended to use the cannon to make their new trench— their new home—even more secure. Some soldiers attempted to rescue the wounded, sending them back, under escort, to the Union side.

Units became entangled and all organization and control were lost. Officers could not find their platoons and companies. Men from oncoming outfits ignored pleas to move on and stay out of the crater. Marshall had no more success in rallying the men than did the lowest-ranking lieutenant. The advance was a shambles, a disgrace, a failure.

Bartlett ambled across the field aided by an ivory-handled malacca cane, his artificial leg biting into his stump with each step. He led his men of the First Brigade to the lip of the crater. Most of the soldiers raced after Marshall's men, drawn by the security of the huge trench. Bartlett and his officers were able to bring only a few hundred under control and lead them north, the opposite of what Ledlie had ordered.

Bartlett had misunderstood Ledlie, interpreting his own left flank as the Confederate's left, and soon men of both brigades occupied the trenches to the right of the crater, leaving those on the other side undefended.

By 5:30 in the morning, forty-five minutes after the explosion, all two thousand men of the First Division had reached the crater, and most of them had gone to the bottom. There was no getting them out. They were too scared to leave. Marshall and Bartlett stood together and looked up at the crest of Cemetery Hill. They saw not a single Confederate soldier. The hill was still there for the taking.

Meade cursed and fumed and shouted. He looked at his watch and saw that it was already 5:30. The sun was up. Grant sat in a camp chair quiet and dejected. He sensed failure. He stared into the distance but could see nothing of the battlefield. Gentle hills cut off most of his view.

"Burnside should have reached the peak fifteen minutes ago," Meade snapped. "I have dispatched two telegrams demanding to know of his progress, and all I receive are vague assurances that the attack is proceeding according to plan. What in God's name that is supposed to mean, I cannot guess. If it was proceeding according to plan, it would be over by now. I knew this was a mistake, General. I should have put a stop to it long ago. Burnside will pay for this."

Grant looked puzzled but said nothing. He recalled that Meade had endorsed Burnside's plan, or at least urged that the option be kept open. The battle, if indeed there would be one, had reached the stage when blame and recrimination, talk of courts-martial and investigations—"someone will pay for this fiasco"—ran rampant, before the bodies were buried. It was time to see for himself.

Grant gestured to Horace Porter, his aide.

"Get our horses, Horace," Grant said. "We have to find out what is going on up there."

"Shall I arrange a cavalry escort, sir?" Porter asked, knowing that Grant liked to wander too close to danger, with Porter in tow.

"Nope," Grant said. "I don't want to make a parade out of this. We'll just mosey up and down the line on our own."

"Leaving us, General?" Meade asked.

"For a while. You don't need me here in the way, and I would like to get a closer look at what is happening."

Meade smiled. And separate yourself from the failure that's in the making, he thought.

"If you find out anything, sir," Meade said, "I hope you will let me know."

Grant nodded, mounted Cincinnati, and rode off. Porter thought the Old Man looked a lot better as soon as he got clear of Meade's camp.

At his command post a half mile due west of Meade's headquarters, Burnside stood outside his tent and lowered his telescope. He had seen enough to know that the attack was in trouble. At first, he could not understand why Ledlie's troops were crossing to the rebel side in small, slow-moving groups rather than a massed assault. Doubts struck him. He could not remember whether he had ordered the engineers to remove the abatis and the other defensive fortifications. It would be too embarrassing to ask the staff. They were watching him for signs of panic. The pity in their glances was obvious. He saw Ledlie's men approach the crater and he willed them to go faster, but they poked along, in no hurry at all.

"There is no fire in the men," he said to Loring. "No spirit."

"No, sir," Loring said, following them with his spyglass. "I am afraid they have been in the trenches too long, General. They have lost their fighting edge."

Burnside tried to be optimistic.

"Still," he said, "if they do not meet any opposition—and I certainly do not see any signs of it—they will not need much of a fighting edge to go on to Petersburg."

His hope died when he saw the Union soldiers peer over the lip of the crater and disappear from view. Others settled themselves in the empty Confederate trenches on one side, setting up defensive positions. It was clear that Ledlie's men were not going anywhere.

"They were supposed to go around the crater," Burnside

said, agitated once more. "They will lose more time going through it. Doesn't anyone obey orders?"

He focused his telescope on the far side of the pit, expecting to see the troops climb out and continue up the hill. The only movement he saw was defensive, a group setting two cannon on the rim. No one else left the crater.

"Send someone up there immediately to order those men to move up the hill."

"Yes, sir," Loring said.

"And tell Potter and Wilcox to move their divisions out."

"What about the Fourth Division, sir—the coloreds?"

"Yes," Burnside said. "Alert them to be ready to move. If they had led this assault, as I planned, we would be in Petersburg already."

Burnside closed his eyes and massaged the back of his neck. He knew he would never have another opportunity like this, or even another command. He had been lucky after Fredericksburg. At least he had been allowed to remain in the army. He did not expect to be so lucky this time.

"It's a disaster," Pleasants said. "The worst mess I've ever seen."

Bobby Lee agreed.

"Where are the other divisions?" Pleasants asked. "Why aren't they advancing?"

"Forget it, Henry," Lee said. "It's too late now. It has been forty-five minutes since the explosion. The rebs will be regrouping and coming at us any time now. The army failed and there's nothing you or I or General Grant himself can do about it."

"I can't just stand here doing nothing. I'm going up there and see if I can get the men moving."

"Won't do any good," Lee said.

"Maybe not," Pleasants said, "but I've got to try, or we might as well never have dug our mine."

* * *

Little Billy Mahone, Brig. Gen. William Mahone, wasn't much of a man sizewise, his troops said, being only five feet tall, and that only if you measured to the crown of his hat, but he was considered one hell of a Confederate general. At thirty-eight, a graduate of the Virginia Military Institute in Lexington and former president and chief engineer of a railroad, Mahone had been wounded at the second battle at Bull Run. He had fought in every major campaign of the war, including Gettysburg, the Wilderness, and Spotsylvania. He was quiet, soft-spoken, and immaculately dressed, a master of infantry tactics and a skillful leader, one of Robert E. Lee's best. The instant the explosion at Cemetery Hill took away part of Lee's line, he thought of Little Billy Mahone.

Mahone did not have to be told how to handle an emergency. He knew what to do the way a hound knows how to tree a coon. He ordered his two brigade commanders to prepare their troops to move out with forty rounds per man and full canteens. He knew that his division was the closest full-size outfit to Cemetery Hill, even if it was only 2,200 effectives. That was not bad for a Confederate division in the summer of 1864.

Mahone's headquarters was three-quarters of a mile from the site of the explosion. His first reaction to the blast was the same as Lee's.

"General Lee's going to want us, boys," he said to his aides, "and I'm going off to tell him so."

He mounted his horse to set off for Lee's headquarters. A half dozen soldiers, hatless, shoeless, and unarmed, walked past. They had fled their trenches after the explosion and had a demented look in their eyes, the stare men get when they have seen too much death.

"What happened up there?" Mahone asked.

"All hell's busted loose, General," one said. "I ain't never seen nothing like it. We ain't gonna stop walking till we get home to Georgia."

"That so," Mahone said politely.

He took off his high-crowned hat, scratched his head, and furrowed his eyebrows as though puzzled.

"Well, boys," he said, "I tell you what. I don't have time right now to shoot you myself, but Sergeant Russell over there, he's got plenty of time, don't you, Sergeant?"

Russell nodded and raised his rifle.

"Of course," Mahone added in the same soft, soothing voice, "if you'd rather join up with my men for a spell and push those Yankees back, that'd be all right, too. You boys decide."

Mahone spurred his horse and galloped off. Glancing back over his shoulder, he saw Sergeant Russell pouring coffee for his new recruits. He was going to need every man he could get before this day was out.

Lee was already riding hard toward Mahone's command post. He met Little Billy at a spot above the line where the gigantic crater and the deserted trenches were easy to see.

"God Almighty!" Mahone exclaimed, quickly apologizing to Lee for the blasphemy.

"That's all right, General," Lee said. "I don't think He would mind your language under the circumstances. Your eyes are younger than mine. How many flags do you count in that hole?"

"Eight, sir."

"Eight regiments," Lee said. "At least two brigades, and no doubt in greater strength than yours. There will be more coming behind them. Grant would be a fool not to push at least one corps through a gap that size. Of course, he should have done that already. He could have been sitting in my tent by now."

Lee paused and cocked his head.

"Is that our fire I hear?"

"Yes, sir," Mahone said. "Some cannon and mortars are firing down on the crater. I hear some small arms, too."

"That's good," Lee said, "but it won't be enough to stop those people, and they must be stopped where they are or we will lose the war right here."

He looked expectantly at Mahone. Little Billy smiled.

"My men are ready, sir."

"Can you plug that gap?" Lee asked.

"We'll do it, sir, or we'll die trying. One way or the other, we'll be in that crater before the day's out."

15

———

"REBEL fire's picking up, sir," Porter said.

General Grant nodded and studied the crater from their vantage point atop the railway embankment. Rebel cannon were lobbing shells directly into the crater and the trench to the right, now occupied by some Union troops. Several hundred rebel infantry survivors who had fled the trench when the mine exploded had regrouped some one hundred feet up Cemetery Hill, above the crater and along both flanks. They fired whenever they spotted a Yankee face peering over the rim.

Caleb Caffee was among them, swearing each time he loaded and fired the rifle he had grabbed from a wounded Confederate soldier making his way to the rear. The soldier had resisted, but Caffee had knocked him down.

"You got no more use for it," the sharpshooter said. "You ain't going to live out the day."

Caffee set himself up in a gully on the hill above the crater, where he could see to the bottom, and began picking off Yankee soldiers one after another, cursing the inaccuracy of the gun.

"Piece of junk," he snarled when the weapon jammed. He blamed the Yankees for the loss of his precious Whitworth, conveniently forgetting that he had cut and run, leaving it behind. He cleared the gun and placed another brass cartridge in the breech. The rifle was one of 55,000 purchased by the Union army. It was called the Burnside carbine, named after its inventor.

Grant spurred his horse on toward the Union trench line and saw that the men of Wilcox's Third Division were beginning to move out. Ledlie continued to deny requests for engineers. The troops had no option but to scale the walls by standing on bayonets and file singly through the small gap in their abatis. They moved faster over the open plain toward Cemetery Hill than Ledlie's First Division troops had done. Enemy rifles and cannon were finding the range, causing numerous casualties. By the time Wilcox's troops had run across the plain and funneled through the gap in the Confederate abatis, they were desperate for shelter. They found it quickly enough in the crater and crowded into it, shoving Ledlie's men back to the walls. The hole was starting to fill up.

Grant clenched the reins and clamped his teeth over his cold cigar. He was furious.

"Where in God's name are the other divisions? Why aren't they advancing? I tell you, Horace, this has all the makings of a disaster."

He glanced toward the other side of the crater to a point about three-quarters of a mile distant, looking for signs of Warren's corps on Burnside's right flank. He detected no movement.

"Why hasn't General Warren attacked?"

Meade had issued orders for Warren and his Fifth Corps to advance in support of Burnside's Ninth Corps if Warren saw an opening—if the Confederates withdrew their troops from opposite his position of the line to plug the gap at the crater. Warren reported to Burnside that no rebel soldiers had moved. The line was still defended and there was no opening for him to exploit.

Warren was wrong. The troops opposite his line were Little Billy Mahone's and they had already vacated their trenches, skillfully withdrawing via narrow ravines out of sight of Warren's men. The Fifth Corps, more than 13,000 soldiers, faced no more than a few hundred rebels—clerks and quartermaster troops—but they might as well have been thousands, so well did they hold the Fifth Corps in place.

Meade ordered Ord's Eighteenth Corps to advance, but it was massed behind Burnside's waiting divisions, unable to move forward. A monumental logjam was developing, with thousands of men stacking up, each outfit unable to go until the one ahead of it moved on. The pace was as slow as a single soldier could walk.

Instead of sending the men double-time across the field between the railway embankment and the forward Union trenches, Wilcox and Potter ordered them up to the front line by way of the deep-pit passageways. That was why the pits had been dug, to provide safe conduct. Not to use them in the past had meant risking getting shot by the rebs dug in around the Cemetery Hill fort. Now the fort was gone, demolished, and the few Confederate troops firing on the crater were too far away to hit anything behind the Union lines. But Wilcox and Potter, acting out of habit and failing to grasp the urgency of the situation, never considered the possibility that the men did not have to use the passageways.

Twelve thousand men of Burnside's corps slowly threaded their way through the winding ditches, walking two and three abreast the way they had done for weeks, colliding with the scores of stragglers, walking wounded, and couriers heading in the opposite direction.

As the troops reached the forward trenches, they followed the men before them, climbing out on sandbag steps and bayonet ladders, filing through the opening in the abatis. They hotfooted it across the open field, raked with increasingly heavy enemy fire, channeled through the gap in the Confederate abatis, and plunged gratefully into the crater. They didn't know where else to go.

Officers tried to rally them to occupy the trenches right and left of the crater, and gradually they filled up, too. And there the Army of the Potomac halted. Nobody advanced.

Pleasants raced across the plain and dashed through the gap in the Confederate fortifications. His saber snagged and held him for a moment until he could jerk it free. He was irate. On the

Union side, he had passed hundreds of troops lingering in the passageways. He urged their officers to get them out and move them on faster, but no one paid any attention to him.

He approached the lip of the crater. One look at the seething mass of men at the bottom persuaded him that it was no longer an army. This was a mob. Officers shouted and men screamed as Confederate musket fire and mortar rounds and cannon shells tore into them. Pleasants plunged down the slope, colliding with a lieutenant who was holding his bloody arm close to his side.

"Get your men together," Pleasants said. "Move them out. Make for the crest. You'll all be killed if you stay here."

The young officer looked at him, dazed and bewildered.

"I don't know where my men are, Colonel. They're scattered to hell and back."

"Round up anybody you can."

The lieutenant opened his mouth to protest. His eyes widened in surprise. A rebel bullet split his head and he dropped at Pleasants's feet.

Pleasants backed away and ran from one officer to the next, trying to find someone to take charge and rally the men. The rebel fire was growing steadily heavier and more accurate, forcing the troops in the crater to pack themselves tighter, pressing toward the sheer far wall, which provided the only shelter from the deadly incoming rounds.

Some soldiers had been prodded to scrabble up to the rim, digging their toes into the dirt to steady themselves as they fired off a few rounds at the enemy. But they were being picked off quickly. Casualties mounted, and still Burnside's oncoming troops were piling into the crater. The last of Wilcox's outfit and now the first of Potter's men were crossing the field. Like Ledlie's troops before them, they sought shelter as soon as they reached the rebel side, following the men in front of them into the pit.

Pleasants searched for Bartlett to urge him to lead his men out.

"My orders from General Ledlie were to proceed this far and

no farther," he told Pleasants. "The general was quite specific about that."

"His orders are wrong," Pleasants snapped. "The whole point of the explosion and the assault is to reach Petersburg. You cannot do that by staying here. Where is Ledlie? Maybe he can rally the men."

Bartlett laughed and gestured with his thumb to the rear.

"General Ledlie is where he always is in battle, somewhere safe with a bottle. I doubt he has any idea what is happening here. Or even cares."

"Won't you try to organize your men and move them up the hill?" Pleasants pleaded.

"I have my orders," Bartlett said.

Pleasants gave up. The troops jammed in the crater were doomed, and he was not prepared to die with them. He scrambled out and ran back across the field, toward the Union line. Around him, many men were doing the same. Some had been wounded; many were deserting. For a moment, Pleasants felt like a deserter himself, but this was not his command. He wasn't even supposed to be there.

Shells exploded, tracking his path. He zigzagged and quickened his pace, determined to make one more try. He would find Burnside and talk to him. Maybe he could save the operation. But before Pleasants had gotten halfway across the field, he spied an old man in a private's uniform walking toward him, pushing his way through the fleeing mob. He was trailed by a smartly dressed colonel. Pleasants recognized the weary figure.

"General Grant, sir!" Pleasants shouted. "It's all gone wrong. The men won't move out and take the hill. They're going to be trapped."

"You don't have to tell me, young man. I have seen for myself."

"It's a disaster, General. You must take over and do something."

"I cannot interfere with my commanders," Grant said. "I will not breach the chain of command."

"Damn your chain of command," Pleasants said. "My men

and I dug that mine for you and blew up a quarter mile of the Confederate line, an open door to Petersburg. You West Pointers let us down, you and General Meade, refusing to allow the black division to spearhead the assault. And Burnside, too. He supported us, but he picked that drunken coward Ledlie to lead the attack."

Grant and Porter exchanged glances. This was the first they had heard about Ledlie. A shell exploded not thirty feet away, but the general did not flinch. Pleasants suddenly became aware of the occasional ping of bullets nearby and realized that they were in danger. Grant knew that one of the most important things a general can do is set the example for courage and morale. It was hard on subordinates, forced to pretend they were not afraid in the midst of enemy fire, and Grant knew that Porter would diplomatically suggest, before the bullets flew too thick and close, that urgent business required Grant's attention elsewhere.

Grant lighted his cigar with a steady hand and studied the line of Union troops moving toward the crater. Men were being shot by the rebels and left for dead not far from where they stood. He shook his head and puffed up a cloud of smoke.

"This is the saddest affair I have witnessed in this entire war. Such an opportunity for breaking through fortifications I have never seen, and I do not expect to ever see again. The entire opportunity has been lost. There is now no chance of success. These troops must be withdrawn. It is simply slaughter to leave them here."

"More are coming, General," Pleasants reminded him, gesturing to the steady stream of soldiers rising out of the Union trench line. "Please order them to fall back, sir. They'll listen to you."

"Yes," Grant said. "I dare say they would. I am sure they would be happy to get the order to withdraw."

Another shell burst nearby, peppering them with tiny clods of dirt.

"Sir," Porter said, "I think it is time to return."

"Yes, you're right," Grant said, but he made no effort to

move. He studied Pleasants for a moment, trying to decide how best to explain why he could not act on his suggestion and call off the attack.

"It's the chain of command, Colonel," Grant said patiently. "Most of the time it functions well, but occasionally it works to our disadvantage. Without it, we would have anarchy. An army needs discipline and control. Commanders cannot have their orders countermanded without their knowledge.

"I will tell General Meade to stop the assault, but I cannot go behind his back and tell General Burnside or one of Burnside's division or brigade or regimental commanders to halt without first informing the man who has overall responsibility. Could you have completed your mine if I had ordered your men to stop or told them to dig in a different direction? You would have been furious, and rightly so. Think about that, Colonel, and while you're at it, pray for those men up there, and for those of us who sent them there. We West Pointers do the best we can, but sometimes it's not enough."

"They are not advancing," Burnside said, training his telescope on the crater.

It was a little before 6:00 A.M., and the day was already hot and sultry. Sweat poured down Burnside's face, soaking his famous sideburns as if he had been standing in the rain. His aides exchanged looks, knowing the battle was lost. Those who had been with Burnside at Fredericksburg wondered whether it was happening again, Burnside stubbornly, obstinately, compulsively issuing order after order to attack. There the troops did attack; here they did not. The staff saw their army careers, inextricably linked to Burnside's, collapsing with his.

Every fifteen minutes, a telegram arrived from an irate Meade demanding to know what was going on. All he knew was what Burnside told him in infrequent and vague replies—all was proceeding as expected.

Then came the peremptory message: "I demand to know more." Burnside exploded with rage and with difficulty forced himself to compose a temperate reply.

"I am doing all in my power to push the troops forward," he wrote to Meade, "and, if possible, we will carry the crest. It is hard work, but we hope to accomplish it."

This did not satisfy Meade. A courier had just brought him a message intended for Burnside but mistakenly delivered to Meade, saying that Burnside's troops were stalled at the crater.

"What do you mean by hard work to carry the crest?" Meade telegraphed to Burnside. "I understand that not a man has advanced beyond the enemy's lines, which you occupied after the explosion. Do you mean to say that your officers and men will not obey your orders to advance? What is the obstacle? I wish to know the truth."

On receiving the wire, Burnside became as angry as anyone had ever seen him. Morally offended by Meade's tone, he found the suggestion that his men refused to obey his orders to be insulting. For Meade to say he wished to know the truth implied that Burnside had been lying! The front was forgotten, replaced by a war compounded of personal outrage and pique. To Burnside, Meade was not a gentleman.

"I did not mean to say that my officers and men will not obey my orders to advance," Burnside wrote. "I mean to say that it is very hard work to advance to the crest. I have never in my report said anything different from what I conceived to be the truth. Were it not insubordinate, I would say that your latter remark was unofficerlike and ungentlemanly."

That should put him in his place, Burnside thought, handing the note to his telegraphist.

He dispatched an aide to the crater with new orders.

"Order General Wilcox and General Potter to move on the crest immediately and at all costs. Tell them I will tolerate no further delays and that if their men refuse to obey their orders, I want to know the reason why."

Wilcox and Potter attempted to organize their troops in the trenches and mount an attack, but the men were too few and too late. Wilcox had no more than one quarter of his division in the trenches to the left of the crater. They had occupied a hundred yards, but when they tried to move beyond the trenches, they were repulsed by well-placed rebel mortar and cannon fire. Confederate infantry had regrouped and dug themselves in, determined to regain the ground from which they had fled. It was all Wilcox could do to hold on. Reaching the crest of Cemetery Hill was out of the question.

On the right side, Potter had been able to get almost half of his Second Division to occupy the trenches instead of plunging into the pit. They advanced some two hundred yards, captured a number of rifle pits, and took heavy casualties. With battle flags flying and officers cajoling, the men fired as fast as they could reload as they charged the slope. The Second Division clawed its way almost to the graveyard of Blandford Church, the cemetery that gave the hill its name.

There they faced Little Billy Mahone and his two brigades, supplemented by hundreds of stragglers, men separated from other units, who were prepared to fight as if the eyes of the entire Confederacy were on them. Robert E. Lee had told Mahone that the life of the Confederacy depended on his success.

From a second-floor window of the Gee House, a short distance from the cemetery, Lee watched the action through his spyglass. He permitted himself a smile as Mahone's troops tore into Potter's Yankees and sent them reeling back toward the crater.

Meade watched tight-lipped as Grant and Porter rode off, back to Grant's headquarters at City Point. He turned to Lyman, his aide.

"At least I will not have him looking over my shoulder anymore. Not during whatever is left of this battle, anyway."

He spat out the words with bitterness, and his large eyes stared malevolently after his commander.

"General Grant has washed his hands of this affair, now that he has seen how it is going," Meade said. "If it fails, he has taken care to minimize the amount of blame that will stick to him."

Meade mimicked Grant's folksy drawl.

" 'Of course, it's up to you, General. It is, after all, your army.' "

He continued in his own voice.

"Yes, it's my army when it fails."

"But, sir," Lyman ventured, "General Grant reported that the troops are all jammed up in the crater and do not seem disposed to move out of it. Those few who are trying to advance do not appear able to get far. If we had more troops up there, maybe the plan would work."

"Perhaps," Meade said. "In any event, he has left it for me to decide, but not before saying that if it was up to him, he would order a withdrawal."

"General Grant may be right, sir," Lyman said, "about withdrawing while there is still time to get the men out."

"No," Meade said. "It is not time for that yet. We must have eleven thousand troops out there in Burnside's divisions. Lee cannot have a quarter of that number opposing them. We have twenty thousand more in reserve. And we have the coloreds; that's another four thousand. I cannot believe that a Union force of that magnitude cannot break through a shattered line held by a demoralized enemy in inferior numbers and get on to Petersburg before noon."

Meade paced for a moment, lost in thought.

"Order the coloreds forward," he said, "and tell General Ferraro that he must not stop at the crater. His soldiers are to seize the hill. When our white boys skulking in that big trench see niggers going for glory where they refused to go, they will climb up out of that crater so mad that they'll race to beat them into Petersburg. To be on the safe side, tell Warren and Ord to move forward on their own, independent of the Ninth Corps. Lee will have to spread his forces so thin to meet their advance that he won't have enough troops to go around. I tell you, Lyman, we will sweep over them like a tidal wave.

"General Grant was correct about one thing. This is my army, and I am going to carry the day, no matter what the cost."

* * *

The tidal wave was only a trickle. Warren, commanding the Fifth Corps, still believed the enemy line opposite his position, where Mahone's men had been, was too heavily defended to attack. He sent a telegram to Meade asking him to come to the front to see for himself. Meade declined, declaring that it was essential that he remain at his headquarters.

Ord's Eighteenth Corps was still far behind the Union line, in back of the railway cut and Ferraro's black division. Ord read Meade's wire directing him to move his corps rapidly to the crest of Cemetery Hill and effect a lodgment there. Instead of sending the entire corps forward to take the hill, he decided to dispatch only one division, with orders to link up with Potter's troops holding the trenches to the right of the crater.

It took nearly an hour for Ord's division to reach the Union trenches, and it was not until 7:30, almost three hours after the explosion, that the soldiers crossed the field to join Potter's men. And there they stayed, pinned down by fire from Mahone's troops. Little Billy had rounded up more cannon and mortars, and his men were dropping scores of shells on the trenches and into the crater. They were killing those damned Yankees right and left.

"We're going up, men!" shouted Ezra Boyce. "The white soldiers are in trouble. They can't take Cemetery Hill by themselves. They need us to do it for them."

The Fourth Division, United States Colored Troops, was strung out in the deep-pit passageways leading from the railway cut to the Union trenches. Ferraro, like Burnside's other division commanders, never thought to bring his men across the field to reach the forward line, even though Confederate fire could not touch them. The passageways were there, and that's the way the men would go. As he led them through the railway cut, they passed the miners of the Forty-Eighth Pennsylvania.

Pleasants and his men watched them go. The Pennsylvanians waved and shouted encouragement, though a few muttered, just loud enough to be heard, about niggers who thought they could do what white troops couldn't.

Pleasants spotted Boyce and ran over to shake hands.

"Good luck, Ezra," he said.

"Thank you, sir. You and your men did one hell of a job blowing up that fort. The rebs must have heard it clear to Atlanta."

"It's pretty rough up there," Pleasants warned.

"We're ready for it, Colonel. My men's spirits picked up as soon as the order came through. I can smell victory in the air—and a hell of a lot of votes!"

Pleasants spotted Corporal Mutesa not far behind Boyce.

"Give 'em hell, Corporal!" Pleasants shouted.

Mutesa glanced at the colonel, his face a mask of anger and defiance. He nodded briskly at Pleasants and snapped his eyes back to the battlefield ahead.

"We'll show them all," he muttered, "every last one of them. They'll know that warriors were here today, and we'll never let them forget it."

Pleasants watched the rest of the black troops file into the passageways. They were not singing, but they no longer had that whipped, sullen look about them. The soldiers walked tall, straight and proud, as tough and determined as any Pleasants had seen. "They look like men a-marching on," he whispered. "They look like men o'war."

"Think they'll carry the hill?" Bobby Lee asked.

"They will or die trying," Pleasants said. "They're not about to hide in any crater. They've got something to prove and they know this may be their only chance to do it."

The black troops stepped quickly and confidently through the passageways, adrenaline pumping, eager to take to the field. Orders came for them to halt, to sit down and wait. Colonel Loring, Burnside's chief of staff, returning from a tour of the crater, met Ferraro at the Union trench line. Loring was appalled to hear that Ferraro had been ordered to advance with the colored troops. Didn't he know the battle was lost? Three divisions were trapped up there, Loring told him. They were all in danger of being slaughtered.

"It's madness to send your men up there," Loring said to an increasingly agitated Ferraro. "It's suicide. Hold them here, sir, until I report to General Burnside. It may be that he does not know how bad the situation is."

The men waited, wilting in the morning heat, listening to the Confederate artillery and resigned to the fact that something more was going wrong. Had the brass decided, again, that the colored troops could not be trusted? Boyce and the other officers paced up and down in the passageways talking to their men, trying to restore their flagging morale.

"We're not bringing up the rear this time," Boyce said, hoping to make the best stump speech of his political career. "We're not carrying supplies or digging ditches. We're going up there to fight. To save the day for the Union army and to rescue the white troops who are pinned down and lead them into Petersburg. By God, this time they're going to be following us. We'll show 'em how it's done."

The men clapped their hands and shouted with him, and Boyce reveled in his ability to fire them up, but it did not last long. No sooner had the cheers subsided when an orderly came through the passage, yelling for everyone to stand aside. The troops were forced to get to their feet and press back against the walls to make way for a caravan of wounded soldiers, casualties being carried to the rear.

There was no avoiding the disturbing sights and sounds, the parade of broken bodies, smashed limbs, litter after litter dripping blood, and the shrieks and moans of the wounded, some thrashing like wild animals, tied down with shreds of their own uniforms. And a few, stiff and silent and white, already dead.

Some bore their pain stoically, the effort showing on their tight, pinched faces. Others, the walking wounded, were cracking jokes.

"It's my ticket home," one said, pointing to his left arm, smashed below the elbow. "It's worth an arm to get out of this hell."

"A thirty-day wound," said another, clamping a bloody bandage on his shoulder. "It's my lucky day."

Others offered advice.

"Don't go up there, boys. It's hell and a half and it's only gonna get worse."

"When you get there, stay under cover."

"Head for the crater. Biggest damn trench you ever saw."

The procession seemed endless. This foretaste of their fate shocked the waiting troops, but they tried not to show it. This was their opportunity, they reminded themselves, their chance to show the world what black soldiers could do.

"We'll never have a better chance, men," Ferraro shouted.

His message passed down the long file of troops from man to man. They heard it and they believed it, and they believed in themselves, but the bottom of the passageway was crimson and slippery with blood, and the screams of mangled men echoed off the walls. The casualties no longer looked like men o'war. When this day began, they were whole men, but they would never be whole again. For them, the war was over, but the black soldiers knew that theirs was yet to begin.

The Fourth Division, United States Colored Troops, waited another hour until Loring returned from Burnside's headquarters with the word Ferraro had been dreading. The attack was on.

"I still say it's suicide to send your men in now," Loring said, further weakening Ferraro's tenuous hold on his own courage. "But General Burnside has no choice. Meade is adamant about taking the hill. Push your men forward, white and black, he said. As far as I am concerned, the battle is lost, but there it is."

Loring shook hands with Ferraro, thinking that he would never see him again. He noticed that the general's hand was cold and limp.

Ferraro summoned his brigade commanders, Henry Thomas and Joshua Siegfried. He told them it was time to move the men forward.

"Your orders are to take the crest of Cemetery Hill, no

matter the cost. Lead them, gentlemen, and your men will follow."

Ferraro wished them godspeed, returned their salutes, and disappeared. He headed for the bombproof occupied by Ledlie, to share his company and his bottle. And there he stayed.

Thomas and Siegfried moved the troops out. The soldiers presented a phalanx of black faces a half mile wide, prepared to charge, to take courage and comfort from the sight of their own line running over the battlefield to meet the enemy. They had practiced and drilled, and now it was time. Some of them almost felt like singing.

But when they emerged from the trenches, they were forced to halt once more. Although nearly three hours had elapsed since the explosion, the engineers had failed to bring up ladders or dismantle the fortifications. And so the men of the Fourth Division advanced, as earlier outfits had done, not as they had been trained but in clusters of three and four, vulnerable in the open field, many of their number falling from rebel bullets and shells. The units became fragmented and entangled. Cohesion, unity, and camaraderie were lost. Momentum dissipated. Confidence threatened to ebb.

The white officers were out in front, and the black troops trusted them, following their orders to the letter, holding nothing back. Not even when they skirted the edge of the crater, so close to Little Billy Mahone's trenches and rifle pits that they came within point-blank range. Not even when they stopped to form into line and heard the order, "By the left flank, march," followed an instant later by the ringing cry, "Charge!"

By God, they were men o'war now! They leapt into the enemy trenches, swinging their muskets like clubs. Corporal Mutesa captured a Confederate regimental flag and waved it defiantly over his head. Rebel prisoners were sent to the rear after officers ordered the troops not to kill them on the spot. "Charge!" came the cry again, and the black soldiers raced forward, Mutesa in the lead. Their battle flags flashed brightly against the smoke of battle, swords shimmering in the sunlight. Rallying, the men shouted themselves hoarse.

* * *

Pleasants watched from atop the railway embankment. He felt like cheering when he saw the ragged blue line, considerably smaller than it had been moments before, climb Cemetery Hill. Whole sections of the formation disappeared in clouds of smoke, but the line did not waver.

From his second-floor window in the house atop the hill, Robert E. Lee peered into the faces of the charging black soldiers and shook his head at the perfidious nature of those people, those Yankees who would stoop to a level quite beneath any gentleman to win this war. "They do not deserve to win," he said aloud, and he gripped the windowsill as the black faces came closer.

Caleb Caffee saw them approach and he cursed all white men who would give arms to niggers so they could kill decent people. He fired at each black head he saw and when they drew close enough, he jabbed them with his bayonet and clubbed them with his Burnside carbine and tightened his hands around their black necks and squeezed the life out of them.

Little Billy Mahone saw them come closer and he fired his revolver so near that he left powder burns on their black faces. He sliced through their flesh and bones with his razor-sharp saber and damned the evil that sent niggers on the rampage, pretending to be soldiers just because they wore uniforms. He shouted to his men, urging them to kill every last one, because if they got past, then their wives and children would never be safe again.

Each rebel soldier watched the black troops come closer and knew, without being told, that if he did not hold his part of the line, it would be the end of civilization as he knew it. If the coloreds won today, there would be no keeping them down.

Their hatred focused on the white officers. Maybe the niggers didn't know any better, but the officers, they were betraying the white race. Those bastards deserved to die. Already more than half the division's officers were down, and with them went the life and spirit of the outfit. The brigade commanders sounded retreat, directing the survivors back to the first line of Confederate trenches.

A message arrived from Ferraro: "If you have not already done so, you will immediately proceed to take the crest in your front."

Thomas and Siegfried looked around at what remained of the Fourth Division and agreed that it would never survive another charge.

"Not a man of us will live to reach that crest," Siegfried said.

"And not a man of us will be able to look himself in the mirror," Thomas said, "if we don't try."

The order went down the line. Men tightened their grips on their rifles and glanced at one another. Lips moved in silent prayer. A thin, pale lieutenant, Charles Taylor, from Lowell, Massachusetts, gripped the brigade guidon. The six other men who had carried it in the last assault were dead.

"Charge!"

The officers scaled the wall of the trench. Taylor waved the guidon. He whirled around, cried out, and fell backward into the trench. A sergeant grabbed the guidon out of his lifeless hand. Mutesa leapt out of the trench behind him, waving the others forward.

"The whole world's watching us," he cried, and the men—most of them—surged forward. It was a ragged and pitifully thin line. The feeble cheers could hardly be heard above the roar of the muskets.

The black troops closed to within twenty-five feet of Mahone's makeshift rifle pits and breastworks before breaking under the withering Confederate fire. Little Billy led a countercharge, sending the Yankees reeling back to their trench.

Ezra Boyce and a private in his outfit tumbled into the trench together, recovering quickly to fire at the advancing rebels. The Confederates pressed their advantage, perching on the rim of the trench three feet away and firing down on the mass of troops. They leapt in, stabbing and slashing with bayonets. Their officers yelled and whooped, reminding their men to take the whites prisoner and kill the niggers.

A rebel soldier eyed Boyce and the black private, upended his rifle, and, with a laugh, stabbed the private in the chest. Boyce shot the reb to death. He rapidly fled the death trap the trench had become.

Soldiers and officers ran, all order and discipline shattered. Even the proud Mutesa ran. It was suicide not to. They raced, crazed, for the only place that offered shelter: to the crater, to the soldiers already massed there, a swarm numbering 11,000. Some had cowered there all morning, helpless despite their superior numbers. Behind them, Mahone's rebels closed in for the kill.

"I knew the coloreds would never take that hill," Meade said. "That was why I refused to allow them to spearhead the attack. I was right."

He seemed almost more pleased to learn that the Fourth Division's assault had not succeeded than upset at the failure of the entire operation.

"Perhaps," Lyman said, "there is still time to send in Warren and Ord on the flanks."

"No," Meade said. "The thing has failed and that is that. I knew from the outset it was a damn fool idea, but no one listened to me. Tell Warren and Ord that all offensive operations are to cease as of this moment. They are not to advance beyond their present positions. Suspend the artillery barrage. Tell Burnside to withdraw his corps back to our lines."

It was 9:30 in the morning, going on five hours since the mine had exploded.

When Burnside received Meade's order to withdraw, he was outraged. He still believed his beloved Ninth Corps could carry the hill and reach Petersburg. His staff had given up on the operation hours ago. And Wilcox and Potter, his division commanders at the crater, had long known the attack was doomed. Their concern was sheer survival, how to get their men back to the Union lines.

They could no longer retreat across the field between the crater and the Union trenches without suffering horrendous casualties. There were too many rebel cannon and mortars and infantry now within range. Burnside was aware of the problem and had begun to arrange for an escape route. He ordered the digging of a six-foot passageway to link the crater with the Northern trenches, and he had men working from both ends. It would take several hours to complete, and until it was finished, his corps was trapped. To attempt a withdrawal prematurely meant death. Burnside had to persuade Meade to delay the order to withdraw.

Burnside mounted up and rode the half mile to Meade's headquarters, recalling Meade's offensive telegrams, the ones that accused him of lying and of being an ineffective commander. By the time he arrived, he was furious.

"General Meade!" Burnside barked.

Deep in conversation with Lyman, Meade looked up, startled. He flushed at being addressed in such a fashion. Lyman wisely backed away and left the tent.

"Didn't you get my order to withdraw?" Meade asked first, before Burnside could say another word.

"Yes, sir. I received it, but I do not agree with it."

"You don't agree!" Meade sputtered. "It is not your prerogative, sir, to agree or disagree. It is your duty to carry out my orders promptly. By God, sir, this is insubordination, and you shall pay for it. Believe me, you will pay."

"A chance of victory remains, General," Burnside said. "My men can take the hill if you send in Warren and Ord on the flanks."

"Any chance of victory ended when your men entered the crater and refused to advance beyond it. That was hours ago, and they are trapped there, along with your colored troops. They are not up to the task, and sending more men on the flanks will not give them sufficient courage to take the hill."

"Are you questioning the courage of my men?" Burnside asked.

"I am indeed, along with your judgment in regard to this entire operation and your ability to command troops in battle. There will be a full investigation of this fiasco, I assure you."

"I welcome it," Burnside said. "It will expose your lack of cooperation and your egregious decision to change the plan of attack at the last minute by refusing me the choice of which of my divisions should lead. We shall see which of us comes off worse."

Meade's eyes popped behind his large glasses and a vein in his forehead throbbed. He pushed himself out of his camp chair.

"You have said quite enough, sir," Meade told him. "Say no more. Withdraw your troops immediately. That is a direct order."

Burnside's shoulders sagged. He knew he was beaten. No matter how blame would be apportioned for this debacle, following an investigation, he could not afford to be accused of failing to obey a direct order. Meade would sack him on the spot.

"Yes, sir," Burnside said, "but at least permit me to delay until the passageway is completed. The men will not survive crossing a hundred yards in the open."

"No delay," Meade roared. "You will issue the order as soon as you return to your headquarters."

"Sir," Burnside said.

He turned on his heels and left without another word.

Boyce and Mutesa rallied the black soldiers and led them to the rim of the crater, trying to hold off the rebels who had dogged their retreat. It was a damnable way to fight. Dig in your heels to cling to the edge, fire, duck, rip open a paper cartridge with your teeth, ram a minié ball down the barrel, and hoist yourself up to fire again.

A bullet grazed Boyce's shoulder. Men on either side of him were flung backward, shot in the head. Other soldiers took their places. White Union troops fired from the far wall and left side of the crater, but the heaviest barrage came on the right side, where Mahone's enraged men were planted, determined to exact full revenge for the attack by the black soldiers.

Little Billy Mahone led his men toward the crater at a run.

Their thrilling, spine-tingling, bone-chilling rebel yell preceded them. Mahone's words hung in the air.

"General Lee is watching us, boys. Don't let him down."

They came within feet of the crater's edge, all but disappearing in the pall of smoke from the rifle fire, and there they halted, stopped by the Union guns. Mahone ordered them back to regroup and to bring up additional ammunition.

"We've got 'em, boys. One more charge and they're ours."

There was no hurry. The Yankees in the pit weren't going anywhere. Rebel infantry held them on three sides. On the fourth lay a flat, open landscape, raked by shell fire.

The Union troops in the crater knew that the rebel line was stretched thin and that General Grant had fifty or sixty thousand troops in reserve. They expected to see them heading their way anytime.

It won't be long now, they told one another. There's the Fifth Corps and the Second Corps, and don't forget the Eighteenth. And five solid miles of men in the trenches ready to rise up and break the backs of these rebs as soon as Grant gives the word. They'll come running and then we can get out of this damn hole. They've got to be forming up now, loading their forty rounds.

But by eleven o'clock, such confident talk was no longer being voiced. Feelings of abandonment took over. The men believed they had been written off. There was nothing they could do but bitch and gripe. They could not attempt to leave without facing charges of desertion. The order to withdraw had not come through.

Burnside still hoped for a miracle, but he was fresh out of ideas as to how to bring one about. And Meade never imagined for an instant that his order to withdraw the troops, issued ninety minutes ago, had not been transmitted.

By 11:30 in the morning, the crater had become a death trap. The casualty rate was increasing and a wound was no longer a passport to a hospital bed and safety. There was no way a wounded man could be transported out.

Many of the wounded could not find space to lie down.

Fifteen thousand men packed a quarter acre of ground. In some places, the living and the dying were jammed so tightly with the dead that they could not raise their arms. The living were helpless to defend themselves; the dying could not rest. Fragments of brain and bone and flesh spattered all indiscriminately as Confederate shells and mortar rounds tore into the mass, gouging and ripping men to shreds. Bodies were trampled underfoot, stomped beyond recognition by terror-stricken soldiers running in aimless circles to escape the continuous rain of shells.

Black flies attacked the corpses and the living dead in swarms so thick, they formed clouds, enveloping the suffering men. The heat was so intense, the temperature near one hundred degrees, that thirst became a terrible need, causing many men to faint. Canteens had long since been drained. Officers rounded up their hardiest men, draped canteens over their shoulders, and sent them racing for the Union lines for water and ammunition. They had already combed the pockets of the dead and wounded for bullets and cartridges, but there was not enough to sustain the troops who were still able to maintain fire at the rebels.

Most of the Union troops had given up, concerned only with finding a place to hide, but in the crater there was no shelter. Only luck and chance protected some from the deadly iron fragments that spewed out from each shell, maiming and killing at random. Some men pushed into the trench that was being dug from the crater back toward the Union lines. Word spread, and soon so many frightened men piled into it that the diggers were overwhelmed.

"Bury 'em if they won't move," the officers ordered, and the diggers beat back their own troops and heaped dirt on them. There was no time for pity or compassion.

The soldiers sent to the rear for water and ammunition were cut down one after another by rebel artillery, and the few who reached the Union trench were so shaken that they refused to return.

As noon approached and the last hope for reinforcements

and relief died and the rebel infantry crept closer to the rim of the crater, a rapidly growing stream of able-bodied Northerners deserted. A few stopped to help the walking wounded, but most pushed past, preferring to take their chances with the rebel bullets.

By 12:15, Mahone's men were near enough to toss rocks, bottles, and spent pieces of shrapnel into the pit, tormenting the trapped mass of Yankee troops. Some threw muskets like spears, bayonets first, the sharp, glinting blades arcing gracefully overhead to impale an unlucky soldier. This was no battle; this was slaughter.

"There's no hope for it, is there?" Burnside said to Loring. It was 12:20.

"No, sir," Loring said. "You must order the men out now."

Burnside buried his face in his hands, and Loring wondered whether the general had heard him. Burnside raised his head and stared glassy-eyed across the open field.

"Oh, those poor men," he whispered. "Oh, those men!"

"Sir," Loring said sharply. "Order them out now."

"Yes," Burnside said, his mind mired in the frozen plain of Fredericksburg almost two years ago, where he had waited too long to stop the killing. But still he issued no orders.

"We must send someone to the crater," Loring prodded, "to deliver the order, sir. Two men would be better, to make sure at least one gets through."

"Yes," Burnside repeated.

"Who, sir?" Loring asked, knowing that the couriers stood little chance of coming back.

"I don't know," Burnside said. "Select someone who doesn't have a wife and children."

Loring went out of Burnside's tent to find the two newest members of the staff. They had been there such a short time that he barely remembered their names. But he knew they were single and young and fresh, not yet played out by the war. If anyone could make it, they could. And if anyone would be among the least lamented, they would.

* * *

"That's it, gentlemen," Bartlett told the handful of officers clustered around him. He perched on a pile of timbers, his wooden leg shattered and useless, fingering the ivory handle of his cane and looking remarkably unperturbed by the carnage around him.

"The battle is lost," he said, "as we knew hours ago, but now we have our orders to withdraw. At last.

"Gather up as many of your men as you can and lead them back. You will lose some in the doing, but if you stay here, you will lose them all, and that would be more senseless than what has already happened here today."

"Aren't you coming, sir?" inquired a major.

"I cannot take a single step," Bartlett said with a smile, "much less a hundred yards."

"We'd carry you, sir."

"No. I appreciate the offer, but I would slow you down. I will not see you sacrifice your lives to save me. My war is over. Good luck, gentlemen. May God go with you."

Each man waited to shake Bartlett's hand before leaving, until shrapnel cut one of them down. Bartlett waved them off.

"Go now," he commanded, "while you still can."

They joined the hundreds of others who clambered up the near side of the crater in a frantic, clawing melee. Those who lost their purchase on the slope slid back and were trampled underfoot. Others stared immobile, too dazed and dispirited to attempt to escape.

Ezra Boyce and a group of about a hundred troops, black and white, remained on the rim facing Mahone's forces, keeping up a steady but dwindling rate of fire. They were down to a few rounds each. Boyce had already emptied his revolver. He slid to the bottom to hunt up a loaded rifle, but he could find no extra bullets. He scampered up to the firing line again, prepared to use his bayonet after he fired his last shot.

Mutesa had two rounds left for his Enfield rifle. He looked at Boyce and smiled sadly.

"Looks like I'm not gonna get home today, sir."

"Day's not over yet, Corporal," Boyce said.

Ten feet away, a line of rebel caps poked above the Confederate line. Boyce and his men opened fire, tearing the caps to pieces. But there were no faces below. The hats dangled from the bayonets on which they had been hoisted. Boyce cursed aloud at being suckered by the old trick, spending his last bullet for nothing.

"Get ready, boys," he shouted. "They're coming."

With a wild yell, Little Billy Mahone's rebels charged, reaching the rim of the crater before the Union soldiers could reload. Boyce and his few troops rose to meet them.

The fight was vicious, with bayonets, rifle butts, knives, and bare hands. The Yankees were overwhelmed by the force and outrage of Mahone's men and they retreated down the blood-soaked walls. Boyce tumbled semiconscious, blood oozing from his shoulder where a bayonet had penetrated and come out his back. He wondered, before losing consciousness, whether the wound would affect his arm-waving oratorical style.

The rebels arrayed themselves along the rim, firing at the trapped men below. At first, they picked their targets at random. Then they turned on the black soldiers.

The cry went out: "Shoot the niggers."

Some of the Union soldiers took up the call and rounded on their black comrades, bayoneting the ones nearby, hoping that their quick action would ingratiate them with the rebs and save their lives.

The colored troops, caught between the Confederate fire from above and the Union bayonets at their back, had no place to run. They pleaded with both sides, with those in gray and those in blue, but it made no difference. Scores went down, victims of the hatred they had enlisted to put an end to, victims of their color, and there was nowhere to hide from that.

Frantic men hoisted white handkerchiefs on their rifles. Others tossed away their weapons and held their hands high, waiting for a bullet or for mercy. Gradually, the firing died down.

Rebel soldiers entered the crater and began to deal with the prisoners. Whites were rounded up. Blacks were shot.

Boyce, woozy and unsteady on his feet, was helped up the slope by Mutesa.

"Tell them you're with the First Division, sir," Mutesa urged. "They'll shoot you down like a dog if they think you're with us. You gotta stay alive so you can tell folks how we fought today. You must be our witness, Colonel; otherwise it was all for nothing."

When they reached the top, a rebel sharpshooter shoved Boyce aside and turned on the black corporal. Mutesa straightened to attention.

"Time you learned a lesson, boy," Caleb Caffee said.

"Leave him alone, you bastard," Boyce said. He flung himself at Caffee.

"Get off me, you goddamn nigger-lover," Caffee growled, knocking Boyce to the ground. "You thank your lucky stars I don't kill you, too."

Caffee lunged and rammed his bayonet through Mutesa's stomach. Placing his foot on the black soldier's hip, he pulled the weapon out. Mutesa moaned and collapsed at Caffee's feet.

"That's enough, soldier," Little Billy Mahone said. "These men are prisoners of war now, the coloreds and the whites."

"We don't take no nigger prisoners, General," Caffee said. "You leave us be to get on with our job."

Caffee turned away to confront another black soldier. A shot past his ear stopped him cold.

"One more step and you're dead," Mahone said quietly. "You are a disgrace to the uniform. Now get the hell out of my sight."

Caffee started to protest but thought better of it. He glanced at the black soldier and walked away.

"We'll get you yet, boy," Caffee muttered, "all of you. Maybe not today or even this year, but we'll get you. You're what this whole war's been about, and it's not going to end when it's over."

16

"IT says here in the newspaper that we lost four thousand men at that battle down in Petersburg the other day. The one where they blew up the mine."

"That many? God Almighty. I don't see how we can keep up this war much longer. Maybe we should let the rebs keep the South and their niggers—we sure as hell don't want 'em—and let us get on with business."

Henry Pleasants opened one eye and stared at the civilians in the seats facing him, two well-dressed men in their forties, prosperous, sleek, and portly. The one-armed private sitting beside Pleasants was asleep, undisturbed by the jerking of the train when it left Washington's Union Station, or by the long, loud whistle the engineer sounded at every crossing and town, or by the voices of the businessmen, raised high to be heard over the clatter and rattle of the rails. They seemed offended when the boy asked whether the seat was free—clearly, they did not want to be so close to the war—and they frowned when Pleasants invited the soldier to sit down.

The boy fell asleep immediately, and Pleasants envied him that. He had slept little in the three days since the battle. Bobby Lee's bottle of whiskey had been no help. Pleasants had lain on his cot, eyes focused on the top of the tent pole, reliving the army's fiasco, becoming more depressed.

He pretended to sleep on the train, slumped in his seat, hat pulled low over his eyes, head resting on his upturned hand. He had never felt so tired, and he asked himself again why he had boarded this train.

"Four thousand men," the first businessman repeated, rattling his newspaper and shaking his head.

Pleasants silently corrected him. More like 4,400. And most of those deaths occurred not during the battle but after Meade ordered Burnside to withdraw. Meade had told him so yesterday.

"More men were lost trying to return to our lines than in attacking the Confederate forces," Meade had said. "Of course, not that many of General Burnside's men attacked, and that was the problem."

"It says here," the businessman continued, "that colored troops were involved. They cut and ran. A rout, it says."

"No surprise," the second man said. "It's a dumb idea, and a dangerous one, thinking you can give niggers guns and turn 'em into soldiers."

Pleasants kept his eyes closed and his mouth shut, knowing that no matter what he said, no matter how vividly he described the glorious sight of the black division twice charging Cemetery Hill under withering fire, the only Union troops to do so, he would never change the minds of those two. Even the soldiers who had cowered in the crater were saying the same thing about the colored troops and were bragging about how many niggers they had killed at the end. Ledlie's men were the worst of the lot.

After the battle, Pleasants had gone looking for Ezra Boyce. On his way to the black soldiers' camp, he stopped to break up several fights the white soldiers had picked with the black troops. Two black soldiers had already been hospitalized because of the beatings, and one was not expected to survive. The troops seemed dazed, in shock and in mourning for the men they had lost, both to the rebs and to their comrades in blue. Pleasants heard no singing, saw few camp fires. General Ferraro was not around, and his men were asking where he had been when they were charging the hill and being cut down at point-blank range. Nobody could tell Pleasants what had happened to

Boyce. One man thought he had been killed, and another said he had been led away by the rebs. Nobody knew what had happened to Corporal Mutesa, either.

The newspaper rattled again.

"You can bet there weren't many niggers among those casualties," the man snorted.

"That's for sure," his companion said.

Pleasants clenched his teeth, recalling that 40 percent of the Fourth Division had fallen, some 1,665 men at last count. More than eight hundred were missing and presumed captured.

"I hope they made those niggers bury our dead. Least they can do is dig the graves of the brave men who gave their lives for them."

The young soldier cried out in his sleep. The businessmen glanced at him in disgust.

"Probably drunk," said the first one.

"Those people ought to ride in a separate car," the other said.

Pleasants had had enough.

"If you two say one more word," he said quietly, "I will throw you out the window."

Startled, the men glared at the tired, unshaven Union officer with the piercing brown eyes and decided not to protest or stand on their dignity. Without a word, they rose and moved to the rear of the car.

Pleasants closed his eyes. The boy cried out again, more of a moan, a sob of pain that reminded him of the sounds that had floated over the Union trenches the night after the battle. The Forty-Eighth Pennsylvania had returned to the trenches to help fill in the depleted ranks of the Ninth Corps line. Several hundred wounded and dying soldiers lay on the open field between them and the Confederate lines, and no one could be sent to retrieve them. The moonlight made them easy targets for the rebel sharpshooters who had resumed their deadly work.

As the night wore on, the moans turned to screams and sobs and pleas for water, for help, for mercy, for a quick death. An occasional shot was heard as a man who still had his weapon chose to end the agony. In the morning, the screams became faint wails, and when the brutal heat of the new day enveloped the men, they grew quiet, lapsing into unconsciousness and death from their wounds or succumbing to a sharpshooter's bullet. Caleb Caffee killed three with his Burnside carbine.

A few men weakly waved sticks with rags affixed to them to brush away the flies, but they could not shield themselves from the sun or find water to slake their thirst. Pleasants saw one man summon the energy to stagger to his feet. He reached out his arms, pleading, first to the Union lines, then to the Confederates. His voice cracked as he tried to shout.

"For the love of God, help us. We're dying out here."

All firing ceased. The man fell to his knees.

"If you can't help, then shoot me. For God's sake, show some mercy."

The answer came from the Union side. The man pitched forward, facedown in the dirt. Sharpshooters on both sides resumed firing and artillerymen sent shells spinning above the field to seek new victims in the trenches.

"Why the hell can't they call a truce and bring in the wounded?" Bobby Lee said.

"No general likes to go begging another for help," Pleasants said. "Their pride is more important than the lives of a few hundred soldiers."

Pleasants was bitter.

"This whole damn war could be behind us, and those poor bastards wouldn't be out there with their lives draining away. Not to mention the ones who died in the crater and the ones captured by the rebs and probably on their way to Andersonville."

He flinched when a chilling shriek arose from some luckless soldier in the field.

"It's my fault," Pleasants said. "None of this would have happened if I hadn't been so stubborn about digging the mine."

"That's stupid," Bobby Lee said. "You know it's not your fault."

"That's right, sir," Bill Cabot chimed in. "Your part of the operation was successful, Colonel. You could not have asked for a more impressive explosion. You delivered what you promised and opened a gap in the rebel line. You gave the army a clear path to Petersburg."

"It's not your fault the generals blew the chance you gave them," Lee said. "They're the ones to blame—Ledlie, Ferraro, Meade, Grant, and Burnside, too. They caused it to fail."

"Still," Pleasants said, "if I hadn't been so enthusiastic and so confident about the explosion, they would not have agreed."

Cabot studied Pleasants and was distressed. The colonel was a wreck, tormenting himself about the casualties and the opportunities lost. He looked thinner, and there were large dark pouches under his eyes. He nervously fingered his beard and tapped one foot on the ground like a loose window shutter flapping in a stiff wind.

"Sir," Cabot ventured, "I thought you were planning to go on leave when the mine was finished."

Pleasants looked at him sharply.

"You're acting like my mother again, Sergeant," Pleasants snapped.

"I think you could use a rest, sir."

"So do I," Bobby Lee said.

"That's none of your goddamn business," Pleasants said.

He leapt out of his chair and paced back and forth, clamping his hands over his ears to hush the cries of the dying. He stopped and shrugged.

"I'm sorry," he said. "I know you're trying to help and I appreciate it. I'm seeing General Burnside this afternoon about a ten-day leave."

"Good," Lee said.

"Will you be going to Lexington to see Miss Anne?" Cabot asked.

"No, I'm going back home to Pottsville to stay with my aunt and uncle."

"Oh," Cabot said, disappointed.

Bobby Lee interrupted him.

"Listen," he said.

"I don't hear anything," Pleasants said.

"That's right," Lee said. "No shots, no cannon, no mortars."

The men peered over the parapets. Cheering erupted from both sides.

"It's a truce party," Cabot said.

"Thank God," Pleasants said. "Finally, we can bring our soldiers in."

"General Grant?"

"Come in, Horace," Grant said.

Colonel Porter stepped inside the tent and saw that the general was lying on his cot, one arm flung over his eyes. He had not been up all day, not even for meals, and Porter was concerned. It was not like Grant to take to his bed, even after such a defeat.

"Still feeling poorly, sir?"

"My stomach aches and my head is pounding like there are mortar rounds going off inside."

Nerves, Porter thought. He was fine until we got the casualty reports last night.

"Would you like something to eat?"

"I can't bear the thought of food."

Grant sighed and sat up, swinging his legs over the edge of the cot. He rested his chin in his hands.

"I keep thinking what a stupendous failure this was and how I might have prevented it."

"There was nothing you could have done differently, sir," Porter said. Except, he thought, to let the black division take the lead, or to have ordered Meade to withdraw.

"You're probably right," Grant said, sounding unconvinced. "But if I had been the corps or the First Division commander, I would have been at the front, not behind the lines."

"You were a lot closer to the front than General Burnside or General Ledlie," Porter reminded him.

"Yes," Grant said, "but if it had been my division, I would have been with it."

"You would have been ahead of it, sir."

Grant chuckled.

"By God, you're right. So I would have."

He ran his fingers through his hair in an effort to bring order to it and pressed his hand against his forehead.

"There are demons in here, Horace, and they are up to no good. It was not the fault of the troops. They were poorly led. I blame their commanders for not doing their duty, and I include myself. The colored soldiers did well, didn't they?"

"Yes, sir. They got closer to the top than anybody else. If they had gone in first and—"

Porter took a step backward and blanched. It was the closest he had ever come to criticizing General Grant.

"I'm sorry, sir. I didn't mean—"

"Quite all right, Horace. You're right, and Meade and I were dead wrong. The battle might indeed have been ours if the blacks had spearheaded the assault. And Ferraro might even have gone in with them. Well, that is for the court of inquiry to sort out now."

"There will be an investigation, sir?"

"Oh yes. General Meade is determined that heads shall roll, and Old Burny's will be the first. It is time he left. He no longer commands the loyalty and respect of his men."

Grant stood and stretched. Some color returned to his face.

"How did Burnside's truce party go?"

"That's what I came to see you about, sir. The rebels rejected it. General Lee himself."

"What did Lee say? No, wait, let me guess. Lee will not honor a truce unless the request comes directly from me."

Porter nodded.

Grant smoothed his beard and pulled a cigar from his pocket.

"Ah," he said. "Vanity of vanities; all is vanity."

He glanced up, to see Porter gaping in surprise.

"Don't look so shocked, Horace. I have read the Bible a few times in my life. That is from *Ecclesiastes*."

"Yes, sir, I know."

"But you did not think I knew, did you?"

"Uh, no, sir."

"Your honesty does you credit," Grant said. "It is nearly always vanity and pride with generals. We have boys dying out there, and all morning long neither Burnside nor Meade nor I would swallow our pride to ask General Lee for a truce so we could bring in our casualties. It is galling to ask a favor of your enemy. It shows weakness, like going cap in hand to family you despise. I have had to do that in my day, Horace, and it is very hard.

"Now look at us, three powerful generals, and none of us giving in, though our soldiers' lives depend on it. It is awful. No man's life should rest on another's pride. I have to hand it to Old Burny. He did what had to be done when Meade and I would not. Of course, now Lee's pride is offended because the request for a truce came from a corps commander when it should have come from me—Lee's equal in rank. He will make me do the begging, as I would do in his place."

Grant lighted his cigar and puffed up a cloud of smoke like an engine building up steam for a long haul. He strode over to Porter and placed a hand on the younger man's shoulder.

"It is time to grovel and beg, Horace. Write a nice flowery truce request. You can do it better than I. I'll sign it and we'll have the thing done."

The men in blue and the men in gray climbed out of the trenches and stared at one another across the open field. No one carried a weapon. The officers had shed their holsters and firearms. Lee had granted permission for the Union army to retrieve the wounded and bury the dead in a ditch to be dug precisely midway between the two lines of trenches.

Colonel Chilton had brought him the letter from Grant.

"That is more like it," Lee said, taking the letter and perusing it briefly. "There is a proper way to transact such business. A gentleman would have known that from the outset and saved those poor men their suffering."

Burnside's division commanders, except for Ledlie, who

stayed in his bombproof like a mole, marched onto the field, followed by staff and orderlies hauling buckets of lemonade. They met the Confederate representatives in the center of the field, saluted, and shook hands. A friendly conversation ensued about the battle, the weather, the whereabouts of mutual acquaintances. Prewar friendships were renewed. Lemonade, and stronger drink, was offered all around, and the Union officers dispensed cigars. It was all quite civilized.

The Union commanders inquired about the identities of the senior Confederate officers who stood aloof behind the lines, arrayed along the rim of the crater to watch the proceedings. Bushrod Johnson was pointed out, clad in a white linen duster and straw hat; and A. P. Hill in an old flannel shirt; and Little Billy Mahone in his tent-cloth uniform of faded gray. General Lee was not present.

A rebel colonel gestured toward General Ferraro, asking who was "that remarkably handsome man." When told he was the commanding general of the Fourth Division, United States Colored Troops, the colonel said he had with him some of Ferraro's papers, taken from a captured Union officer.

"Let me introduce you," Potter offered.

"No thank you, sir. We are not in the habit of recognizing as social equals those who associate with Negroes."

The enlisted men of both sides, save those Union men treating the wounded and gathering the dead, traded stories, tobacco, coffee, food, and pictures of loved ones. The gibes and taunts were taken in good spirit, like members of opposing teams meeting on a playing field after the game has ended.

A regiment of black soldiers from the Fourth Division crossed the field. Conversation ceased. Men eyed them with suspicion and hostility until they noticed that the coloreds were carrying shovels, there to dig a ditch one hundred feet long to serve as a communal grave.

Pleasants wandered over the field, with Bobby Lee and Bill Cabot in tow. They tied handkerchiefs over their noses and mouths to mask the stench of death. Pleasants studied the bodies, looking for Boyce and Mutesa. He quickly realized that he would not find them. The soldiers were no longer recognizable.

The blistering sun had turned the bodies the color of coal, and the faces of the dead were so shriveled that it was impossible to distinguish white men from black, enlisted man from officer. This time, race did not matter, for the dead were buried together, tossed into the trench three deep. The job was done in a hurry—General Lee had permitted them only three hours—and the men sifting through the graveyard were anxious to have it behind them.

The bodies were bloated from swelling gases, torn and mutilated by shell fire. Some bore the marks of boots, trampled by others in their panic to return to the lines. Swarms of flies attached themselves to the corpses; maggots feasted on open wounds. Occasionally—five times that afternoon—a cry was heard when a man was found alive; five men out of the hundreds who had cried through the night.

"If the generals saw this," a doctor said, "maybe next time they would arrange a truce sooner. Who knows how many we might have saved?"

More than seven hundred men were buried, each body searched for some mark of identification, a letter, a slip of paper in a pocket. The name was written down and pinned to the soldier's shirt, then added to the roster so that the next of kin could be notified that their son or husband or brother was dead, not missing in action, not left in that yawning limbo that caused relatives endlessly to hope that one day their men would return.

Burnside had aged years overnight. He sat alone in his tent, sweat glistening on his forehead, resting his elbows on his desk. He felt ill, despairing, and remorseful, but he managed a smile when Pleasants entered. He rose and shook the colonel's hand with surprising strength.

"Colonel Pleasants. Do come in and sit down. I want to congratulate you most sincerely on the success of your mine. You did precisely what you promised and you did so in the face of skepticism, opposition, and downright interference. You and your men deserve a great deal of credit. You have my gratitude, sir. I will express it officially in orders, but I also wanted to thank you in person.

"The blame for our failure is shared by others, but I bear a large portion of it. I let you down, I let my men down, and myself, as well. It was inexcusable to have my division commanders draw lots to determine who would lead the attack. I cannot explain why I did not choose Potter or Wilcox. And I should have been closer to the front to take more direct control of the battle."

Burnside looked at the floor and shrugged.

"The thing is done and there is no undoing it. I shall pay the price for my ineptness. I fervently wish, however, that I will be given another chance to serve my country before this war ends, and that the others who bear responsibility for this fiasco will be admonished. I refer, of course, to General Meade and General Grant. If they had not changed my battle plan and forced me to replace the colored troops, we would be celebrating a victory instead of holding a wake.

"General Meade has formally preferred charges against me, so I shall have to answer to an army court, and probably to the United States Congress, as well. They like nothing better than to investigate someone else's folly. It takes their mind off their own and keeps them from having to act on more pressing concerns. I am certain your testimony will be required. I am sorry about that, but your slate is clean and you have no reason for concern."

"Sir," Pleasants said, "I will be glad to help in any way I can. I will testify that you supported the mine operation, whereas General Meade and Major Dunne opposed it and tried to thwart it. I hope that will be of some help."

"I appreciate that, Colonel," Burnside said, "but do not jeopardize your career by being too critical of General Meade. He is vindictive, a most troublesome enemy, and I do not want to see you hurt. Exercise discretion when you testify."

Burnside smiled at Pleasants and wiped his forehead with his bandanna.

"Enough of this somber talk. I promised you leave and you shall have it, beginning tomorrow morning. You look like you need it. Take the advice of an old soldier and guard your health and vitality while you are young."

"I welcome the chance to get away, sir."

Burnside rummaged among the papers on his desk and extracted a form. He handed it to Pleasants.

"This authorizes twenty days' leave. It occurred to me that ten days would not give you sufficient time to travel to Lexington and back and enjoy a restful interlude with your young lady."

He smiled at Pleasants like a father bestowing a generous gift on his son, and waiting for praise in return.

"I was not planning to go to Lexington, sir," Pleasants said.

"Now that you have more time, of course you can go to Lexington," Burnside said, beaming like a cherub. "Send your young lady a telegram and tell her you are on your way."

Pleasants looked uncomfortable. The general's smile faded.

"Oh," he said. "Perhaps I am overstepping my bounds. I do hope nothing is amiss between you and your intended. In any event, you can catch the morning train from City Point to Washington and transfer from there to wherever you wish to go."

"Thank you, sir," Pleasants said. "I appreciate the extra time."

"Use it well, Colonel. One more thing. General Meade wishes to see you."

"I would rather not see him, sir, if it's all the same to you. I am not too kindly disposed toward him at the moment."

"It is not all the same to me, Colonel. It is in your best interest to call on him. Also, he must approve your leave. Do be circumspect in your dealings with him, however. Do I make myself clear?"

"Yes, sir. I will take care in what I say."

"That is always wise when dealing with the commander of the Army of the Potomac."

Pleasants glanced at the imperial pennant hanging slack over Meade's tent. He saluted the patrician colonel who barred his way.

"Can I help you?" asked Lyman.

"Colonel Pleasants. He's expecting me."

"Ah yes," Lyman said, looking Pleasants up and down for wrinkles, dirty shoes, and tarnished brass, as if he was the rawest recruit.

"Do I pass inspection?" Pleasants asked.

"You'll do."

Lyman cocked an eyebrow, warning Pleasants not to go too far.

"The general prizes neatness," Lyman said.

"Surely a comfort to those who died yesterday. I was just out with the truce party. The soldiers I saw didn't look so neat."

"General Meade is not in the best of moods," Lyman said. "I would urge you to be temperate in your remarks and to keep them to a minimum. Junior officers should be seen and not heard."

Lyman announced Pleasants with the formality the occasion demanded and ushered him into Meade's tent.

Meade smiled and gestured to a camp chair in front of his desk.

"I wish to congratulate you on the success of your project, Colonel Pleasants. You did an outstanding job. Your mine was entirely satisfactory from a military standpoint. If the attack following the explosion had not been bungled, the whole affair would have been a considerable victory. There will be an investigation to apportion blame, but I do not think your testimony will be required."

Meade detected disapproval in Pleasants's frown. Silently, he thanked Lyman for suggesting that Pleasants be given a long leave, making him unavailable to the court of inquiry.

"As to who bears the greatest responsibility," Meade said, "I think you will agree that is General Burnside. He managed this badly from the outset. His selection of General Ledlie is one of the worst blunders of the war. Then Burnside proved incapable, despite my best efforts, of getting his troops to obey his orders to advance. He has left me with no choice but to apply for his relief. He will never return to the Army of the Potomac while I remain in command.

"I must admit that I was not much in favor of your project to begin with, but once it was decided to proceed, I did everything I could to ensure its success. I hope you appreciate, Colonel, that I tried to give you every assistance."

Pleasants could not let Meade's assertion pass unchallenged.

"I would take issue with you on that point, sir."

"You would take issue?" Meade said slowly.

"Yes, sir. Perhaps I should testify at the inquiry, along with your Major Dunne, about the type of support I received from your command."

"Major Dunne is on leave and will not return until after the inquiry. He needs a rest, as you obviously do, too. Do you have your leave authorization with you?"

Meade snatched the paper out of Pleasants's hand, scribbled his signature across the bottom above Burnside's name, and handed it back.

"Good day, Colonel," Meade said.

Pleasants felt a hand on his shoulder and found Lyman ready to escort him outside. Lyman led him away from Meade's tent.

"That was not smart, Colonel Pleasants. Try to remember that General Meade is not a man to be trifled with. You will not be asked to testify at the army inquiry, although if Congress decides to investigate, you may be called. I advise you to be careful of what you say."

"I'll try to remember that, Colonel," Pleasants said.

"I sincerely hope so. The Union Army cannot afford to lose men like you."

"Why, look at that, sir," Bill Cabot said, feigning surprise. "There's a band at the station."

It was a little before six o'clock in the morning. Cabot eased the wagon through the crowd at the City Point railway depot. The engine was steaming up and men were boarding the four passenger cars for the daily run to Washington City.

"That's Ledlie's band," Pleasants said.

"So it is, sir. I wonder what they're doing here. They must be seeing off somebody important."

"Of course you know nothing about this, Sergeant?"

"Me, sir? I just got here."

Pleasants had been silent and morose on the long ride to the station, trying to ignore Cabot's bright, steady chatter about the regiment's days in Lexington and his remembrances of our Miss Anne. Pleasants folded his arms across his chest and pretended to sleep, but Cabot knew better.

He stopped the wagon beside the musicians and retrieved the colonel's bag. Pleasants climbed down and glanced at the band director. The man was watching Cabot from the corner of his eye. Cabot nodded and the man gave the downbeat with his baton. The band broke out with an enthusiastic version of "The Girl I Left Behind Me."

Cabot grinned.

"Isn't that the song the band played when we left Lexington, sir?"

"You know damn well it is. You set this up," Pleasants growled.

Memories of the day at the train station rushed over him. He blinked and looked away. In his mind, he saw Anne standing on the platform, tears streaming down her cheeks, smiling bravely and waving her handkerchief as the train pulled away.

Cabot saluted.

"Good-bye, sir," he said.

"Good-bye, Bill. Take good care of things."

"I have something else to say," Cabot said, "as a friend. Don't go home to Pottsville. Remember that Anne Shaw saved your sanity once, and it looks to me like it needs saving again."

"You're incorrigible, Sergeant."

"I know, sir."

* * *

The one-armed private got off the train at the first stop after Washington. Pleasants watched him awkwardly retrieve his bag from the overhead rack. He had learned not to offer help to amputees—they needed to do things for themselves. He stared out the window at an elderly couple, farmers, he guessed, not very prosperous ones. He saw the woman embrace the boy, her body shaking with sobs. The father shook hands with his son, and the couple drew apart so the boy could see the young woman standing a few feet back.

She was crying as she ran toward him and threw her arms around him. She clung for a long time, until the mother spoke to her and she pulled away, embarrassed. She smiled at the boy and he smiled and laughed in return. He had not seen what Pleasants had, the look of revulsion and horror on her face when she first spied the empty sleeve pinned to the shoulder of his jacket. Pleasants knew she would keep that feeling hidden from him as long as he lived.

That was not what she had bargained for, he thought. It was the same for him. Anne was not what he had bargained for, either. The train pulled out of the little station and he settled back and tried to sleep. He found himself staring at Anne's photograph with no memory of taking it from his pocket. The clacking, rhythmic sounds of the wheels hypnotized him, lulling him into a trance that transported him over space and time.

"Sometimes I think men prefer women who are ninnies," Anne had said the night they met. "I think most men are afraid of a woman who speaks her mind. What do you think, Colonel Pleasants?"

"I think you're right," he'd heard himself say.

"Do you plan to come calling on me? If you do, I hope you will not be slow about it, Colonel Pleasants."

"I'll never change my mind about you," Pleasants had told her as they sat on the wrought-iron bench beneath the now-dead magnolia tree.

He heard her soft laugh, felt the cool touch of her hand and her lips on his cheek. He heard the rattle of paper, the letter that disturbed him so much. He saw the words, the handwriting magnified in his mind.

"I have told you that I cannot be the kind of wife your Sallie was," he read. "I do have confidence that you will understand and accept me for what I am, the person who loves you more than anyone else can and who will be, if not always the perfect wife, still the best friend and partner you could ever hope to have."

"I love you for what you are," Pleasants had written in return, wondering whether he was being honest.

A ghostly image of Sallie rose before him, the Sallie of his dream, wearing a white silk dressing gown, her hair cascading down her back. She held her arms out, imploring him to come to her, trying to tell him something he could not hear.

He cried out her name and moved toward her, groping through the fog. The more frantically he tried to reach her, the farther she receded, until she disappeared. Only her voice remained, calling to him. This time, finally, he understood.

"I won't be here when you get back," she said. It was what she had whispered to him before she died.

"I won't be here when you get back."

He woke with a jolt. The train had stopped. He opened his eyes to find the conductor waiting.

"We're here, Colonel. Lexington. And on time, too."

Aftermath

THE stalemate in the trenches outside of Petersburg continued for nine months after the Battle of the Crater. As the war raged on, charges, countercharges, and recriminations grew.

On Saturday, August 6, 1864, one week after the battle, the United States Army Court of Inquiry opened at City Point. Burnside objected to the composition of the court, arguing that its members, selected by Meade, were under Meade's command. Further, the judge advocate was a member of Meade's personal staff. Burnside appealed for a new court, composed of officers who were not from the Army of the Potomac, but his request was rejected by Secretary of War Stanton.

Meade testified first, describing the events that had led up to the explosion of the mine and his impressions of the failed assault. He read into the record every dispatch sent to and received by him the day of the attack, including the one in which Burnside accused him of conduct unbecoming an officer and a gentleman. He noted that Burnside had been uncooperative in supplying information on the attack's progress and that now, a week later, Burnside had still not submitted to Meade a report on the battle.

"I have very little knowledge of what actually transpired," Meade told the court, "except from the dispatches you have heard read here. I have been groping in the dark since the commencement of the attack. I did not wish to take any unpleasant measures, but I thought it my duty to suggest to the

President of the United States that this matter should be investigated and that the censure should be made to rest upon those who are entitled to it. What I have done has been to show that I tried to do all I could do to ensure success."

Burnside testified next, endeavoring to defend his conduct of the battle. He was questioned for three days. He said that he had tried to keep Meade informed of the progress of the attack and that he had replied to every dispatch Meade had sent. He admitted that one reply had been insubordinate.

Burnside praised the conduct of his troops, arguing, perhaps unwisely, that he did not know of any order issued by him that had not been carried out by his division commanders. He defended Ledlie, again unwisely, arguing that Ledlie had been ill the day of the battle, unable "to stand the oppressive heat." He asserted that the Fourth Division, United States Colored Troops, would have carried out "a more impetuous and successful assault" than the First Division. Had he been allowed to use them to spearhead the attack, as he had planned, the outcome would have been different.

In sixteen days of testimony, thirty-two officers appeared before the court, including Potter, Ferraro, Wilcox, and Ord. Pleasants was not called. The findings were released on September 9. Burnside was found "answerable for the want of success," for his failure to obey the orders of his commanding general in regard to "not giving such information to his assaulting columns as to ensure a reasonable prospect of success; not preparing his parapets and abatis for the passage of the columns of assault; not employing engineering officers who reported to him to lead the assaulting columns with working parties; [and] neglecting to execute Major General Meade's orders respecting the prompt advance of General Ledlie's troops from the crater to the crest."

Also censured were Ledlie and Ferraro for not being with their troops, and Wilcox for failing to carry out Burnside's orders to advance to the crest of Cemetery Hill.

Ledlie left Petersburg the day the court of inquiry began—for a twenty-day sick leave. He remained indisposed for four months. When he rejoined the Army of the Potomac in December, he was told to return home to New York and await orders. Sensing that there would be no further orders, he resigned his commission a month later.

Ferraro was retained as a divisional commander and promoted to the rank of major general the following December—for "meritorious service."

The Committee on the Conduct of the War of the United States Congress held hearings on the Battle of the Crater from December 17, 1864, to January 16, 1865, interviewing witnesses in Washington and Petersburg. Most of those who testified at the army inquiry also appeared before this body. In addition, Pleasants reported at length on the lack of support for the mine from Meade and his engineering officer, citing their comments that the idea was "claptrap and nonsense," and that "such a length of mine had never been excavated in military operations and could not be." Pleasants related in detail how his requests for tools and supplies were ignored, something the committee emphasized in its report.

The committee concluded that the "first and great cause of the disaster" was the last-minute decision not to allow Burnside to use the black troops. "The conduct of the colored troops when they were put in action would seem to fully justify the confidence that General Burnside reposed in them, and General Grant himself, in his testimony, expresses his belief that if they had been placed in the advance as General Burnside desired, the result would have been different." Grant had testified that the attack would probably have succeeded if the Fourth Division had led the assault.

Congress was lavish in its praise of Burnside for supporting the mine project and for selecting the best troops available to spearhead the assault. It criticized Meade for rejecting Burnside's choice of troops and for providing little assistance.

The praise for Burnside came too late. On August 13, two weeks after the battle, he was given a twenty-day leave of absence. Pleased not to be relieved of command or dismissed from the service, Burnside went on vacation with four members of his staff at a hotel in New Hampshire's White Mountains, expecting to return to active duty with the Army of the Potomac.

On August 25, he sent a telegram to Grant: "Shall I report with my staff at your headquarters or shall I wait further orders? We would like a few days more if consistent with interest of service." Grant replied to Burnside at his home in Providence, Rhode Island, authorizing him to "remain absent with your staff till further orders."

Burnside may have suspected that he was being eased out. Six days later, he wired Grant: "My leave of absence expires Friday next. Shall we await orders here?" The blow came the following day, eight days before the United States Army Court of Inquiry released its report censuring him. A telegram from Grant instructed Burnside to "Await orders where you are. Your staff may remain with you." Later that day, Burnside received a second wire: "Lieutenant General Grant directs me to say to you that under existing circumstances, he does not deem it best to return you to the command of your corps at present, but that he will not relieve you from it, unless to assign you to some other command. He therefore desires that you remain at Providence or such other place as you may select until further orders from him."

Four weeks later, on September 28, Burnside was ordered to return his staff "without delay" to the Army of the Potomac. His military career was over. He offered to serve as aide-de-camp to Grant or Sherman, even as a bearer of dispatches from Washington to the front. He received no reply to that pathetic request. Seven months later, his resignation was formally accepted.

In 1866, Burnside undertook a career in politics, serving three terms as governor of Rhode Island. He was twice elected to the United States Senate and died in 1881, during his second term.

Meade remained in command of the Army of the Potomac

for the duration of the war. The day after the surrender at Appomattox, he met Robert E. Lee, with whom he had served before the war. Lee did not recognize him.

"Don't you know me? I'm George Meade."

"Oh, is that you, Meade? What are you doing with all that gray in your beard?"

"You have to answer for most of it," Meade said.

A month later, Meade rode at the head of his mighty army to lead the two-day grand review down Washington's Pennsylvania Avenue. After he passed the reviewing stand, he joined Grant and President Andrew Johnson to take the salute of more than 200,000 Union troops.

Meade stayed in the army as commander of the Military District of the South, in charge of administering the reconstruction of the former Confederate States. With Grant's accession to the presidency in 1869, the position of general of the army became vacant. That would go to Sherman. Meade assumed that Sherman's rank of lieutenant general would then be his, the final reward for the years of service in an army he had never wanted to join in the first place.

Rumors spread that Grant did not intend to promote Meade. Meade, upset by the talk, called on Grant and told him he believed he was due the promotion. It would be an injustice to deny it to him. When Grant made no reply, Meade knew the rumors were true.

One of Grant's first acts after his inauguration on March 4, 1869, was to appoint Sheridan, junior to Meade in age and years of service, the new lieutenant general of the army. "The blow has been struck and our worst fears realized," Meade wrote to his wife from his headquarters in Atlanta. "You can imagine the force of the blow, but it is useless to repine over what cannot be remedied, and we must find consolation in the consciousness we have that it is the cruelest and meanest act of injustice, and the hope, if there is any sense of wrong or justice in the country, that the man who perpetrated it will some day be made to feel so."

Meade went home to Philadelphia to assume command of

the Military District of the Atlantic, a position that rarely required him to leave his house. He died three years later, in 1872, at the age of fifty-seven, the same age as Burnside when he died.

At the surrender ceremony at Appomattox, General Grant was vividly reminded of the last time he had seen Robert E. Lee, when, as a shabbily dressed lieutenant in the Mexican War, Grant was admonished for his appearance by the elegant, impeccably attired Lee.

"I met you once before, General Lee," Grant said, aware of his dirty boots. He wore a private's uniform with dingy straps, no sword, and one coat button in the wrong hole. "I have always remembered your appearance, and I think I should have recognized you anywhere." He described the circumstances under which they had met.

"Yes," Lee said, dressed in a new uniform with embroidered belt, shiny high boots with red silk stitching around the tops, gold spurs, a scarlet sash, and a sword with a hilt in the form of a lion's head. "I know I met you on that occasion, and I have often thought of it and tried to recollect how you looked, but I have never been able to recall a single feature."

Ulysses Grant never again went unrecognized or suffered another such humiliation. Friend of the rich and powerful, rich and powerful himself for a time, he traveled in grand style, a guest in mansions and castles and yachts, feted by kings and governments the world over.

The riches rolled in within a month after Appomattox, first a lavishly furnished house in Philadelphia, complete with fine silver and a wine cellar, then other houses, in Galena, Illinois, where he had clerked in a store, and in Washington, D.C. Businessmen in New York gave him $100,000 in cash, and a group in Washington added $75,000. The government rewarded him with four stars, the highest military rank ever given.

In 1868, Grant was elected President of the United States; he was reelected in 1872. He had no program for the country and was not all that interested in affairs of state, but his old friends, family members, and wealthy new acquaintances profited from their government appointments. His administrations were tarnished by graft and corruption on a gigantic scale, but Grant himself remained untainted. He never took a bribe, although he innocently accepted presents, naïvely trusting anyone who claimed to be his friend. Sherman tried to warn him about the fortunes being made by men to whom he had given government jobs and contracts, but Grant refused to listen. He could not believe that others would take advantage of him.

After his second term ended, he and his beloved wife, Julia, decided to tour the world for "as long as the money holds out." For more than two years, the Grants traveled, hailed and entertained throughout Europe and Asia. Disraeli invited them to dinner, Wagner played his own compositions for them, and the Greek government illuminated the Parthenon. The Pope blessed Julia's diamond cross, the Tsar assembled the Imperial Russian Navy for their inspection, and the Japanese Emperor shook hands, the first time any Japanese ruler had touched a commoner. Grant remained the same portly, ill-dressed, plainspoken, unassuming person he had always been. Of his travels, he said, "Venice would be a nice place if they drained the streets."

When he returned home late in 1879, wealthy New Yorkers provided another house, an income, and some railroad bonds, and Grant joined his son in a Wall Street brokerage firm, buying in for $100,000. They were paid three thousand dollars a month by the other partner, Fred Ward, who did the work and kept the books. Many of Grant's relatives and friends gave money to Ward to invest. He was making them all rich, he insisted, telling Grant that his investments had appreciated to $2.5 million. Grant sold his Washington residence and borrowed on the New York house to give Ward additional capital.

On May 4, 1884, Ward fled, leaving an empty safe, stripped bank accounts, and more than $15 million in obligations. He had built a pyramid scheme, a gigantic swindle, and had never invested the money in anything.

"I don't see how I can trust any human being again," Grant said. Impoverished, as in the days before the war, he was forced to rely on charity. A stranger sent a thousand dollars, "for services rendered during the war," and the Mexican ambassador left another thousand on the parlor table.

The only way Grant could see to provide for his family was to write his memoirs. Mark Twain offered an advance of fifty thousand dollars. Grant said it was too much and settled for twenty thousand. His manuscript grew apace with his throat cancer, diagnosed the same year. He died on July 23, 1885, at the age of sixty-three, one week after completing his memoirs. They ultimately earned half a million dollars and sold twice as many copies as Twain's popular *The Adventures of Huckleberry Finn.*

Henry Pleasants left the army on December 18, 1865, choosing not to reenlist when his term of service expired. He remained despondent about the army's failure to break through the gap his mine explosion had torn in the Confederate defenses. He blamed the fiasco on Meade and Grant and was greatly upset by Burnside's dismissal and the fact that Meade received no official censure by the United States Army Court of Inquiry.

Pleasants took part in another unsuccessful Union attack against the Confederate line in late October 1864, at Hatcher's Run, Virginia, another failure to break the stalemate. Promoted to colonel, his last post was commander of Fort Sedgwick, so close to the rebel trenches that it came under constant fire. His men called it Fort Hell.

In April 1866, President Johnson signed Pleasants's commission as brevet brigadier general of volunteers, for "skillful and distinguished services during the war, and particularly in the construction and explosion of the mine before Petersburg."

He married Anne Shaw and they moved to Pottsville, where Pleasants became chief engineer of the Philadelphia and Reading Coal and Iron Company. The nation's industries were demanding abundant fuel resources and the coal regions of Pennsylvania were soon awash in prosperity.

Anne Shaw Pleasants bore three children, one girl and two boys. History has not recorded whether she became a modern or a traditional wife, or successfully balanced the demands of the two.

In 1873, Pleasants became general superintendent of the Coal and Iron Police, an organization established to combat the Molly Maguires, an Irish-American society whose stated goal was to improve living and working conditions in the Pennsylvania coal fields. The Molly Maguires conducted a widespread terrorist campaign until put down by Pleasants's police.

On a family vacation in the summer of 1873, at a hotel in Cape May, New Jersey, Pleasants encountered Grant, who entered the dining room accompanied by a large retinue. Pleasants noticed that the President was staring at him. Grant leaned over to talk to one of his aides and gestured in Pleasants's direction. A few minutes later, the man approached and asked whether he was General Pleasants. When Pleasants nodded, the aide said that the President would like him to come to his room after dinner.

Grant received Pleasants graciously.

"I have tried to meet you personally many times," he said. "I know that you left the army with harsh feelings, for which I was as responsible as anyone. I have asked you to do me the honor of coming here today in order that I may express to you the regret I have always felt in the failure of your magnificent project. It was no fault of yours, and I am only sincerely pleased that the Senate saw fit to honor you with the brevet of brigadier general after you left the service. It was little enough for them to do. I do want to congratulate you, even at this late date."

They chatted for nearly an hour, and by the time Pleasants left the President's suite, he had revised his opinion of Grant. He came to believe that Grant was a kind, generous, and basically honest man who had been overawed by the suave, sophisticated, and clever Meade.

In his mid-forties Pleasants began to experience fierce headaches, which doctors attributed to the stress of his work. He was urged to take frequent rest periods, but the headaches worsened. In the late 1870s, while he and Anne were on an extended holiday in Europe, he consulted a French neurologist who diagnosed an inoperable brain tumor. He did not tell Anne, and spent the remainder of the trip buying expensive gifts for her, including a five-hundred-dollar black silk shawl. He died at home on March 26, 1880, at the age of forty-seven.